Blackhawk

Far Stars Legends I

Jay Allan

system 7 publishing

The Far Stars Series

Also By Jay Allan

www.jayallanbooks.com

Blackhawk

Blackhawk is a work of fiction. All names, characters, incidents, and locations are fictitious. Any resemblance to actual persons, living or dead, events or places is entirely coincidental.

ISBN: 978-0692701751

Acknowledgements

Blackhawk is a prequel to my existing Far Stars series, which was published by Harper Voyager. I'd like to take the opportunity to thank my entire team at Voyager for their part in helping to bring this universe to life. The Far Stars wouldn't be what it is without the contribution of their time, effort, and talent.

A special thanks to my editor, David Pomerico, whose patience and advice was invaluable in working through the manuscripts for Shadow of Empire, Enemy in the Dark, and Funeral Games.

I'd also like to shout out a heartfelt thanks to Rebecca Lucash, Shawn Nicholls, Angela Craft, Dana Trombley, Lauren Jackson, Caroline Perny, Pamela Jaffee, and Richard Aquan …the whole Voyager team. You guys are the best, and I'm looking forward to working with you all on the upcoming Flames of Rebellion series, and hopefully a return one day to the Far Stars

Jay Allan

Prologue

The galaxy. Unimaginably vast.

Mankind inhabits a huge swath of this massive conglomeration of stars, an entire spiral arm explored and colonized eons ago. Humanity's origins are forgotten, its birthplace long a lost legend, buried in the endless depths of the past. Little is known of mankind's expansion into the stars, of how so many worlds were settled and tamed. There are vague histories, as much legendary as factual, of civilizations that rose and fell, leaders who achieved great glory and were remembered...and then mostly forgotten. Great fleets that clashed, deciding the fates of billions. Armies that marched across worlds, cities destroyed and then rebuilt. Humanity pushing out ever farther from its home world, settling a thousand worlds before falling into a dark age.

But now, mankind's lost glories are forgotten, the independence and spirit of its early adventurers gone, replaced by terror, by slavery. For the empire that now reigns over those worlds of humanity knows only one way to rule. Fear.

On a thousand worlds, people live in terror, crushed by their masters at the slightest signs of disobedience. For a millennium the emperors have ruled humanity with an iron fist, and everywhere men and women look up to the sky, they live under imperial control. Everywhere save the Far Stars.

A remote sector, a star cluster separated from the rest of human space by the great emptiness of the Void, the Far Stars are a difficult and dangerous journey from imperial space. It is to the mysterious natural phenomenon of the Void that the people of the Far Stars owe their freedom from imperial rule.

Into this untamed frontier a man fled. He had been a warrior, a soldier of great ability, the product of a select breeding program...but that time had passed, and it was a broken man who fled to the frontier of humanity's dominion, haunted by a dark and terrible past.

He left his old name behind, took a new one, one utterly anonymous, but not for long. For where he goes, violence and death follows...and soon his new name will spread throughout the Far Stars, a cry of hope to some, a bitter curse to others.

Blackhawk.

Chapter One

West Hill
"The Badlands"
Northern Celtiboria

The bar was dusty, rundown…a filthy shack. It sat on the edge of a town boasting no more than a few dozen buildings, most as ramshackle as the tavern itself. The walls were dark and grime covered, and the floor was built from coarse boards, old and stained with spilled liquor and more than a little blood. It was a place soldiers went, to get drunk, to gamble, and sometimes to get into fights, mostly non-lethal brawls fought with fists and bar stools instead of assault rifles and artillery.

There were about two dozen people milling around, wearing a variety of mostly worn and filthy uniforms, sitting at the bar or at one of the half dozen broken down tables scattered around the room. Most of them were busy drinking—or playing poker. Gambling was always popular with the soldiers, and many of them rushed to find a game just as soon as their paymasters handed out the nearly worthless scrip for their habitually overdue pay.

There was a rickety stair in the back corner, leading up to a second floor with a half dozen small rooms, where the saloon provided the other service soldiers with pay in their pockets tended to seek. A private was stumbling down the stairs, trying unsuccessfully in his drunken state to fasten his pants with one hand as the other gripped the loose and wobbling rail.

West Hill wasn't much as towns go, but it was the biggest settlement in the Badlands, and the only significant population center within ten day's march in any direction. The scrubby desert had little more than sagebrush and a few meager farms clustered around the river, nothing of significant value. Save that it was a crossroads of sorts, laying between the rich ports of the White Rock Coast and the fertile plains and the river cities farther inland. A dozen trade routes passed through its desolate landscape, the motor caravans carrying all manner of goods to waiting markets. And that made it worth fighting over.

The armies of four Warlords were nearby, men of war who had struggled for this scrap of arid rocky plain, and the power over regional commerce it would provide its owner. The soldiers were mostly huddled in their armed camps now, licking their wounds after more than a year of nearly constant combat. They had fought themselves to exhaustion, and worn, tired, and low on supplies, the respective commanders had agreed to a truce. No one expected it to last very long—ceasefires on Celtiboria seldom did—but for now the guns were silent. At least mostly silent. With almost a hundred thousand grim veterans in the area, there was no such thing as perfect peace, and men were still dying, just at a slower pace.

"Give me the bottle." The man tossed a coin down on the bar. It was an imperial copper, worth twenty times its weight in any of the debased and almost valueless Celtiborian currencies…and an almost obscene price to pay for the bottle of throat-scarring rot gut the bartender dropped in front of him. But the man didn't care. The money was ill-gotten, so it only seemed right to him it should be ill-used as well. Besides, it was worth it to him if the bottle got him drunk. A glass at a time wasn't accomplishing anything, so he figured it was time to escalate things.

"Sorry, buddy, but I can only give you the set exchange rate on that." The bartender stood, staring down at the coin with poorly disguised greed. Imperial currency was accepted everywhere in the Far Stars, with far greater enthusiasm than the various local coins and scrips. But most of the worlds established official exchange rates that owed more to fantasy than reality. And on Celtiboria, fractured and perpetually mired in civil war, each Warlord enforced his own valuation, generally with even greater avarice and wishful thinking than the central banks of the other worlds.

The man knew the bartender was full of shit. There wasn't an establishment on Celtiboria that wouldn't happily give three times the official rate, regardless of local laws and regulations. But he didn't care. The barkeep had to earn his way, and if cheating his customers was the only way he could do it, so be it. He'd have even found it amusing…if he'd had time for anything beyond misery and the temporary relief offered by extreme drunkenness.

"S'alright, just keep the change…and keep this swill coming until I'm under this stool instead of sitting on it." The man wasn't really drunk, not yet at least. The slurred words were more wishful thinking than real impairment. Getting drunk was a challenge for him, something that took a lot of effort. And one hell of a lot of booze. He grabbed the bottle and filled his glass right to the top. Then he picked it up and drank it down in one slug. It was shit, some kind of bathtub brew that burned like battery acid going down, but right now he'd have guzzled Stegaroid piss if it would dull the pain…erase the memories, even for a few hours. But that was easier said than done.

He wasn't a normal man, born with a random assortment of his parent's traits, with memories of old Aunt Jenny telling him how they had the same eyes. No, his genetics were far more complicated, the product as much of manipulation in a lab as whatever DNA he got from his mother and father, whoever they had been. Many people would have considered his genes a gift. They made him stronger, faster, smarter…more capable than pretty much anyone else he'd ever encountered. But they also made it damned difficult to get drunk, and most of the time that was all he cared about.

He realized people would consider him ungrateful for the

capabilities he so despised, but he didn't see things that way. He was doing his best to throw away his talents, and he radiated contempt for the things he could achieve if he chose to. Indeed, he was far too aware of just what he could do, the terrible uses to which he'd put his capabilities in the past…and it was that more than anything that made him want to crawl into the bottle. He wanted to be left alone, and usually that's what he got. Most of all, he hated his hyper-charged digestive and immune systems, and the efficiency with which they purged poisons like alcohol from his system almost as speedily as he could imbibe them.

A group of four soldiers walked through the door, their green and black uniforms identifying them as General Ghana's men. Bako Ghana was one of the strongest Warlords in the area, and he'd been expected to chase the others out of the Badlands in a single campaign season. But the rival Warlord Lucerne had gotten the better of him, beating his forces in the field three times, and taking West Hill away from him.

The truce that followed gave the soldiers of all sides access to the town, as long as they didn't bring anything heavier than sidearms with them. The word was Lucerne didn't like it, but even in victory, his forces had been worn down, and he needed time to rest and resupply them. Giving his rivals' soldiers access to the only place in the Badlands they could get their fill of booze and women didn't seem like too much of a price to pay for the break in the fighting.

The new arrivals carried themselves not with the demeanor of an army that had been thrice defeated and chased halfway across the Badlands, but rather a swagger that suggested their side had gotten the better of the fighting, that West Hill was their town, and not just someplace they were allowed to come lightly-armed to do their drinking and whoring. The man would have quickly seen through the pretense, realized the soldiers were overcompensating, covering for their bruised morale. That is if he'd noticed them at all. Which he didn't. Apathy had become his religion, and he was deep in prayer, with no interest in anything save the bottle in front of him.

"Barkeep, four whiskeys…and be quick about it." The soldier's voice was coarse. He and his comrades sat down at the bar, the speaker at the end of the group, right next to the man. The four of them were puffing on foul-smelling cigars, cheap ones, the man realized as the noxious smoke wafted in his direction.

The soldier next to him reached out and grabbed his drink as the bartender set it down. "Another," he barked as soon as he'd tossed it back and set the glass down. Then he turned his head and stared at the man.

"So, what the hell do we have here?" he asked, the disrespect unmistakable in his tone. "Some homeless wanderer in off the scrub?" He paused, his gaze locked on the man. He made a face. "You stink, you know that? You reek like the trail." He paused, turning back and downing the drink the bartender had just poured for him. "You got any scrip on you? Cause one of them fine women upstairs'll give you the bath you need for half a ducat. You might even enjoy it." He laughed at his own insult, followed immediately by his three friends. They all looked over at the man, waiting to see if their target had the guts to stand up to four of the great Ghana's soldiers.

But the man didn't react, didn't respond at all. He'd seen his share of soldiers, killers with frozen blood who would make these Celtiborian bullies piss themselves with a stare. And from the stench drifting his way, the loudmouth needed to bathe even more than he did.

"What are you, deaf? I'm talking to you, boy."

The man remained silent. He stared straight ahead as he grabbed the bottle and filled his glass again. He wasn't there to fight…or even to socialize. He was there to drink himself into unconsciousness.

The soldier's face turned red, and he looked back at his companions. "This drifter thinks he's too good to talk to us, boys." He stared back at the man. "He don't look like much though, does he?"

The man turned toward the soldier, staring with cold gray eyes. "I'm not looking for trouble, soldier. Now, drink your drink, move the fuck along…and keep your shit to yourself. I'm only gonna say it once." His voice was icy. He held his gaze for a few seconds, eyes fixed on the soldier and his friends. He was fighting to stay calm, to beat back urges from the past, dark ones...to try to ignore the soldiers, not to take the bait. But the normal involuntary response stirred in his mind, and he analyzed each of them, coldly assessing the threat they represented, and deciding it was minimal. If it came to fighting, he didn't doubt he would prevail. But wasting four troopers would draw a lot of unwanted attention. So he turned back to his drink and put it to his lips, downing it in one quick gulp before he put the glass on the bar and filled it again.

The soldier hesitated. There was something in the man's stare, the frozen sound in his words. Something unsettling, threatening. He hesitated, but then he looked back at his friends, saw the chuckles forming on their lips, waiting for him to back down. Finally, he turned back toward the man.

"Hey, boys...we got ourselves a real tough guy here." There was a nervousness in his voice, but he pressed on anyway. "You know what, shithead? You picked the wrong guys to fuck with. You hear me?" His voice was thick with false bravado, but there was an uneasiness there too, even fear. The soldier took his cigar and put it out in the man's glass, the lit end hissing as it was extinguished by the low proof, watered down whiskey.

"What about that, tough guy?" The soldier laughed, flashing another glance back to his comrades, clearly expecting his target to back down. But the man just sat still for a few seconds, silent, unmoving. Then his arm whipped up, striking out in a motion so quick it was just a blur. The soldier stood still, looking straight ahead, his eyes transfixed. Then he fell to the ground, his hands grasping desperately at his crushed throat as he gasped for air.

The man was on his feet now, his eyes fixed on the three other soldiers. He was dressed all in black, though the dust from the trail had covered him with a light gray coating. His hair was dark brown, long, pulled back in a ponytail held by a small silver clasp, the only thing of apparent value on his person. "Now get the hell out of here," he said, "and take this piece of shit with you." His voice was ominous, the threat of death heavy in every word.

The soldiers were stunned. They had jumped to their feet, and they stood staring at the man…then at their friend, lying at his feet, still in the final stages of his death struggle. The bar was silent, every conversation hushed. Those closest to the door had run out into the street in search of relative safety…or one of General Lucerne's patrols. The others shied away, moving back against the walls, watching nervously as the scene unfolded.

"Go," the man said. "Walk away. Live."

The soldiers glanced back and forth for a few seconds. They were clearly scared, but in the end their rage won out. Almost as one, they reached for the pistols at their sides. They were combat veterans, men who had killed before. They moved rapidly, decisively. But not quickly enough.

The man's hand dropped down as well, faster. He gripped the well-worn pistol he wore and brought it to bear before his enemies had even gotten theirs free of their holsters. The heavy gun cracked once, twice, a third time, in rapid succession…and the soldiers fell backward, a single red hole dead center on each of their foreheads. The man slipped the gun in its place, and he turned back to the bar.

He looked down, pushing the glass with the cigar to the side. Then he grabbed the bottle and took a deep gulp. Then he reached into his pocket and pulled out another imperial coin, tossing it on the bar. "Clean up the mess," he said with no detectable emotion. He turned and walked toward the door, carrying the half-empty bottle with him as he did.

He'd gotten halfway to the exit when he heard the commotion in the street. He stopped just as a group of uniformed troops poured in, weapons drawn. "Hands in the air," the leader shouted. "Now!" His voice was tense, but the man could hear the control of a true veteran in the words, a real soldier, not like the bullies in uniform he'd just wasted. Through the layers of apathy and contempt, a small spark of respect flickered.

"I don't want to hurt you…" The man stood, unmoving, the still warm pistol hanging on one side, and a bronze-colored shortsword sheathed on the other. His eyes darted back and forth assessing his opponents. There were seven of them, and he could tell immediately they were better soldiers than the four thugs he'd just killed. They all head weapons drawn…and leveled at him.

"This is the last warning you're going to get." The lead soldier, a lieutenant from his insignia, stared at the man, his eyes focused, ready.

The man could see the soldier's hands, the whiteness in his fingers as he gripped his weapon tightly. He knew he could win the fight one on one, even two or three to one. But these were good soldiers, he could see that clearly, and there was no way he could take them all down. Not before they killed him.

He felt an urge to fight despite the odds. Death didn't seem like such a terrible option. Life was a burden anyway, a constant effort to keep moving, to push back the memories, the dark side of himself…usually with the help of a river of alcohol. *Yes*, he thought, *die now…die gun in hand in this filthy saloon in the middle of nowhere. A fitting end to a life so wasted, so ill used.* His hand tensed. He was ready to draw.

But something stopped him, something deep inside, as it always did. The indomitable will, the refusal to yield to death. It had saved him many times, even when he hadn't wanted saving. And there it was again, hardwired into his psyche. The will to survive, by any means necessary. Any means at all.

He cursed silently to himself, feeling the wave of anger at his inability to simply allow himself to die. But even as his mind railed against itself, he felt his arms moving outward, away from his weapons. He stared right back at the officer and simply nodded.

The lieutenant jerked his head toward the man, a signal to his troopers. Two of them ran forward, grabbing the man, reaching down and removing his weapons belt. One of the soldiers handed the pistol and sword to another, and then he grabbed the man's arms and pulled them behind his back, attaching a set of shackles. He pushed the man forward. "Let's go."

The man felt a wave of anger, an urge to strike, to kill the soldier who shoved him. He knew he could…the shackles wouldn't stop him. But it wasn't the time. So he moved his leg forward, walked slowly toward the door. He was testing his captors, expecting the soldier to push him harder, to take the bait his defiant shuffling pace offered. But the soldier didn't touch him. He just said calmly, "Let's move."

The man stepped through the door and out into the dusty main street of the town. There was a sparse crowd gathered, looking on cautiously. Trouble at the saloon wasn't exactly an uncommon occurrence, and Lucerne kept a tight grip on events in West Hill. Most days his soldiers made arrests two or three times, but the majority of those were routine fights and other situations involving too much alcohol. They typically held the prisoners overnight, letting them dry out before releasing them. But this was something else entirely. It seemed different than most fights, even ones with fatal endings. It had been so lopsided, over so quickly, it looked at first glance like an ambush, cold-blooded murder and not a real fight.

The man walked slowly down the street, silently staring ahead. The soldiers led him toward a light transport vehicle, two of them running ahead and opening the rear hatch. The man just continued forward, his eyes darting around, taking constant assessments of the situation. He would go along quietly. No doubt these soldiers would believe whatever cell they locked him in would hold him…but the man thought otherwise. The soldiers were professionals, there was no doubt in his mind about that. But he was equally sure he could break out of whatever jail they put him in. They might be good soldiers, but they were utterly unprepared for someone—some*thing*—like him.

He could see the crowd growing larger, hear the background noise of the townspeople speaking to each other. His hearing was vastly superior to human norms, and he could understand much of what they were saying. Word was spreading that this drifter had killed four soldiers, Ghana's men. That was noteworthy enough as the start of a legend, the stranger who'd bested four adversaries, and all the more enticing because of who the victims were. The people of West Hill still resented the callous rule and atrocities they'd suffered when Ghana had controlled the town…and no one mourned for his dead soldiers. But the situation sparked another kind of gossip, and people were already whispering fearfully, wondering how General Ghana would react, if the killing would endanger the fragile truce.

He turned his head and took one quick look at the crowd. *They're really scared. Did I just restart the petty little war in this backwater?* He paused for a second. Then he decided he didn't give a shit. He looked up and stepped into the transport.

Chapter Two

General Lucerne's Headquarters
"The Badlands"
Northern Celtiboria

The man sat on the cot. It was a hard metal platform, bolted to the stone wall and covered with a thin foam pad. There was nothing comfortable about the cell, but it was clean and orderly, more so than the man had expected. He'd seen far worse prisons.

He'd sat quietly since they had brought him in the day before, watching, taking note of everything...the bars, the schedule of guards coming in, delivering meals, returning to retrieve the trays. He had a plan, a way to make his escape, one he had calculated offered a considerable chance at success. But he'd held off. There was something about these soldiers, a discipline, a professionalism he'd hardly expected to find in a Warlord's army on Celtiboria. In truth, he was curious. About the troops...and about their commander. And he found being interested in anything to be a refreshing change from the crushing apathy that ruled his life.

The man had served in armies before, forces with veteran soldiers trained to a sharp edge. But those troops had all had a malevolence he didn't see here. These soldiers were sharp, capable, and he had no doubt they could unleash a fearful fury on the battlefield...but the casual brutality he'd seen in his own service was nowhere in evidence. They were controlled…and that said something about the man in command.

He was sure these troopers would enjoy the pleasures of a good sack when they took a city. He didn't think them immune to the customary callings of war. But there was a hint of morality at work in this force, one that had rarely been in evidence elsewhere were he had fought. He wanted to know more about the man who commanded this army. So he didn't try to escape. He waited to see what happened next.

The air was musty, damp, a coldness coming from the walls despite the adequate heat pouring from the ceiling vent. Like most deserts, the Badlands could be brutally hot during the day, and surprisingly cold at night. And it was early morning still, the heat from the blazing sun still hours from penetrating to the depths of the huge stone building. Lucerne had taken an old castle as his headquarters, a massive fortification he suspected had once been built to protect the very trade routes the general and his adversaries battled over now.

The man wondered about his…host. He'd heard the name in his time on Celtiboria, but little else. Lucerne wasn't one of the top tier Warlords, he was fairly certain of that, but he'd heard good things about the general, both in terms of his military skill and his temperament. And he suspected total control over the Badlands trade routes would propel him a long way toward the top of the hierarchy, doubling or tripling his resources in an instant.

These soldiers are well-trained. And led. If this Lucerne is able build a larger army of this quality, he could shake up the power struggle for sure.

The man couldn't help but analyze strategy and tactics, it was hardwired into his brain, and no matter how much effort he made to ignore such things, the response was almost automatic. Even with a conflict that didn't involve him, an insignificant struggle in the Far Stars. A fight in which he had no stake, no real interest.

The man didn't know all that much about Celtiboria, only that it was the most populated world in the Far Stars, and that it had once been the most powerful as well, until the republic that governed it collapsed almost three centuries before, ruined by generations of corruption and incompetent leadership. The fall ushered in a period of protracted civil war that still showed no signs of ending. The planet was ruled now by dozens of Warlords, local nobles who styled themselves as generals and raised armies to fight an unending war for planetary hegemony. That struggle had seen its increases and decreases in intensity, but in three hundred years none of the Warlords had achieved the sought after planetary rule…and while they continued to fight, the people suffered, the resources that should have supported Celtiboria's wealth squandered on hundreds of pointless battlefields.

He'd thought the whole situation to be fitting. The Far Stars was a wild and untamed sector, overrun by pirates and mercenaries, half its worlds relegated to a kind of semi-modern squalor, while others were ruled by an eccentric variety of kings, oligarchies, and religious sects. And then there was Celtiboria, the greatest planet, mired in a centuries-long nightmare that made the bizarre happenings on the fringe worlds look sane by comparison.

He heard a sound, and his head snapped up. His mind cleared itself, shook away any ponderings that might distract him. His eyes were bright, focused, despite the fact that he hadn't slept in over two days, and while he wasn't planning any action, his body tensed nevertheless, every muscle ready for battle.

The cell door slid to the side, and an officer entered, with two guards in front of him and four behind. It was a good level of protection, but the man couldn't help but suppress a bitter laugh. He was sure the grim soldiers were confident in their ability to protect their leader. But he had already analyzed the movement of the forward guards, and he'd catalogued their apparent weaknesses. They were poorly positioned, close enough to each other that he could take them both down with a single compound move. He figured his chance of disabling the two guards and killing the officer, if he so chose, was north of ninety percent. It was a lot less certain he could drop the other four before they took him down, probably right around fifty-fifty. And of course, he was in the middle of a military installation, full of troops who would probably react badly to his killing seven of their comrades. He wouldn't guess he had no chance at all of an outright escape under such circumstances, but it wasn't a particularly good one. Of course, all of that only mattered if he was worried about his own survival. And, in truth, he was quite ambivalent about it. He didn't fear death, and some days he came close to craving it.

Still, he always held back, chose tactics, even desperate battle, over suicide. There was something inside him, some force that made the thought of giving up anathema. He might be tired of living, tormented by the things he'd done and seen. But he knew in his heart he was incapable to yielding, of accepting death willingly. Even allowing himself to be captured was but a tactic, one acceptable because of his confidence in his ability to escape. No, whatever future lay ahead of him, he knew when he died it would be gun and sword in hand, fighting to the last.

Besides, there was something different now, a feeling he hadn't experienced for years. He was intrigued. The officer, the expression on his face. He seemed different from the others, he had a greater presence. There was something in his eyes, a spark of some kind...and the man was curious to hear what this solider had to say.

The officer nodded, a generic greeting. "I'm not sure 'welcome' is the appropriate word for these circumstances," he said, "but when I heard the story of what you did, I decided I had to meet you myself." His voice was calm, but there was something there, a quiet authority. The man could tell this officer was accustomed to being obeyed.

"You may not know this, but the penalty for breaking the peace in West Hill, for murdering four soldiers there, is death. By all rights, you should already be on the gallows. Or worse, I should give you to General Ghana and let him do with you as he would, since it was his men you killed." The officer paused. "That, I can assure you, would be rather more unpleasant than the hangman's rope."

The officer stood just inside the cell door, his eyes locked on the man's, taking his stock of the prisoner. He wore the uniform of a general, and there were three silver stars on each collar.

The man looked up at the figure standing before him. The officer was young—very young for a Warlord—though he suspected the general's baby face made his age appear less than it truly was. The man's eyes paused on the three stars on the officer's collar. He had been on Celtiboria for months now, and while he couldn't have been less interested in the savage politics that had the planet's Warlords fighting each other for power, his genetics and training made it hard to ignore what he saw. It was natural for him to acquire information from happenings around him, and he had picked up the basics of the ranking system in his first week planetside.

He'd considered it strange. Celtiboria's Warlords fought each other with undisguised hatred. Their armies marched across the tortured world, fighting battles, requisitioning the supplies they needed, leaving farmers and townspeople on the brink of starvation. They lied and stole and cheated their way through negotiations and sacrificed honor and trust in their naked grabs for power. They sent assassins after their rivals and fought each other over the smallest disputes. But on one thing they mysteriously agreed. The ancient rank structure of the Celtiborian army was respected, and each Warlord wore a number of stars commensurate with the size of the army he commanded. And only the lord who controlled the ancient planetary capital could style himself Marshal.

The officer's three stars meant he was a Warlord who commanded at least 75,000 soldiers. That was a considerable achievement for an officer who didn't look all that much older than the man's own thirty-four years. It had been a long time since the man felt anything but misery and disgust for those he encountered, but there was something about this young general, a strength of character he could sense, despite his tendency to stand behind angry misanthropy, to think the worst of all those he met. In spite of himself, he liked something about this officer.

"Then hang me and be done with it. Or try to, at least." The man's voice had an uncommon hint of respect in it, but the last sentence also dripped with undisguised menace.

"I don't intend to hang you." The officer looked down at his prisoner, firm, neither provoked nor concerned by the man's threatening tone. "There is little enough justice on Celtiboria, but one can find it in this camp. At least whatever battered version of it I can provide."

"Justice?" The man's voice was thick with mockery. "You believe in justice? It is a useful fiction, I'll admit, often well-employed in controlling the weak minded masses. But I have no place for fables, for fantasies of fairness and men of wisdom and compassion. I have seen enough of this universe—indeed, more I'd wager, than you have—and I know what it is. Nasty and brutish. I have hatred aplenty for those who make it so, but my pity is reserved for the idealistic, for the believers. For their role is that of prey, the wounded herd animal limping around the watering hole. And worse even for those who follow them, eyes glittering with idealistic dreams as they march to their slaughter."

The man rarely spoke, and never more than a few words or a sentence to convey his meaning. But there was something about this officer, and he found himself unloading, sharing the grim thoughts he usually kept to himself.

"That is a bleak view…though I understand how one can come to feel that way. Indeed, there is little enough honor on this world, but I wouldn't say there is none."

The man felt a wave of anger, and he almost snapped back. But he didn't. Something stopped him, and he just sat there, staring back wordlessly.

"And I wouldn't speak so sharply of a lack of justice. The men you killed provoked a fight with you. I have no doubt of that…or you would be at the end of a rope even now. But I also give you tremendous benefit of the doubt. It seems to me that killing those men, or at least the first one, was rather more aggressive an action than was called for. Perhaps true justice requires you to hang for what you have done. You could have simply moved…or gone out into the street and called for my patrol to deal with the matter."

"I do not seek other men to fight my battles."

The officer stood stone still, calm. "I see. But I submit a battle could have been avoided entirely. The patrol would have ejected the soldiers from the saloon. And that would have been the end of it."

The man frowned. "That is not my way." He paused. He was not accustomed to offering detailed explanations. But once again he felt the strange charisma of the officer, and he continued. "And what would that have served? Would they have returned to their camp, not to be seen again? Or would they have been waiting for me, somewhere outside...to ambush me, to take their vengeance? At a time of their choosing, when I was drunk, when I would have been least able to defend myself?" The man was speaking hypothetically...he didn't have a doubt he could have taken down the four soldiers, drunk or not.

The officer just nodded, though the man thought he caught the hint of an amused smile, one the officer was clearly trying to suppress. Then the general took a few steps forward, his escorts scrambling along with him.

"You are clearly not from Celtiboria. That is evident in many ways. I would ask some questions. What brings you here? Where are you from? I would ask also what trade you ply, though I believe that is self-evident. You are obviously a warrior of some kind." The officer paused. "But let's start simply. What is your name?"

"I have none. I have no need for a name. Names are a burden. Things attach to them—reputations, rumors, accusations. People expect things of a name, and I have chosen the life of the nameless, ignored, disregarded. Invisible."

"And how is that working?" The officer looked around the cell. "Your namelessness didn't prevent Ghana's soldiers from singling you out. It didn't keep you from this prison cell. It wouldn't save you from the hanging that awaits you without my commutation. There is more to you than meets the eye, of that I am certain. But I submit to you that your namelessness is of far less value than you suppose."

The man looked back, silent. No angry response. No wave of invective. Just a cold, focused stare.

"Well, whatever your thoughts and motivations, I'm afraid you need a name," the officer continued. "If you don't tell us who you are we will assign you one anyway. But I would prefer to engage you with mutual respect rather than pointless attempts at intimidation. So I will tell you my name first, and then perhaps you will tell me yours. I am General Augustin Lucerne."

The man stared back, still silent. He found himself surprised by his reaction to this officer, Lucerne. His usual shield of disrespect and anger had failed him. In the grim swirling vortex of guilt and rage that ruled his mind there was a spark of light. He liked this Lucerne, and against all odds, he was beginning to respect him.

But he couldn't give his name. It was unthinkable. No, he would never go by that name again. He hadn't uttered it in years. That man was dead, gone…or at least buried in the darkest reaches of his mind. If he was to have a name, it would be a new one…a life that would begin here, a man with no past…but perhaps with a future. He thought for a few seconds, trying to come up with something appropriate. Then, suddenly, he knew.

"Blackhawk," he said. "You can call me Arkarin Blackhawk."

"Very well, Mr. Blackhawk." Lucerne turned and looked behind him, waving away the guards. "Leave us…I would speak with Mr. Blackhawk alone."

"Sir…" The lieutenant looked nervous, and he stood with the rest of the guards, hesitating and nervously eyeing Blackhawk.

"Go…for the love of Chrono, go. Must I repeat every order? I would speak with this man…and I would do it alone."

The guards scrambled out the door, still uncomfortable leaving their leader alone with the prisoner, a man they all knew had killed four enemy soldiers in a few seconds.

Lucerne turned and watched impatiently as his guards walked slowly out into the corridor. "Close the door," he yelled after them. "And shut down the surveillance systems." Then he turned and walked toward Blackhawk, sitting down on the cot next to his prisoner.

Blackhawk was even more impressed than he had been. This general was a brave man, there was no question of that. He knew

Blackhawk had killed the four soldiers in the saloon…he was surely aware of the danger of being locked in this room alone with his prisoner. Yet whatever fear he felt was well-hidden.

"Let us talk more. I am intrigued. You are a man of a sort I have rarely encountered. I will not ask you about your past…little would be served by compelling you to lie to me. And that is all that would happen if I pressured you to provide information."

"We can agree on that, at least." Blackhawk stared at the general. "Assuming I didn't just tell you to go fuck yourself."

Lucerne smiled. "Come, Mr. Blackhawk, there is no need for hostility. I have already told you I will not try to force you to tell me anything. But a few minutes of civil conversation hardly seems too much a price to ask for a pardon from a death sentence, wouldn't you agree?"

Blackhawk sat still for a moment. Then he just nodded.

"I know our conflicts here on Celtiboria are not your fight. But I would speak with you about changing that, at least for a short time. I need a man, one unknown to my enemies, one with a great range of capabilities. I have a proposal for you, Mr. Blackhawk." Lucerne spoke softly, calmly.

"A proposal? What…do you want me to kill someone for you? One of your rivals? Do I look like some kind of gun for hire? I don't work well with others, General. All I want is to be left alone."

Lucerne nodded. "And how has that worked for you?" He looked at the disheveled state of the prisoner, the worn and tattered clothes, boots patched in half a dozen places. "You may not consider yourself a gun for hire, but you look like a homeless drifter, wandering around without a ducat to your name." He paused. "And yet, I can see there is so much more to you. You can fight, that much is abundantly clear. But I daresay there is more than just that lurking inside you. You do not hide the strength of your intellect as well as you think."

"You think you know something about me?" Blackhawk stared back at Lucerne, a doubtful expression on his face. "You believe you have some idea what goes on in my head?" He felt a hint of amusement…no, not amusement. It was respect. He didn't think Lucerne had any massive insight into what drove him, and certainly not the dark things he'd done, but he'd met few enough people with any perception at all. And Lucerne's insight was surprisingly good.

"I wouldn't presume to understand your motivations, certainly not in any detail, nor whatever has happened to you, what burdens you carry. But I can recognize someone with great talent and ability, a man haunted by demons from his past. I don't know what you have been through, but I am familiar with how it feels to have men die carrying out your commands...and sometimes because of your mistakes."

Blackhawk stared back at Lucerne, startled at how close to the mark the general had come. *Though at least you seem to be on the right side...*

"You're not from the Far Stars," Lucerne continued. "I'd bet fifty thousand imperial crowns on that. You're not the first one to flee to the Far Stars, to escape from imperial authorities or bounty hunters...or to try and outrun whatever memories or regrets fuel your torment."

Blackhawk still didn't respond. He just sat quietly and thought something he hadn't in a very long time. *This man is worth listening to.*

"I won't ask you if I am right. Your past is yours...if you wish to speak of it one day, I will listen. If not, I will respect your privacy. But I can see quality in you, and I have come to trust my judgment in such matters. Redemption does not require confession. You are here, by whatever means. Let us move forward from this point and not look back."

"Move forward?" Blackhawk's voice was soft, and without the skepticism he'd expected to hear in his words. "My only concern is being released from of this prison...and being on my way." He paused. "Or taking matters into my own hands." His words were still soft, but the menace drifted back into his tone.

"That will not be necessary, Mr. Blackhawk. If I intended to hold you—or worse—I can assure you I would not be in here with you alone. While I suspect I could give a credible fight, I have no doubt you would kill me before my men could get back in here. If that was what you wanted." Lucerne looked right at Blackhawk. "But I fancy myself a good judge of character, even when it is deeply buried. And I do not believe that you are, at your core, the type of man who kills for no reason."

Perhaps…but your perception is shaky on this one. I was that type of man. For a long time.

"That is a dangerous assumption. Do you take chances like that on the battlefield?"

"I do not believe I am taking a chance, Mr. Blackhawk, at least not a significant one. I have no doubt you would kill without a second thought to avenge a wrong done to you or to defend yourself. Indeed, the affair in the saloon is proof enough of that. But you have nothing to gain by killing me. If you did, you would never leave here alive. My men would kill you immediately. I don't doubt your courage, but I'd wager you are not a man to lash out for no reason, for no gain. I see a coldness in you, but not a lack of discipline."

Blackhawk listened quietly, and his estimation of Lucerne grew. He had been many places, fought alongside—and against—highly capable warriors. But he'd never seen in anyone what he was starting to sense about his jailor.

Is this really…an honest man? Does such a creature exist?

"That is a significant wager, especially since the stakes are your life."

"And yours, Mr. Blackhawk. And you strike me as a man who knows how to survive, whatever demons are driving you."

Another comment close to home. Lucerne had Blackhawk's attention.

"If you release me we have no quarrel, General. I will leave your occupied territories at once. To be honest, I've had enough of Celtiboria. This world has its own problems, and I have mine."

"I would try to convince you to stay, at least for a short while. I have a mission in mind, and I think you are the ideal man for the job."

Blackhawk shook his head. "I am not a hireling, General. I am not for sale."

"I will pay a thousand imperial gold crowns." Lucerne's eyes were locked on Blackhawk's. "I do not wish to buy you, only retain your services for a short while. After that you may leave… or stay. Whatever you wish. You may even find a home with us."

Blackhawk held back a derisive laugh. He had no home, not anymore. And he didn't expect he'd ever find one again. "That is unlikely, General. I appreciate your offer, as I know it was made in good faith. But I do not need your money. So, if you are true to your word, I will take my leave now."

That is a lie. You do need the money. And you have wallowed long enough in the filth, wasting the days…

"My word is good. You may leave at any time." He walked over to the door, putting his hand on the small communicator. "Lieutenant, you are to get Mr. Blackhawk's weapons and possessions at once. He is free to go."

"Yes…sir." There was surprise in the guard's voice, concern.

"There. The guards will return your sidearms and your pack, and you are free to go. I ask only that you not speak of this to anyone…neither my offer to you nor that you are the man apprehended in the saloon affair. I will have enough trouble over that without you causing me more. Do not go back to West Hill."

Blackhawk nodded. He was tense, suspecting a trap, as he always did. But something told him Lucerne was telling the truth, that he was free to go. And that made him consider staying.

"I will repeat my offer, however." Lucerne stood next to the door, standing aside as the hatch opened and a lieutenant came in carrying Blackhawk's things. The general gestured toward the bed, and the officer stepped across the room, laying the items down. Then he turned and looked at Lucerne.

"Dismissed." Lucerne watched as his officer saluted and left the room. "As I was saying," he continued, looking back at Blackhawk, "you may leave now. Or you can stay and discuss what I have in mind. And perhaps leave with your pockets full of crowns."

Blackhawk sat quietly. He'd held back the response that had tried to push its way past his lips, another empty denial that he

needed Lucerne's money. But he knew this man was no fool…
and that Lucerne's people had gone through his pack. He knew
what they'd found there, what they'd reported to Lucerne. Eight
copper crowns. Eight. And a single change of clothes, as filthy
and tattered as the ones he wore.

A thousand gold crowns was real money, enough to take
him anywhere in the Far Stars he wanted to go. And the idea
of doing something, of having a purpose, even as a mercenary,
sparked something he hadn't felt in a very long time. It was a
good feeling.

Chapter Three

Gray Company Refuge
Western Badlands
Northern Celtiboria

"We tried, Cass, we really did. But they've doubled the patrols. There was just no way to get in. If I'd gone any closer, my whole team would have been killed or captured." Meln Haggin stood at the base of a line of large rock outcroppings, a geological feature that stretched more than two days' march north to south...and provided the Grays with their secret base.

Cassandra Cross stood in a narrow cut between the two sheer rock walls. The split between the cliff faces didn't lead anywhere, it just petered out and ended when the two sections of rock connected a short way to the west. At least that's what the maps said. But Cross knew her way around better than the last mapmakers to visit the Badlands. There were caves under these mountains, interconnected and very difficult to find, especially since Cross and her people had camouflaged the entrance.

She stared at Haggin, her expression one of frustration. "We've got to do something, Meln. We can't just leave them there."

Haggin didn't say anything. He just held her gaze for a moment, and then he turned away.

"What is it?" The concern in her voice became more pronounced. "C'mon, Meln...what the hell is going on?"

"They killed five of them, Cass." Haggin's voice was clipped, his anger and sadness clear in every word. "Yaz and Gans for sure. I couldn't get IDs on the others."

Cross just stood there, her body tense with rage. Her eyes glistened for a few seconds, the hint of tears about to come. But then her anger pushed them back, hatred replacing sadness, at least for the moment. "We've got to get the others out of there, Meln. Now." She shoved aside thoughts of her dead people. The loss hurt—deeply—but there was nothing she could do for them now. But the other five of her Grays...if they were still alive, they needed her now. Because it wouldn't be long before they followed their brethren to the scaffold.

"I know, Cass, but damned if I know what to do. Unless you've got a spare army laying around."

She didn't reply, didn't move. She just stood there, thinking, growing increasingly restless at the lack of any idea what to do. Finally, she reached out and put her hand on Haggin's shoulder. "Forgive me, Meln...you've had a long journey...and a hazardous mission. Come, let's get inside, out of the heat. Let us share water, food." She turned and gestured toward the crack in the mountain, the long hidden path to the Grays' refuge.

Meln nodded and walked up next to her as they headed toward the secret entrance. They were quiet for a long while, and Cross knew her comrade's thoughts were in the same place as hers...on their captured friends. Wondering how long they had before General Ghana finished questioning them—an unpleasant process she was sure—and ordered them executed. Just like the others.

The description of Cross' trade varied depending on who was commenting. She considered herself—and all the Grays—to be adventurers, rogues, even freedom fighters, doing only what they had to do to provide for their people. At worst, smugglers of sorts, and ones who sought gain only to help those back home, the families and children they had left behind in the ruins of the Galadan.

Their adversaries however, mostly the Warlords fighting to

control the trade they preyed upon, called them thieves, pirates, albeit ones plying their trade on land rather than the sea. They'd branded the Grays outlaws, pronounced death sentences on all of them...and especially on their shadowy leader. But as far as Cassandra Cross was concerned, Ghana and the other murdering psychopaths who called themselves Warlords could kiss her ass. The Galadan had been a virtual paradise once, a rich and fertile plain dotted with prosperous farms and pleasant small towns. At least until the Warlords brought their conflict there, drawn by the need to feed their ever-growing armies.

The Galadan was a burnt out ruin now, its fields mostly barren and fallow, its once-pristine small rivers poisoned and polluted by the detritus of war. The people, at least those who'd survived the last years of invasions and occupations, huddled in the small woodlands around the edges of the province, beaten down, terrified, starving...and scarred by the images of the atrocities they had witnessed, the memories of friends and loved ones tortured, raped, murdered. Their home was a once peaceful province on the verge of utter destruction and depopulation. At least until Cassandra rallied a group of Galadan's young adults, and formed them into the Gray Company, a band of adventurers/smugglers/pirates, whatever one chose to call them, whose name came from the colors of the cloaks they wore.

She'd led her group of followers north, toward the Badlands, determined to hijack enough caravans to support their families back home, and for more than two years they'd done just that. General Ghana had eventually penned them in and was on the verge of destroying the entire company, but then Lucerne's invasion compelled him to cease the pursuit, and for more than a year the Grays had been wreaking havoc among the under-escorted caravans. She'd sent a dozen expeditions west, upriver, to sell their booty to black marketeers from the river cities, happy to take all she could deliver at half its value. And the flow of gold had been sent home, to buy food and medicine for the families and friends they had left behind.

Cassandra knew the battles that had kept the soldiers from chasing her people had cost thousands of casualties, and she sympathized, on some level, with the suffering of the soldiers. They were young people gathered from their homelands, much like her Grays, who had chosen their dangerous careers more through a lack of other options than any great desire to live an often short life of marching and combat. But the carnage on the battlefields took the heat off her and her followers, and she was grateful for the conflict…and the ceasefire had frustrated her, ramped up the danger for her raiding parties.

"Cass, what are we going to do? You know they're going to kill the others." Haggin's voice was hoarse, finally showing the fatigue he'd tried to hide earlier. "And they have us shut down. We've got almost twenty dead since they stopped fighting. And five more sitting in a cell, waiting to be executed."

The truce was bad for the Cassandra and her raiders, and Ghana had taken advantage of having Lucerne off his back to try and wipe out the Grays and the other groups attacking convoys.

And if the peace lasts too much longer, that's exactly what is going to happen…

Cass had been waiting impatiently for the truce to end, for the day the soldiers returned to killing each other and lost interest in her people. But there was nothing she could do now but wait, and hope. And she hated the helplessness she felt.

"I don't know, Meln." She had the feeling in the pit of her stomach, the one she got when she felt trapped, when there were no answers. "I just don't know."

* * *

"I'm going to ask you this once again, you piece of cave slime…where is your headquarters?" The jailor was a big man, tall and muscular, but overweight too. He wore the brown pants of a uniform, but he was stripped down to a torn, white undershirt, discolored around the arms with sweat stains. He had a large apron strapped on in front, light brown and liberally splashed with blood. His face was twisted into a nasty scowl, but there was the hint of a smile there too. It was clear he enjoyed his work.

Balon Tahl stared back at his tormentor. He was against the concrete wall, his arms shackled above his head. He was groggy, semi-conscious from the beating he'd gotten over the past two hours, but the defiance inside him was still sharp, strong. "Go screw yourself," he said, his voice rough, hoarse.

He looked at the jailor. His vision was blurry, his eyes swollen from the repeated blows, from blood pouring down out of the large gash on his forehead. "You're a sick, fat piece of shit, you know that? You're gonna make one helluva sound when somebody finally drops you."

The jailor's face turned red, and he swung hard, slamming the heavy metal baton he was holding into Tahl's gut. "You're a funny guy, you know that?" The jailor pulled the club back and struck again, hitting Tahl in the side. "I like that." He leaned forward, staring right into his victim's eyes. "Because I like this too." He hit Tahl again, harder this time.

The captive Gray howled in pain. He'd been struggling to remain silent, to deny his tormentor the pleasure of hearing his agony. But the last blow broke his arm, and the pain was too much to hold in. He gritted his teeth, steeled himself to endure. He tried to stop the tears from pouring out of his tortured eyes, but they came anyway, and slid down his swollen cheeks. He knew he had to hold out, to deny his captors the information they sought. If he broke—if any of his comrades did—they would all die almost immediately. The enemy's need to find the Grays' refuge was the only thing keeping him alive. Keeping his friends alive.

He still remembered the nightmare of three days before. They'd lined ten captives along a wall, all the Grays who had been captured in the last disastrous raid, and an officer had walked down, pointing at every other one of them. A pair of soldiers took each of those selected and dragged them across the courtyard, lining them up on a large wooden gallows and placing a rope around each of their necks.

It had been the odds who'd been chosen to die, and Tahl had been an even. It had been luck only that had spared him from the group selected for execution. It had been no preference, no action he'd taken, no effort to spare himself at the cost of his friends...but he felt guilty nevertheless. He'd seen his comrades murdered...the soldiers had left the evens lined up where they had stood and forced them to watch. Indeed, that had been the point of the whole exercise. Five could divulge the location of the Grays' base as well as ten...and watching their comrades killed was the first part of breaking the survivors. The trips to the dungeon chamber and the long and brutal beatings were the second. But so far, none of them had broken. Tahl knew he hadn't, and he was just as sure his comrades had remained firm. He'd know when one finally talked, because he'd find himself in the courtyard with a rope around his own neck.

He knew there was a death sentence on all of them, that only withholding the knowledge the enemy sought could preserve their lives. But every man had his limits, and enough pain and fear could wear down rationality. Eventually, one of them would talk. Then they all would die, the five prisoners...and when Ghana's forces used the information they had gained to trap the others, the rest of the company would be destroyed too.

He felt himself fading, the darkness taking his vision. Unconsciousness was welcome. It would provide a break from the pain...though he knew it would also cause the torment of one of his fellows, as he was dragged back to the cell and left to recover while another Gray was selected for a beating. It was selfish, he knew...to wish for the blackness, to trade his place with one of his friends. But he did it anyway.

Then he felt the cold...water hitting his face, shocking him back to awareness. A man stood behind the jailor. He held an empty bucket, and he laughed as he saw Tahl's eyes open wide.

"No sleep for you," the jailor roared, erupting in his own laughter as he did. "We still have so much to discuss, don't we?"

Tahl saw him moving closer, the metal baton in his hand, droplets of blood running down the weapon.

Stay strong...stay strong...

"We have to try…there is no other way." Cass stood in the large cavern, the space the Grays used as a meeting place. They were all gathered, all eighty of those that remained, save the six out on guard duty, watching the desert approaches to their secret refuge.

"But Cass, we don't even know if they're still alive. If Meln saw five of them executed, how do we know they weren't all killed? Just because no one saw it?"

"We don't give up on our people, Rinn. Not unless we're sure they're dead." She sighed softly, trying to keep it to herself. Rinn was right, she knew. Sending ten or twenty of the Grays to almost certain death wasn't going to do a thing for their five comrades, whether they were still alive or not. But she didn't abandon her people…and she didn't intend to start. She was responsible, she'd convinced them all to come, led them here. But she had just as much obligation to the others, the ones who would risk their own lives on any rescue mission. She couldn't just send people in…she needed a real plan, one with a chance of success.

"And they're alive," she continued. "We can be sure of that. They wouldn't kill everybody. They want answers, the location of this headquarters. As long as there are none of Ghana's kill teams outside, you can be sure the others are still alive. And they're sitting there wondering if we'll come for them…or if we'll write them off, decide it's too difficult, too dangerous to save them." She knew that was unfair, but she was also aware Rinn had a point. Cass had no intention of abandoning her people, whether it made sense or not. Regardless of the risk. Sometimes honor and morals meant more than rationality. It didn't make sense, not in a logical way, but it was also part of what made her someone a bunch of farmhands had followed on a crazy quest to save their homes and families. And she had been true to her word, led them from one success to another. Until now.

The truce had caused a few close calls, instances of Ghana's men arriving just too late to catch her people. Those final missions had given them a surplus of goods to sell, and enough crowns to send home to sustain their families and neighbors for the foreseeable future. Several of her people had called for her to halt the missions, to stay in hiding until the armies started fighting again. No one doubted that would be soon. But she had insisted on continuing. Just one more, she had said. She remembered it clearly. It had been a rich convoy, a prize worth enough to double the provisions sent home to the Galadan, to keep the people there safe and fed for years to come.

And a trap. It had been a trap. She'd rethought it all a hundred times…the ambush. Eight of her people killed, ten captured. And a dozen more wounded, half of them seriously. All because she had insisted. She told herself her decision had made sense, that it had been worth the risk to send so much aid back home. But that was bullshit, and she knew it. The crisis in the Galadan had been averted, and enough food, medicine, and supplies had been sent back to ensure the entire population would survive the winter, and most of the following year too.

No, it was hubris, my own ego. We've done too well, gotten away from too many near misses. I thought we were so good, that Ghana's men were fools. But they showed us…

"Cass, it wasn't your fault." It was Rinn again, his expression softer than it had been, his tone sympathetic.

Yes…it was my fault. All my fault.

"Thank you, Rinn, but that doesn't matter now. The only thing that is important is rescuing the prisoners. And I don't have any ideas. None." She looked out over the gathered Grays, her eyes begging for one of them to speak up. "Anyone have any suggestions? Other than leaving our people behind?"

The cavern was silent, only the hum of the portable reactor deeper in the cave to break the stillness. Cass looked out, panning her eyes back and forth.

Please…one of you…

"I have an idea, Cass…but it's pretty out there." It was Elli Marne, and she was sitting along the back row, wearing a baggy tunic and a pair of trousers tied around her waist with a rope. Everything was baggy on Marne. She was a tiny little thing, barely fifteen years old when the Grays had first marched out of the Galadan for the Badlands. Cass had twice rejected her pleas to come along, declaring her too young to leave home on such a dangerous expedition. But she'd stowed away in one of the transports and managed to stay hidden until they had ridden halfway to the desert. Cass had vowed to send her home with the first shipment of supplies, but Marne's pleas, and the demonstrations of courage and ability she'd put on during the first raids, had kept her with the group ever since.

Of course…who else would it be?

"Okay, Elli, what do you have in mind?"

Chapter Four

General Lucerne's Headquarters
"The Badlands"
Northern Celtiboria

"I am pleased you have decided to stay." Lucerne looked across the conference table at Blackhawk. The adventurer had agreed to remain in the general's stronghold and listen to his proposal. But he hadn't committed to a thing. Not yet.

"I haven't decided anything. Except that I will listen."

Lucerne nodded. "That is all I ask. As I said before, you may leave at any time. You will find I am a man of my word, Mr. Blackhawk, though I know you are skeptical." He paused. "Meanwhile, is there anything I can get for you? Perhaps we can share a meal while we talk." Lucerne didn't wait for an answer, he just turned back toward the guard standing next to the door. "Tell the chef to serve lunch immediately."

Blackhawk appreciated the gesture…and Lucerne's efforts to make charity appear as simple hospitality. In truth, it had been a long time since Blackhawk had eaten a decent meal… and two days since he'd had anything at all. He wasn't sure if it was simple defiance that had caused him to send back the meals that had arrived like clockwork during his imprisonment or just the unappetizing nature of the food. Lucerne's prison was clean, humane, orders of magnitude better than others he'd seen. But the meals were the same kind of slop common to most prisons.

"So, General, why don't you tell me why I'm here." Black-hawk didn't know if he was going to do what Lucerne asked, but he felt an energy that had long been absent from his thoughts. Ever since he'd...left...the empire. There had been a time when Blackhawk craved action, when he chafed in boredom at inac-tivity. Most of his life, in fact. And this Celtiborian Warlord had impressed him, not an easy thing to do.

"I am concerned about the truce, Mr. Blackhawk. I was reluctant to agree to it. My forces had the momentum in the conflict. But modern war cannot be won with morale alone, and my logistical situation was perilous. I managed to hide that well, but my troops were down to a dozen cartridges each when the ceasefire took effect. I moved my heaviest units forward, tried to give the impression I was planning a final offensive, a bit of posturing to induce the others to accept the truce. But in truth, my soldiers didn't have enough ordnance to sustain half a day's fighting."

"I applaud your counter-intelligence efforts. And your skill at bluffing. That couldn't have been an easy bit of deception." Blackhawk was surprised at Lucerne's candor. He suspected the general had already addressed his supply problems, but still, it said something about the man that he would admit how he'd almost made a tragic miscalculation. Most men in his position would rewrite history, turn even nearly disastrous miscalcula-tions into displays of wild self-aggrandizement. He started to understand Lucerne's reputation as a no-nonsense leader, beloved by his soldiers. It made sense that they followed him with unshakeable loyalty...he was one of them. In a way few generals could be.

"No, it wasn't. I have since been able to get several convoys through, and my soldiers are resupplied and reprovisioned...but the truce still has almost ninety days to run." He paused. Then he continued, his discomfort clear in his tone. "Now that my forces are resupplied, the peace works against me. My soldiers' morale is still very strong from the recent victories...and my other forces, those outside the Badlands, are tied down elsewhere. I'm afraid I have no additional strength to deploy here. In three months, my enemies will only be stronger, and my forces will be the same as they are today…but the memories of victory will be older, fading."

"You didn't bring me here to tell you to violate the truce and launch a surprise attack. That is what most generals would do. Certainly in the empire." Blackhawk paused, silently scolding himself. He didn't talk about the empire. Ever. No good would come from anyone knowing the extent of his knowledge.

"Yes, you are right, Mr. Blackhawk. Most generals would break the truce without warning. They would deploy treachery to gain a victory."

"But not you?" Blackhawk's tone was odd. He'd intended the comment in an almost sarcastic way, but it came out more as a deadpan question. He tended to disregard claims of honor and trustworthiness, having found such traits to be very rare indeed. But he was beginning to believe Lucerne, to accept that the Celtiborian general was the genuine article.

"No, Mr. Blackhawk. Not me." Lucerne paused. "It is not that I am some paragon of virtue…far from it. But I have based my dealings on honesty, on keeping my word when I give it. Even my enemies know they can trust me, at least to a point. My reputation has served me well. Indeed, this current truce, which saved me from destruction as my forces ran out of ammunition, was only possible because my opponents believed I would honor the terms."

"But they will not…not if it is to their advantage to strike."

"You come to the heart of the matter, Mr. Blackhawk. My strongest adversary is General Ghana. I have fought him before, and I have excellent intel on his holdings and his various forces. I have examined the data a dozen times, and I am sure of my conclusions. He has greater forces here than he should be able to support in this country…by a considerable margin."

"And you want to know who is behind him."

"Yes, Mr. Blackhawk. That is exactly what I want."

"Why me? Why not send your own people?"

Lucerne hesitated. "I am afraid my intelligence operation is rather less developed than my field forces. I lack operatives of your…ability. And there is too much chance one of my people would be recognized. I'm more of a military officer than a spymaster. The cloak and dagger comes far less naturally to me."

"And you think I am a spy?" Blackhawk felt a wave of amusement. He had far more experience himself in the blunter ways power was employed. Skulking around in the shadows playing the games of intelligence was not in his skillset. He was an able warrior—more than able—but he knew for all his skills he was a blunt instrument of sorts, accustomed to using naked force to attain his goals.

"No, not necessarily. But I do believe you are an extraordinarily competent individual…with a range of capabilities far beyond those in evidence. And, while you killed four of Ghana's men, it is very unlikely you will be recognized, not with the surveillance footage from the saloon destroyed and all of his people who saw you dead. And that anonymity will facilitate your gaining entry into his service…that and a bit of cover manufactured by my people."

"So you want me to go to General Ghana's camp…and what, volunteer to serve in his army? That is a little convenient, isn't it? Don't you think it will seem a bit suspicious?"

"No…why would it? There is war here, and all the armies seek recruits. You are an offworlder, clearly one possessing military skills. You will be a mercenary, here seeking pay in one of the Warlords' armies. You'd hardly be unique in that regard. My forces are 99% native, but many of my rivals aggressively recruit offworlders. Including Ghana. He is in the middle of a massive recruiting effort right now, though I can't even begin to guess how he is funding it. His people are offering huge bounties to new recruits, especially those who can demonstrate military experience."

"This sounds like a dangerous mission." Blackhawk's voice was matter-of-fact, with no hint of fear.

"It is. Certainly. I didn't think that would be a major obstacle for you."

"I didn't say it was. But I've done my fighting, General. I've fought my battles. Now I just want to be left alone."

"And how has that worked for you? Four bullies walk into a bar and draw you right into a dangerous mess. Don't forget, you could easily be hanging from a rope right now if things had gone differently. If you truly want to be left alone, you need wealth and power, enough to enforce your solitude, to protect it. And I am offering you a thousand gold crowns…a good start toward that."

Blackhawk almost argued, but he stopped himself. Lucerne was right. He'd been wallowing in self-pity and misery for too long. He knew he could never kill himself, never even give up in a fight…and while his anger and bad attitude had gotten him into a number of scrapes, his extraordinary abilities had ensured he'd prevailed in those. He was even sure—pretty sure—he could have escaped from Lucerne as well if he'd had to. But if he was going to live, wallowing in misery and poverty didn't make sense. He carried a lot of guilt about his past, but it was time to leave that behind, or at least put it in its place. And Lucerne seemed like a good man, almost certainly more admirable than any of his adversaries.

He thought about the discipline of Lucerne's soldiers… and contrasted them with the four loudmouthed troublemakers who'd walked in the saloon and picked the fight that killed them. Ghana's men.

"Tell me why?" he said suddenly.

"Why? Because I need warning if Ghana is going to violate the truce. I need to know who is supporting him."

"No," Blackhawk said. "Why are you fighting? Why are you in this war instead of sitting home protecting your estates?" Blackhawk had been in many wars, but he couldn't have answered his own question. He didn't know why he had fought before, what had driven him to do the things he had done, at least he had no reasons that made sense to him now. But Lucerne was different, and Blackhawk was curious. "Why does a good, honest man choose a life of war?"

"That's an interesting question, Mr. Blackhawk, one with two answers. The first is simple, straightforward. Because peace is not a viable choice on Celtiboria. Because just as your own desire to be left alone didn't prevent Ghana's men from picking a fight with you, so this world's nobility is drawn into its never-ending wars. Those who remain weak, who fail to grow their holdings, build greater armies...they are conquered, reduced to serving one of the stronger lords...or worse."

"And the second reason?"

Lucerne paused. "The second reason is a bit more complicated...and one you might find far-fetched." His voice was tentative, uncomfortable. "And somewhat boastful as well, I'm afraid."

"Try me." Blackhawk looked intently at his companion. "If I am going to do this, it is because I believe you are different from a hundred other paymasters. If money was my only concern, I could sell my skills to the highest bidder, couldn't I?"

"Indeed you could." Lucerne sighed softly. "Very well, your point is taken. I will share my motivations with you. I intend to unite Celtiboria, Mr. Blackhawk. I am not the most powerful of the Warlords, not by any measure. Not yet. But when I am finished, I intend not just to be the strongest. I will be the only one left."

The words were, in fact, boastful, and extremely aggressive considering Lucerne's place in the Celtiborian hierarchy. But Blackhawk found himself accepting them at face value, and for reasons he couldn't quite pinpoint, he believed Lucerne just might achieve his goal one day. If he was able to prevail in this struggle, at least.

"So, I help you become king of Celtiboria, or whatever title you choose to give yourself? I'll acknowledge you seem to be an honorable sort, General, but what do I care who rules this planet?"

"It is more than the planet, Mr. Blackhawk. I intend to unite the Far Stars...the entire sector."

Blackhawk felt like a laugh was about to emerge, but it never came. Lucerne was serious...he could tell that immediately. And, more amazingly, he again believed the general just might achieve his goal. It didn't make sense. Blackhawk wasn't an expert in

Far Stars history, but he knew, like everyone else, that it was an unruly, disordered frontier, with planets far more likely to fight each other than join together for the greater good. Uniting all one hundred worlds would require conquering the other five Primes, the technologically advanced planets that dominated the sector...not to mention defeating dozens of planetary kings and dictators, eradicating fleets of vicious pirates, crushing mercenary companies...

"So you want to be king of the Far Stars..."

"No, Mr. Blackhawk," Lucerne interrupted, "not king. I intend to form a confederation, one that will guarantee certain basic freedoms and liberties to all residents of the sector. But more than that, I intend to ensure that the Far Stars is ready to protect itself. That it is never conquered, never forced into the empire."

Lucerne's mention of the empire pricked at Blackhawk, and he focused even more intently on the general's words.

"It is only here that men live without the imperial yoke on them. The Far Stars has its share of conflict and oppression, but if these last worlds in all of human-settled space fall under the emperor's rule, the last embers of freedom will be gone from the galaxy."

Blackhawk knew the empire was already in the Far Stars. Six of the one hundred systems contained imperial worlds, including Galvanus Prime, considered the sector capital by an empire that already claimed suzerainty over all of the Far Stars. That was a claim without basis, he knew, at least beyond the six systems of the imperial demesne, but one the emperors had made for centuries nevertheless.

"That is quite a goal. You really think the empire is a threat to the Far Stars?" Blackhawk was just curious what Lucerne would say. He knew for certain that the imperial threat was very real.

"Yes, I do believe it. The Far Stars owes its independence to the Void, and the difficulty of navigating across that treacherous expanse of nothingness. No emperor has been willing to risk his battleships and legions on a crossing that claims so many of the ships that attempt it. But I find scant comfort in that.

There are six imperial worlds in the Far Stars now…and we owe the fact that there are no more to a long sequence of foolish, incompetent governors. Even with the Void, and without the massive fleets the emperors command on the other side, the Far Stars are vulnerable. They are exposed because they are fractured, because they fight each other over nothing. The economic strength of the sector is drained by pirates and freelance mercenaries and raiding parties. An imperial conquest wouldn't be a war…it would be a mopping up expedition, one planet at a time, while the others watched, and scooped up what crumbs they could. Until their turn came. It waits only on the day a competent man comes to take the governor's chair, armed with enough resources to make imperial rule a reality."

Blackhawk was impressed. Lucerne's observations were spot on, and his fears were very justified. All it would take was a determined emperor…and a capable governor with some additional resources. Then six worlds would become ten, and then twenty…each taken one at a time, isolated, with no help from its neighbors. Until imperial might in the Far Stars became too powerful to resist.

He found himself nodding gently as he considered everything Lucerne had said. And he knew one thing for certain. He didn't want to see the Far Stars fall. Not to the empire. Not ever. It wasn't any particular love for the sector or for the people who lived there. But he didn't want the last resistance to the empire to disappear.

"That is a long way from where you are now, General, is it not? Even if you are successful—as no Celtiborian general has been in three hundred years—it will take you decades, just to conquer the planet. And more time to force the other worlds into your confederation." Blackhawk knew—and he realized Lucerne did too—that most of the worlds of the Far Stars would resist, that to make his confederation a reality, he would have to be a conqueror first…and only then a lawgiver, a guardian of freedom.

Blackhawk didn't know if the general could achieve his audacious goals or not. But he was certain of one thing…and that realization surprised even him. He wanted to help if he could.

"Very well, General. I will do it. But I'm going to need a lot of information first. Impressions from the saloon incident notwithstanding, I do not rush into things unprepared."

There was a soft buzz. Lucerne leaned down over the communications console and said, "Enter." He turned back to Blackhawk. "Lunch is here." He paused a moment as a line of soldiers walked in carrying several trays. "Just set them down. We will serve ourselves."

He sat quietly as the men put the trays on the table. Then they each bowed to the general and walked swiftly back into the hall.

"Let us eat, Mr. Blackhawk, while we discuss further. I will answer your questions…and get you whatever information you require. And there is also the matter of your cover. You will need an identity, perhaps an Antillean outcast, a member of a modestly upper class family expelled for some disgrace and turned mercenary. That is not terribly uncommon among the Antilleans."

"Your people can create a cover for me? I thought you didn't have much of an intelligence operation, General."

"I didn't say I had none, Mr. Blackhawk. And I assure you that when I send you into Ghana's maw, you will have every possible tool I can provide to ensure your success…and your survival."

Lucerne reached out to one of the trays, grabbing a large loaf of bread and tearing off a piece before handing it to Blackhawk.

"Let us start with what you really want from this mission," Blackhawk said, taking the bread from Lucerne as he spoke. He paused for a second. It was soft, fresh…even still a little warm. Blackhawk had ingested more alcohol than solid food recently, but he couldn't remember the last time he'd had a decent meal. Or something as simple as freshly-baked bread.

"And what do you think I want, Mr. Blackhawk? Besides what I have told you?"

Blackhawk took a bite of the bread, chewing quickly and swallowing before he answered. "I think what you say is true…

you'd like to know who is backing Ghana…" He looked over and stared intently at Lucerne. "…but I'd also guess you are really hoping to entice Ghana into breaking the truce…or gaining some information you can use to justify your own attack, a casus bellum of some kind."

It was Lucerne's turn to stare wordlessly for a few seconds. He was a man who hid his thoughts well, but now they were on his face to be read. He was impressed. "You are an insightful man. And very correct. I cannot allow another three months of inactivity…and I cannot launch an unprovoked surprise attack." He paused. "So, we must make something happen by other means, Mr. Blackhawk. We must find a way to engineer a resumption of hostilities as quickly as possible."

Blackhawk took another bite of the bread. He was seeing Lucerne more clearly, and his esteem was growing. The men he'd seen in his life he'd have called good were few in number… and almost without exception they were weak fools. Their motivations might have been positive, but they were idealistic, believing what they needed to believe to sustain their outlooks. And, eventually, they were all destroyed by the nature of a universe they refused to see for what it was.

But Lucerne was different. He was a good man, Blackhawk believed that more with every additional moment he spent with the general, with every word spoken. But he wasn't weak…nor foolish, blind to the realities of the world. This was a man people would follow, a man soldiers would die for. He was a man who just might achieve the goals he'd set for himself.

If people helped him. Blackhawk didn't know if Lucerne would be able to attract all the skilled and capable supporters he would need in his fight. But he was sure about one thing. He would be one of them. He would help.

"Very well, General," he said as soon as he swallowed. "I will do it. I will help you."

Chapter Five

Marshal Carteria's Palace
The Turennian Archipelago
Equatorial Celtiboria

The room was massive, at least a hundred paces from the great, bejeweled bronze doors to the raised dais at the far end. It was built from pure white Celtiborian marble, the floors, the walls, the great columns supporting the ceiling far above the gleaming floor. It was an architectural marvel, and every bit of it had been constructed for a single purpose, to sate the vanity of a one man, and to proclaim his greatness to all who entered.

Demetrius Targus Ellian Carteria was the most powerful of Celtiboria's fractured and feuding class of Warlords, the absolute ruler of more than a quarter of the planet, including the ancient religious capital. Control of Celtiboria's primary city was a dubious prize in many ways, bringing with it the need to provide bread and circuses for its large and disorderly population as well as to treat with the elders of the planetary church headquartered there. But it also bestowed a right acknowledged by all the combatants, that of its possessor to style himself Marshal, the ancient title of the supreme commander of Celtiboria's armed forces.

The city had little military or economic value, and the Marshalate carried with it no wealth, no power over the others, nor a single additional soldier. But it appealed to the narcissism that ran deep in Carteria, and he'd celebrated his conquest of the capital by restyling his dress uniform, adding a considerable amount of lace and braid and creating a bit of foppery that matched his idea of what the Marshal of Celtiboria should wear.

Carteria had inherited his father's rich estates at a young age, and he'd expanded the breadth of his domains more than fivefold in the past twenty years, as much through backroom deals and base treachery as military skill. He was a hated figure, both in the lands he controlled and those he didn't, but he was feared more...for his cruelty, and for his seemingly random and unpredictable nature. The people in the provinces he ruled were cowed, beaten down...and they suffered under the harsh occupation by his soldiers, who projected the frustration caused by their own fear of their master onto the unfortunates over whom they were placed.

He had allies too, other Warlords, who were dazzled or intimidated by his power, so much so they ignored the many instances when he'd betrayed his compatriots, sold out those who had sworn to follow him. Some fooled themselves, invented excuses for past treacheries, reasons why they were different. They told themselves they were Carteria's true allies. Others simply accepted they had no alternative and made the choice to embrace the Marshal as an ally rather than face his forces in battle...and endure far more certain destruction as a defeated enemy. To serve Carteria—as an ally, as a soldier, as a citizen of his occupied lands—was to know fear every moment.

The small group of officers walked slowly forward. Jinn Barkus stood in front of his two aides, wearing a freshly pressed dress uniform. He was a major in Ghana's army, a veteran of many battles, but he found himself on edge, an uneasiness beyond the direct fear he felt in combat. Carteria was a volatile and dangerous man, one Barkus knew was not above killing a messenger in a fit of rage. And he was not there to report good news.

He walked forward, standing perfectly straight, trying not to look at the discolored areas of the floor, spots where the marble had been stained with blood. His eyes focused on Carteria, sitting in his chair on the highest part of the raised area. He'd been told where to stop, just short of the steps up to the platform. He moved to that point and stopped. Then he snapped to attention and bowed...deeply.

"I would hope you are here to report that your master has secured control over the trade routes through the Badlands...if I had not already had considerable intelligence suggesting things are rather less satisfactory." There was annoyance in Carteria's tone, but not outright hostility. Yet. Still, Barkus didn't think the total lack of a greeting or any customary niceties was a good sign.

"Marshal Carteria, General Ghana sends his respects, and be bade me tell you of his undying..."

"Yes, yes, yes...no doubt General Ghana has many pleasantries he sent you to convey. But let us skip all that and focus on results, shall we? General Ghana came to me, and he offered friendship in exchange for my aid in taking the Badlands. And when he came, I welcomed him with open arms, as a brother. Did I do as I promised? Did I provide the money I had pledged to finance his campaign?" Carteria gazed at Barkus with a withering stare. "Yes, I did...and more. Ten million ducats, the funding that allowed your master to sustain an army large enough to crush anything that opposed it. Yet he did not crush his opposition, did he? No, instead, he lost battle after battle...and finally his forces were driven from West Hill itself, in an ignominious retreat."

Barkus could hear the tone in Carteria's voice increasing in intensity, his anger growing with each word. He wanted to speak, to answer some of the Marshal's statements, to do his best to explain the army's losses...but he didn't dare interrupt.

"Your general has failed, Major. He has failed me. He assured me he could gain total control over the Badlands within six months if I provided the aid he requested. I gave him everything he asked for, and now here you are more than a year later with naught to offer save excuses."

Barkus stood still, at respectful attention, struggling to maintain his calm under the Warlord's blistering attack. He wasn't sure if Carteria was done speaking, if he should respond. But after ten seconds of silence he took a deep breath and began the speech he had been rehearsing all morning.

"Your excellency...my master, General Ghana, has fought nobly, true to his alliance with you. He would have prevailed, but one of the other Warlords present in the Badlands...his army... it is extremely well-trained and led."

"General Lucerne." Carteria glared down at Barkus. "I have heard of this man before, of unlikely victories won by his out-numbered armies. It appears he is a man of some ability, but his army, however capable the soldiers, is nothing. He wields only regional power, and the Badlands is far from his base in the Riverlands. He is overextended and at the end of a long and tenuous supply line. And your master had nearly twice the strength in the field. Yet still Lucerne was victorious."

Barkus swallowed hard. Carteria obviously had excellent intel...and he knew what that meant. Spies. Probably some of Ghana's own soldiers, taking Carteria's coin to report on their commander. The idea sickened Barkus. He was afraid of Carteria, no question. But he'd sworn to Ghana's service, and he would fight his battles for the general whose oath he'd taken. And he despised those whose loyalty was available for purchase. The thought of such men among those he served with sickened him.

"Marshal Carteria, I can only say that General Lucerne's forces are extremely well-trained and..."

"And?" Carteria glared at Barkus with a withering stare.

"And General Lucerne is an extremely skilled commander." He paused. "Extremely skilled," he repeated.

"Perhaps I should have entrusted General Lucerne with my investment in the Badlands campaign. No doubt then I would be celebrating news of victory rather than enduring excuses for defeat."

"General Lucerne would not have accepted your aid, Marshal." Barkus' stomach tightened. His words sounded harder edged than he'd intended them, and if Marshal Carteria got angry enough…

"And why is that, Major? Warlords from across Celtiboria beg for my support, they petition for my friendship, promise me their unending loyalty. Yet you think this General Lucerne would spurn my backing? I find that difficult to believe…and suspiciously self-serving for you and your master."

Barkus stood facing Carteria. He could feel his heart beating, hear it in his ears. "I meant no disrespect, Marshal. But this Lucerne, he is a…zealot. He is arrogant, he believes he can defeat anyone, that he needs no one's help. And he will not yield. Were he here, great Marshal, he would spurn your offers of friendship, refuse your aid."

Barkus stood trying to stand firm, to suppress the shivers he felt trying to take hold of him. His gaze was fixed on Carteria, watching, his imagination running wild with images of the Marshal waving to his soldiers, commanding them to seize Ghana's impertinent messenger.

"I presume you have come to seek further aid," Carteria said. There was annoyance in his tone, but not the deadly rage Barkus feared. He relaxed…just a touch.

"Yes, Marshal. General Ghana seeks to crush this upstart once and for all…and he sent us to renew his vows of friendship and ask for your continued aid and indulgence."

Carteria was silent for a moment, staring at the terrified ambassador. Barkus had the distinct impression that the Marshal enjoyed the fear and discomfort he caused.

"Very well, Major. I will consider General Ghana's request. Leave your data pack with my chief of staff, and I will review it all and make a decision." He waved toward an officer standing at his side. The man, whose uniform bore the rank insignia of a colonel, stepped forward immediately, taking a small pouch from Barkus.

"In the meanwhile, Major, allow me to show you my hospitality. You and your aides will be my guests until I have reviewed all of this…then you will carry back my reply."

"Thank you, Marshal Carteria."

"You may leave," Carteria said, gesturing again, this time to a different officer, one standing next to a large column to Barkus' side. "Captain Wrik, you will take Major Barkus and his people to their accommodations. See that they are fed and that all their needs are attended to."

"Yes, my lord Marshal."

Barkus bowed, making sure to dip down as low as he could. Then he stood up and turned around, following the captain and feeling a bit of relief with every step he took toward the door.

* * *

Carteria sat at a long dining table, one large enough to accommodate more than a dozen diners. But he was the only one seated. A cluster of attendants stood behind him, silently waiting for him to issue a command. And in front, standing next to the table, was a man in Carterian uniform, a senior colonel, whose riotous bunch of multi-colored ribbons indicated, among other things, twenty-five years of service.

"What are your thoughts, Colonel Eleher? How do we proceed?"

The officer stood more or less at attention, though Carteria had already told him to be at ease. "My intelligence suggests General Ghana is a moderately competent commander, capable of occasional moments of brilliance. He has certainly enjoyed a level of local success, including a number of major military victories." He paused. "That is, of course, before he encountered General Lucerne."

Carteria picked up a small fruit in his hand. It was a blood date, from the deep deserts in the south of the planet's largest continent, a delicacy that had cost Carteria a king's ransom to import...before he'd defeated the cabal of local chieftains who had ruled the area and added it to his growing domains.

The fruit had a wrinkled, dried out appearance from the outside, but it was full of deep red juice that poured out and trickled down his chin as he bit into it.

"The utility of controlling the Badlands and its trade routes is self-evident. But I wonder now, if defeating and destroying

Lucerne is not an even greater priority. I'm not inclined to accept the reports of his ability as presented, but it seems likely that there is some truth there. Allowing him to continue to expand his lands and his army seems unwise…and letting him gain control over the Badlands trade routes is out of the question."

Carteria held his arm out to the side, and an aide rushed forward, putting a wet towel in the Warlord's hand. He wiped off his hands and then his mouth, tossing it to the side when he finished.

"I am inclined to agree, Marshal. General Lucerne represents an unknown…there is no way to predict what strength he could attain, especially if General Ghana and the other local Warlords fall to him. He could quickly become a much more significant problem…one that could make us wish we'd dealt with him earlier, when he was weaker." Eleher paused. "I know it is frustrating, Marshal, but I do not see how we can abandon General Ghana now. That would hand the victory to Lucerne. And our future plans on the Northern Continent require control of the Badlands trade routes, either through a proxy like Ghana…or directly."

Carteria tore a piece from a hunk of bread. "Directly? Are you proposing we send a force to the Badlands, one large enough to defeat all the contending armies there?" The doubt was heavy in Carteria's voice. "That would take what, perhaps seventy-five thousand soldiers? One hundred?" He looked down at the table, his face twisted into a frown. "We have considerable commitments now…I don't see how we could spare that much strength without some additional notice, and even less the transport capacity to ship the troops and supply them so far from our bases."

"No, sir…I wasn't proposing we take everyone on. Simply that, instead of more financial support we send a ground force, perhaps twenty-five thousand. That, combined with Ghana's forces, should give us enough to overwhelm and destroy Lucerne. Then we would have forces there, in place…and the ability to exert greater control over General Ghana, ensure that he does not become, shall we say unreliable, after the battle is won."

Carteria looked at his officer, and he began nodding his head. "Yes, Varn…I believe you have a good idea there. We'll be moving more forces to the Northern Continent soon anyway. A foothold would be useful."

"I thought so, sir. And it puts us in a good position to keep an eye on Ghana longer term, to enforce his loyalty."

Carteria didn't answer, he just sat quietly for a few seconds, staring at the plate in front of him. Then he looked back at Eleher. "Yes, Colonel. I approve your plan. See to it immediately. You may choose your units from the household area forces… twenty-five thousand strong. I will authorize sufficient transport capacity to ship the troops and ordnance."

"Me, sir?"

Carteria had just shoved a chunk of meat into his mouth. "Yes, Colonel, you. If we are to lay the groundwork for the conquest of the Northern Continent, I would have a commander on the scene whom I trust completely…and that is you."

"Yes, Marshal." Eleher wasn't sure how he felt about the assignment. Ghana was likely to be hard to handle, especially once Lucerne was gone and he wasn't as afraid anymore. And battle assignments were risky, not just in terms of combat itself but also because Carteria tended to be extremely unforgiving of defeated generals. There was no better way to advance in his service than to achieve victory…and no better way to end up on your knees with a gun pressed against the back of your head than losing in the field.

"I want this matter expedited. The truce in the Badlands may have ninety days to run, but that assumes everyone adheres to the terms…and we can't count on that. I will provide you will air travel assets to get your forces on site as quickly as possible."

"Yes, sir…" Eleher knew he'd just been given an opportunity…and a risk as well. And very little time to prepare for a major operation. "With your permission, Marshal, I will get started immediately. I have considerable preparations to begin."

"Yes, Colonel, you are dismissed." Carteria held a leg of roast fowl in his hand, and he moved it toward his mouth, stopping suddenly as Eleher saluted and turned to leave. "And Colonel…"

Eleher stopped and turned back toward Carteria. "Yes, sir?"

"I like your earlier thought of direct control over the Badlands. I will give you a hundred thousand silver ducats for bribes and special operations…and when Lucerne is defeated and the Badlands secured, you are to move against Ghana as well. Choose your moment for maximum surprise." Carteria stared at his officer, a sinister look in his eyes. "And then kill him, Colonel…and seize his lands."

Carteria stared at his subordinate, a crooked smile forming on his lips. "And then we will begin our campaign on the Northern Continent in possession of its most valuable trade routes… and with the two most dangerous Warlords already dead."

Chapter Six

West of Lucerne's Headquarters
"The Badlands"
Northern Celtiboria

Blackhawk walked across the open sand, pulling the hood of his cloak over his head, sheltering his face from the searing sun. The territory north of West Hill was open desert, with nothing more than a few tufts of scrub brush to break up the endless expanse of sunbaked sand. It was hot, hot as hell, and Blackhawk was covered in sweat, despite his body's superior ability to adapt to hostile conditions. He was surprised Lucerne's men were doing as well as they were, but they were still slowing down, and forcing him to do the same.

They've been fighting in this furnace for over a year...otherwise they'd all be on their backs, panting for air and guzzling the last drops of their water supplies...

The group was small, one of Lucerne's operatives and half a dozen soldiers, all wearing the garb of Badlands dwellers, desert nomads who eked out a sparse living traveling from oasis to oasis in the bleak countryside, and selling food and water to the caravans passing through. It was a reasonable cover, but Blackhawk had his doubts. The nomads he'd seen in his travels through the Badlands had a different look to them, their bodies adapted to lifetimes of chronic dehydration. Lucerne's soldiers had the right clothes, but they looked like plump melons compared to the natives...and they were covered in sweat, even more so than Blackhawk.

"Perhaps I should be on my own," Blackhawk said, turning toward a tall man standing just to his left. Aton Pellier was one of Lucerne's top people, a major from the main army seconded to the sparse intelligence service. He was the closest thing Lucerne had to an expert on Ghana and his operations, and the general had ordered him to get Blackhawk around to the other side of the enemy camp, where he could approach from the direction of the deep desert, giving him maximum believability as a wandering mercenary or recruit.

"The general was very clear, Mr. Blackhawk. I am to escort you around the perimeter of General Ghana's forces...and see that you have a clear approach."

Blackhawk sighed. He wasn't used to diplomacy, to worrying about relationships and fitting into a group. His actions in his past life had been more...direct. But he'd accepted service with Lucerne, and he was determined to make the best of it.

"Very well, but perhaps we should find someplace to hide during the day...and then travel at night." He gestured toward the soldiers. "Your men look like they're about to pass out." *And you don't look much better, Major.* "Darkness will provide some extra security, make it easier to avoid any patrols."

"That's impossible," Pellier replied. "We have a timetable. We have to be there by midday tomorrow." There was something odd in the officer's voice. It was nothing specific, at least nothing Blackhawk could place. But something.

"Timetable? I didn't discuss any timetable with General Lucerne. His only instructions were to proceed as I feel practicable." That wasn't exactly true...Lucerne hadn't said anything at all about timing. His last words to Blackhawk had been about the importance of the mission, and a last heartfelt thank you for accepting the job.

"He told me." Pellier's voice was cool, matter-of-fact, but Blackhawk was uncomfortable. He'd already decided he didn't like the officer. Pellier hadn't done anything suspect, not really.

But Blackhawk had a strange feeling of unease. He tried to tell himself he didn't work well with others, that he'd been on his own a long time, and he was uncomfortable relying on anyone else. But the feeling was still there, not suspicion really. More discomfort.

"I agreed to do this job as I saw fit, Major. Not adhere to deadlines I didn't even know about."

Pellier stopped walking and turned toward Blackhawk. "I am a military officer, Mr. Blackhawk. I just follow the orders I am given by my superiors. I know nothing about your past, nor do I wish to. If we are being candid for a moment, I do not understand why General Lucerne would choose to entrust such a crucial mission to someone he hardly knows." He looked at Blackhawk, and his mask dropped, his true disdain showing in his scowl. "You are an unknown, a wanderer who, at least at first sight, offers little to assure one of your ability or trustworthiness. But it is not my place to question the general's decisions. Now, you agreed to carry out this mission, and I was ordered to get you to the approach point. I do not like you, you do not like me...but mutual friendship is not a requirement for our respective missions. I suggest we make the best of things. I will get you to the other side of Ghana's occupied zone, and then you will complete your mission however you see fit. Can we agree on that? A meager bit of détente that allows each of us to focus on what we were sent to do?"

Blackhawk looked back at the officer, surprised at the strength on display. Oddly, both his respect and his dislike grew. He wasn't convinced, not entirely, but Pellier had a point. He'd go along. He'd keep an eye on his new comrade, but he'd go along with Pellier's wishes. For now at least.

"Very well, Major. But if we're going to travel through the day, you and your soldiers are going to have to pick up the pace." Blackhawk was uncomfortable in the heat too, but he knew he could handle it better than his companions, who had to face the elements without the myriad benefits of genetically-engineered bodies.

"Don't worry, Mr. Blackhawk. We will have you at your destination on time." Pellier turned and started walking again, Blackhawk following suit. "I can promise you that."

* * *

Blackhawk was lying on his back, looking up at the inky black sky, splattered with a dazzling array of stars. He'd looked at it with various thoughts in his mind, the extreme clarity of the night, how much brighter and crisper the stars appeared in the deep desert, far away from any cities and the light pollution they gave off. But there was something else, the kind of thing he'd rarely considered in his life, or even noticed. It was beautiful.

Blackhawk had been bred—no, created was probably the better word—for a purpose…and he'd lived most of his life without deviating from his assigned role. His old life had left little room for appreciation of things like a perfect, starry night, and now he struggled with it, feeling…something…but not understanding it, at least not completely. He was a grown man, a warrior who had killed many times. But in some ways he felt like a child, truly seeing some things for the first time.

He also felt like he was awakening from a deep sleep, one infested with dark dreams. He'd spent the last several years traveling from planet to planet, from tavern to tavern, supporting himself with one act of petty theft after another. He'd sought one thing only. Escape. And he'd mostly found that in the bottle, when he'd been able to drink enough to overwhelm his body's own defenses.

But even those respites were brief, and ultimately unsatisfying. He had memories, terrible memories…not only of things he'd seen, but also deeds he'd done. Those images had tormented him, driven him to keep moving, to medicate with whatever mind-numbing substance he could lay his hands on. But that was a dead end, and he knew it. He'd come to a stark choice. Move past the guilt, the nightmares…find a new life, build one…from scratch, if necessary. Or die. He knew he couldn't kill himself, that his mental defense systems wouldn't allow it. But he could pick a fight, one he had no chance to win.

He could die as he had lived, weapons in hand.

He'd known all of this for a long time, but he'd hidden the direct choice from himself, stumbled forward through the wreckage his life had become, seeking only pain relief and taking no real steps to address the choice head on. Until now.

He knew what had changed. Lucerne. He hadn't known the Celtiborian general long enough to call what he felt loyalty, but he realized he deeply respected the man. And his encounter with Lucerne, the realization that there were good people out there, causes worth fighting for, had pulled him back from the abyss. He wouldn't seek his own death. He would complete this mission for Lucerne. And then he would build a new life, one separate from that he had lived before. He would become the man he'd never been allowed to be, one whose actions didn't overwhelm him with self-loathing. And he would remember his debt to this Celtiborian general.

But what about Pellier? Why do I have this uneasy feeling? Am I worried I misread Lucerne? That I am wrong, that the general really sent his people to murder me in the desert? No, that doesn't make any sense. He could have killed me far more simply in his headquarters…and no one would have cared. So what is it? Why do I feel such concern?

He took a deep breath, enjoying the cool, fresh air, amazed at how cold it got in the desert at night. He shivered and slid down deeper into the light sleeping bag. It didn't provide an enormous amount of warmth, but it was enough.

His thoughts were on Pellier, on the day's march. He recounted every moment, every word the Celtiborian officer had uttered. There was no reason to suspect the man of treachery. But Blackhawk was still uneasy, concerned enough that he'd decided to remain awake through the night. It was another benefit of his engineered body, the ability to go a number of days with no sleep without a significant degradation in his abilities. But for all his precautions, the unease he felt in his gut, he couldn't make a rational case to suspect the officer. He told himself it was paranoia, that he was creating an issue where none existed. And he forced it back, out of his mind. But he also stayed awake, lying quietly, staring up at the stars.

* * *

"We're almost there." Pellier was at the front of the group, looking out over the landscape with a small scope. "We'll stop just behind that low ridge." He turned toward Blackhawk. "Then you'll get your wish, Mr. Blackhawk. You'll be on your own."

Blackhawk stared out in the same direction. He wondered for a moment how the view his enhanced eyes gave him compared to that Pellier had through the scope. He knew he didn't have the same magnification with his bare eyes, but he could still make out the ridge. It was a long stretch of rock outcroppings, narrow but running on as far as the eye could see. There were breaks in the rock wall, places where sections had long ago been blasted away to make an easier path for the transports of the trade caravans. But it was more than enough cover, and Blackhawk was grateful they'd gotten this far without being discovered.

"Will your people be heading back before nightfall?"

He was debating spending the night along the rocks and setting out for Ghana's camp in the morning. He'd have preferred the cover of darkness on the journey here…getting spotted with a pack of poorly disguised soldiers wouldn't have been helpful. But now he intended to be seen. He was a wanderer who had come to enlist in Ghana's army, and all of Celtiboria's Warlords recruited from the dispossessed and desperate of the planet. Traveling now at night was dangerous…and sneaking around this close to Ghana's base in the darkness only invited the guards and patrols to view him as a threat. Better to walk in, openly, in the sunlight of morning.

"Perhaps," Pellier replied. "We might take advantage of the cooler weather and get some distance behind us."

Blackhawk had stopped listening. He'd heard something, and he tensed immediately, his eyes darting to the side, looking off beyond the rock outcroppings.

Airship.

"Let's go, Major…we've got to get to those rocks. Now."

Blackhawk moved forward, turning his head back and repeating himself. "Now!"

Pellier had a surprised look on his face, one that changed quickly to anger at the imperiousness of Blackhawk's tone. But then he heard it too, and he yelled out to his troopers. "Let's go, men...we've got to get under cover."

Blackhawk was moving forward, quickly, definitely a run... but far from the fastest he could go. There was no point in outpacing his companions. His idea of a new life didn't include racing off and leaving comrades in trouble. He hadn't exactly sworn an oath of loyalty to these soldiers—or Lucerne either for that matter—but running away and leaving them behind didn't sit that well with him.

Besides, if the enemy spots them, they'll search the whole area...if they get caught, I get caught too. And it's going to take Ghana's people about ten seconds to figure out they're not desert nomads...and another ten to decide they're Lucerne's men.

No one is going to believe I'm not with them, that it's just a coincidence we're both here in the deep, empty desert...

"Move," he yelled, knowing the soldiers were already running as hard as they could.

There was more than one airship now. Blackhawk could make out at least three...and when he looked up, he saw a glint in the bright sky, the lead bird heading directly toward the group. He cursed their bad luck...but deep in his mind he couldn't believe it was fortune that had failed them. They hadn't seen so much as a scout flyer zipping over the truce-quieted battle zone the entire day before. Now, on the verge of reaching their destination, a flight of what he was willing to bet were gunships, was heading straight at them.

Blackhawk didn't believe in coincidence, and he damned sure didn't trust Pellier. Had the major simply screwed up, had they been detected by Ghana's people somehow as they trudged across the desert? Or was something darker happening?

He glanced back over his shoulder at Lucerne's officer. He was cursing himself for getting involved, for trusting the general...and worse, for not listening to his gut instinct on Pellier.

He wasn't sure yet the major had set him up, but he *was* sure of one thing. As soon as he knew for certain, Pellier would die. Whatever else happened.

The airships were closer now, louder. They were less than halfway to the ridge, and Blackhawk knew…they weren't going to make it. He wasn't even sure he could get there if he broke into a dead run. And he wouldn't do that, not until he was sure about Pellier.

"We're going to have to fight, Major," he snapped out. He knew the airships could gun them down with strafing runs, but he figured they would land instead. Either this was a setup, and Pellier was involved…or Ghana's people would want to investigate, to discover who they were before taking any action that might threaten the truce. If the airships landed, that meant there would be a fight on the ground, and that gave them a chance.

"Don't provoke anything," Pellier snapped back. "We should be able to talk our way out of this."

Blackhawk didn't reply. He just wondered if Pellier was really stupid enough to think his water-fat soldiers would really pass for desert nomads, or…

The lead airship swooped lower, kicking up a cloud of dust as it came down just in front of the group. Blackhawk watched as the other ships—there were six of them now, and they were indeed heavily-armed gunships—set down in a wide circle around them.

He'd stopped running…there was no point. They weren't going to make it to the rocks. He stood still, holding back from any moves that might appear threatening. That much of Pellier's advice, at least, made sense.

The noise from the airships' engines was loud, almost deafening as the other ships landed, and the sound came from all sides. Blackhawk could see Lucerne's men standing, their poses similar to his, not threatening, but ready to reach for their weapons on an instant's notice. He could tell they were afraid—any rational person would be. But they were hiding it well, and anyone less perceptive than Blackhawk might have been fooled.

He watched as the hatches opened on the lead airship, and a

group of soldiers scrambled out. They were clad in desert camo, and they wore partial body armor. They had assault rifles in their hands, and heavy swords at their sides.

"Stay where you are," the leader yelled, his voice almost lost in the din of the airship's turbines. "Hands out…don't move."

The squad of troopers moved forward, fanning out, weapons pointed toward Blackhawk and his companions.

"We want no trouble. We are Emiridani, desert dwellers…we are traveling between Hermami…oases." It was Pellier, managing a credible version of a Badlands accent, complete with a few words of the native dialect.

"You are on territory claimed by Lord General Bako Harrian Ghana. You are under arrest. You will be taken to our headquarters…if you are who you say you are, you will be released. If not…" The leader waved to his troops, and they moved forward, rifles extended in front of them.

Blackhawk watched, trying to appear nonchalant as he inspected the soldiers, their armor, weapons…weak spots. He was aware there were troops pouring out of the other airships too, taking position around his group. But he didn't look, didn't take any action to give away the degree of his focus.

One of the soldiers walked right up to him, a suspicious scowl on his face. "Open the cloak," he said gruffly. His comrades were doing the same with the others. Blackhawk paused, just for a second. He knew they wouldn't pass for desert nomads. Their looks were all wrong…and their weapons were far superior to the old bolt action rifles the Emiridani would be carrying. He needed to make a decision, in a split second. If he was going to fight, now was the time. The alternative was allowing himself to be disarmed, and probably shackled.

Attack…

He didn't figure it offered great odds of success, but he knew even if these soldiers couldn't tell, it would take Ghana's interrogators about five minutes to figure out his companions were Lucerne's soldiers. And even if they didn't assume the same of him, the plan was shot to hell. There was no way he was going to explain away being captured with a group of Lucerne's men.

He could feel the strange feeling, the tingling in his muscles, the alertness in his mind, adrenalin in his bloodstream. He'd never fully understood the battle trance, the physiology behind it, at least...but he'd experienced it countless times, and he knew how to use it. It wasn't voluntary...it came on him when battle called, and it increased his already-impressive abilities.

He was about to lunge forward against the soldier in front of him when he heard the sounds of fighting off to his side. It was Pellier, moving, grabbing the rifle of the soldier in front of him and pushing it aside.

Blackhawk launched his own attack, spinning to the side, away from his enemy's weapon...and then swinging hard, one quick strike, his open hand slamming into his foe's neck. The stunned soldier dropped to his knees, a shocked look on his face as he fell forward to the ground. Dead.

Blackhawk was already on the move, pulling the assault rifle from under his cloak, and bringing it to bear on two soldiers in front of him. He pulled the trigger, a burst of three bullets almost taking the head off the first man. His eyes were fixed on the second as the trooper moved to bring his own weapon to bear. But Blackhawk was faster, and he put his target down.

He swung his head back and forth, evaluating the situation. Most of Lucerne's soldiers were already down, only Pellier and two others still standing. There were enemy fighters closing from the other airships, but only one left between Blackhawk and the closest bird. He reacted on instinct, without conscious thought, and he dropped the last soldier with another burst. He knew what he had to do...if he could get to the ship...

Eight troops had come out. Blackhawk's eyes focused for an instant, estimating the ship's size. There would be a pilot inside...and possibly a co-pilot. But the payload wasn't more than eight troopers. He was sure. Ninety percent sure.

If he could get there quickly enough...he could kill the pilots, take the controls himself. He felt the tension in his legs as he readied himself for an all-out run for the airship. But Pellier and the other man...should he just abandon them? Could he?

He was confused, in a way he'd never been in battle before.

He knew what he'd have done before. He'd have left Lucerne's men behind to their fates. But there was something else there now, in his mind. And it kept him in place.

Fuck, he thought, glancing once at the airship before he turned toward his comrades. He disliked Pellier…and he'd deeply suspected the gruff major of treachery. But here he was fighting against Ghana's men, just as Blackhawk was.

One of the other soldiers went down, shot at least five times by two enemies…clearly dead even as he fell.

Two left. Plus me.

Blackhawk whipped up his rifle, flipping it to single fire as he did. Quarters were tight now…his targets were too close to his comrades for anything but aimed shots.

He fired once. Then again. Two enemy soldiers dropped. They had been moving around Pellier's flank, about to fire.

Blackhawk ducked to the side even as he took the shots, lowering his body in a jerky motion, an almost random movement, as he heard the fire whizzing by, passing through where he'd been an instant before.

He fired again. And again. Two more dead. But it wasn't enough. There had been three. And the third soldier fired… taking Pellier right in the chest. Blackhawk felt the frustration, the anger, as he saw his comrade fall back. He fired again, and the soldier who'd shot Pellier dropped, the top half of his skull gone.

He felt the urge to run to Pellier, the hope that the major was only wounded. But Blackhawk had seen enough battles to recognize a killing shot when he saw one. Pellier's wound was mortal, and if the major wasn't dead already, he would be in a matter of seconds. The regret hit him hard. He hadn't like Pellier, hadn't trusted him either. But the major had died fighting at his side, and now Blackhawk felt regret.

He spun around, toward the other survivor. But he was too late again. He shot, took down a trooper moving in from one of the other gunships. But the rest of them opened fire, riddling the last of his escorts. He was alone now.

He turned, going back to his old plan…a mad dash for the

airship. But he'd lost time, his abortive efforts to save Pellier and the others had cost valuable seconds. He wouldn't give up…it was still the best option. But he knew he wasn't going to make it.

"The general wants him alive."

Blackhawk heard the words. They were distant, but his enhanced ears picked them up.

Why? Why would they want me alive? How would they even know I'm not just another of Lucerne's soldiers?

He spun around, flipping the rifle to full auto…and emptying the clip, dropping another six of Ghana's troopers before throwing the weapon aside and turning back toward the airship. He zigzagged as he ran, avoiding the gunfire that wasn't coming. His comrades were all dead…and the enemy wanted him alive.

He felt the urge to reach for his pistol, but he remembered he'd left it behind at Lucerne's headquarters. His sidearms were too distinctive, completely unlike anything a desert nomad would possess. The pistol was of imperial manufacture, and though it was old and well-used, it was a formidable high tech weapon. The sword was even older, its blade short but razor-sharp and forged of the best hyper-steel in the empire. If he'd wanted to draw unwanted attention to himself, either would have done the job. But now he wished he had his own weapons. He'd fought many battles with that pistol and sword, killed countless enemies with them.

He was almost to the airship. Just few more steps. Then something hit him. It was like an electric shock, and he felt the energy drain from his body. A stun cannon…a powerful one. He staggered for half a second. Then he pushed forward, putting all that remained of his strength into keeping himself moving.

Again. A wave of pain, blackness for an instant. A dull ache in his legs. He fell down to one knee, gasping for air. His body twitched, and his vision was blurry. But still…somehow…he climbed back to his feet, took a step. And another.

Then a third blast, one that sent him face forward to the sand. He was lying, his mind fuzzy, clouded, his body immobile. He tried to force himself up, but there was no response. He struggled, pushed with everything he had…his arm lurched forward, then his leg. Slowly, he crawled forward, hearing the sounds of his enemies gathering around him. He could see their legs, the shadows they cast in the blazing desert sun.

They were talking, but he couldn't hear, couldn't focus on what they were saying. Someone was yelling to him. He heard the words, but the meaning was slow to come. Stop. The man was ordering him stop.

Fuck you, he thought, the defiance giving him back some clarity. He reached out ahead of him, shoved forward with his foot…another lurch toward the airship. Then pain, the stun cannon again, from close this time. He felt his body spasm, pain in every nerve. His mind was lost, floating. He had only one thought…he'd suspected Pellier, but the major was dead, a victim of the ambush even as he was. All the men were dead. There was only one answer, one possibility. Lucerne. Lucerne had betrayed him. He had betrayed them all.

How could I have been so wrong? And why…what does he have to gain?

And then there was nothing but the dark.

Chapter Seven

Ghana's Main Base
"The Badlands"
Northern Celtiboria

Blackhawk sat on the bare metal bench along the wall, looking out at the large cell. Ghana's prison was considerably less humane than Lucerne's, and far more representative of the genre in his experience. There were a dozen prisoners in the cell, with just a single bench large enough for perhaps half that many to sit. There were no cots, no place to sleep save sitting up on the bench for those lucky enough to have a spot…or on the damp, filth-strewn floor for the others. There was a single trough along the far wall, clogged and overflowing with urine and feces, adding mightily to the overpowering reek in the room.

Blackhawk felt a tug on his pants leg, and he kicked hard, sending the sand rat flying across the room. The rodents in the prison were extremely aggressive, climbing up legs to get at the slightest morsel of food…or to take a bite out of a prisoner if nothing else was available.

This is just great, he thought, looking around with a disgusted expression on his face. He'd been in worse places, in greater danger, but somehow that was of limited comfort to him now. He was pretty sure he would be able to escape when the time came. Ghana's operation didn't come close to Lucerne's in efficiency, and his soldiers were typical rabble, brave enough in a fight, but most of them seemed dumb as a box of rocks. And they were arrogant. Arrogance and stupidity were Blackhawk's favorite combo in an adversary.

He leaned back, stretching, trying to twist the kinks out of his back. His body ached, but he mostly ignored it. He'd done about an hour in one of Ghana's interrogation cells getting worked over by an inquisitor. It hadn't been pleasant, certainly… but his main impression was these frontier folk had a lot to learn about effective torture. They wanted him alive, and more or less unharmed, at least it seemed that way at the moment. That had held them back, prevented them from using any truly brutal methods.

Blackhawk was grateful for their ignorance, for how far behind imperial methods they were. There were many ways to inflict unimaginable suffering without causing permanent damage, but Blackhawk hadn't gotten anything more than a moderate beating…a few bruises that were already healing, courtesy of his improved bodily functions.

He suppressed a laugh. Every man would break at some point, though he knew he could take a lot of punishment. He had advanced training in resisting questioning…and an ambivalent attitude toward survival. It would take a lot for these yokels to make him talk. A lot more than a few kicks and punches.

He was more troubled by his thoughts of Lucerne than by the immediate prospects of an interrogation session he couldn't handle. He had really taken a liking to Lucerne, respected the man. He was rarely wrong about people…and almost never completely in error. He tried to convince himself this was a lesson, a reminder in why never to get involved in the affairs of those around him. But he still hated facing the realization he couldn't counter. Lucerne had set him up…and sacrificed one of his own officers and a group of his men to do it. That ran counter to every impression he'd had of the general…and also of the reputation Lucerne had among his own men.

Blackhawk knew a general's image among the population, even with his rivals, was subject to all manner of tricks and playacting. But the men who fought his battles, who followed his commands, quickly took his measure. And Lucerne's men seemed to take the concept of loyalty to a new level.

But what else could have happened? That was no random encounter… half a dozen airships, fifty men. Heading straight for us. No, they knew we were there. And everybody else who knew our route is dead. Except Lucerne.

The more Blackhawk thought about it, the surer he was. He put himself in Lucerne's place, and he knew he'd have never trusted an unknown drifter, no matter how adept he was at fighting. Not in a million years. He cursed himself for his folly, for believing the Celtiborian general. But he still couldn't figure out what Lucerne had to gain by betraying him.

He put those thoughts out of his mind. Now his focus was on getting out. Of the prison, of the Badlands. Off Celtiboria entirely. He was angry, disappointed in his own judgment…and he'd had more than enough of this miserable planet. It was time to go. Past time.

He wasn't going to crawl back into the bottle, though. No, he'd wallowed long enough in his misery. There was plenty of work in the Far Stars for a man as good with a gun and a blade as he was…on planets whose dysfunctionality was far more straightforward, at least, than Celtiboria's. Lucerne's efforts—his treachery—had produced some benefits…they had shaken him out of his self-indulgent stupor.

Yes, it was time to get out of here. The only question he hadn't answered was, would he leave Celtiboria immediately? Or would he kill Augustin Lucerne first? He knew he wouldn't know the answer…not until it was time to make that decision.

His eyes panned around the cell, his mind working, making a plan. There were a couple guys in filthy brown uniforms off to the one side…Ghana's men who had apparently gotten themselves into some kind of trouble.

Or they're spies, hanging around, trying to overhear something useful from the other prisoners.

Blackhawk wondered. He would have had operatives in his prison, but he decided Ghana wasn't that sophisticated. He was a blunt instrument, like most of the Warlords, born into a noble class with an inheritance of some lands and a force of retainers, assets he'd used more effectively than some of the others, mostly because his neighbors had been weaker than he was. He had some military skill, Blackhawk acknowledged that, but far less, he expected, than Lucerne. He glanced back at the uniformed men. *Not spies, he thought again. Just soldiers who got in trouble.*

There were a few others in the cell, clad in the light khaki garb of desert dwellers. Probably locals who'd resisted some outrage or another perpetrated by Ghana's troops. It was one of the perversions of war that the father trying to prevent a soldier from raping his daughter was usually the one dragged away as a criminal. Or perhaps they were starving locals who'd been caught stealing from military supply depots. Whatever the specifics, there was injustice of one sort or another on display, just as Blackhawk had seen everywhere else he'd been. He looked at the men for a few seconds, some part of him wishing he cared more than he did, that some sense of outrage at these helpless nomads being imprisoned—and likely killed eventually—pushed him to want to help them. But he'd seen enough of the galaxy to know that fairness was a fool's dream, one he had no time or patience to indulge.

There were five others, in the far corner. They'd been clustered together the entire time he'd been there, except when one had been dragged off for questioning. They were obviously together, and while he could tell at once they weren't military regulars, there was something about them, a hint of the toughness veterans acquired in battle. They reminded him of seasoned militias and rebel groups he'd seen on different planets, civilians at heart, but with some strength and discipline too. They were more watchful than the other prisoners too. More than one of them had flashed a glance his way.

Perhaps they were some kind of fighters, a local resistance group or something similar. He didn't care who they were or what cause they followed. But he knew they could be useful in his escape. Half a dozen prisoners would be a lot more trouble for Ghana's men to handle during an escape attempt…and he'd be able to slip away while the guards were chasing down the others.

He stood up slowly and walked across the room, shifting to the side to avoid a particularly large pile of unidentified slop on the floor. Then he moved directly toward the group, making no effort to disguise the fact.

The conversation stopped abruptly, and all five turned toward him. There were four men and a woman, and as soon as he got a close look at their faces he decided they had all seen some kind of combat. It was their eyes...these were people who had faced death, who had watched friends and comrades die... he was sure of it.

"Can we do something for you, stranger?" It was one of the men who spoke, and Blackhawk decided immediately he was the leader. His tone wasn't overtly hostile, but it wasn't friendly either.

Blackhawk stared right into the man's eyes. "Perhaps. I am going to get out of here...and I thought you might want to join me." He preferred bluntness whenever possible, and a few minutes of pointless banter would serve no purpose here.

The man started to laugh, but it died quickly on his lips. Blackhawk's stare was intense, his words heavy with deadly purpose.

"Is this some kind of joke?" the man replied. "A setup?"

Blackhawk's eyes darted to the sides, surveying the others. They were all covered in bruises and cuts, their clothes stained with dried blood. One of them had an arm in a makeshift sling, and another had a bloody rag tied around his head, covering one eye. Where one eye should have been.

Interrogation. These people have been questioned harshly...and from the looks of things they haven't broken yet.

His respect for them grew.

These are not simple locals...definitely not...

He almost felt a wave of guilt for his intention to use them as diversions in his own escape. Almost.

"I am quite serious. You do not look like you have enjoyed your captivity. It occurred to me you might wish to end it."

He noticed a few hostile stares, a rustling among the group. But the leader held up his hand, gesturing for his people to stay calm. Then he said, "And just how do you propose we escape?"

Blackhawk looked at the leader. "I have considered our options. The cell has two ventilation ducts. Both are on the ceiling, which makes it difficult to reach them. It might be worth the effort if this was an old castle or similar structure repurposed as Ghana's headquarters. But it appears to be some sort of modern prefabricated building, and these are purpose-built cells, which means there is likely some sort of obstruction in the ventilation system anyway, blocking an obvious avenue of escape."

Blackhawk clearly had the attention of all five prisoners now, even the ones who'd been looking at him a moment before with undisguised menace. His description was concise, complete, unemotional. Professional.

"The walls are made of some kind stress resistant polymer, so breaking through is unlikely, at least without tools we don't have. It might be worth the effort if we were on the outside of the structure, but we're not...we're deep in the center."

"How could you know that?" the leader asked.

"I kept track of distance and direction changes when they brought me in. The structure is roughly rectangular, and based on the path to this cell, it is apparent we are nowhere near the exterior wall."

The leader turned to look at his companions, and then his eyes moved back to Blackhawk. He was silent, as were all the others, trying to decide if they believed the man speaking to them truly had that kind of awareness of his surroundings.

"That leaves only more direct options as possibilities. The guards will be here with the evening meal in approximately one hour. Their doctrine has been absolutely consistent over the past three days. Two prisoners will bring in the pushcarts, with two guards standing behind them. The guards will have assault rifles, and pistols holstered at their sides. There will be another guard out in the hall, to the left of the cell door, armed similarly to the others. I observed a shadow from farther down the hall on two of three occasions, so we must assume a potential fourth guard…my guess is about three meters from the cell door."

The prisoners stared at Blackhawk in wonder…and rapt attention. The details he'd amassed on the prison, on the activities of the guards, were nothing less than astonishing.

"You want us to jump the guards?" There was surprise in the leader's voice, and fear too.

"Yes, simply put." Blackhawk could see the hesitation in the faces looking back at him. "Direct action is often the correct tactic, as much because it is unexpected as any other reason. Many efforts fail because those involved mistake added complexity for useful additions to the operating plan."

Blackhawk paused for a second, looking around him, checking on the status of the other prisoners. What he had to say was for the four men and women he was speaking to and no one else. "A jailor anticipates prisoners trying to tunnel out of a prison or escaping through the ventilation ducts. But unarmed prisoners assaulting four guards…the very audacity of the plan gives it an edge. On a simplistic level, the presence of the armed guards is intended to thwart any such effort, and once they have deployed significant force—as is the case here—they will likely discount the possibility of a direct assault. They will feel they are strong, that they have enough strength in place to prevent any such attack. And that is what makes them vulnerable."

Blackhawk felt an energy he hadn't in a very long time. His mind was awake, alive, analyzing his proposed plan even as he spoke with the prisoners. They stared back at him, eyes wide as understanding sunk in that this was no random loudmouthed inmate speaking to them.

There was a long silence. Then the leader spoke. "And just how do we disable four guards…armed guards?"

"Kill," Blackhawk said coldly. "We kill the guards. Don't even think 'disable.' There is no time for half-measures. It is easier to strike a fatal blow than one certain to incapacitate an opponent…and a man who is still alive is still dangerous. I have seen 'disabled' men, even dying ones, kill their attackers. If we do this, we shoot to kill. We stab to kill. We punch or kick to kill. There is no time for hesitation, for softness. Any escape will be a race against time. If we allow General Ghana's people enough time to respond, the escape attempt is doomed."

"So you want us to attack the guards and what? Take their weapons? Fight our way out of Ghana's main base? Past all his troops? And then what? Into the desert?"

"Yes." Blackhawk's voice was calm, matter-of-fact.

The leader looked back at him with shock in his eyes. "That is a desperate plan, isn't it? One more likely to end in our deaths than escape."

Blackhawk stared back. *Your deaths maybe.* He was still thinking of his tentative compatriots as cover, diversions. If they made it out, fine. If not, also fine. But he figured he had a good chance, maybe eighty percent. Ghana's soldiers weren't completely incompetent, but they'd never run into anything like him before either.

"Is that a valid reason not to try?" He looked over the group. "Is it better to stay here and endure Ghana's torture sessions? He clearly wants some kind of information from you. Surely you know the instant one of you breaks, you are all dead." Blackhawk's tone was without emotion. He'd seen suffering, enough to desensitize him to it, to view it as an antiseptic fact. "Is it better to remain here like sheep, to endure pain and degradation until one of you falters? And then to die? If you must die, is it not better to die on your feet, trying to escape?"

Blackhawk watched the leader's face, saw the realization there. His people were doomed if they did nothing, whether they told Ghana's people what they wanted to know or not. They had nothing to lose by even the most desperate escape attempt. Blackhawk knew that, and he could see the leader coming to the same realization. The others looked less certain, their faces covered with masks of doubt. But Blackhawk was willing to bet they would follow the leader.

"I'm going to go whether you come or not," Blackhawk said decisively. "We all have a better chance together than alone. Are you with me?"

The leader turned for a moment to look back at his people, but Blackhawk already knew the answer.

"Yes," he said, struggling to keep the doubt from his voice. "We're with you."

He extended a hand toward Blackhawk. "I am Jarvis Danith. And this is Balon Tahl." He gestured toward the man with the sling. Then he turned his head to look back at the others. "And Tig Arhn, Mog Poole, Cyn Larison."

Blackhawk paused. It had been a long time since he'd had any real interaction with comrades of any sort. He told himself these were not new friends, they were cover, a diversion...that he intended to keep it that way. He had no place for connections, for relationships based on anything except utility. He'd allowed himself to feel respect for General Lucerne, and now he felt like a fool. He should have known better...and he didn't intend to make the same mistake again.

Still, there was no harm in playing along with social conventions. Anything to get the best out of his new comrades. "Blackhawk," he said. "Arkarin Blackhawk." Then he reached out and took Jarvis' hand.

* * *

"The prisoner's possessions offer no hint of his origins, General." Dav Roogen stood at attention, holding a small datapad in his hand. He was clearly on edge, fully aware that what he was reporting would not satisfy the Warlord. Ghana wasn't a bloodthirsty psychopath like Carteria, but he wasn't a patient or tolerant man either.

"That is unsatisfactory, Captain. We must know more. This man is clearly not from the Badlands...and I'd wager he is not Celtiborian either. His skills and abilities are beyond impressive. We are fortunate to have received warning about him. But we must find out who he is...and where he came from."

Ghana was sitting behind his desk. He was a tall man in his mid-fifties, his head completely shaved except for a small goatee, black frosted heavily with gray. He was clad in a dressier version of the brown uniform his troops wore. His sleeves were rolled up, and his desk was covered with data chips and tablets. His workstation screen displayed a map, with symbols designating troop positions in the area.

"He was questioned, General. The inquisitor was instructed to do no permanent damage, but it was still a thorough session. The man said nothing, sir. Not even a grunt of pain."

Ghana stared back at the officer, his hand absent-mindedly playing with a stylus laying on the desk. "That is unfortunate… though not entirely unexpected."

"We can question him again, sir, if you wish. The head jailor has been focusing his primary attention on the prisoners from the Grays, but I can instruct him to…"

"No," Ghana said, his voice deep. "This man will be hard to break. It will take considerable time, if indeed we are able to compel him to talk at all. Finding the terrorists' secret base is still the priority. The disruption of what is left of our trading revenue has become intolerable." He paused, staring down at his desk for a few seconds as though he was looking for something. Then he gave up and stared back at Roogen. "I can't find it now, but I just read it. The most recent report suggests several of the prisoners are close to breaking."

Of course they're probably lying to me about that. They should have broken these pirates long before now.

"Yes, sir." Roogen's tone suggested he thought the same thing.

"Still, we must know more about this prisoner. Perhaps a DNA scan will shed some light on his origin. If he is Celtiborian, we should be able to pinpoint his region of origin…or at least that of his parents and immediate ancestors. And if he is not from this planet…" Ghana let his voice trail off. He had a number of thoughts, but they were still formative, nothing worth speaking of yet.

"Yes, General. I will order a complete scan at once."

"I want the results as quickly as possible."

"Yes, sir." The aide waited for Ghana to dismiss him, but the general was silent, staring down at his desk. "I want more guards on duty in the detention area as well, Captain. Two more. Every time someone enters the cell. And two more in the hall."

"General, we already have additional guards..."

"Then we will have even more won't we?" Ghana snapped. "Perhaps that will eliminate any risk of problems with the prisoner...problems I can assure you would not go well for those in charge down there. After all, this man has already killed, what, twelve of my soldiers? And that despite the fact that we vastly outnumbered his party and had warning? We were supposed to be ready for him...and yet he almost escaped. Indeed, had he been in any terrain save the open desert I have no doubt he would have eluded us. So let's just say I want to be sure. Post the additional guards. Now."

"Yes, sir."

"Dismissed."

The soldier saluted and turned on his heels, walking quickly to the door and out of the office.

Ghana leaned back in his chair massaging his temples. He was tense, about the mysterious prisoner, about the unexpected endurance of the captured raiders...but mostly about Marshal Carteria. He'd been hesitant to ally with the Marshal at all. Carteria's reputation, not just for betraying allies when it served his purpose, but also for intolerance of failure, was well-known.

Ghana had convinced himself it would work, he'd succumbed to the temptation to gain an edge on his rivals, overruling his caution and reaching out to Celtiboria's Marshal. It had succeeded at first. Carteria's gold had financed his campaign, allowed him to bring overwhelming force to bear. The Warlords who had controlled the Badlands before were all but defeated now, but the fight for the precious trade routes was still in doubt.

His plans had been so clear when he'd accepted the Marshal's overtures. Control of the Badlands and its trade routes was a major step toward dominance on the Northern Continent, and with Carteria's aid, he'd been sure he could seize the stretch of barren desert in a single campaign season...so sure, the thought of failure hadn't entered into his calculations.

That was before Augustin Lucerne turned up.

And now he was on the verge of total defeat at the hands of the upstart. He'd taken Carteria's coin...and he had not lived up to the promises he'd made. He knew that was dangerous.

He was still amazed he'd found himself in this position. He'd been worried about a few of the other Warlords becoming involved—or at least rattling their sabers—but Lucerne hadn't been one of them. The general had a reputation as a strong tactician, but he was from the Riverlands, a backward province inhabited mostly by farmers and fishermen. By all accounts, Lucerne ran his economy well, but it was hard enough to sustain a modern army with revenue from farms and fishing villages. Ghana hadn't imagined for a moment that Lucerne had the wealth and strength to project power as far from his base as the Badlands. But he'd been proven wrong in that. Catastrophically wrong.

The two local Warlords who had controlled the Badlands had indeed seemed beatable...and he had quickly thrown them onto the defensive. Hagerod and Elemando were both near total defeat, crushed by his Carteria-financed forces. They were sitting on the periphery now, watching as the final battle approached. Their battered forces were waiting to see who would gain the advantage.

The battle had become one between Ghana and Lucerne. Ghana knew the others would stay uninvolved, wait until either he or Lucerne was on the verge of final victory. Then they would commit...and work out the best deals they could for themselves.

And I will give it to them...as much as I'd like to grind the opportunistic bastards into the ground, it doesn't make sense. I'll let them keep a piece of the trade revenue, ten percent maybe...and they will become my allies. At least the kind of allies money buys.

But Lucerne will do the same...and he is far closer to victory than I am...

He had to rally his forces, turn things around and defeat Lucerne...and he knew he couldn't do that with his own empty treasury. He needed more help. He was far from sure Carteria would provide it, but he had nowhere else to turn. The Marshal had proven himself reluctant to throw good money after bad, but control of the Badlands trade was valuable...and Ghana was sure of one thing. General Lucerne...the honorable, the unspotted…he would never deal with a creature like Carteria. If the Marshal wanted influence on the Northern Continent, he needed Ghana.

I just hope he realizes that…

Jinn Barkus had been gone for days now…and he'd sent no communications, not a word. Nothing. Ghana knew that Carteria had a streak of paranoia, that he blocked all outgoing communications from his palace. But the lack of an officially-sanctioned update wasn't a good sign. Carteria had been known to answer petitioners by killing their ambassadors. Ghana had been reluctant to send Barkus…Jinn had been with him for a long time and was one of his most trusted aides. But the matter was too important to entrust to anyone less capable. Barkus was smart, experienced…he knew what he was dealing with in Carteria.

He will succeed.

I hope…

Chapter Eight

General Lucerne's Headquarters
"The Badlands"
Northern Celtiboria

"We are certain, sir. We've confirmed it with General Horatii. He has a man in Carteria's court. One of the Marshal's retainers he keeps on his payroll." Rafaelus DeMark stood in front of Lucerne, his uniform wrinkled and stained from travel, not at all how he'd usually present himself to the general. His face was twisted into a frustrated scowl. The news he'd come to report wasn't good. It wasn't good at all.

"Well, that explains how he funded an expedition the size that he did, doesn't it?" Lucerne sat staring at his desk, his head cradled in his hands. Normally, he'd have made more of an effort to hide his concern in front of one of his soldiers, but DeMark was very much one of his inner circle, an officer he considered not only a gifted tactician, but also one of his few true friends. Indeed, that is why he'd entrusted DeMark with the mission to find out who was backing Ghana.

Lucerne had been sure his adversary was getting help from someplace, and he needed to know where. And now he did. He couldn't say he was truly surprised. Carteria had always been a possibility, but he'd hoped it would turn out to be one of the other alternatives. Any of the others. Fighting against the most powerful Warlord on the planet was dangerous business, even when the Marshal was only a financier. Lucerne was disgusted by Carteria, and he'd long ago decided he'd never ally with the man, no matter what the situation. But he wasn't ready to openly oppose him either, not even when the bulk of Carteria's strength was an ocean away.

"Yes, sir. General Horatii's source believes it was at least ten million ducats, possibly more." DeMark took a deep breath. He'd just returned from Horatii's capital on the southern coast, a difficult and dangerous journey. It was late, and he looked exhausted. It had been a long trip there and back again, but Lucerne hadn't wanted to wait to hear DeMark's intel…and he'd given the officer strict instructions not to trust any over the air communication, subject to interception. There was no way of knowing where any of his rivals had set up a listening post.

DeMark was trying to hide his fatigue, with limited success. He hadn't slept since before he'd left, but as soon as he landed he raced right for Lucerne's quarters. He'd had a bit of a fight to get the guard to let him through to wake the general, but Lucerne had heard the argument and come out of the office, ordering the sentry to stand down.

Lucerne had recently given into the pressure from his officers and created a guard company charged with escorting him and managing his personal security. The veterans assigned to the new duty took it very seriously, standing up even to superior officers whenever their perception of the general's needs were at stake. Lucerne went easy on the guard…his zealousness came from pure loyalty, after all and not any disrespect or insubordination to DeMark. But he'd been wide awake, sitting at his desk, waiting for his officer. He wanted to see DeMark as soon as possible.

"I know you're exhausted, Rafaelus, but you were right to come here immediately. General Ghana doesn't worry me, not too much at least. We can handle him. But if Carteria is involved, we must be careful. The Marshal didn't get where he is by being foolish…or by easily accepting defeat."

"No, sir. And I'm afraid I have more news. One of General Ghana's officers was at Carteria's stronghold. Jinn Barkus, a major. Close to the general, a trusted aide. He arrived three days ago, and he was received several times, the last two in private."

Lucerne sighed. That *was* bad news. Ghana's man was seeking additional support, there was no other explanation… and while Carteria would no doubt be enraged at the setbacks, Lucerne knew the Marshal wouldn't throw away the chance to gain control over the Badlands trade routes. He'd been after a foothold on the Northern Continent for years now…and there was no question. This was the best opportunity he'd had. Whatever mistakes Ghana had made, Carteria would continue to back him, at least until he'd secured the Badlands. And Barkus was one of Ghana's top aides, his equivalent of DeMark. He would get the job done.

"We need to know what Carteria is planning. Will he give Ghana another ten million ducats?" That would be bad. Lucerne knew the Warlords along the continent's western coast had just made peace, putting an end to six years of war. While no one doubted hostilities would come again, the nearly-bankrupt combatants had dismissed thousands of their hired soldiers. The mercenary markets of the river cities were glutted, individuals, small groups, even large companies looking for employment. Lucerne had considered supplementing his own forces, but the campaign had already stretched his resources to the breaking point. He simply didn't have the cash to hire mercenaries. But if Ghana had another ten million ducats from Carteria…

"I'm sorry, General. There was no way to get more information. General Horatii's source is skittish…and he wasn't a party to the discussions. We're lucky we even know about Barkus. And the informant made it clear there would be no more updates for a while. He was planning to lie low to keep suspicion off himself."

Lucerne nodded, a grim expression on his face. That was the problem with buying off other peoples' retainers. The backstabbing swine who would take coin to sell out their masters were, by definition, unreliable and untrustworthy.

"If Carteria gives Ghana more coin, he'll hire half the mercs in the river cities. He'll put another fifty thousand experienced troops in the field against us. And those mercenary companies are ready to go, fully armed and equipped. He could have them here in a matter of weeks…before the truce expires."

DeMark just nodded. Then he stood silently for a moment, an uncomfortable expression on his face. Finally, he said, "General, perhaps we should hit Ghana now, before any help can get to him."

Lucerne paused for an instant. Then he shook his head. "Break the truce? Without clear provocation? No, Rafaelus, we can't do that. That is not our way. I would not become like them to defeat them."

"Yes, sir…but…"

"No buts, Rafe." Lucerne looked right at his officer. "That is how it starts. Just this one time, I wouldn't do this except…" Lucerne shook his head. "No, Rafe. We are not like them. Our success has been based on winning the people's support…by treating them with respect instead of brutality. On showing our allies—and even our enemies—that our word is good. Can you name another Warlord who can maintain control over his provinces without stationing troops there? We are alone in that, Rafe…our people support us, they recognize that we are honest, that our promises to them are worth something. I would not sacrifice all that with a surprise attack. I will not violate the truce. Not under any circumstances."

Lucerne meant what he was saying, at least to a point. He tried to conduct himself with honor, at least whenever possible, but he wasn't quite the paragon of virtue his public persona suggested. He wouldn't violate the ceasefire, that much was true. But he wasn't above trying to trick or provoke his enemies into doing it for him.

"Then what do we do, sir?"

Lucerne stared back at DeMark, silently. In truth, he had nothing to say, no idea of how to proceed. He'd think of something…he always did. He knew he was close to victory in the Badlands, and also to defeat. And which way things went relied far more on matters out of his control than he liked.

"What do we do, Rafe? Well, for now, you go relax. Get a hot meal...and then some sleep. Our problems will still be here tomorrow."

"Yes, sir," DeMark said, his tone heavy with concern. He looked like he was going to add something, but in the end he just said, "Goodnight, sir." Then he turned and strode out of the room.

Lucerne watched him go. Then he stood up, walked across the massive chamber he'd taken as his office. It was cold, cavernous, uncomfortable. Built for war, for defense. Just like his own stronghold.

He scooped up a small picture frame on a table, a woman, young, smiling. Eliane. His wife. She'd been in her early twenties when the image was taken, just months before they'd been married. He still remembered the first time he saw her. He'd been dumbstruck, speechless. He'd come to her father's estate to discuss an arranged marriage, one that would seal an alliance between the two houses. But the instant he laid eyes on his bride to be, all thought of strategy and tactics, of adding to his lands and his army, vanished from his mind.

She was dead now, and he knew she hadn't remained that smiling, happy girl in the photo. Lucerne had given his new wife everything she could want...everything except his time. Life with a Warlord had proved lonelier than she'd imagined. Campaigns had kept him away most of their married lives, and she had spent her days in the cold confines of Lucerne's ancestral castle, a fortress designed for defensibility, not for comfort. She'd longed to travel, begging to stay at his side as his armies marched. But he'd always refused, too afraid to expose her to the rigors and dangers of the field. Like any man with enemies, he feared they would seek to hurt him through his family, and he'd kept her as a virtual prisoner, protected around the clock by his most trusted men. His mandates had been acts of love, his almost obsessive need to keep her safe...but in the end he'd killed her spirit, destroyed the natural happiness that had once been so much a part of her personality. And, he feared, he had also killed the love he knew she had once felt for him.

Eliane had died alone, feeling abandoned. He'd had word that she was ill, but it was only days later, after a new dispatch came, that he realized how serious things were. Red Fever was sweeping through the Riverlands. Hundreds were dying...and Eliane's illness was far more serious than the influenza he'd assumed it was when he'd first been informed.

He knew he had to rush home, to be at her side. But the dispatch arrived on the eve of battle, with his army in a desperate situation. He'd almost walked away, turned command over to his officers and raced home immediately. But he didn't. He stayed and commanded his army...and he won his first great victory. As soon as the battle was clearly won, he boarded a transport and raced back to his stronghold. But he was too late. Elaine was dead.

He knelt long that day at the side of the bed, holding her cold hand in his. He spoke to her, told her he loved her, shed tears for her loss. He ached to feel her grip his hand back, to speak words to him, any words. But she was gone.

It had been three years, and the pain cut as deeply as it had that day. He ignored it most of the time, slammed his iron discipline down on it, as he did with most of his emotions. He was a man driven...he belonged to the quest. If he was to unite Celtiboria one day, it would take all he had, every last measure of devotion. Other men could take time to indulge their heartbreak, to mourn for those they lost. But not Augustin Lucerne. There was little room in his life for anything save duty.

He set Eliane's image down on the desk and walked over toward the fireplace. It was a massive hearth, and it was ablaze with a pile of logs. He sat down in one of the two leather chairs flanking the fire and stared into the flames. He'd always enjoyed a fire, it was one of the few indulgences he allowed himself.

He stared at the hearth, felt the hypnotic effect of the flames. His mind drifted away, his thoughts turning to Blackhawk. *Is he dead? Or a prisoner in Ghana's torture chambers?*

He'd liked the wanderer...there had been an immediate connection between the two of them, one he somehow knew Blackhawk had felt too. He had sensed the stranger carried a lot of pain with him, and he'd hoped one day they would become friends, that Blackhawk would confide in him, join his quest.

He'd had a lot of faith in Blackhawk, more than he could explain on such short acquaintance. But he had learned to trust his instincts on such things. He'd placed a lot of trust in his new comrade, and he'd hoped the mission would succeed in its true purpose of ending the truce, of tricking or provoking Ghana into making a premature move.

Now he felt the bitterness of futility, of guilt. He'd convinced Blackhawk to step out from the past that was dragging him down, to undertake the mission for him. But that mission had turned out disastrously, and now, if Blackhawk wasn't dead already, he soon would be.

It was strange. Lucerne had led thousands to their deaths in his campaigns, all soldiers who'd willingly followed him. But there was something about Blackhawk. Was it the waste, a man of such ability reduced to wandering the Far Stars like a drifter... and then killed the first time he tried to rise above his misery? Or was it something more?

It was just a feeling, one Lucerne knew was ridiculous. But it was there, and it seemed so real. He'd felt it the minute he'd met Blackhawk in his cell. The man had a destiny, something more than being killed by Ghana's people.

I was so certain. But I was wrong.

Still, he didn't believe it. It didn't make sense, but he had a feeling he hadn't heard the last of Arkarin Blackhawk.

Chapter Nine

Ghana's Main Base
"The Badlands"
Northern Celtiboria

Shit.

Blackhawk knew immediately. Four guards behind the conscripted prisoners. Twice what he'd expected, what he'd seen
with every other food delivery. Ghana's people had changed their
routine...and that meant they were suspicious, that they were
afraid of him. He sighed softly to himself. That wasn't good. He
figured his eighty percent chance at escape had just dropped to
even money. And the others...well, they were totally fucked. He
considered calling off the attempt, but things weren't likely to
get better, and he was sick of sitting in the stinking prison. He
knew his allies in the escape were likely to end up dead, but was
it better to leave them here, to reduce his own chances so they
could remain and endure more torture...and ultimately sell out
whomever they were protecting? No, sometimes death was a
better option. Besides, his own chances were a lot better if they
went too.

He turned and glanced over at Jarvis and his people. They
were nervous, uncertain, staring at the extra guards as Blackhawk himself had been doing. He flashed them a stern glance, a
silent communication. *We're still on.*

They'd planned the operation expecting to have a maximum of four guards to deal with, but now it was at least six…and eight if the hallway sentries had been doubled up too. Blackhawk had intended to kill one of the guards in the cell and leave the other to Jarvis and his crew. Then he would rush into the corridor and take down the two guards in the hall. The outer guards would have more time to react…and he knew he could get there faster than any of the others. But now there were four in the cell…and four outside. And he didn't have time to think, to plan. He only had time for a decision.

His eyes focused on the guards standing behind the two food carts. They were attentive, not overly so, but not as distracted as they'd been before. Obviously, a lecture on staying alert had accompanied the increase in personnel.

Blackhawk's eyes darted around, to the guards, the prisoners in front, the quickest route to get to the soldiers. His mind was fast, sharp. He knew attacking would be a big risk…but waiting didn't offer much promise of a better opportunity. And that meant go now. It also meant taking all the guards himself. That was going to be difficult, and dangerous, but he'd had too little time to prepare Jarvis and his men. The best chance was doing it himself.

He lunged forward, the enhanced strength of his legs propelling him with great speed and control. He looped around the carts, his hands striking out, breaking the neck of the first guard before anyone could respond. He grabbed the already dead man's rifle as he fell, even as he was moving forward toward the second. The new target was still staring at the body of his comrade as it dropped, when Blackhawk's hand smashed into his chest, crushing his sternum and driving a dozen bone shards into his heart.

Two…

His eyes were on the other two guards. They'd been farther away, and now they stepped back, leveling their weapons. But Blackhawk was faster. He pulled the trigger, putting a shot right into the third guard's forehead, lunging to the side as he did.

Three…

The fourth guard opened up, his weapon on full auto, spraying the area were Blackhawk had been an instant before. But he was too late. His body lurched to the side as Blackhawk put three shots into him, and he fell hard.

Four...

"Arm yourselves," Blackhawk yelled as he leapt to the side, giving himself a field of fire as the two guards just outside the door ran in, their weapons ablaze. Two of the other inmates were hit, and the rest ran toward the back of the cell, screaming in panic. Jarvis and his people had frozen for a few seconds, but now they were scrambling toward the dead guards, grabbing whatever weapons they could get their hands on. The situation was pure chaos. Everywhere but in Blackhawk's head.

His mind filtered out the hysteria, held his own fear in check. He was disciplined in a way no normal person could understand, a way only years of conditioning could achieve. His brain was silent, his thoughts crisp, rapid. He flipped the rifle to full auto as his finger pressed down on the trigger, firing a burst at each of the two guards just inside the door, killing them both in an instant.

Six...

Just two left, in the hall.

He knew those would be the hardest, the most dangerous. He'd had surprise on his side in the cell, total in the case of the first two guards, and partial with the others. But the troopers in the hall had heard the gunfire. They wouldn't be as accommodating as the last two, running into the room, making perfect targets of themselves. They would stay in the hall, cover the door, ready to fire as soon as any of the prisoners came out.

Blackhawk's eyes were on the door, looking, watching for shadows, for any signs of movement. Nothing. He risked a quick look behind to make sure Jarvis and his men had grabbed weapons. They had. Then he crept up to the door. Nothing. Silence.

He gestured toward Jarvis and one of his people, then to one of the dead guards. His eyes were still fixed on the door. The guards outside were waiting for his people to come out. It was a standoff. And a standoff was certain defeat. The soldiers outside just needed to buy time for reinforcements to arrive. Blackhawk and the other prisoners had to get out. Immediately.

He waved toward the form of one of the dead guards. "Okay, when I give the word, push the body out the door... slowly." He spoke softly, leaning toward Jarvis as he did. His comrades had understood his gestures perfectly, and they stood next to him, holding the body of the dead guard.

Jarvis just nodded. Blackhawk could see the tension, the fear in his ally's face. But the raider stood firm, looking back, waiting for the signal.

Blackhawk leaned down and grabbed a pistol from one of the other guards, shoving it inside his jumpsuit. He'd used half his rifle's clip already, and the guards didn't seem to have extra cartridges on them.

He moved back, pressing himself against the door, opposite Jarvis. "Now," he whispered.

Jarvis pushed the body forward, struggling to move slowly, not to let it fall forward. An instant later, bursts of gunfire erupted, and the body was yanked from his grasp, blasted out into the hallway and riddled with bullets.

The instant the shooting started, Blackhawk dove through the door, low, dropping to the floor, firing the whole time. He hit the concrete hard, rolling at the last second to blunt the impact. It still hurt like hell, but he hadn't taken any serious injuries.

He popped his head up, looking down the hall. Both guards were down. He jumped to his feet, tossing the spent rifle and pulling the pistol out from inside the jumpsuit. He took a step forward, bringing the weapon to bear. The first guard was clearly dead, his head almost completely destroyed by Blackhawk's fire. The other was lying face down. Blackhawk moved slowly, carefully, his eyes fixed on the man. He leaned down, the pistol at the ready, and grabbed the soldier's uniform, pulling hard and flipping him onto his back. There were three bullet holes on his chest, two of them dead center on his heart.

Eight.

"Okay," Blackhawk said, turning back for an instant, checking on Jarvis and the others. "Let's go. Time's the one thing we don't have."

He moved down the corridor, quickly but deliberatively, his eyes wide, alert, watching for any movement. The hall ended just ahead in a T, and he jogged forward, pistol out in front of him.

"Everybody good?" he asked without turning around again.

"Tig took a round in the arm, but he's okay."

Blackhawk didn't respond. On some level he wished he cared more whether Tig—or any of the others—made it, but there was only one thing on his mind now. Getting out.

And taking his revenge on Augustin Lucerne.

* * *

"Quiet, all of you. We don't move. Not until dark." Cass peered out of the half-crushed concrete pipe. It was old, the relic of a project that predated Celtiboria's three century long civil war. The plan had been to install piping all the way from the river cities to the coast, where a string of desalinization plants would be built. The project had never been completed, and the half-finished plants had long ago been pulled down to salvage their parts. But the pipe was still there, at least the half of it that had been laid. And a long stretch made its way through the badlands, unknown to the Warlords and their armies.

Cass' people used the pipeline to pass unnoticed through the desert, with egress points positioned near the trade routes they preyed upon, making the conduit extremely useful. But it hadn't offered a way to Ghana's headquarters, at least until Elli Marne had somehow managed to map out the route of the thing...and pinpoint a spot that was close. Cass had been skeptical, but Elli had earned her trust many times, and she'd chosen to accept her friend's judgment. They'd followed the pipeline, measuring their movement carefully until they reached the designated spot. Then they spent half a day pounding a hole in the reinforced concrete and digging through the dirt above, almost burying themselves alive in the process. But when she finally poked her head out and looked around, she could see Ghana's complex off in the distance, no more than an hour's march away. Elli's measurements had been spot on.

She slid back down into the pipe. It was uncomfortable, its circumference large, but not quite big enough to stand up. Her people had been in the conduit, twisted up like pretzels for two days now. Her legs ached with a ferocity she wouldn't have thought possible, and she wanted nothing so badly as to stand up straight and walk.

Not yet…wait until it gets dark…

There was no room for carelessness, no place for stupid errors. Not if they were going to get their people out. Not if they were going to survive this operation themselves.

It was dusk now, but she intended to wait until night was fully upon them. Only one of the moons would be out tonight, and that wouldn't be until just before dawn. So the night promised to be a dark one. That was good. Because they needed every edge they could get.

She slipped down into the conduit, leaning back, trying to get as comfortable as she could…which wasn't very. She wondered—for about the millionth time—if what she was doing was foolish, misguided. She'd lost people before, more than the five who were prisoners in Ghana's headquarters. But they had been killed in action, not abandoned while they were still alive. She knew there was a good chance a lot more of her people would die in the rescue attempt…but she found it difficult to apply that kind of brutal mathematics when her friends were in trouble. She knew the others were having similar thoughts, their fears struggling with their loyalty to comrades.

And it's more than that. If you leave them in there, Ghana will break them…and soldiers will come to the refuge…

Cassandra Cross had been born on a farm, just like virtually everyone in the Galadan. She'd grown up working with her brothers and sisters in the small vegetable garden near the house, and later out in the main fields. That had always been enough for most of those born in the Galadan, to follow the same paths as their parents, their grandparents. But not Cass. She'd always craved more, and from an early age her intelligence and drive had been obvious, to her parents, to everyone who knew her.

She'd longed for a life away from the fields, from the relent-less monotony of a farmer's life. But even in good times, the existence of a Galadan farming family was a simple one, and there was rarely much coin left after the harvest was sold off and all the expenses paid. Certainly not enough to send children off to university. Cass had two brothers and two sisters, and she knew her life's script had already been written for her. But her father hadn't accepted that. His other four children were normal Galadaners, content enough with their future roles on the farm. But Alexi Cross had watched his brilliant oldest daughter wast-ing away. He had seen the sadness in her eyes that she thought she hid. And he'd resolved to do something about it.

Somehow—and Cass could never quite figure how—he saved almost enough to send her to University, to give her a chance to find a life beyond the farm, outside the Galadan. Two years, he had said. Two more years, and there would be enough for her to go.

She'd been stunned, and she had thrown herself into his arms and burst into tears. She still remembered that feeling… hope. It was the most amazing thing she'd ever felt, a joyous sensation still unmatched in her life. But it was a lie, a self-indul-gence she had vowed never to allow herself again.

Less than a year after her father's revelation, the soldiers came. The first group was small, perhaps a few hundred strong. They were disordered, defeated in battle and retreating. They were in no condition to fight another battle, but they were still armed, and they took out their anger and rage on the helpless farmers of the Galadan. They pillaged the farms, killed most of the animals. They feasted on their pillage and took off what they could carry, leaving the rest behind, rotting carcasses of cows and pigs…and the trampled fields of a ruined harvest.

The soldiers devastated the Galadan, but they'd done worse to Cass. Her father had sent her away, with her mother and brothers. There were stories, civilians beaten, raped, murdered. Alexi Cross wanted his family safe…so he insisted they go to woodlands at the edge of the province to hide. Cass had argued with her father, begged to stay with him…or for him to flee with them. But he'd been adamant. So she'd agreed to go…a surrender she still regretted.

Though if you stayed, you'd only be dead too now. And it wouldn't have been a pleasant way to go…

A band of soldiers came to the Cross farm, not long after Alexi's family had gone. They trampled the crops, shot and cooked the animals…and burned two of the outbuildings for no reason save to watch the spectacle of the flames. Then they stormed up to the house, looking for women, for civilians to terrorize. But they found only Alexi Cross.

He told them his family was dead, killed by an epidemic two years before. It was a reasonable story, but one not supported by the evidence on display, closets full of clothes and other indications that the house had been occupied by more than a single man. The soldiers beat him for lying, taking out their rage that he'd denied them his wife and daughters, that he had so little coin for them to steal. And then, she imagined, one of them found the strongbox with the money he'd saved for Cassandra's tuition.

She could see the images in her mind, though she hadn't seen it all happen. The soldiers' anger flaring, rage that Alexi had lied to them, that he'd tried to deny them their spoils. She had pieced most of the rest together. The soldiers had beat Alexi Cross savagely, almost to death. And then, just before they left to move on to the next farm…

She could see one of them, the image clear, though she hadn't seen it happen, looking down at the bleeding, battered farmer…and shooting twice, leaving him behind to die.

But Alexi Cross hadn't died, not right away. Somehow he'd managed to crawl into the house's main room, to fashion some makeshift bandages from a small blanket he'd pulled off the couch. And he lay there, for two days, with no food, no water, no care. Until Cassandra found him.

She'd come back to the farm with her oldest brother, moving cautiously, by night. It was almost dawn when they reached the house…and as soon as she saw the fields, the still-smoldering ruins of the outbuildings, she knew something terrible had happened.

She ran into the house, frantically looking for her father. And she found him, bleeding, in pain...near death. He looked up at her as she leaned over him, her tears dripping on his face. "Cassie," he said. "I'm so sorry. They took the money, for your education." He looked at her, his own eyes wet with tears. "I'm so sorry," he repeated.

She still remember how she felt, kneeling there in a pool of her father's semi-congealed blood. He was dying, the farm virtually destroyed. And he was apologizing to her about the money for her schooling. Something changed in her in that room, that terrible morning. She became harder, grim hatred replacing her friendly demeanor. Her father died on that floor, with her holding his hand and sobbing uncontrollably. And part of her died there too...replaced by something dark, terrible.

She'd tried to help her mother rebuild the family's lives. They buried her father...and then they cleaned up, replanted a section of the fields, desperately trying to preserve all Alexi had worked so hard to build. But another group of soldiers came...and then more after them. The battles of the Warlords had come to the Galadan, and the fury of war was all around. And by the time the battling armies moved on, the province was ruined, its lush fields burnt and ravaged, its wells and once-clear lakes poisoned.

The people, those who had survived the relentless onslaughts, had taken refuge in the forests, surviving as they could on what little food remained, struggling with the pestilence and the epidemics that raged among the weakened populace. Cass had watched her mother wither away, her mind broken. She had been a strong woman, loving and caring, but the trauma of losing everything was too much for her. Then her oldest brother got sick. He was sixteen and strong, built like a tree trunk...but she watched him wither away until his legs were so thin he could barely stand. Near the end, she could pick him up from his bed and carry him herself. She took care of him, refused to surrender, gave him her meager rations to supplement his own...but he died anyway.

Cass shed no tears this time. Tears were for the weak. She buried her brother next to her father, and what fragile remnant remained of the girl she'd been died as she dug the grave. Then she went back to the forest refuge and began gathering recruits. The Grays were born in an open glade in the shade of the trees, amid the poor shelters and tents of a once prosperous people. The time for hiding in the woods was over, she had declared. The young people of the Galadan would strike back. All they'd possessed had been taken…so now they would become the takers. They would steal from others, as they'd been stolen from. They would kill if need be, instead of cowering, waiting for others to kill them.

And so it had been for two years now. She'd lost people in her raids, many of them old friends she'd known her whole life. But there hadn't been another tear, not a single one. Cassandra Cross didn't cry. There was no room in her life for weakness. None. And no place for doubting her decisions. Yes, it was risky trying to rescue their comrades. But that meant exactly nothing to her.

"Cass?"

She heard the voice, distant at first through her thoughts.

"Cass?"

She looked up. It was Elli. She got the feeling the girl had been there calling her for some time.

"Yes, Elli?"

"It's dark out. Should we get ready to go?"

Cass twisted her head, stretching the kinks out of her neck. She pushed the rest of the old thoughts from her mind. The events of the past had brought her here. But now she had to focus on what had to be done now.

"Yes, Elli. Tell everyone we leave in ten minutes."

The girl nodded. "Yes, Cass." She turned and crawled down the pipe toward the others.

Cass reached down to her side, her hand moving over the pistol hanging there.

Yes…it was time.

Chapter Ten

Airship White Condor
Somewhere Over the Azure Sea
Northern Celtiboria

The airship shook, hard, the high winds too much for the pilots to offset. The weather was spotty, and Barkus had considered rescheduling the departure, leaving the following day, when all the forecasts called for a clear, calm day. But Carteria had been insistent. There would be no delay. The initial wave of ships would depart on time…carrying the first thousand soldiers to the Northern Continent. And so it had.

Barkus was edgy, nervous. He wasn't fond of flying, and the turbulence had been uncomfortable for him. He'd already rushed to the bathroom twice, and he'd avoided all the food he'd been offered, and the drinks too, save for a few small sips of water. But it wasn't his flying phobia that was truly stressing him out. His mind was deep in thought, and all he could see was trouble ahead.

He'd been outright scared to death when Ghana had sent him to Carteria's court to request additional aid. The brutal Warlord was the strongest of Celtiboria's dozens of feuding nobles, and his reputation for casual brutality was well known planetwide. Carteria had a history of taking terrible vengeance on those who let him down, and Ghana had failed in delivering

on his promises to the Marshal. That was dangerous for him…
but even more so for whoever was sent to deliver the bad news.
Carteria had shot more than one messenger in his day.

But the Marshal had taken the news better than Barkus had
dared to hope. There had been some anger, and his stomach had
been twisted into knots as he stood in Carteria's great hall, waiting to see what would happen. But he'd endured nothing more
than a light tirade, and then he'd been sent to palatial quarters to
await the Marshal's decision. Much rode on that determination.
Without additional support, Barkus knew Ghana was unlikely to
prevail against General Lucerne…and a defeat in the Badlands
would have been damaging enough under any circumstances.
One coming after Ghana had spent ten million crowns of Carteria's money and still lost would almost certainly prove to be
fatal.

Barkus still remembered his relief after he'd been summoned
back to hear Carteria's decision. The Marshal had even been in
a good mood. He'd assured Barkus of his continued support,
and told him to advise Ghana that they were still allies, that they
would always remain so. He'd felt a lightness, a relaxed feeling he
hadn't had since the moment Ghana had made him ambassador
to Carteria. Success! With more funding from the Marshal, he
was confident his master would overwhelm and defeat Lucerne
and his stubbornly effective troops.

Then the hammer fell, and with it his spirits. He could still
remember Carteria's words, his cheerful, enthusiastic tone. "I
have decided to reinforce General Ghana. Even now, twenty-
five thousand of my troops are preparing to embark. We will
defeat this upstart Lucerne together…and then we will unite the
rest of the Northern Continent."

Troops. The thought still troubled him. He'd been sent to
secure financial aid, money that Ghana would use to increase
his own strength. But that was not what he was bringing back
with him. It was an army, its lead elements even now flying in
the airships formed up around his own. And it was an army not
answerable to him, nor to Ghana himself. Carteria had turned
the defeat around on his ally. Instead of acting out of rage, of

abandoning Ghana to his fate—or worse—the Marshal had recognized an opportunity to get a foothold on the Northern Continent. It was brilliant, a coup that Barkus hadn't even seen coming. He understood now how Carteria had achieved his position. The Marshal was no great tactician by all accounts, nor an inspiring leader who extracted love or loyalty from his followers. But he was a ruthless politician and a master at using people, at making them allies and then pitting them against each other to serve his own ends. And he was expert at creating fear, at intimidating his enemies into making mistakes…and his friends into accepting anything he imposed on them.

Barkus knew General Ghana would be upset. There was no other way he could react. He had been allowed to contact Ghana, but he'd held back the full report, merely telling the general things looked good. The situation was too complicated to discuss over an open signal…and Barkus had no idea how Ghana would respond to the news, and no doubt that Carteria's people would have been listening.

Carteria's soldiers were coming to help Ghana's forces, but Barkus didn't fool himself for a moment that they would return home after the campaign was won. No, the price Ghana was paying for support was clear. He would share his gains with Carteria, become one of the Marshal's minions.

He cursed himself for not refusing, for not finding a way to prevent Carteria from sending the troops. He knew that was unfair, a pointless waste of time. There had been no way to refuse the Marshal's offer, no way that didn't end very badly. Carteria was overlooking the wasted millions of ducats, the failure to secure the Badlands last season, as promised. By his standards, that was enormous magnanimity. If it had been thrown back in his face…that was something Barkus didn't even want to contemplate.

Besides, it's not like there's a choice. We're going to lose without some kind of support.

Even if there had been a way to refuse Carteria's troops, the lack of any aid would have led to defeat at the hands of Lucerne. And for all the Marshal's well-known brutality, there was probably a better chance of making a decent deal with him than with the sanctimonious Lucerne.

Yes, that's how I'll put it to the general. He understands the situation. He'd have rather had money from Carteria, funds to buy enough mercenaries to destroy Lucerne. But if the choice was between troops, and all that entailed, or nothing…well that was no choice. Not now.

* * *

"I held you back, Varn, because I have considered the operation in greater detail, and I wanted to have a final discussion on strategy with you, one I did not wish to trust to the vulnerabilities of long distance communication. When we are finished here, you will take one of the hypersonic speedsters. You should be able to catch up to the first wave of airships and be there when they land."

"Yes, Marshal. Of course. As you wish." Eleher stood silently, waiting for Carteria to elaborate.

"Varn, I believe we may have a greater opportunity here than we'd believed. I have reviewed the latest intelligence reports. The Northern Continent is extremely divided, and looking beneath the immediate surface, even greater weakness becomes apparent. Most of its Warlords control modest resources, and there is no true dominant power. I believe there may be an opening for us to take control, not just of the Badlands, but also of the entire continent…not years in the future, but now."

"Yes, Marshal. I am inclined to agree. Though I urge some degree of caution. There is opportunity certainly, but our knowledge of the Northern Continent, specifically the capabilities of the various Warlords, is partial at best."

"We will be cautious, Colonel. You will proceed as originally planned. Your forces will serve alongside General Ghana's army. You will see to the destruction of General Lucerne by whatever means. By all accounts, he is a man who cannot be suborned. And that means he must die in the Badlands."

"Yes, sir. I agree. General Lucerne would never ally with us…and from what I have heard, he is a dangerous man. Allowing him to expand his power only assures us a greater fight down the road."

Carteria nodded. "Then we are agreed. General Lucerne dies in the Badlands…whatever it takes. To that end…" He paused. "I am sending Zoln Darvon with you."

Eleher hesitated, a cold feeling moving through his body. He knew all about Zoln Darvon. The man was a specialist. An assassin.

"He will be under your command, Varn. You can use him if you need him…or you can handle it your own way. But however you proceed, I want Augustin Lucerne dead, his army destroyed." A pause. "And when the fight is over, you will waste no time. You will spread some coin around among Ghana's top people, seek to prepare a smooth transition. Ghana himself is to die, of course—he failed me and I must make an example of him—but I want his organization as intact as possible. With their general dead, they will have no choice but to willingly join us."

"Yes, sir." Eleher's voice was edgy, nervous. Carteria had dumped a lot on his plate.

"I will be mobilizing an expeditionary force while you are seeing to the Badlands campaign. As soon as you have secured control over the area, we will begin moving troops. By the end of the year we will have 500,000 sets of boots on the ground… and we will be ready to begin the conquest of the Northern Continent in earnest."

"Yes, Marshal." Eleher knew he was being given a tremendous opportunity. If he won the victory, he would be at the center of the invasion, one of the top officers in the conquest of the Northern Continent…perhaps even the commander, with full viceregal authorities. He felt a wave of excitement.

But there was something else as well, a coldness, a yawning pit of fear. Carteria had set his sights on the Northern Continent, and he'd laid out the promise of rewards and glory to his subordinate. But there was another side, a darker one. Once Carteria decided on something, he became obsessed with it. Varn Eleher had served the Marshal for years, long been one of his most trusted aides. But he knew if he failed, he'd likely end up on the gallows…or with Zoln Darvon's blade in his back. It was dangerous to fail Carteria, and his long service was unlikely to save him if he was defeated.

He took a deep breath, sucking in the air slowly, trying to hide his tension. Things had moved rapidly over the past few days. The decision about whether to provide more financial support to Ghana had turned into a decision to send troops instead. And that had escalated into plan to kill two Warlords and seize control of the Badlands…and a new strategy, one calling for no less than the total conquest of the Northern Continent.

Eleher understood the importance of the operation. If Carteria was successful, if he managed to seize all of the Northern Continent, his power would be irresistible. The wars might go on for a few more years, the holdouts might dig in, fight to the bitter end. But in the end his master would achieve the goal Celtiboria's Warlords had pursued for three centuries.

Carteria would be the master of Celtiboria, and he would place the crown of the planet's ancient kings on his head. Carteria I, the ruler of the most powerful world in the Far Stars.

* * *

"You called for me, Marshal?" Ganz Jellack stepped forward, squinting, trying to see through the clouds of steam floating through the room. He was wearing his full uniform, and he could feel the sweat building up under his arms, on his back.

"Yes, Ganz. I have a mission for you."

Jellack moved toward the sound of Carteria's voice, taking another few steps before he saw the Marshal before him. Carteria was lying on his stomach on a cushioned platform, naked save for a towel wrapped around his torso. Two women—Jellack recognized them from Carteria's cadre of regular lovers—were leaning over him, one on either side, giving him a massage.

Jellack stood at attention, hiding his revulsion at his master. Ganz Jellack had been an independent man once, a trader and entrepreneur, a financial genius well on his way to building a considerable fortune. Until Carteria's armies marched through his homeland. The Marshal had seized the property of all locals who refused to submit to him...and he'd done worse to many. Jellack had a wife and two young daughters, and he had shuddered to think of what his resistance might cost his family. He'd briefly harbored thoughts of continuing the fight, of joining the small bands forming in the fringe areas, swearing to continue the struggle. But then his mind was consumed by images...of his wife and daughters assaulted, murdered, his home burned to the ground. Jellack the rebel had lasted a few brief, defiant moments. Then Jellack the husband and father took control, and he submitted to Carteria.

But fate had decreed the price of his family's safety would be greater than the levy of half his wealth and the pledges of loyalty that the other notable inhabitants of his homeland had endured. Carteria had heard about Jellack's success, and he'd offered the trader a place on his staff, charging him with no less a task than reordering the finances of the greatest war machine on Celtiboria.

The Marshal's offer had been generous. To allow Jellack to sell his businesses...and keep all the proceeds. And he'd moved Jellack's family to a large palace on the Golden Coast of the Southern Continent, for a millennia the playground of Celtiboria's elite. Jellack's wife lived there in unimaginable luxury...and his daughters were educated by a corps of renowned scholars. But he knew that their home, as gilded and magnificent as it might be, was a cage, his family little more than comfortable and pampered prisoners. Hostages, whose purpose was to guarantee his loyalty.

He stood in front of Carteria, watching as the Warlord waved his masseuses away and hauled himself up to a sitting position. Carteria had been a legendary warrior once, and while he'd never been a brilliant tactician, his physical prowess had been known throughout Celtiboria. But age and success had not worn well on the Marshal, and in recent years he'd put on considerable weight and spent less and less time sparring on the training field.

"Sir, I am at your command." Jellack had been troubled serving Carteria at first, disgusted by his new master and the casual brutality of his regime. But that had faded quickly as he'd buried himself in his work. He spent little time worrying about moral considerations, though when he occasionally did, he was more likely to be disturbed at how quickly he'd become comfortable serving a master like Carteria. He always reminded himself he did what he did to ensure his family's safety. But there was still something, deep, ignored most of the time, but still there. Self-loathing.

"I want you to go to the Northern Continent, Ganz, to the river cities. They are awash with mercenary units for hire, veterans fighters released from service after the Warlords of the western coast made peace." Carteria shifted his bulk, swing his legs around and sitting up straight. "I want those mercs, Ganz. All of them. We will be invading the Northern Continent, and I want as much force in place there as possible." He paused. "There is a very glutted market…and few potential paymasters right now. With enough coin, you should be able to hire at least 100,000 soldiers."

"Sir…I appreciate your confidence, but I am not a soldier, not really." Jellack carried a colonel's commission, but his role had never strayed beyond duty on the staff.

"Don't worry, Ganz…your job is to hire the mercenaries, to build and organize them into an army. Varn Eleher will assume command before any real fighting occurs…and you will return here, to my immense gratitude for a job well done."

Jellack wasn't convinced. The idea of going to a foreign continent, to territory far from any Carterian holdings, was daunting. He felt out of his depth. And scared. But he knew there was no choice. Carteria was giving Jellack a great honor, at least in his own mind, and expressing anything but gratitude and acceptance would be dangerous. His mind flashed back to his daughters, images of them standing on the terrace of their waterfront palace, turning and screaming as the soldiers kicked open the doors and moved toward them…

"Yes, Marshal," he said, hiding the hesitancy that tried to force its way into his voice, "as you command. I will begin preparations. When do you want me to go?"

"Now, Ganz. I have ordered five airships to be ready for you, as well as two hundred soldiers as an escort. You will draw whatever coin you feel you will need and be ready to leave at dawn."

Jellack caught his objection before it crossed his lips. It was already late evening. He would have to wake his staff, choose the key ones he'd need to accompany him. And he had to find several million ducats and have it all loaded on the waiting airships. In six hours.

"Yes, Marshal. And again, thank you for your confidence. I will not let you down."

"I know you won't, Ganz. I know you won't." Carteria's voice was cheerful, and he sat there with a smile on his face. But Ganz felt the chill, the vague but ever present threat in the Marshal's words, in his stare.

He swallowed hard, pushing back the thoughts of his family that struggled to divert his attention. "With your permission, sir…I have considerable work to do before morning."

"You are dismissed, Ganz."

Jellack snapped rigidly to attention, and he snapped off a salute. Then he turned and walked toward the door, his pace accelerating as he got closer to the door, to escape from Carteria's chilling presence.

Chapter Eleven

Ghana's Main Base
"The Badlands"
Northern Celtiboria

Blackhawk continued down the hallway. It was odd, he thought, ironic that Ghana's guards were chasing him. He wanted to get out of there, escape from captivity…and deliver payback to the man who'd set him up. If Ghana had known Blackhawk's intentions—to rid him of his most dangerous enemy—he'd not only have called off his guards, he'd have opened his arsenal to Blackhawk and given him the choice of any weapons and vehicles on the base. And probably fifty thousand ducats as a bonus. But there was no time, and no way to convince Ghana that they both wanted Lucerne dead. So it was still plan A. Get out the hard way.

He could see something ahead, the hint of a shadow. Someone lurking near the corner up ahead. He stopped running, holding his hand up, a signal for the others to follow suit. He stepped forward slowly, silently, repeating the gesture to make sure no one followed him. He was surprised at how well his fellow-escapees were following his commands. They hadn't known him for more than a few hours, but they had not questioned anything he'd told them to do, not since they'd begun their escape attempt, at least.

His makeshift comrades had handled themselves well so far, much better than he'd expected. There had been no panic, no hesitancy. He knew they weren't real soldiers, but they had heart…and they were right behind him, showing no signs of faltering.

But none of them can move quietly. They sound like a herd of Stegaroids rampaging across the open plain.

He had the pistol in his hand, aimed forward, ready to fire if anyone came around the corner. He was pressed against the wall, creeping ahead, one careful step at a time.

He reached the corner, and he froze. He could hear more noise, loud breathing, hushed voices. Footsteps. There were at least three people there…possibly four.

He turned and looked back, holding his hand up yet again. Just to make sure. The last thing he needed was the lumbering herd racing forward and giving their presence away. He crept forward, right up to the edge, careful to angle his body so the lighting panel on the wall didn't cast a shadow where it would be visible. Then, suddenly, decisively, he lunged around the corner, his head snapping up, eyes focusing almost immediately. Four. His hand snapped up. A shot…then another. Two down.

The others were staring back, shock on their faces, weapons coming to bear…

Another shot from the pistol…a third man down. Then, one left, his rifle moving, even as Blackhawk brought the pistol to bear. It was a race, a close one. Blackhawk felt his finger tense, the kickback as the heavy pistol fired. The soldier fell backwards, his own weapon firing as he did, the burst slamming into the ceiling, sending chunks of the white polymer material to ground.

Blackhawk turned back down the corridor. "Let's go," he yelled to his comrades, even as he moved forward. He knew Jarvis and his people would have trouble keeping up with him, and he reminded himself he'd brought them as decoys, that it wasn't important for them to escape. But he still found himself holding back, lagging behind so he didn't get too far ahead. That wasn't how he would have done things before. He wouldn't have hesitated to sacrifice a few recent acquaintances—or even close comrades—to achieve his goal. But a lot of things had changed since then, him not the least. He was a different man than he'd been, and he was beginning to realize just how much he'd changed. Still, it was a hard adjustment, and confusion threatened to push away the rigid discipline that existed at his core. He told himself he wouldn't get killed trying to save them, but if he could get them out safely he would. But he wasn't sure what he'd do if it came to that.

He ran to the end of the hall and turned left. He was following the path he'd taken on the way in, when they'd led him to the cell. It was a long way, with a large number of turns, but he was fairly certain he had it all memorized. They soldiers had brought him in somewhere in the rear of the complex, a service entrance of some sort. The corridors had been almost empty then, and they seemed to be the same now.

That's a lucky break…if a convoy had just pulled in this hallway would be full of enemy soldiers…

He glanced quickly back, frustrated again with the speed his companions were managing. He was tense, his chest tight. Confidence came easily, indeed he knew on some level it had been bred into him. But he could still recognize danger…and they were in the middle of an enemy base, one that probably had a least a thousand soldiers in it. It was no time to be slow.

They're not slow, he reminded himself. *They just aren't manufactured things like you, with twice the muscle fibers of a normal human being…*

His eyes darted up to the top of the walls. There were lamps at intervals along the hallway, and they were flashing red. The whole installation was on alert. And even if he and his makeshift team got outside they would still be in the middle of the desert. They'd never manage to get away on foot…not as a group, at least. So they'd need to steal a vehicle of some sort, something that could get them far enough away to disappear into the desert wastes. And if they couldn't get some kind of transport…then he'd have to leave his new comrades behind. He would be fast in the desert, swift, silent. He could go far in the night, without water, untroubled by the cold. And then he could continue in the blazing sun of day, his body pushing itself to exertion levels that would kill a normal man. He could get far enough away to elude pursuit...as long as he was traveling alone.

His comrades wouldn't make it three hours before they needed rest, before the chill of the desert night had them shivering uncontrollably in their light prison jumpsuits. They couldn't go on for a day or two in the blazing sun of the desert without water like Blackhawk could. He didn't want to leave them behind. It was a new feeling, one he was still learning to understand. But if it came down to all of them getting caught and him escaping alone...

He snapped out of his deep thoughts, his finger already tightened around the trigger of his weapon, firing on instinct as a cluster of guards ran into the hall ahead of him. He had scooped up another assault rifle from one of the last group of soldiers he'd killed...but none of those troopers had any reloads either. Apparently, a single clip was deemed sufficient to handle whatever crises Ghana's sentries were expected to face. But then they'd never planned to deal with Arkarin Blackhawk.

He'd already dropped two of the enemy troopers before the others opened fire. There were three still standing, and Blackhawk dove forward, dropping to the ground for cover while he continued to fire. He took down a third just as he slammed onto the hard composite surface...but the impact knocked off his aim, and he missed the others.

He pulled the trigger again. Nothing. He was sure the clip wasn't empty. He'd paid close attention, and he couldn't have fired more than half the rounds. Jammed.

Shit.

He tossed the rifle to the side, reaching down for the pistol. But it was under him, and he had to shift to the side to get to it. And even as he did it, he knew it was going to take too long...

Crack. Crack.

He heard the gunfire, steeled himself for the incoming rounds. But there were none. Instead the guards both dropped to the ground. Blackhawk watched, realizing the shots had come from behind. His comrades had taken out the remaining troopers.

He leapt to his feet, turning toward Jarvis and nodding. A silent thank you.

All five of them were still there. That was a surprise. He'd expected them to drop pretty quickly. Inexperienced combatants tended to make mistakes that got them killed, and it didn't usually take too long. Perhaps they weren't as raw as he'd thought.

Tig Arhn was standing just behind Jarvis, his hand on his arm, blood pouring through his fingers. Cyn Larison was standing next to him, trying to pry the hand off so she could take a look. But Arhn was still on his feet, clearly in pain, but not making a sound.

Blackhawk nodded. "You okay to go, Tig?"

"I'm good." His voice was clipped, tense. His face was twisted into a painful grimace. But he stared right back at Blackhawk and nodded.

"Good." Blackhawk turned back around. "Let's move. We're not too far from the entrance they brought me through." He remembered the guards escorting him into some kind of doorway, one near the supply dump and vehicle storage. If they were going to manage to hijack some kind of transport, that was where they would do it.

Blackhawk stopped at the next corner, staring both ways down the hallway. He was about to turn left when something caught his eye. It was a conduit, a thick pipe fastened at the top of the wall, just under the ceiling.

"What is it, Blackhawk?" Jarvis was right behind him, alarmed at the pause in their escape.

"This is a power conduit…and it looks like a pretty major one. If we can sever it…"

"And how are we going to do…" He never finished. Blackhawk reached out, grabbed the rifle from the Jarvis' hand…and he started shooting, pouring at least thirty rounds into the conduit. It erupted in a shower of sparks, and Jarvis and his people backed away, throwing their hands in front of their faces as they did.

Then the lights went out.

* * *

"You get 'em, you stay alive…you understand me? Dig out whatever lamps or electric torches you can get…but just keep moving. If they escape, I promise you all a power failure is going to be the least of your problems." Jangus Sand stood in the hall-way, screaming into his portable com unit. His tone was harsh, angry.

Sand was in charge of security for Ghana's complex, and he was mad as hell. Not only had his people allowed the prisoners to escape, they'd failed in every attempt to stop them, losing more than a dozen of their number without recapturing—or killing—anyone. He was angry with himself too. Since the pris-oner exchanges that accompanied the recent truce, the deten-tion area had become a bit of a backwater, a few soldiers who'd gotten in trouble, a handful of raiders under interrogation… nothing that had seemed like a threat. Now he was cursing him-self for not paying more attention to the newest prisoner…a man who had proven himself to be a far greater danger than Sand had anticipated.

And now the lights are out. Just fucking great.

Sand's anger was fueled by his own frustration, but also in no small part by thoughts of what General Ghana would do to him if the prisoners got away. His men were responsible to him. And he was accountable to Ghana. He had no idea how he would explain that the prisoners made their way through the army's main headquarters and walked out into the desert. No, there was no way to say that, not without risking a firing squad. That left one option. Find the prisoners. Now.

He turned back toward the small column behind him. Two of the men had portable lamps, and they had turned them on, illuminating the utter blackness to a dim dusk. "Give me one of those," he snapped to the nearest soldier holding one of the lamps.

"Sir!" the trooper responded, and he stepped up toward Sand, handing him the light.

"Converge on sector G," he said, moving swiftly as he spoke

into the com unit. He was close to G himself, and he had a full squad with him…veteran line soldiers, not the trumped up babysitters that pulled security detail in the detention area.

He moved forward, his men close behind. Sand had an assault rifle in his hands, and unlike the prison guards, he had a bandolier across his chest with almost a dozen reloads…as well as two grenades. A pistol hung from one side of his belt, and a sword from the other. His troopers were identically armed.

Sand whipped around the corner and then he stopped as his com unit crackled to life.

"Captain, we just found half a dozen bodies. Looks like there was some kind of firefight here." It was one of his squad leaders, Sergeant Zahg. His mind focused, remembering where he'd sent Zahg.

Near the main freight delivery zone.

Of course. That's where they brought the new prisoner in.

And the main power conduits run through that area…

"All units, forget sector G. Move to Sector M immediately." He flipped the channel on his com unit. "Central Command, I want troops in the transport area immediately. All incoming and outgoing traffic is to be suspended."

"I'm sorry, Captain…I'm going to need authorization from Colonel Belwar to shut down transport ops." The voice on the com was soft, lethargic. Morale had been poor since General Lucerne's army had defeated Ghana's forces in three consecutive battles. Sand had struggled to deal with the problems the army's despondency was causing in his own command, but he knew victory was the only real cure.

And if we can't even hold on to a few prisoners, how are we going to beat Lucerne's army?

"You will obey my orders at once, Lieutenant, or you will explain to General Ghana why you allowed the prisoners to escape. Is that clear?"

"Yes, Captain." The lieutenant's voice was crisper, more alert, though tinged now with fear. "Issuing shutdown orders now."

Sand closed the com line and cursed under his breath. He'd exceeded his authority…but no one would care as long as he recaptured the prisoners.

And if he didn't…

* * *

"Leave him. He's dead." Blackhawk's voice was cold, more so than he'd intended. But he'd been on enough battlefields to know there wasn't a damned thing you could do for a dead man, no matter how valued of a comrade he was. And the bleeding hole in Mog Poole's head left little doubt he was dead.

The others stared back at him with undisguised rage, but Jarvis Danith pulled back from Poole's body and said, "Blackhawk is right. There's nothing we can do for Mog now…and the last thing he'd want is for the rest of us to get ourselves killed for nothing."

Blackhawk looked at Jarvis, impressed by the raider's poise. He was certain none of them had military experience, but someone had instilled an impressive esprit de corps in these people.

I'd like to meet their leader…

He snapped his head right then left, looking down both sides of the corridor. Nothing. He listened as well, his ears straining for any signs of more enemy troops approaching. There were alarm bells ringing now, and the noise made it hard to pick up subtle things like footsteps or far away voices, but as far as he could tell, there was no one nearby.

His eyes turned back, panning over the area. There were seven bodies on the ground, and six were from the other side. The raiders were upset by the loss of their comrade, but Blackhawk realized his ragtag group had actually acquitted itself quite well. He wasn't ready to admit he was better off for having them along…but he knew it would have been tough to fight his way out alone.

"Alright," he said, his voice that of a man used to command, "You heard Jarvis. Let's move. Now."

He paused for a second, until he was sure they were all responding. Then he stepped forward. The exit was at the end of the hallway, and unless Ghana's people were total idiots, they had to have a good idea where the escapees were.

He was halfway down the hallway when the door swung open, and soldiers stared pouring in. He reacted on instinct, and his rifle was down, firing with deadly accuracy before the enemy troopers could respond. He dropped three of them before the others pulled back outside, closing the door behind them.

Blackhawk's mind was deep in the state he called the battle trance. He was thinking rapidly, so much so that events around him seemed to be happening in slow motion. His legs tensed, lunged forward. He had to get to the door before the enemy could lock or bar it. If his people were trapped in this hallway, the escape attempt was over.

He bolted forward, slammed into the door, his hand moving toward the panel, pulling down the cover over the emergency controls. His hand reached inside, twisting the latch…and the door popped open.

He swung around slipping through the opening, and out into the night air. It was crisp, cool…but as bright as day. There were at least a dozen soldiers in the area just outside the door, and the whole area was lit by floodlights…clearly not on the same circuit he'd disabled. Ghana's people were surprised when he emerged so quickly, and Blackhawk knew that gave him an edge…the only one he was likely to have.

His eyes snapped back and forth, scanning the area almost by pure instinct, looking for cover. There was a large transport close to him. A few second's mad dash could get him there. But those seconds were all the advantage his surprise would give him. He could race for cover, knowing his comrades would come through the door, that the enemy would be ready for them, firing. It was a chance, he knew, to get away, alone at least. To slip into the desert and disappear. While his allies died.

Blackhawk was still analyzing his options when he opened fire. He was never sure how he'd made the decision, what had driven him to stand there in the open, to give away his best chance at escape. He owed his life to his comrades, he knew that much…though that wouldn't have meant anything to him in the past. But now the thought of leaving them behind, of using their deaths to slip away, was unthinkable.

The rifle was on full auto, and he hosed down the entire area. Two enemies went down. Then four. His arms jerked around, directing the deadly spray in meticulous order, dropping those closest to him, the ones his mind singled out as the greatest threats.

He leapt to the side, just as the others came through the door, adding their fire to his. The enemy was shooting back now, but the ferocity of his attack had unnerved them. Their fire was panicked, wild. And the raiders were all out now, their own shooting far more effective than he'd dared hope.

He felt the kick vanish from his rifle. His clip was empty. He tossed it aside, lunging forward toward the nearest enemy. The soldier had time to fire, to drop Blackhawk before he could close the distance. But he just stared at the oncoming warrior, his eyes wide with shock and fear. He only hesitated for an instant, but against an adversary like Arkarin Blackhawk, that was too long.

Blackhawk shifted his body, avoided the single shot his enemy managed to get off before he slammed into the soldier. Blackhawk felt the impact, and even as the two were falling backwards, his hand lashed out, slammed into his opponent's chest. He could feel the resistance give way, hear the sickening sounds of breaking bones as he drove the soldier's sternum into his heart. He saw the man drop his rifle, and before they hit the ground, he knew his enemy was dead.

He reached out, but the rifle had fallen too far away. He twisted to the side, eyes snapping down to the soldier's body, hand reaching out, grabbing the pistol hanging from the man's belt. He hopped up onto one knee, whipping his head around, looking for enemies. His hand moved like a blur, the pistol firing once, twice…a third time. Three more enemies down. But there were fresh troops moving in, from around the side of the massive structure.

He leapt up to his feet, his eye catching the glint of metal alongside the slain soldier. A sword. Blackhawk reached down, pulling the blade from its sheath. It felt good in his hand, natural, like an appendage he'd been born with. He'd left his own sidearms back at Lucerne's headquarters, but these would do for now. He stared toward the wall in front of him, at the line of troopers coming around, moving toward the fight.

He threw himself forward, coming at them from the shadows, too quickly for the lead troopers to react. His blade slashed out, a spray of blood flying through the air. Then again, his eyes focusing for an instant on those of his enemy, seeing the shock as the soldier reached up in a panic, felt the flow of blood from his slashed throat.

He swung around the wall, pistol firing, taking down the first two soldiers in line. Then pain. His leg. He'd been hit, somewhere in the thigh. He gritted his teeth, ignored the wound, firing again…and again. He'd taken down all but three of the enemy soldiers when his comrades swung around the wall and fired, taking down the last of the enemy.

"You're hit," Jarvis yelled, as he raced toward Blackhawk. The others were right behind him, Rinn Largon and Elli Marne holding Tig Arhn between them. Arhn was bleeding badly from a wound to his abdomen. Blackhawk's training told him it was serious, but not mortal. At least not if he got some kind of help.

Which isn't going to happen.

"I'm alright," Blackhawk snapped back. "Let's just get the hell out of here."

He moved forward, a wave of pain shooting up his leg. He knew the wound wasn't dangerous, at least not on its own. The bullet had missed the artery, and it was embedded in the muscle. Not too deep. Given a little time, he could get it out himself. But time was one thing he didn't have. Not now.

He could feel the weakness in his leg, and he knew he couldn't run. Not full out. Not without falling.

He staggered forward, flashing a quick look behind as he did. There were more soldiers, just inside the door to the building. They would be out in a few seconds…and his people needed to be away from the lights, out into the cover of darkness.

"Go," he shouted, his voice harsh, angry. "Run as fast as you can! You have to get away from the lights…and keep moving. It's your only chance."

He hobbled forward, gritting his teeth, pushing himself as hard as he could. The pain was bad, but he could handle that. Falling was another matter. That would only slow him down more.

He took another step, struggling to keep his leg from giving out. Then he felt something. A hand on his shoulder, an arm slipping under. It was Jarvis.

"What the hell are you..."

"I'm not leaving you, Blackhawk. Now throw your arm over my shoulder...take some of the weight off that leg."

Blackhawk was speechless. His first thoughts of the raiders had been to use them as cover for his own escape...and now one of them was trying to save him. Finally, he managed to croak out, "Go, you fool. I'm fine on my own."

"To hell you are," Jarvis answered, a strength and firmness in his voice Blackhawk hadn't heard before. "Now let's move or we'll both get killed."

Blackhawk leaned on his comrade, taking most of the weight off the injured leg. The two of them hobbled away from the lights, out into the darkness of the desert. They were moving slower than Blackhawk could have done uninjured, even than Jarvis could have managed on his own. But they were faster than a wounded Blackhawk, and they slipped past the last of the lights and into the deepening darkness.

Blackhawk turned his head, looking back. There were several dozen enemy soldiers forming up just outside the door... and moving to follow them. Night would be a help, he knew that much. If it had been daylight, they wouldn't have had a chance. But the desert was a wide open place, and in a matter of minutes the enemy would have airships deployed and multiple platoons searching. His original plan had been to race off into the desert, quickly putting distance behind him until he slipped away. But now he was part of a group of five, two of whom were wounded, crawling slowly away. He kept walking...it wasn't in his nature to give up. But he knew they didn't have a chance.

They continued on for another few minutes. The desert was quiet, hardly a sound save their own footsteps and grunting. And something else too. From behind. The enemy, closing on them.

"They're behind us, Jarvis. It's time for you to leave Arhn and me and run for your lives."

"That's not going to happen, Blackhawk. If they catch us, we fight." Blackhawk could hear the fear in Jarvis' voice, but also the firmness. He believed the raider. He wasn't going to leave Arhn behind…and he wouldn't abandon Blackhawk either.

"Then we better find a good spot to fight, Jarvis. I figure we've got two minutes…and if they catch us in the open, hobbling along, it's over. Even with the darkness."

"There is no good spot. It's all open desert."

Blackhawk looked around, seeing a lot farther into the gloom with his superior eyes than the raider…but coming to the same conclusion. There were no rocks near them, no major elevation changes. Nothing. Just the dark of night standing between them and a perfect killing zone.

He reached down to his side, where he'd shoved the pistol into his pocket. If he was going down, by Chrono he was going down fighting. He almost told Jarvis to stop, but he kept silent. They might as well push a bit farther, for all the good it would do.

He could see light behind them, the portable lamps of their pursuers. They're following our tracks. Blackhawk knew a few things about covering his trail, but they were all slow and time-consuming. He'd counted on the dark to give them some cover, but how he knew they were as good as dead. The enemy had picked up their trail…and they were closing.

Another few steps, perhaps twenty. Then the sounds behind, louder now…and the light, moving closer. Now voices, clearer. Shouting, officers yelling commands. Then gunfire, too far away in the dark, wasted shots.

"Here they come, Jarvis." Blackhawk squeezed his hand around his comrade's shoulder, a sign of gratitude, of respect. *Die well, Jarvis Danith*, he thought but didn't say. Then he pulled away from the raider, turning back toward their pursuers. He could see them, still far back but close enough for his eyes to make them out in the light of their own torches.

Crack. His pistol fired. One shot, and in the distance he saw a shadowy figure fall, a beam of light moving wildly across the sky as the stricken man dropped his lamp. Crack. Another shot…and in the murky light he saw another man fall.

The fire from the enemy soldiers picked up, at least a dozen men firing. Then more, perhaps twenty in total. The shots were still random. Blackhawk and the raiders had killed their own lights, and the mask of darkness hid them. But enough random fire was dangerous.

Blackhawk dropped to the ground, on his stomach, pushing forward to dig himself into the sand, gain what little cover he could. He arm was out in front of him, pistol aimed at the enemy. Crack. Again, he saw a falling figure, lit by the cluster of portable lights. They were closer now, and pretty soon…

The light erupted from behind him, bright, a phosphorus grenade. Then another, off to the side. He saw Elli in the light, rushing to the side, back into what remained of the darkness. But Blackhawk knew the damage had been done. In another few seconds the enemy would be close enough. They would take losses…but they would overwhelm the escapees. Blackhawk again felt the temptation to run off into the darkness. He was wounded, slow…but he still figured he could slip away while his comrades fought their death struggle.

His eyes were locked forward, watching the enemy approach. Crack…crack. His pistol continued to take its deadly toll, but enemy shots were whizzing by, impacting into the sand all around him. Eventually one of the enemy would score a lucky shot. And that would be the end.

He'd kept count on his shots, and he knew he only had three left. His mind raced for options, for some tactic to save his tiny command. But there was nothing…nothing save running for it while his comrades fought to the death. And that he would not do.

He gritted his teeth, prepared himself for the end. He didn't know if the enemy would try to take them prisoner or simply wipe them all out, but he'd made his own choice already. They wouldn't take him alive. Arkarin Blackhawk would fight to the end…and if he was fated to die there, deep in the desert, on the miserable rock of Celtiboria then so be it.

He saw a pair of figures, running, out in front of the others. They'd shut off their lamps, and they were trying to sneak forward in the dark. But Blackhawk's eyes needed only the tiniest bit of illumination, and he saw them both, their silhouettes clear to him. He moved slowly, bringing his pistol to bear. Then he fired, twice in rapid succession, watching as both of the enemy troopers dropped.

One shot left…

He looked out, squinting, focusing, looking for a final target. Then he saw something behind him, a quick movement. And another. There were bodies moving. They were all around him.

He jerked his head back toward the enemy, even as he heard the sounds of fire erupting from behind. There were figures all around now, leaping out from camouflaged positions in the sand. He turned again, seeing shadowy clouds…clouds of dust flying through the air as hidden combatants threw off the sand covered cloths they'd used for cover and opened fire on the enemy.

Blackhawk could see the troopers in the distance, halting, falling in groups, the survivors turning, running back toward the safety of the fortress. But the mysterious fighters were on their heels, following, firing mercilessly on the broken security forces.

Blackhawk jumped to his feet and moved toward a pair of the new fighters, his pistol at the ready. He saw one of them move, reaching for a weapon. Then: "Cass, no! He's a friend!"

Blackhawk froze. The voice was familiar. Jarvis? He stared at the figure facing him, let his own arm drop to his side, still holding his pistol. Was it possible? Were these friends?

"Blackhawk…" It was Jarvis, he was sure now.

"Jarvis…what is going on?"

"These are friends, Blackhawk. The rest of the Grays…here to help us escape."

Blackhawk took a step forward, his eyes locked on the gray-robed figure next to Jarvis. He was tense, still uncertain. Then his eyes caught something. A wisp of dark brown hair, poking its way out of the figure's hood. He stopped, just looking forward.

The raider stood still for a moment, clearly staring at Blackhawk. Then two hands came up and pulled back the hood of the cloak, revealing her face. It was a woman standing in front of Blackhawk. Her hair was long and wild, and she took a step forward, extending her hand. "Hello, Mr. Blackhawk," she said. "Jarvis tells me you helped my people escape…so I suppose we owe you an assist in return." She looked off into the darkness of the desert and then back again. "My name is Cassandra Cross, Mr. Blackhawk. Come along with us." She paused again. "That is if you'd like to get out of here without half of Ghana's army and air force hunting you down."

Chapter Twelve

Ghana's Main Base
"The Badlands"
Northern Celtiboria

The flyer slowly came to a complete halt. The airstrip outside Ghana's headquarters was far from minimum specs for a hypersonic transport, but the plane had come in anyway, and its pilot had earned his pay, bringing his bird down with room to spare. It was a job well done, even if the cost of the rapid braking had been an uncomfortable ride for those in the passenger compartment.

Varn Eleher sat in one of the seats, strapped in, a bit pale from the landing. Carteria's hypersonic planes were incredibly useful, if far too expensive for routine use. But the Marshal had holdings on four continents, and he'd insisted his research teams develop a faster way to move messengers and staff officers around. The planes themselves were plush, built to transport top brass and other VIPs, but that didn't mean a trip at seven times the speed of sound was a pleasant one. Eleher unstrapped his harness. He would be glad when he felt the ground beneath his feet.

"Well done, Jacques," he said, leaning over the com unit as he stood up slowly, giving his stomach time to settle before he challenged it with any sharp moves.

"Thank you, sir." Jacques Paridan was one of the most experienced pilots in the Carterian service, and Eleher had make liberal use of the Marshal's authorization to select his own people. He'd awakened the pilot in the middle of the night and given him barely enough time to complete his preflight procedure before liftoff. But he knew landing at Ghana's makeshift airstrip in the dusty reaches of the Badlands would take a good pilot… and Paridan was just about the best there was.

He turned and walked toward the hatch, just as it began to open, and the retractable stair extended slowly. He took a deep breath, hoping for fresh air, but sucking in the hot, dry wind of late morning in the desert. He stood at the top of the stairs, his hand sheltering his eyes from the blazing sun. It was bright, as bright as he'd ever seen it anywhere.

This must be a fun place to fight, he thought. Then: *You're probably going to find out.*

He stepped out onto the stairs, feeling the sweat begin to drip down his back almost at once. It was winter in the subtropical Southern Continent, and while he was used to the heat, it was the dryness that got to him almost immediately. It felt like an oven, and he wasn't dressed for it.

He put his feet down on the grayish-black of the runway, some kind of composite material that he could tell had been hastily laid to create an airstrip in the middle of this hell. He'd been well aware that the Warlords of the Northern Continent were very divided—and vastly less wealthy than his own master—but now he felt as if he'd traveled back in time, to some primitive past era.

He looked up, squinting in the relentless brightness of the morning. There was an officer approaching, with a ragtag group of soldiers following behind him. Eleher sighed. He knew Ghana had been a Warlord of note on the Northern Continent for thirty years, but he couldn't reconcile that fact with what he saw rushing toward him.

"Colonel Eleher, welcome to the Northern Continent. I apologize that the general isn't here…well, we just found out you were enroute, and I'm afraid General Ghana is tied up with…another matter." Dav Roogen wore his dress uniform, but the signs of haste were evident in a number of places, the crookedness of the line of medals on his chest, the wrinkles in his jacket. He had an honor guard behind him, a sergeant and ten privates who looked like they'd donned their own formal uniforms even more quickly.

"That is quite alright, Captain. I appreciate your welcome." Eleher's eyes darted to the slightly slovenly group of soldiers standing more or less at attention in their rumpled dress browns. Any unit in Carteria's army that looked like this one would have found itself in a world of hurt.

Rumor is Ghana's men are close to defeat…and this looks like a demoralized bunch of losers…

"Though, I do hope the General will not be long. I have much to discuss with him."

"Yes, sir…I mean, no, sir. He won't be long. May I show you to your quarters? Perhaps you wish to freshen up after your long journey."

My journey wasn't that long, not at Mach 7. And I look a lot fresher than you and your men…

"Yes, Captain. That will be fine."

Eleher nodded, and he followed the officer.

I don't know if they fight better here on the Northern Continent than they look, but if they don't I may yet live to see Carteria crowned king of Celtiboria…

* * *

Ghana stood in front of the cowering group of soldiers, glaring at the one closest to him, an officer wearing the insignia of a captain. He hadn't said a word…he didn't need to. The anger radiated off his body, the expression on his face, the rigidity of his movements. None of the soldiers could doubt their general was angry. They could only hope his rage wasn't enough to stand them in front of a firing squad…because at first glance it looked like it was.

"Eight guards," Ghana said, his tone menacing, though he

did not raise his voice. "Four in the cell and four just outside. And a cell full of unarmed prisoners. And that doesn't even take into account two dozen more soldiers in the halls…and more than fifty outside in the pursuit. And one enemy body recovered. One!" He panned his gaze over the entire group before returning his stare to the officer in front. "Is my information accurate? Or am I wrong?"

"No, sir…you are not wrong." Jangus Sand stood in front of the general, his arm throbbing from the wound he'd taken when his pursuing force was ambushed. He was trying to decide how to proceed, whether he should try to explain…or simply wait and see if Ghana's anger burned itself out.

"Then perhaps you can enlighten me, Captain, as to why six prisoners were able to outfight and outwit my entire security force. A force you command, I might add."

"Sir, the one prisoner…the last one who was brought in. He is no normal vagrant, not even a soldier. He is extremely capable…like nothing I've ever seen before. He killed at least twenty of my men by himself."

"Because your men came at him in small groups, three and four at a time. You had over two hundred soldiers at your command. Are you suggesting this was an inadequate force to apprehend six escapees?"

Sand struggled to stay at attention, to communicate as much respect as possible to Ghana. The general wasn't a raving psychopath like some of the other Warlords, but he was prone to fits of anger…and even Sand had to acknowledge there was reason for rage over the escape.

Ghana didn't see that man…what he could do…

"General, respectfully, while I understand it appears that way in retrospect, at the time I was trying to get any forces I could in position as quickly as possible."

"Yes," Ghana said. "Well, *in retrospect*, that wasn't a very good plan, was it?"

"No, sir…" Sand shifted nervously on his feet. He knew he was a good soldier, a capable officer who had performed his duties with distinction in the past. But now he was at a loss, still trying to figure how a small group of escaped prisoners had gotten the better of him. "General, it wasn't just the six of them. We were ambushed in the desert, just as we were about to catch up with the prisoners." He paused then added, "I saw several of them, sir…it was the raiders, the comrades of the five we had in custody. Those damned Grays."

Ghana sighed hard. "That would be a valid explanation, Captain, for why you were beaten back in the desert. But I still have difficulty understanding how you allowed them to get out of the fortress. It reeks of a level of incompetence that makes a mockery of the term 'security.'"

"General, again, I cannot express to you how capable that last prisoner…"

"Yes, yes, I'm sure he was a virtual demigod, smiting your men with a giant hammer. Yet your guards were able to stop only one of the other escapees, the Grays. And that by killing him in a firefight where you lost half a dozen men. You do understand that we have missed our best opportunity to track down those infernal raiders, don't you? I seriously doubt the dead man will tell us much…and the others are gone. And despite over a thousand men and fifty vehicles deployed in the search, we haven't found a trace of the others. It appears they simply vanished."

Sand stood and looked back at Ghana. His throat was parched, his voice hoarse. Every word was a painful effort. "We know the raiders have some means of traversing the desert in secrecy. We must find how they escape detection as they move about, despite the best efforts of our scouts and aircraft to track them down."

"That is a wonderful idea, Captain." Ghana's voice dripped with sarcasm. "I wonder why I never thought of that." He turned a withering stare on Sand. "Now that you have lost our interrogation subjects, pray tell…how exactly would you go about discovering their location? Or their means of transit?"

Sand was silent, struggling to meet the general's gaze.

"I should punish you for this incompetence, Captain. I should put you in private's stripes, send you to dig holes in the desert."

Sand stood. He felt the full intensity of Ghana's disapproval…but perhaps a spark of hope too. *Did he say 'I should?'*

Ghana held his gaze, staring at Sand for a few seconds before he continued. "But your past services has been spotless, Captain, and so I will give you a chance to redeem yourself. You will go, you will take a force with you…and by whatever means necessary you will find the refuge of these criminals who call themselves "Grays." You will track down their mysterious means of transit, you will find their base…and you will destroy them utterly."

Sand felt a pit in his stomach. The army had been trying to track down the Grays for almost two years now, with little to show for the effort.

"If you succeed we will forget this entire shameful episode. Indeed, I will reward you, and you will have your major's cluster."

Sand could hear the flipside of that coin, even before Ghana continued.

"But if you fail me again…"

The general didn't finish. He didn't have to.

* * *

Rhiombe was a bustling city, a trading center and the informal capital of the four rivers region. The half dozen cities situated along the banks of the great waterways formed a sort of loose federation, and they had managed to remain free of the control of any of the Warlords on the Northern Continent. Jellack knew they owed their relative freedom more to a strange power balance between the half dozen Warlords whose power bases surrounded them than to any real military strength of their own. But as long as any general who seized the cities could expect his rivals to band together against him, an uneasy independence continued.

Jellack looked around at the crowds of people moving about their business. There were guards too, the green-uniformed members of the city watch in evidence in most of the public places. For the most part they walked around patrolling, giving a sense to the people that they were maintaining order...and discouraging crime.

He'd also spotted a few members of the militia, the light-blue uniformed troops that were tasked with defense if one of the river cities was ever attacked. Jellack wasn't a soldier himself, but he'd worked closely with them for a long time now, and he had to force back a callous laugh. The few troops he'd seen seemed to wear the same arrogant scowl, one he'd witnessed before in Carteria's men, and those of the other Warlords. Celtiboria had seen constant war for three centuries, and the soldiers had risen to a place of prominence in the overall hierarchy. But Jellack could tell the uniformed fops walking around Rhiombe were mostly pretend soldiers. He doubted, if they were ever forced to fight against the veterans of one of the local Warlords, the battle would last more than an hour.

Rhiombe, like the other river cities, was far from a democracy, but the Council of Elders ruled with a light hand, one that allowed trade to flow...and to bring wealth and prosperity in its wake. Jellack had been a trader himself, before he'd been forced into Carteria's service, and he appreciated the value in allowing private businesses to flourish. Carteria had assumed total control over the regions his armies had conquered, and the Marshal had howled in anger and frustration as output and standards of living plummeted under the commissars he appointed to keep a heavy boot on his new subjects. Jellack had tried to explain how the heavy-handed policies drove away commerce and diminished wealth, but Carteria had refused to loosen his iron control.

There was poverty in Rhiombe, certainly, as there was everywhere in war torn Celtiboria. But there were jobs in the city for those willing to work, and that offered the Riverlanders opportunities that were only dreams to many elsewhere.

He glanced down at the small tablet in his hand, his fingers moving across the map that was displayed, zooming in on one area. He nodded to himself and turned right, down the Place D'Alhas...toward the Piazza Dromonde, where the main mercenary markets operated out of a cluster of taverns and inns.

It was technically illegal for mercenary companies to sell

their services in Rhiombe or any of the other river cities. Indeed, even discussing possible terms of service was forbidden, at least in the written books of laws. But the reality was far different. As the closest thing to neutral ground on the Northern Continent, the river cities were an ideal location for conducting such discussions. The officers and men of the merc forces brought a steady stream of revenue into the cities, bolstering their economies, and the agents who negotiated with the representatives of the Warlords kept the city officials satisfied and well-greased with bribes.

The nature of the business conducted in the taverns surrounding the Dromonde was an open secret, one ignored by the city watch and the militia. For almost a century, the river cities had been the center of the market for mercenary forces on a continent constantly at war, and much of their wealth was built upon that blood trade.

But the D'Alhas was almost empty as Jellack walked along the wide pedestrian promenade. He'd expected to find a bustling avenue, but now as he walked he noticed boarded up storefronts and other signs of economic distress...including a number of beggars wearing tattered uniforms in a variety of colors and styles. The mercenaries of the Northern Continent were well known for providing for their disabled veterans, at least more than many other forces did, but even here, the signs of economic distress were clearly in evidence.

Jellack reached into his purse and pulled out a handful of ten ducat coins, handing them out to the veterans. "Where would I go," he asked them, "if I was interested in hiring a mercenary company?"

"To Tigranes' Tavern," one said.

"At the Endless Bottle," said another.

He held out a coin to the last soldier in the line. The man reached leaned forward, bringing a small pouch around his neck toward Jellack. He had no arms.

Jellack was no stranger to wounded soldiers, and he was ashamed to admit, Carteria tended to be callous with his troopers when they became useless to him. But it was still a shock to see men in such condition, unattended, uncared for. It was the true face of war, the reality the Warlords hid behind parades and banners and bands playing raucous marches. Jellack was a trader at heart, and even after years in Carteria's service, the harsher side of war was still a shock to him.

"You want to go to The Raven Inn," the man said. "Turn left at the Dromonde, down the Rue Malazar. Ask for Dolakov. He books for the Red Wolves. Best mercenary company on Celtiboria."

Jellack nodded, noticing the worn wolf's head patch on the soldier's tattered uniform and wondering how impartial the advice was. "Thank you," he said softly, leaning forward and dropping a second coin in the soldier's pouch.

He turned and walked into the piazza and stopped, looking up at the fountain, with its sculpture of a dozen mythical warriors fighting a dragon. It had been a gift from some of the mercenary companies over a century before, he'd heard, a blatant attempt to quell the populace's opposition to the mercs' use of the area to conduct their business. The true powers, the politicians and ministers in positions of power, were won over by more discrete—and expensive—means. But it was worth a sculpture or the occasional sponsorship of a festival day to keep the masses content.

He scanned the area. He'd heard the Piazza was one of the busiest areas of the city, filled with agents from the Warlords seeking to hire soldiers, and with the troops themselves, spending their coin in the gambling halls and brothels that lined the side streets all around. But it was quiet now, almost dead. Jellack could tell immediately the rumors were true. The companies had fallen on hard times. The wars along the Northern Continent's west coast had raged for almost a decade, providing a steady source of employment and an uninterrupted flow of coin to the combatants. But the battling Warlords were bankrupt now, their subjects bled dry of everything they had to support war.

He shook his head, a frown on his face. Jellack was good with money...very good. But he knew soldiers well enough to realize they quickly squandered whatever came into their hands.

I will get a good deal here, he thought. *They are all desperate for work.*

He looked around off to the left, his eyes fixing on a sign reading, Rue Malazar. He turned and walked toward it. The Malazar wasn't a broad avenue like the Place D'Alhas, but it wasn't one of the crooked little alleys that had little to offer save dive bars and affordable sex for sale.

He walked down the street, his head panning back and forth until he saw what he was looking for…a small wooden sign with the image of a black raven. He stepped up to the door, pausing for an instant and assessing his surroundings. It wasn't the plushest—or the safest looking—establishment, but it wasn't the filthy deathtrap some of the other places appeared to be. He walked through the door.

The tavern was almost empty, perhaps half a dozen soldiers sitting at the tables…and a few more along the edge of the bar. There had been several conversations going on, but they stopped the instant he walked in.

He stepped up to the bar. "Black Hills," he said to the bartender, referring to one of the local whiskies he'd seen the soldiers in the area drinking. "A double."

In truth, Jellack wasn't much of a drinker…and when he did partake, it was usually one of the Gold Valley reds, and he was picky about vintage. The thought of guzzling soldiers' rot gut was less than appealing. But he knew he already looked more like an accountant than a warrior, and there was no sense feeding that image.

The bartender dropped a glass in front of Jellack and filled it from a smoky-colored glass bottle. "Half a deci," he said, his voice gruff, disinterested.

Jellack pulled out another ten ducat coin—two hundred times what the bartender had asked him for—and he threw it on the bar. "I'm looking for Dolokov," he said, trying to sound as tough as he could. He glanced down at the yellowish liquid in the glass, hiding his hesitancy. Then he took a quick breath and raised it to his lips, slugging is down in one gulp.

The whiskey was harsh, perhaps not quite a bathtub brew

distilled in the back of the bar, but not far from it either. Jellack's stomach rebelled, but he didn't let it show as he stared at the bartender, his expression demanding, impatient.

The bartender was a large man, a good bit taller than Jellack and a lot heavier. He stared at Jellack, his eyes dropping down to the coin and back to the stranger in the non-descript, but clearly expensive suit.

He raised a thick, hairy arm, pointing across the room to one of the tables. "That's Dolokov over there."

Jellack turned toward the table. There were three men sitting there, all wearing what were clearly officer's uniforms. He pointed toward the empty glass, without looking back at the bartender. Then he scooped up the refilled drink and tossed a second coin on the bar.

He walked over, not reacting as the men at the table watched his every move. "I'm looking for Dolokov," he said.

The three men exchanged glances. Then the one in the center said, "You are, are you? And who might you be?" His tone wasn't exactly hostile, but it wasn't inviting either.

"My name is Jellack. I represent a party interested in retaining a force of mercenaries."

The man looked back, not speaking for a few seconds. Jellack could see skepticism in his eyes, but also interest.

They really do need work…

"And who exactly is this…party?"

Jellack paused. It was his turn to play for effect. "We're not there yet. There is a lot to discuss before we start talking names."

The man stared back, his expression turning to a scowl. "Well, we're not going to get there unless I know who I'm dealing with."

Jellack stared at the man, struggling to keep his cool. "You're dealing with me," he said coldly. Then he reached out and pulled a chair from the table, sitting down and staring across at his counterpart. "Now, shall we talk details?"

The mercenary officer stared back, clearly trying to maintain his cold demeanor, but Jellack caught a flash of surprise on the man's face.

"Or am I wasting my time here?" Jellack added before the man spoke. "Because there are plenty of other places I can go to hire…"

"No, we're not wasting time," Dolokov said, a hint of respect creeping into his voice. "What do you have in mind?"

"A long term contract…three years with an option to extend."

"For how many troops?"

Jellack didn't flinch. "All of them, of course."

"Look, Mr. Jellack, I'm sure you think you need a lot of men, but the Wolves are the biggest mercenary company on the Northern Continent. We can put ten thousand men into the field almost immediately…and another ten thousand on six weeks' notice." The man paused. "So, let me ask you again, how many men do you need?"

"Twenty thousand," Jellack said. "That's a good start." He stared right at Dolokov. "And I trust you can assist me in reaching out to some of the other companies."

"Other companies?" Dolokov stared back, no longer able to hide the surprise in his face. "How many soldiers are you looking to hire?"

"That depends on what is available," Jellack said, reaching down to his side and pulling a small purse from his belt. "Perhaps one hundred thousand, if that many are available." He paused, savoring the look of shock in Dolokov's face. He dumped the purse over, and a pile of gold hundred ducat coins spilled out. "And we will pay in good coin, none of the debased garbage that passes for money on the Northern Continent. Six months in advance for any company signing a three year contract." He stared at Dolokov. "So, Colonel," he said, dropping the subtle fact that he could read the Wolves' rank insignia, "do we have a deal?"

Chapter Thirteen

Just Outside Ghana's Base
"The Badlands"
Northern Celtiboria

Blackhawk crawled through the conduit, biting down hard trying to ignore the pain in his leg. It was far from an ideal way to travel, and they been moving for hours now, but he was wise enough to realize the raiders had saved his life. He'd have fought to the death, and surprisingly, he believed his comrades would have done the same, but he didn't have any doubt death would have come. There had just been too many of Ghana's soldiers.

The raiders had led the escapees across a section of open desert, skillfully using the slight changes in elevation to provide as much cover as possible against any pursuers equipped with infrared scanners. They'd heard an airship overhead, and the leader ordered them all to hit the sand and lie perfectly still. Blackhawk knew that had been a desperate attempt to avoid detection, but he also had to admit it had worked.

They'd run for almost an hour when they came to a hole in the ground, surrounded by a pile of displaced sand...and mixed in, several chunks of concrete. On closer inspection, Blackhawk realized it was some kind of underground pipe...and the debris from a hole that had been dug through it. A pipeline, a conduit of some kind. And in an instant, Blackhawk knew how the raiders got around undetected, confounding Ghana's efforts to track them down.

The group had slipped through the opening into the pipe one by one, the last of them pulling as much dirt and sand as possible back over the hole as they did. He knew it was far from perfect camouflage, that a close inspection would reveal there was something there. But the desert was large, and the makeshift entrance to the conduit was small…and in a matter of hours, a day at most, the wind would blow more sand over the hole, erasing the last hints that the Grays had a secret tunnel less than an hour from Ghana's headquarters.

He was surprised by the turn events had taken, by the unexpected rescue operation. He'd only had a moment to speak with Cass, and all she'd told him was they had been on the way to break her people out when they saw the floodlights, heard the sounds of combat. They'd halted at once, created what cover they could, intending to ambush any of Ghana's soldiers that came their way.

Whatever the sequence of events, Blackhawk knew he owed his life to these raiders. That wouldn't have mattered to him once, but now it did. He might have called it even…Jarvis and his people would never have gotten out of Ghana's stronghold without his leadership and combat abilities, and as capable as Cassandra seemed to be, her people would never have succeeded in some desperate rescue attempt from outside.

But there was more than an analysis of who did more for whom at play. He was intrigued by Cassandra—and more than a little stunned at what he perceived in her. She was beautiful, all the more because he knew he was seeing her in her combat garb, crawling around in the desert, her face covered with dust and sweat, her hair tied up in a greasy ponytail. He felt the stirrings of affection, something new to him. Before, his women had been amusements, enjoyable diversions certainly, but nothing more. Indeed, he'd spent most of his life conditioned to view all those around him for their practical worth…whether that was for a romp in bed or their capabilities on the battlefield. He'd never had a real friend, nor a woman he'd cared for on any level beyond the physical. But he pushed it all back…now was not the time for such thoughts. Perhaps later…

He realized it was more than just physical attraction he felt, even affection. He was a leader. It had been bred into him, it lived in every fiber of his being. And he knew immediately, she was one too. He suspected she was in over her head, that she didn't have the training, the knowledge to prevail. Yet, she had done precisely that, apparently for a considerable period of time…and he felt his respect growing.

He wanted to know more about her…and he felt the urge to help her. He didn't like the idea of leaving her on her own, of taking off once they'd cleared the immediate danger zone. She was smart, and her people were clearly devoted to her. But Blackhawk had seen enough rebels and raiding operations to realize that eventually they would all be wiped out. And the thought of Cassandra Cross lying in the desert, her pretty face shattered by a spray of bullets, was upsetting to him.

If I leave, she will die. Perhaps tomorrow, next week, next year. But she will never leave this desert. None of them will.

He struggled with himself, his resurgent apathy trying to push back his new thoughts, feelings.

It isn't your fight. Cassandra is an attractive enough woman, but she and her people will live or die…and it has nothing to do with you.

He could feel the argument in his head, the debate between himself and…himself. There was coldness, the old feelings stirring, the frozen rationality, the disregard for all those around him, for everything save victory.

And victory here is unlikely. Besides, you have your own agenda. Vengeance on the man who betrayed you. And then to leave this miserable rock…and its Warlords, raiders, downtrodden people. None of it has anything to do with me. Their problems are their own…not mine.

He continued crawling forward, mostly ignoring the worsening pain from his leg. He listened to the old thoughts, and he saw the cold logic in them. But that wasn't him anymore. And he couldn't stop thinking about Cass and her people…and the anger he felt at the thought of them all dying.

* * *

"The first flights will be arriving within the hour, General. Marshal Carteria didn't want to waste any time in rushing support to you." Varn Eleher sat in the guest chair, perched uncomfortably on the spare wooden seat. Ghana's stronghold was a field fortress, not an ancestral castle, and comfort was a relative thing.

Ghana sat in his own, slightly plusher, chair, staring across the desk at the Carterian officer. He understood what he was hearing, but he was still having difficulty accepting it. He'd sent Jinn Barkus to negotiate additional funding, hard currency that would enable him to hire enough mercenaries to vanquish Lucerne's army. He'd been prepared for a refusal, for the need to find a way to prevail on his own. He'd even considered the possibility that Carteria would take his anger out on his longtime aide, that Barkus would never return from his desperate mission. But this...this was something he'd never imagined.

"Colonel Eleher, I...ah...appreciate the marshal's show of confidence...and his willingness to help in so significant a manner, but I requested financial support. The mercenaries of the river cities are a short march from here. We could have reinforcements in position before the truce expires. Marshal Carteria couldn't possibly have enough soldiers here in time to..."

"Your information is inaccurate, General. You underestimate the Marshal's capabilities and his commitment to your cause. The incoming flights will deliver combat troops, fully supplied and ready for action. And they will continue to arrive, around the clock. In three days we will have five thousand men on the ground. In two weeks, a combat ready force of twenty-five thousand will be fully deployed." Eleher paused, clearly trying to suppress—slightly—the arrogance he felt as one of Carteria's top commanders. "Armored vehicles and heavy equipment will take more time to transit, I'm afraid, thought I submit even the light infantry forces will be rather better equipped and trained than your men...or General Lucerne's." Ghana knew the words were an intentional jab, a boast meant to remind him of

Carteria's power. But he was well aware they were also the truth. The Northern Continent Warlords couldn't match the financial resources of the Marshal, and that showed itself in a number of areas, including providing leading edge equipment to field forces.

Ghana bolted himself to his chair, his posture upright, radiating pride...and not a little of his own controlled arrogance. He wasn't about to show this lackey of Carteria's how unnerved he was at the actions his plea for aid had unleashed. Bako Ghana had been a warrior all his life, starting as a common soldier in the army of General M'tara almost four decades earlier. He'd risen steadily through the ranks, and one day he caught the eye of M'tara's daughter. The ensuing marriage had made him heir to all the lands south of the River Caragian, and it had given him the Warlord's stars less than four years later when an enemy sniper killed General M'tara on the eve of battle.

Ghana had avenged his father-in-law, not only winning the battle, but killing both of the allied enemy Warlords responsible. And he had proven to be a competent commander, if not a brilliant one. For thirty years he had steadily expanded his domains, defeating all those who stood against him. Until he ran into Augustin Lucerne.

Lucerne was nothing, a petty general from a forgotten backwater. But Ghana had never seen anything like his army in action. The Warlords generally commanded a combination of retainers of varying degrees of loyalty along with mercenaries fighting for pay. But there was something different about Lucerne's soldiers. They were devoted to him, in a way that transcended even the generational loyalty of longtime retainers. He'd seen images of them on the eve of battle, or after a victory. Thousands of them, arms raised in the air, screaming Lucerne's name, carrying the Warlord on their shoulders.

And they were skilled, trained to a level Ghana had never seen before, their discipline almost indestructible, even in the most desperate battles. He'd seen units of Lucerne's army, surrounded, hopelessly outnumbered, fighting to the last man. He'd learned to respect Lucerne's soldiers. To fear them.

Ghana had never been one to seek help before, and certainly not from a man like Carteria. But he'd been unnerved by his first encounter with Lucerne, and he had reached out, driven by fear as much as logic, offering trade concessions in exchange for financial backing. But even with Carteria's coin, he continued to lose to Lucerne, and now he was on the verge of total defeat, his position far weaker than was generally known. His battered army hadn't even been able to stamp out the bands of raiders and smugglers that had plagued the trade moving through the Badlands, choking off his largest source of revenue. When the struggle resumed, he knew his army was doomed. But he hadn't been idle. He had a plan, a way to strike at Lucerne, to paralyze his army. And it had nothing to do with Carterian troops pouring onto the Northern Continent.

"Perhaps we should limit the number of troops for now, Colonel. Say, ten thousand. That should be…"

"The twenty-five thousand are already in transit or preparing for departure. The Marshal's orders are clear."

Ghana fought back against the anger trying to bubble out at this Carterian lackey for daring to interrupt him…and at the thought of Carteria's orders dictating affairs on the Northern Continent, in Ghana's own occupied lands. But he knew rage would only undermine him now. Even now, his machinations were in progress, his scheme to overcome Lucerne. But he still needed more troops to be assured of success. And there was no way to stop Carteria's soldiers from coming, no way save attacking them as they land. Rage or no, Ghana wasn't about to start a war with the most powerful Warlord on the planet.

"Perhaps we can feed the arriving units into our OB, replacing losses in many of the frontline units."

"The Marshal was quite clear. The expeditionary force will fight as a whole." Eleher paused. "The Marshal does not wish to see any degradation of combat capabilities. I'm sure you are aware, our forces have different doctrines, equipment."

It was a small concession, an explanation where Eleher might have offered none. But Ghana knew it was bullshit too. Carteria had a hidden agenda, almost certainly. But what? Ghana's mind raced, trying to analyze things from every possible direction.

What does Carteria want? Is he looking to force better terms, a larger share of trade revenue? Or is it something…worse?

* * *

"Nothing. Absolutely nothing. Eight hundred men, more than a hundred vehicles, a dozen airships on constant patrol duty…and we've found nothing." Jangus Sand was angry, not just normal anger, but the frantic rage that only fear could feed. Ghana had been straightforward, the general had given him a chance to redeem himself, to rescue his career. And he'd been very clear. *Find the raiders.* But Sand's people had been searching for days, and they hadn't found a trace.

He'd had airships covering the area within hours of the escape, patrolling a radius far beyond what the escapees could have covered in that time. But there was nothing. Just endless, open desert. Rolling hills, sand. And not a soul to be found.

It didn't make sense. They had to be out there somewhere. He'd ordered the airships to continue their sweeps, flying lower, overlapping each other's search areas. But still, there had been nothing. He'd even airlifted ground patrols, dropping them at intervals far beyond what the raiders could have covered on foot. But still it was the same. Nothing.

"Sir, the patrols are still…"

"The patrols are going to have to do better, Lieutenant," Sand said, his voice cold, angry. "Even if these raiders had some vehicles hidden out here, there have to be some signs. Tracks, discarded food and water canisters…even a makeshift latrine. Something!"

The lieutenant shifted uncomfortably, moving his weight from one leg to the other, struggling to maintain Sand's angry gaze. He was about to speak when the captain continued.

"Your men had better look harder, Lieutenant…because no one is going back to base until we find these criminals. Do you understand me?"

The lieutenant looked back, hesitated. Then he said, "Yes,

Captain. I understand."

Sand turned and looked out over the desert, silent for a moment. Then he said, "We would have found them if they were out on the open desert...even your lackluster, lazy patrols couldn't have missed them. The airships would have had a sighting by now." His voice trailed off, as he stared intently, looking at the endless sandy, rolling hills. "They would have had a sighting by now..." he repeated.

"Sir?" The lieutenant had a confused look on his face.

"Double your patrols, Lieutenant. I want them to scour this desert step by step. The raiders must have a hideout somewhere...a cave, something. If they'd continued across the desert we'd have found them by now. That means they didn't just keep marching. They went somewhere."

"Somewhere?"

"Yes, Lieutenant...somewhere. There must be a refuge out there...and judging from how quickly the escapees disappeared, it has to be close to our base. No more than a day and a half's hard march." He turned and stared at the still-confused officer. "I want all units equipped with seismic detectors. There's a cave out there somewhere, or an old underground complex of some kind. And our escaped prisoners are hiding there. It's the only answer." He paused. "And you're people are going to find it, Lieutenant, or by Chrono, I will hang every one of them up by his heels and sit and watch as the sun bakes them to death."

Chapter Fourteen

Dark Shadow Valley
"The Badlands"
Northern Celtiboria

"I said focus! Those are your comrades up there, counting on you to cover their moves. If you let them down, they die." Blackhawk stood looking down the line of raiders lying in the sand in a rough formation. They had weapons extended in front of them, an assortment of modern assault rifles mixed with a few backcountry shotguns and pistols. It was far from ideal armament for a fighting force, but it was what they had.

He turned his head to the left, watching another line of men and women, moving forward swiftly, crouched down, their own weapons at the ready.

"Evens stop," Blackhawk yelled. "Covering position." He turned back to the line of raiders on their stomachs right next to him. "Odds, forward." He saw them scrambling to their feet, their paces varying widely, the whole line taking on a disordered look. "Now!" he yelled, dissatisfied at the effort he was seeing. Leapfrogging was infantry tactics 101, and the Grays looked like shit trying to manage it. But he had to admit, they had shown a lot of improvement. Three days before they'd been an uncontrollable mass, resembling a wild mob rather than a military unit. But Blackhawk still shuddered to think of how they would perform under fire...or even when they were shooting themselves. The Grays didn't have enough supplies to expend ammunition on exercises, and besides, too much shooting in the desert only increased the chances of detection by one of the armies.

They don't look like soldiers, but they were good enough to pull your ass out of the fire at Ghana's fortress...

He looked out at the odds, moving forward, toward the rough line the now prone evens had formed. The advancing troops moved up to their comrades' position and then beyond. No one was firing, but all Blackhawk could see was phantom friendly fire, men and women dropping as their scared and confused comrades fired wildly, carelessly. He'd seen it with trained and experienced troops, and for all Cass had done with her people, at heart they were still farmers, young men and women far more at home with a plow in their hands than an assault rifle.

He watched as the odds moved up, about as far ahead of the evens as they'd been behind. "Stop," Blackhawk screamed, loud enough for his words to carry across the valley. That was another problem...the Grays didn't have much in the way of coms, just six units, of varying types and in marginal condition. Worse, they could only those in emergencies. They had no stealth capability...they transmitted wide, easy to intercept signals. One careless transmission, and they could find a thousand enemy troops moving on their hideout.

Which is going to happen anyway. These Grays are good, and Cass is a strong leader...but they've been lucky too. And that always ends. Eventually.

"They're not used to anyone like you." The voice was friendly, almost affectionate. Cassandra Cross walked up behind Blackhawk, quietly, carefully. He had to admit, she had a light step. He'd heard her, of course, and he'd monitored her movements from the instant she'd come out of the small opening in the ridge, from the tunnel that led from the Grays' headquarters out into the valley. But he didn't let on, even giving her a quick look of surprise.

"You are quite the special ops master," he said, doing something he hadn't done in years, smiling. Blackhawk certainly wasn't a romantic, not by any means. But the grim, morose depression that had ruled his life for the last few years had lifted, at least a bit. He still had guilt, and nightmares that would have driven a normal man to lose his sanity. But Cass was different than most of the people he'd known. She had a little of what he'd recognized in Lucerne…and some other things too. He respected her. And he liked her.

"Stop bullshitting me, Ark. You knew I was here…you probably had me the instant I poked my nose out of the tunnel."

"Maybe, he said. But you're still pretty sneaky."

"You know just what to say to a woman, don't you?"

The two had been exchanging mildly taunting comments for days now, a kind of clumsy flirting between two people to whom combat and death were far more real than romance and frivolity. Blackhawk, so confident in battle, so relentless when facing an enemy, felt like a child as he realized he had feelings for Cass. He was so different than he had been before. Breaking his conditioning had been a rebirth of sorts, and he found himself feeling almost childlike in many situations. He'd been a warrior before, a fighter, and he'd retained his cool capability in a fight. But he'd treated comrades, even those close to him, poorly before, in ways he regretted…and vowed never to repeat. He still didn't have much use for most people, but he could feel something inside now that he hadn't before…loyalty, honor. A respect for those who stood by him, fought at his side.

Cass had been hostile to him, at least at first. She didn't give her trust easily…another reason Blackhawk respected her. But in the month since the escape, she'd warmed to the mysterious stranger. He'd proven himself to her, in the only way she recognized. He'd come along on their last two raids. The first had been an almost effortless success. The second had come to the brink of disaster, and in the thick of the crisis, Blackhawk had effectively taken command, snapping out orders with such intense authority and power, every one of the Grays—Cassandra Cross included—had obeyed him without question. And that had saved their lives, most of them at least. They'd had two dead on that mission, but there had been no doubt…they'd all have been wiped out without Blackhawk.

Since then Cass had warmed considerably, and the two sat long and talked, often into the depths of the night. Sleep didn't come easily to Blackhawk, he knew the nightmares awaited him there. He'd always been able to get by on a few hours of rest, and even without any for an extended period. Now he'd met a kindred spirit of sorts in Cass, though he knew that she didn't have his genetic improvements, and the lack of rest wore her down. It was likely to get her killed one day, he knew, but he also understood how the guilt, the burden of command weighed one down, especially in the still quiet of the night.

He realized he wanted to do all he could to help her, to keep her and her people alive. He'd intended to leave almost immediately after the escape, to set out on his vendetta against Lucerne. But he'd put it off one day at a time…and after the near disaster of the second raid, he'd offered to train the Grays for a few weeks before he left.

"So," she said, her voice soft, friendly. "Do you think they can spare you for a while?" She smiled mischievously.

Blackhawk looked back at her. Cass was a tall for a Celtiborian woman, her brown hair loose, hanging about her shoulders. She wore the same gray cloak all her people did, but underneath, Blackhawk could see the leather breeches, the same pants she'd had on the day her people had rescued the escapees. He'd noticed them then too, even as they were running for their lives…as she was staring at him as though he was an enemy, a spy trying to infiltrate and harm her people. But even her hostility hadn't driven the image from his mind.

"Jarvis," he yelled, turning his head to look out toward the maneuvering Grays. "Take over. The same thing…over and over until it's second nature." He looked over at Cass and then back toward Jarvis. "I'll be back in an hour," he said.

He flashed another glance at Cass, standing there smiling at him. "Make that two."

"Samis, you take your people to here." He pointed to a spot on the map. "It's an ideal position to ambush the caravan."

"Yes, Blackhawk...I see. It's a perfect spot."

Blackhawk wasn't sure be believed the raider actually 'saw,' but he knew the man would obey...and that was enough.

"I want you to hit it hard. Lay down fire with everything you've got for thirty seconds. Don't worry about damaging cargoes, just lay waste to everything you can."

Samis looked up from the map nodding, his eyes fixing on Blackhawk's.

"And then I want you to break off. Run like hell, and get your people out of there."

Samis had been nodding steadily, but now his head froze. "Get out? I don't understand. When do we take the caravan?"

"You don't. You just shoot it up and then get out of there. Fast."

"I don't understand..."

"We're not going after that caravan. It's the richest one that's been through here in a long time. Ghana's people will be waiting for an attack. There are probably three times as many guards as you expect...and as soon as you open up, they will send out the word. Every airship and roving patrol will head that way..." Blackhawk pointed to a spot on the map. "...and when they're all concentrated, the rest of us will strike here."

He pointed to another location on the map. "It's not a rich caravan, nor a big one, so it won't be a huge prize. But it's one we can take...and come back alive."

Samis looked up at Blackhawk. "But if we hit the first caravan hard...maybe from multiple directions..."

"It won't matter, Samis." Blackhawk glanced around at the others. It looked like about half of them were following him. *That's better than none...*

He looked back at Samis. "It's clear...or at least it should be. You've been a drain on Ghana for the last two years...and now you humiliated him, five prisoners breaking out of his man base. Like it or not, you've graduated. You're not a thorn in his side anymore...you're a priority. And that means the heat has been turned up. Way up."

He looked over at Cass, saw the comprehension in her face. Then he turned back toward the others. "The last mission should have taught you that. We walked right into a trap there. We went after the richest caravan coming through, walked right into the place Ghana would have guessed we'd go." He paused, his eyes sticking on Elli Marne. He older brother Tyke had been one of the two killed in the last raid. "And we were lucky to get out of there…" He glanced back at Marne. "Those of us who did, at least."

"So what are we supposed to do, Blackhawk? Pick the worst targets, the ones barely worth the effort?" It was Samis again. He wasn't challenging Blackhawk as much as he was working his way through the facts verbally.

"Yes, Samis. That's what you do. Or you die." He paused. "Look, all of you need to hear this. You've done well, you've made a real difference for your people back home. But you've been lucky too. Never forget that. You let your successes go to your head, and it's just a matter of time before you're all dead. You think you've bested Ghana? He's got forty thousand troops…more now that he's been reinforced. You've survived because you were more of a nuisance than a major threat. But that's over now, people. He's mad…and he's determined to take you all down. And if he puts enough resources into it, that's exactly what's going to happen." He paused again. "You will die. All of you. Hunted down relentlessly. But if you listen to me, if you settle for moderate prizes and let the obvious ones go…we can put that day off."

"For how long?" It was Jarvis Danith. He'd seen Blackhawk in action closer than any of the other Grays.

"I'm not going to lie to you, Jarvis." Blackhawk looked out over the others. "To any of you. It could be today, tomorrow. In a month. In a year. It will be sooner if the peace holds. If the armies start fighting again, that will probably buy you all time." He turned and looked back at Cass again. "And we've got to get out of this headquarters. I know it's a good spot, but you've been here for too long. Ghana's people will find it eventually.

And when they do, they'll surround it, cover the area all day and night with airships. Then they will come down into these tunnels, wave after wave of heavily-armed troops, and they will root you out one by one." He could see the uncertainty in Cassandra's expression. The two of them had become close, spent a lot of time together, but she was still having trouble accepting his insistence that the Grays abandon their base. The hideout had been one of the key factors that kept them alive for a very long time, and he knew it was hard to give up, even after it had gone from being an asset to a liability. Blackhawk suspected she understood...but he could also see she needed time. Time she might not have.

He pushed his concern for her out of his mind. There was no time for it now. He was going to lead them on this last raid, show them how to pick targets, to avoid enemy traps. And he would spend a few more days with Cass. But then he had to go. He had to go see Augustin Lucerne. Vengeance had been too long delayed.

Chapter Fifteen

General Lucerne's Headquarters
"The Badlands"
Northern Celtiboria

"At least ten thousand, General. Perhaps more. They appear to be drilled, and extremely well-equipped. It's just a guess, but I'd say they're all veterans." DeMark stood in front of Lucerne's desk, his face twisted into a worried frown. He'd just read the scouting reports, and he'd rushed to report them to the general.

"So there's no doubt, not really. Carteria is supporting Ghana, not just with coin, but now with troops." He sighed. "I thought Bako Ghana was smarter than this. He has to know Carteria is just using him to get a foothold on the Northern Continent." He shook his head. "The fool would have done better to reach out to me, at least try to make a deal to share control of the Badlands...before he sold his soul to the devil."

DeMark stood at attention, staring at Lucerne.

"By Chrono, Rafe, sit down, will you? It's making me uncomfortable just looking at you."

DeMark nodded. "Yes, sir." Then he sat down in one of the chairs facing Lucerne's desk, managing to look as uncomfortable sitting as he had standing.

Rafaelus DeMark was a young officer, one who had risen to his rank of major ahead of all his peers. He'd become one of Lucerne's most trusted officers, and a friend as well. His skills and intellect warranted his rapid advance, but he'd lagged in one area. He still had difficulty managing his intensity. He approached every problem with an urgency that was certain to wear him down long before his time. He'd watched Lucerne, how the general handled bad news, urgent problems...and he'd tried to emulate the cool but attentive demeanor of his commander. But his progress had been slow. He was cool and calm on the battlefield, but in the offices and meeting rooms, discussing the overall strategies and problems the army faced, he tended to overload on stress.

"What do you think, Rafe? Can we take an extra ten thousand...or more?"

DeMark paused. He knew very well Lucerne already had his own answer to that question. The general was a military genius, and his officers were continually amazed at his grasp of both the tactical and strategic situations. But he valued the input of his aides too, and DeMark took his question very seriously indeed.

"I don't know, sir." He felt like the answer was a cop out, a dodge to avoid taking a clear position. But it was also honest. DeMark knew the army's capabilities, he realized the troops were more than a match for Ghana's mix of retainers and hirelings. But Carteria's troops were a question mark, and he just wasn't sure what to expect. He wanted to think they could take ten thousand...but he knew the Marshal's forces would be superbly equipped. They just didn't know enough.

"Don't worry, Rafe. My answer is the same. We need a better estimate on their strength. And we just don't know enough about Carteria's troops...about these units specifically. If they are easily shaken, our odds are good. But if they are solid, if they're armed with leading edge weapons..."

"Yes, General. As I said, from what I've seen, I'm inclined to think these are at least seasoned units...and perhaps long service veterans." He paused. DeMark was under Lucerne's spell, just like the other officers on the staff, and he tended to hesitate when offering advice.

"Go on, Rafe...say what's on your mind."

"Well, sir…" Another pause. "Beyond the question of can we win…do we dare to engage Carteria's soldiers?"

Lucerne exhaled loudly. "I get your meaning, Rafe. But what choice do we have? If Carteria's forces stand off, if they don't aid Ghana's men, we will not engage them. But they didn't fly across an ocean to sit and watch, so I'm inclined to doubt we'll have much choice."

"Yes, sir." DeMark still looked uncomfortable.

"You're worried about provoking Carteria? About a wider war with the Marshal?"

DeMark looked back at Lucerne. He admitted it to himself…he was afraid of Carteria. And he was ashamed for feeling that way. "Yes, sir," he finally said.

"Don't worry, Rafe…I'm scared of Carteria too. He's got twenty times the resources we do…probably more." He looked at DeMark, and his expression softened. "But since when do we let our fears govern what we do? Or overrule our rationality?" He paused. "Carteria is powerful, Rafe, there is no question about that. But if he's got his sights set on the Northern Continent, we're going to have to deal with him one way or another. The only way not to fight his people now is to pull back, leave the Badlands to Ghana. But aside from the other ramifications of that strategy, Ghana isn't Ghana anymore. He's a tentacle of Carteria. If we give the Marshal this beachhead we won't avoid conflict with him…but we will ensure it will be far worse when it comes. If we let Ghana and Carteria prevail here it won't be twenty or thirty thousand troops we face. It will be a hundred thousand. Or two hundred." He paused. "Or five hundred."

DeMark found himself nodding as Lucerne spoke. The general was right, he realized. There was no place for fear in this analysis. Carteria was a reality, one they would have to deal with sooner or later…and their best chance was now.

"We can't wait, sir. If we sit idle until the truce expires, we may have to fight twice as many Carterian troops…or three times." He took a deep breath. He knew Lucerne was an honest man, that he'd repeatedly rejected pleas to break the cease-fire, to launch a surprise attack on Ghana's army. But things had changed now…and waiting simply wasn't an option anymore.

Lucerne was silent for a moment, shifting slightly in his chair as he looked back at his aide. Finally, he locked his eyes on DeMark's and said, "Major, I believe the movement of foreign troops into the theater of war is a violation of the underlying principles of the truce agreement, don't you?"

DeMark looked back for an instant, a confused look on his face. Then he understood. "Yes, sir…I certainly think so. That would put General Ghana in default…and invalidate the cease-fire." DeMark had read the entire truce agreement, and he knew Lucerne was twisting its words with a virtuosity that would have impressed the most aggressive and grizzled counselor or politician. But there was a thread of truth to what he was saying, enough, at least, to manufacture a violation.

"Yes, Major. It would." Lucerne smiled. "Send an envoy to General Ghana's headquarters immediately. I will draft a communique demanding the immediate withdrawal of foreign troops from the Badlands…within 48 hours."

"Yes, sir." DeMark nodded as he rose from the chair. "I will see to it at once."

Lucerne looked up at his aide. "And while you're at it, Rafe, put the army on alert. All leaves are cancelled, effective immediately. All troops are to report to their units and be ready to march within 24 hours."

"Yes, sir!" DeMark smiled. Lucerne was an honorable man, but not a fool. He knew when to bend his word, even if he was unwilling to break it. And there was no doubt, Augustin Lucerne's loyalty was to his soldiers, above and beyond any other considerations.

He turned and walked toward the door, feeling better than he had when he'd entered. He was still worried about Carteria's involvement, but Lucerne's decisiveness was contagious. And the army would be on the move by the next day. Action always calmed him. It was odd, there was no time he was in greater danger than he was in the battle line, but he always knew what to do there. It was the planning, the scheming, the backstabbing so prevalent in Celtiboria's wars that twisted him into knots. But he could put all that aside now.

They were going back into battle.

* * *

Ghana was silent, sitting motionless at his desk. The room was dark, only a single dim light holding off total blackness... and yet it was brighter than his mood. Carteria's soldiers had been intolerable, demanding preference for supplies, treating his own troops like inferiors. He'd issued stern orders, a warning to all his men to hold their tempers. The last thing he needed was his own soldiers brawling with Carteria's...though part of him wished for it, delighted in the thought of one of his people pounding the hell out of one of the Marshal's snotty troopers.

The door opened slowly, and an aide peered in. "General Ghana, sir?"

"What is it?" His voice was gruff, but not overtly hostile. He could see the relief in the lieutenant's face.

"Sir, I'm sorry to disturb you, sir, but Captain Sand is here. He says it is urgent."

"Let him in." Ghana had so many problems he'd forgotten all about the raiders...about his ultimatum to Sand. But he looked up and stared at the door. Perhaps something had gone well recently. Probability suggested it had to eventually.

"General Ghana, sir..."

He could tell immediately Sand had good news. *Refreshing...*

"Yes, Captain, what is it?"

"We have found the raiders' means of transit, sir. There was an underground pipe in the desert, a large one, big enough for men to move through. I searched the databases...apparently it is part of an old project, from before the war, a system to bring water to the inland cities. It was never finished, but it appears the raiders found a large section of conduit that had been laid. That is how they have appeared and disappeared in the open desert, escaping time and time again from our patrols."

Ghana felt a small rush of energy. This was good news.

"Excellent, Captain. You are to be commended. You have

made up for any past…errors."

"There is more, sir."

Ghana could hear the enthusiasm in the captain's voice. He looked up expectantly.

"We have found their headquarters as well. At least I believe we have. I pulled the scouting parties and airships back at once so we didn't give them any alarm. It appears they are based out of a series of caves and tunnels along the Mezzara Ridge."

"Outstanding, Captain. You are to waste no time. The raiders are to be wiped out…to a man. Take whatever resources you need, and go immediately." He paused. "Use whatever force is required, Captain, and risk whatever losses…but none of them are to escape…do you understand me?"

"Yes, sir. Understood. The strike force is loaded up and ready to go. All I need is your orders, General."

"Then you have them, Jangus, along with my congratulations. Well done."

"Thank you, sir." Sand saluted. "With your permission."

"Yes, by all means. Go. Rid us of these parasites."

Ghana leaned back, savoring an uncommon bit of good news. He realized it didn't really help him with his bigger problems, but it felt good nevertheless. And he wanted to savor it, at least for a few minutes.

But that was not to be.

"General…" It was the aide at his door again.

Why do I even bother to turn the com unit off?

"What is it?"

"Sir, we have an officer at the front gate. He says he is a messenger from General Lucerne."

Great…what the hell can that be about?

"Very well, have him brought here at once."

The aide hesitated.

"What?" Ghana snapped, the pleasure from Sands' report all but gone. "What is it?"

"Sir, I also have a report from operations…"

"By Chrono's beard, man, just spit it out!"

"We have multiple reports of troop movements, sir. General

Lucerne's men. They are more active than they've been at any time since the ceasefire."

"Go," Ghana roared, get that messenger down here now!"

He watched the messenger slip out, the heavy door closing behind him. He kept staring, for a minute perhaps. Then he leaned back and took a deep breath.

What fresh hell is this?

Chapter Sixteen

Aquitania Oasis
"The Badlands"
Northern Celtiboria

"I can see the dust cloud coming. It's heavier now. Definitely the caravan." Minth Samis crouched down behind the clump of bushes, looking out from the edge of the oasis. Aquitania was a common place for caravans to stop and camp for the night. There was no real reason the line of trucks needed to stop at the tiny patch of lush terrain in the otherwise dry and inhospitable desert. The caravan wasn't some ancient procession of camels and horse-drawn wagons, making their way slowly from oasis to oasis. The motor transports carried food, water, fuel...everything the convoy needed to cross the desert. But human beings made decisions for various reasons, and not all were based on logic. The traders in the caravan longed to feel the grass beneath their feet for a night, to sleep among palm trees and picturesque little ponds. And so, the oases remained major vectors of cross desert travel.

Blackhawk had told Samis that is where the convoy would stop for the night. He looked up. The sun was almost down. It looked like the stranger had been right. Again.

Samis had wanted to hit the convoy at midday, when the heat was at its worst. It was what the Grays usually did. But

Blackhawk had his own ideas. 'Attack just before they stop for the night,' he had said. 'They will be least on their guard, their minds already on the evening meal and sleep…and the growing darkness will cover your withdrawal.'

It was the withdrawal part that rubbed Samis the wrong way. The caravan was a big one, the richest they'd seen in a long time. It would be heavily guarded, no doubt, but the Grays had taken on escorted caravans before. Still, Blackhawk had been insistent…and there was something about the man, something that made it hard to refuse his advice.

Advice, my ass. He's been giving us orders.

Samis resented that, the way Blackhawk had just shown up and started telling everyone what to do. The Grays had been in this desert for a long time. They knew how to take care of themselves. And Cass was their leader, not some adventurer none of them knew. He'd never known Cassandra Cross to let anyone influence her.

Even when he's sharing her bed…

Samis felt a surge of anger, but it subsided. Part of him resented Blackhawk, as much because he'd wanted Cass for a long time, and he'd been painfully aware she viewed him as no more than one of the Grays. But even his jealousy was insufficient to overcome Blackhawk's strange power of command. He would stew about the newcomer, grumble to himself, or even to one of the others. But the idea of disobeying Blackhawk was a more difficult proposition. He wasn't sure if it was fear or respect—or some combination. But the thought of challenging Blackhawk scared him to death.

He turned and glanced down the makeshift line. He had ten of the Grays with him, and they were all in position, including the two with the autocannon. The heavy weapon was one of the Grays' most prized possessions, but the truth was, they were almost out of ammo for it, and they had little prospect of getting more…so Cass had sent it with Samis. The small squad had to make the enemy believe the Grays' entire corps was attacking the convoy. The longer the enemy bought it, the better chance the diversion would work.

Samis leaned forward, his eyes focused on the now-visible column. The trucks were heavy ones, but there was nothing else. He'd expected an armored vehicle or two in the lead, a few squads of soldiers doing escort duty, but the convoy looked entirely unprotected.

Blackhawk told you to fire and then run...

Fuck Blackhawk...if we can take this convoy, it's worth two years' supplies for back home...

His thoughts struggled with each other, resentment, obedience, thoughts of securing a great victory. Seeing Cass' expression when she discovered he'd taken the convoy with just ten of the Grays...

His eyes focused on the lead vehicle. It was close, and slowing down. It looked like the convoy was going to camp at the oasis. Just as Blackhawk said.

He's been right about everything since he showed up. Listen to him...

Fuck off...it's right there in front of you. All that plunder. Cass...

He turned toward the autocannon.

"Open fire."

* * *

Blackhawk raced along the narrow ridge. There were drops to each side, not deep, but enough to break half a dozen bones if he lost his footing. But his balance was true, as always, and he felt a spark of relief that Cass had let him go alone. He'd been sure she was going to insist on coming...and she did, at least for a while. In the end, she'd made him do what he'd hoped to avoid...tell her point blank he could move faster and stay safer alone than with her along. He knew that was tough medicine for a proud leader like Cass, but if the choice was between hurting her feelings or getting her killed...

The convoy was moving between the two open ridgelines. It was a perfect spot for an ambush, and Blackhawk would have disqualified it for its obviousness save for two facts. First, the convoy wasn't a rich one, and this shipment was probably where Ghana least expected any kind of raid.

And second, in about one minute, the radios in those transports were going to crackle to life with news that the other convoy was under attack. This was Grays country...none of the other bands of raiders dared to poach in the areas staked out by Cass' people. And the Grays had never hit two targets simultaneously. As soon as word hit the convoy down below that the other caravan was under attack, the guards would lose their edge, let themselves feel safe. And that was all Blackhawk needed.

He glanced down at the chronometer Cass had given him, but it only confirmed the countdown that was already true in his head. Thirty seconds. Assuming Samis and his people were spot on time. And Blackhawk had emphasized the importance of that. He looked across to the other ridge, to the last bits of the bright sun slipping down behind the rocky spine. In a few more minutes the light would be gone, replaced by a dusky semi-darkness. Perfect.

The trucks were almost at the point he'd designated. Cass and her people would attack any second...and then he would slip in behind and take out as many guards as he could. He didn't doubt the Grays could take the convoy with or without his efforts. But he knew they were up against a new reality, an increased urgency by Ghana to crush them before he ended up back at war with Lucerne. They were going to have less time to compete the raid. Even if the caravan didn't get out a distress call, they would miss their regular check ins...and Ghana's people would respond by sending a flight of airships. The diversion would probably delay any response, buy a little time. But it still made sense to get in and out as quickly as possible.

Blackhawk also knew he could kill a lot of guards quickly... and possibly save some of the Grays. It was no coincidence the raiders had begun to suffer greater losses on their raids. They were victims of their own success. When they'd started, they were inexperienced, but they were motivated, and they were up against private security forces. Now, for all their own experience, they were facing convoys protected by veteran soldiers...and for all their own seasoning, they were still ill-equipped for that kind of battle.

He counted down to zero in his head. Still nothing. Then, a few seconds later, he heard sounds, the Grays scrambling down from the ridge. He knew he was the only one who would have heard the sounds, but he still made a note to himself. Teach them to be fucking quiet.

He made his way down, grabbing hold of a rock outcropping as he pivoted around, moving swiftly. His feet found the right spots, avoiding loose rocks that might slide down the slope, giving him away to anyone listening carefully. He had a rifle in his hands and a blade at his side, a heavy survival knife. It wasn't his trusty shortsword, but it would do in any fight he was likely to encounter around the caravan.

He heard a shot. Then another. The Grays were in position…and they were opening fire.

He swung around another large rock, staring forward to the last of the transports, slowing quickly, coming to a stop. He raced over, pulling the blade from its sheath. He could see the rear hatch of the transport opening, two men emerging.

Guards. Protecting the rear.

His mind raced, analyzing what he saw, making his own projections on the fly.

Regulars, well drilled ones. Ghana's men.

He'd hoped—but not expected—that a secondary caravan like this one might have relied upon private security. But if there were soldiers here there would be more elsewhere in the convoy.

He leapt forward, almost without conscious thought, acting on instinct, and on conditioning he still knew ruled much of what he did. The guards saw him coming, but too late. His blade flashed. A spray of blood, and one of the soldiers fell, his throat cut so deeply, his head rolled back as he fell.

The other had a fraction of a second more, and he moved his rifle toward the attacker. But Blackhawk had been ready. He pivoted hard, moving his body to the side, even as his blade struck again, plunged deeply this time instead of a slash. Blackhawk could see the expression on the dying guard's face. Shock, fear, pain…then he pulled the blade out hard and the body dropped.

He looked into the back of the transport. There were crates stacked inside, but no other soldiers. He swung around the side of the truck, rifle in one hand and the blood-covered knife in the other. He saw the forward hatch slide open, a man climbing out. The driver. Obviously a civilian.

Blackhawk felt something unfamiliar, a wave of doubt, of regret at what he was about to do. The concern for killing an innocent, a civilian who'd done nothing more to him than taking a job as a caravan driver, was new to him. Collateral damage was part of war, and he'd rarely given it a thought in the past. But now it was there...not strong enough to stay his hand, but notable nevertheless.

He ran up to the man, plunging the blade deep into his chest. It was the most merciful death he could give the driver. Quick, too fast even for the man to feel much pain. Sparing him simply wasn't an option. The attack had just begun, and he had no way to watch a prisoner.

He ran up the line of trucks, his eyes snapping around, looking for other guards. There weren't any, but he saw too more drivers, running for the ridges, fleeing for their lives. His eyes fixed on them.

If they don't have weapons or com units, I can let them go...

But he couldn't tell, not for sure. He pulled the trigger once, then again, dropping both of the men.

More innocents, trapped in the horror of war...

And he knew that's just what this was. War. Cass and her people hadn't become bandits out of greed. They were fighting for families, for husbands and wives and children and parents left behind, loved ones who faced starvation if their young people hadn't marched off to do battle, to take by force the sustenance they'd once had on their own but had lost to the ravages of the armies.

He ran forward, continuing his gruesome task, making sure no one escaped, sent in a warning that the convoy was under attack. He could hear the sounds of combat ahead. The Grays had a variety of weapons, but he'd noted the sound of Ghana's rifles...and he could tell there were still guards ahead, fighting Cass and her people.

He moved forward quickly, his eyes snapping around, picking out the soldiers still resisting. He was coming up from behind them. His rifle snapped up. Crack. One of the men fell. He leapt out from his position right next to a transport, expanding his field of view. Crack. Crack. Another two guards down. He listened carefully…the shots coming from the convoy.

One left…

He looked around, trying to zero in on the guard. He could hear the rifle fire, sporadic, aimed. But he couldn't find the man. He heard other sounds, screams, distress. At least one of the Grays was down.

This is no normal soldier. He's a specialist, a sniper…

His eyes snapped over toward the ridge, focused, looking for the slightest sign of movement. Another shot…and more yells from the Grays. The sniper had them pinned down…and he'd shot at least two of them. Blackhawk had no idea how badly the two victims had been hit, but this was a skilled sniper. And he knew more than likely that meant the two Grays were dead.

He moved slowly to the side, slipping behind the transport, staring out over the rugged terrain. Nothing.

Wait…

There was something, movement.

His body lurched hard to the side, his subconscious acting on its own, just as the sniper's shot ripped through the air where he'd stood.

Fuck, Blackhawk, pay attention. This guy is good.

He crouched down, leaning slowly forward, looking out at the rocky hillside. Nothing. The sniper hadn't hit him, but he'd forced him to duck. And that had been enough time to make a move. Blackhawk had no idea where the sniper had gone…but he knew he was facing a very capable foe.

He moved his head slowly, almost imperceptibly. He knew he had far outmatched the soldiers he'd fought so far, but here was an adversary that could kill him if he was careless…and one that could decimate Cass' people if they tried to rush forward.

He had to get the sniper. Now. Or the Grays would be cut down one at a time. And he knew Cass well enough to realize she'd be in the lead once she realized the danger. And that would get her killed.

Unless I get there first…

* * *

"Let's go…forget the diversion. We're taking this convoy."
Samis had burst out of the oasis, and he was rushing toward the
stalled line of trucks. Half a dozen soldiers had taken position
in the front of the column, but they'd been surprised, and they
were disorganized, slow to react. Samis and his people fired as
they ran, taking all six of the soldiers down before they could
respond.

"We've got them surprised. Keep going…take down all the
guards!" Samis felt a rush as his eyes glanced down the long line
of transports. The Grays had good intel on the caravan, and he
knew it was a rich one. High tech imports, rare minerals, luxury
goods…even the small part of the convoy his tiny force could
grab would net a fortune, enough to send money home, buy new
weapons. And to impress Cass.

*She'll see me differently when I come back with this booty…she'll forget
Blackhawk, and see that I've been here all along…*

He saw another cluster of guards running along the edge
of the line of transports. He fired, missing. Then again, hitting
one in the shoulder. The man fell back, behind the cover of one
of the trucks. His comrades had dived for cover themselves,
and now they were returning the Grays' fire. Samis could hear
the bullets whizzing by, and he felt a wave of panic. He and
his people were out in the open. He felt the urge to dive to the
ground, take cover. But he knew they had to defeat the guards,
secure the trucks.

"Move it," he yelled, increasing his own pace. He saw one of
his people go down. It was Uri Hart. Samis thought his comrade
was still alive…as far as he could tell, he'd been hit in the leg. But
then Jin Fallin took a hit, and Samis knew it had been a kill shot.
Fallin had been hit in the head, and the bullet had taken off the
top third of his skull.

"Fuck," Samis muttered to himself as he lunged toward the

front of the first transport in line. He looked around him. At least four of his people were down. He felt the urge to run, but he looked back out over the open ground, at the bodies of his friends who hadn't been fast enough—or lucky enough—to make it to cover. The area he'd advanced over was now a killing ground, and he could hear the fire increasing as more guards took up position.

He stood where he was, frozen, the panic ruling him now. His mind raced…what to do? But there was nothing. Only fear.

"Minth, what do we do?" It was Rehn Kleren, his second in command. He'd run up behind, and he put his hand on Samis' shoulder.

Samis jumped at his friend's touch. He turned and stared wordlessly at Kleren.

"Minth! We have to do something!" Kleren was clearly scared, but he wasn't paralyzed by it like Samis. "Minth!" He grabbed his commander and shook him hard.

"I don't know," Samis said, his words choked with tears. "I don't know…I don't know…" He kept repeating himself, even as his words slipped into unintelligible sobs.

Samis saw a shadow, a familiar face. Winn Salvas scrambled over. "We're in trouble," he said. "Everybody else is down. There are at least two dozen guards, maybe more. We can't hold them…maybe if we can get back to the autocannon…"

"No," Kleren said, his own voice starting to show signs of panic. "We'll never make it."

"Then what are we going to do?" Salvas stared over at Samis.

"Minth? What are we going to do?" He paused, peering around the edge of the transport before snapping his head back. "Minth? Minth?"

But Samis just leaned down into a fetal position, crying uncontrollably.

* * *

Blackhawk eyed the terrain, a whole series of outcroppings slowly climbing the slope up to the rugged ridgeline. Dozens of places to hide. His training was there, a constant reminder. Patience. It was patience that won this type of battle. The first man to give himself away was lost. That didn't hold true in all situations, but it was almost always the case between two masters.

Blackhawk knew he had the edge, at least in inherent ability... but it was an uncomfortable one. The sniper had the advantage of ground...but he also had to deal with Cass' people, and when he fired he risked giving away his position. Blackhawk knew that meant using the Grays as bait...but he also knew it was the only way to get the sniper.

He waited and watched, breathing regularly, deeply. His rifle was in his hands, his eyes fixed on the rocks, scanning constantly, relentlessly. In all likelihood, one of Cass' people was about to die...and if Blackhawk didn't use that, if he allowed his enemy to get off a shot without giving himself away, that loss would be for nothing.

He could hear his heart beating in his ears, feel his mind focusing, ever more tightly, on his purpose. His other thoughts receded, slipped away. There was his target—and his rifle. Nothing more. Silence. Concentration.

Blackhawk had been in many fights, felt the call of battle more times than he could easily recall. He could have been on any of a dozen worlds. More. It was always the same. The focus. The cold blood of a killer...

Then he saw it, barely visible, the rustling of a clump of tumbleweed. It was nothing, the slightest move, something he'd have blamed on the wind in most cases. But not when facing a master sniper.

His rifle snapped around, targeting the rock. And then he saw. The muzzle of a rifle. And a shot. He felt the bullet himself, not literally, but in sympathy for a comrade he suspected was now dead or dying.

Maybe even Cass...

But there was no time, and his mind clamped down, maintained its focus. He knew where his enemy was, but he was blocked, with no shot. He weighed his options, and in a fraction of a second he made his decision. He knew patience could win the fight, but he wasn't willing to pay with the deaths of more of his allies. He lunged forward, flipping the rifle to full auto, spraying the rock and the area all around the sniper. He knew he wouldn't hit his enemy, but he might keep him pinned for a few seconds. And that would keep Blackhawk alive as he made his move. He was running forward, crouching, using what he could for cover, but emphasizing speed. He had to get around, find a spot where he had a shot.

He kept track of his shots…he couldn't burn the whole clip. He wouldn't have time to reload. And he had to be in position before he stopped firing. Or he'd be dead.

His legs pushed, driving up the hill. He let his finger relax on the trigger, ceasing fire for half a second before squeezing it again. He could feel his inbred abilities, mixing with training and conditioning. His body functioned with extreme efficiency, running faster than any normal human, dodging around rocks and rugged terrain, all the while firing at his hidden target with almost perfect accuracy. But he was running out of time…and he still had a distance to go to get to a place where he'd have a shot.

He felt the battle trance, the strange feeling of both calm and tense awareness that came over him in life and death situations. His legs moved faster, pushed harder…driving him up the hill. His head snapped around, and he could see his enemy. Moving, already trying to escape. But Blackhawk was too fast. His rifle snapped around, his eye staring down the barrel, aiming, adjusting for his target's movement, for the wind.

He had a second, no less…a fraction. But in his mind everything moved in slow motion. He saw the target, focused…then he fired.

He saw the sniper recoil, stumbled backwards and slip out of sight. He'd hit the target, but he knew he hadn't scored a kill shot. He could grab some cover, wait, see how badly he'd wounded his enemy. Or he could charge now, take advantage of whatever time he had, gamble his wounded adversary couldn't get up and back into position before he got there.

He felt his legs tense…then lunge forward, his decision

made, almost without conscious thought. He raced over the broken ground toward the spot where he'd seen his enemy. He knew his gamble might fail at any moment, that the sniper could leap back up and put a shot in him while he was in the open. It felt like an age before he reached the rock outcropping, though he knew it had only been a few seconds. He leapt over the rock, rifle extended, held in one hand.

There he was! The sniper. Lying on his back, his left side covered with blood. But he was alive, and he had his rifle in hand. He brought it around, his eyes focused hard on Black- hawk. His maneuver was death, and Blackhawk knew it. But the sniper was too slow. Just.

Blackhawk's rifle cracked loudly. Then again. And again. But the first shot had been enough. The soldier lay on the ground, a bloody hole where his eye had been.

Blackhawk felt a wave of fatigue, but also of elation. It was far from his first victory…or his first desperate battle. But the feelings were always the same. He was a creature of the battle- field, and however hard he tried to fight it, he felt something primal after a fight. There was something about killing. He could regret it later, feel guilt for his actions. But on the field, he felt like a predator standing over its kill. It was natural. On a level he detested, but one he couldn't help but acknowledge, it was where he belonged.

"Ark! Are you okay?" It was Cass, scrambling up the hill with half a dozen of the Grays. There was concern in her voice. He found it gratifying, but the affection he heard gave him concern too. He liked her…he liked her a lot, and he could imagine feel- ing more. But the feelings he'd just unleashed had jarred him, the fury, the cold-blooded killer, willing to sacrifice comrades as a diversion. It shook him to reality. He had changed, and he'd sworn he would no longer wander from place to place, seek- ing solace in whatever bottle he could find. But staying with the Grays, with Cass…and going back to the Galadan with her, to tend a farm…house, home, love. He knew that was impos- sible for him. If he'd had any doubt before, the feelings that had surged through him in the fight put them to rest. The thing he had been, the ruthless, cold-blooded killer…it was still there, inside him. He could control it, at least he thought he could. But house and home was not for him. Not now, at least. Someday, perhaps, though he had doubts.

"I'm fine, Cass. Is the convoy secured?"

"Yes," she said, clearly relieved to find him more or less unscathed. "We've got it all. The others are organizing, loading the best cargoes onto a dozen transports. We should be out of here in twenty minutes, maybe less."

"That's good." He paused, and when he continued his tone was darker. "Losses?"

"Four dead," she said, her own tone becoming grim. "Three more wounded."

Blackhawk just nodded. He knew those numbers were high for Cass and her people…but he was also aware that was their new reality. They had made themselves too great a threat…and now they would have to face real resistance. He knew it would destroy them, that the losses would tear them apart. Some would flee…and the others would fight on, weaker, suffering increasingly severe losses until the Grays were gone.

The thought made him sad. He wanted to save Cass, to get her to give up her raids, convince her she had done enough for the people back home. But he already knew that was doomed to failure. She was a warrior…as he was. And he knew she could never give up the fight.

Chapter Seventeen

Marshal Carteria's Palace
The Turennian Archipelago
Equatorial Celtiboria

Carteria's eyes moved over the dispatch. Normally, he'd have allow his steward read it to him. It was all part of the show, the great Marshal, surrounded by attendants and servants, at the head of the largest army on Celtiboria. But now he was in his office, seated at his antique desk. There were legends that the ancient wooden desk was the same one used by the last king of Celtiboria nearly nine hundred years before. Carteria knew all about those rumors...because he had started them. He wanted more than to be the dominant Warlord, more than to make the other generals kneel down and subordinate themselves before him. He wanted to reinstate the monarchy, establish a dynasty that would rule the planet for a thousand years. That would require power...and a certain amount of showmanship as well.

The office was empty, quiet. For all the pomp of his court, for the attendants constantly buzzing around him and the silent, respectful rows of officers typically following him around, the truth was sometimes Carteria craved nothing so much as quiet. It didn't fit with his public image, and most of the people outside his inner circle would be shocked. But he often sat alone in his office, working late into the night. His goals were enormous…and he was always ready to put in the work required to attain them.

He smiled as he read. Ganz Jellack's report was better even than he'd expected. Jellack had started his service for Carteria the way so many of his other ministers and officers had, conquered in war and offered the chance to serve as a well-compensated subordinate…rather than enslaved, or lined up against a wall and shot. Jellack was a financial wizard, and he had served Carteria well. His skills had been worth millions of ducats, and Carteria had rewarded him. Jellack's wife and children lived in an oceanfront palace, denied nothing. Nothing save their freedom. For in their luxury, amid the piles of silks and the gourmet means, they were guarantors of Jellack's loyalty. As long as the financial minister remained true, his family would want for nothing. And if he ever betrayed Carteria…then soldiers would go to that palace, and his wife and children would pay the price for the crimes of their husband and father.

But betrayal was far from Carteria's mind as he read the dispatch. Jellack had performed well, securing contracts with almost two dozen different companies, almost one hundred thousand veteran troops, fully armed and equipped and ready to march on a few weeks' notice. It was perfect. Eleher and Ghana would defeat Lucerne…and then Jellack's mercenaries would march on the Badlands. They would crush the other Warlords in the theater…and then they would ensure that Ghana was eliminated, and his survivors drafted into the new Carterian army on the Northern Continent.

Carteria hadn't gotten where he was by missing opportunities. Ghana had been given his chance, and his stupidity and incompetence had sealed his fate…and that of the Northern Continent. Carteria was mobilizing his reserves, assembling more forces to ship to the Badlands. By the time Ghana and Lucerne were eliminated, he would have close to two hundred thousand troops in the field…and the conquest of the continent would begin.

The Warlords of the Northern Continent were a fractured and bickering lot, most of them rulers of small areas, with armies twenty to fifty thousand strong. They would be kept apart, prevented from banding together in an effective alliance. Carteria's agents would travel among them, inflaming old feuds, offering alliances to the best of them, positions within the new Carterian regime. And his army would sweep up the others, crushing them utterly. Their shattered armies would be conscripted, their families killed or enslaved, their wealth and lands absorbed. It would take two years, perhaps three, but then Carteria would be the undisputed master of the Northern Continent. And with that conquest, his power would reach the tipping point. He would be invincible, his domination irresistible. The campaign in the Badlands would be the springboard to the final crusade that would put the crown on Carteria's head.

Carteria was a selfish man, one ruled by his own runaway ego. But he wasn't irrational. His conquests hadn't been accidents. He was sly, sneaky, a master strategist who knew how to use fear and greed to manipulate people. And he wasn't beyond feeling appreciation. Jellack had done a magnificent job, and he would make certain the finance minister was rewarded. He would be part of the new nobility, the holder of a ducal title under King Carteria, just as Varn Eleher would be if he succeeded in the Badlands.

He leaned forward over his desk, tapping the small control for his com unit. "Get me Bulg Trax," he said.

"Yes, Marshal," came the reply. Carteria had three personal secretaries, and one was on duty at all times.

He stood up slowly, walking across the room, stretching out his legs. The years were catching up with him, the endless time spent in vehicles, walking across battlefields. He delegated most of that these days to his subordinates, but Carteria had done his time knee deep in mud and blood. And he carried the scars and pains to prove it.

He'd had a plan before, of course, one that led to his placing the crown of Celtiboria on his head. But he'd guessed it would take at least another ten years...and the Northern Continent would be the last to fall. But Ghana's plea for help—followed by his utter failure and need for even more aid—had created an opportunity. The Northern Continent was fractured, worse even than the rest of the planet, its Warlords almost constantly at each other's throats. But it was big…and wealthy. Control of its resources and manpower would make him invincible…and move the timetable to total victory up four or five years.

He heard the sound at the door, a loud clumsy knock. He'd know that sound anywhere. "Enter," he said, turning around to face Bulg Trax. The soldier wasn't just large, he wasn't just strong and powerful. He was a colossus, a veritable mountain of a man. And he was Carteria's creature, body and soul.

"Marshal," he said in his deep voice, snapping to attention as he stood just inside the room.

"Come in, Bulg. Close the door."

Trax turned, slid the door shut. Then he walked toward Carteria.

"I have a job for you, Bulg…an important one."

"Yes, Marshal. Whatever you command."

Carteria motioned toward a chair…the largest one in the palatial office. "Sit, Bulg." Carteria moved to another of the plush seats. He could see Trax had moved next to the chair, but he was still standing. He was about to motion for his subordinate to sit, but then he decided it was just easier to plop himself down first. Trax took loyalty to often absurd extremes, and Carteria knew how uncomfortable his subordinate would be sitting while he still stood.

"Bulg, I have a cargo to transport, a very valuable and vital one. I must be certain of its security, of its safe arrival." Carteria leaned back in his chair, watching his minion stare back in rapt attention. Trax wasn't the sharpest blade in Carteria's arsenal, but there wasn't a man in his service who could match the giant's pure, unabashed loyalty…or his raw power in a fight. "I want you to command the escort, to ensure that it arrives on time… and safely."

"Yes, Marshal…as you command."

"You will be transporting coin, Bulg, forty million ducats to pay the mercenary forces Ganz Jellack has hired." The disorganized and fractured state of Celtiboria had rendered the various electronic currencies almost valueless. Paper money wasn't any better, widely scorned by soldiers who had endured far too many inflationary devaluations. To quickly retain the numbers Carteria had wanted, Jellack had been compelled to promise payment in silver coin, six month's wages upfront. And that was a lot of currency to transport to another continent.

"I will protect it with my life, Marshal."

"I know you will, Bulg." There weren't many people Carteria would trust to take that much money across an ocean, but he knew Trax wouldn't pocket so much as an errant coin that fell to the ground. He was the perfect man for the job, perhaps even the only one.

"I want you to take one thousand men, Bulg. Your pick of the guard." Carteria rarely committed his elite guard to any mission. He tended to protect the veteran soldiers, never forgetting they were his last resort in any emergency. But the entire plan to conquer the Northern Continent depended on getting this shipment of coin through.

"Yes, Marshal." There was surprise in Trax's voice. Carteria's parsimony with the deployment of his guards was well known in the army.

"You will fly to the edge of the Badlands, but we cannot risk travel by air over the battle zone…there is too much AA capability on both sides, and Ghana's forces cannot know what we are doing. Even if we could risk moving by air, the river cities would inspect any cargo landing at their airfields. While they allow the mercenary companies to operate, I think it is unwise to test their restraint when such a sum is in play. We will have to meet the mercenary commanders at a designated place at the edge of the Badlands." Forty million ducats was a lot of money, even to Carteria.

"You want us to move by land, Marshal? Through the battle zone?" Carteria knew Trax would have jumped from the highest battlement in the palace if he'd commanded it, but he could hear the doubt and concern in his henchman's voice. "Isn't that just as risky?"

"Yes, Bulg, it is. That is why I am sending you. And my

guards. Varn Eleher and his troops will be engaged with General Lucerne when you arrive…and you will move behind their lines. That should insulate you from contact with the armies… and a thousand of my guards will be a sufficient force to protect against any raiders or other threats. With any luck, a convoy across the desert will slip by undetected…a flight has no such chance."

"Yes, Marshal. Understood."

"The coin will be gathered in two days, Bulg. You will select your forces in that time and be ready to leave as soon as the planes are loaded."

"Yes, sir."

"Very well, Bulg…you may go and attend to your duties."

"Sir!" Trax stood abruptly, snapping to attention and saluting. Then he turned and walked toward the door.

"Bulg?"

Trax stopped and spun around, looking back toward the Marshal. "Sir?"

"There is no one else I would trust with this mission. Your loyalty is known to me, my old friend…and greatly appreciated."

"I serve you, Marshal, as I shall until death takes me. And I shall protect this convoy with all my skill and ability. With my life, if need be."

"Thank you, Bulg." Carteria stood up, walking across the room. He stopped in front of Trax and extended his hand.

Trax looked back, surprise on his face. He hesitated. Then he reached out, took the Marshal's hand.

Carteria held the handshake for a few seconds. Then he let his hand slip away. "Good luck, my old friend."

Trax stared back for an instant, his visage taken with emotion. "I will not fail you, Marshal."

"I know you won't, Bulg. No one has my confidence like you." He paused. "Now go, prepare. And complete your mission so you can return. We have much to do in the coming months."

"Yes, Marshal." Trax saluted again and then marched toward the door.

Carteria stood, watching him leave, hearing the sound of the door closing behind him. He knew his own reputation, what they said about him...ruthless, arrogant, bullying. And he knew it was deserved. But there had been more to his rise than just those traits. The art of manipulating subordinates was a complex one, and Carteria was good at it. Very good. Bulg Trax was like a force of nature in combat, and Carteria had worked his henchmen into a near-frenzy. Failure was unthinkable to the huge soldier, and he would remember Carteria's words, the sound of the Marshal's voice calling him 'old friend.' Bulg Trax would obliterate anyone who came near the treasure convoy... and he would die, along with the thousand men under his command, before he would relinquish a single ducat.

Carteria turned and walked back to his desk, sitting in the chair. He sighed softly. The forty million ducats he'd placed in Trax's hands was the price of the Northern Continent. The war would go on, of course, and the end cost would be many times forty million. But the mercenaries would ensure the total conquest of the Badlands...by allowing the establishment of an invulnerable beachhead. The destruction of Lucerne and Ghana would open the door to the Carterian forces...and the ultimate fate of the Northern Continent—and then all of Celtiboria— would be sealed.

He sat silently, his mind consumed with a single thought, an image that played over and over again. The great Basilica in the capital, his own hands, raising a crown of gold over his head. And the sounds, a voice, deep and booming, echoing under the dome, the words clear, unmistakable.

Carteria I, king of Celtiboria.

Chapter Eighteen

Abandoned Underground Fortress
"The Badlands"
Northern Celtiboria

"You can't go back, Cass. You know that too. You should have bugged out of there the second Ghana took your people prisoner." Blackhawk paused. "You should have moved months ago. Rebels, smugglers, whatever you are...your kind of warfare depends on stealth, surprise. And if you stay in one place for too long, your enemies will find you. You can be careful, but you are never careful enough. In the end it is simple mathematics. You're lucky they hit the place while we were out. Your people dodged a bullet there."

After the raid, Blackhawk had insisted the Grays find a new headquarters. He'd argued against going back at all, but Cass had insisted they at least gather the weapons and equipment they'd stored there. He suspected Cass had been pushing her luck for a long time already, but he'd given in, agreed to return and secure what supplies they could move.

Cass sighed. "We were lucky you insisted on sending a scouting party ahead." She paused. Blackhawk knew she was beating herself up. They'd sent three of her Grays forward as scouts... and none had returned. Blackhawk had gone after them...and he'd found them dead, the base surrounded by Ghana's forces.

He'd rushed back with the news...and he'd led them all away... before Ghana's people expanded their coverage area and bagged the whole company.

"Cass, you're a leader. A damned good one." He looked over at her, saw the self-loathing in her eyes. "You've lost people. All warriors lose people. That is war. It wasn't your leadership that killed them...it was your leadership that kept the rest of them alive." He could see she wasn't listening. She was hell bent on blaming herself, and the fact that she'd led her people for more than two years, saved countless hundreds or thousands back home, meant nothing to her. Blackhawk knew the images of her dead friends, their faces staring back at her in her dreams, were powerful. It was something he wouldn't have understood before, but now he was different...and it made sense.

She didn't reply. She just leaned closer to him.

He put his arm out around her. She was strong, as strong in her own way as anyone he'd ever known. But she still saw her Grays as friends and neighbors. He knew she would have to acquire a coldness, an ability to see her people as soldiers, and to acknowledge that whatever she did, some of them would die. He wasn't sure if she would manage that transition, but he knew she'd drive herself crazy if she didn't.

The loss of the base—and of the three scouts—was bad enough, but then she'd immediately had to deal with the disappearance of Samis and his people. Something had clearly gone wrong with the diversion, and she blamed herself for that too.

"I'm sorry, Cass," he said, realizing what was going through her mind. "The diversion was my idea." He knew it had been the right move, and he suspected Samis had done something foolish, stayed too long. But he didn't think that would help her right now, so he kept the thought to himself.

"No, Ark...you're right. We have to think like a military unit. And people die in war. If we hadn't followed your plan, we'd all have been in the headquarters when Ghana's troops attacked. We'd all be dead." She paused, and he felt her face pressing harder into him. "It's just so hard for me to think that way, to look at dead friends like so many marks on a ledger."

Blackhawk put his hand on her head, rubbing her hair gently. "It's not quite that cold blooded, Cass." Though he knew, for him it had always been just that cold. "But it is the reality. Your people are here to fight for their families back home. They are heroes…and heroism carries a heavy cost."

"Why did all this have to happen? Why did the armies have to come to the Galadan? We were peaceful people, no threat to anyone. Whatever the Grays are now, whatever I am, they made us. If they'd left us alone, I'd be at university. And most of the others would be working family farms."

"It is tempting to think that way, Cass. But that is not the reality of the universe. The strong will always take from the weak, and those who cannot defend themselves will always face the choice you did. Die or live as slaves. Or become killers yourselves." He paused. "You are strong…so you chose the latter. And your people were lucky to have you to lead the way for them. You punish yourself over every one of your Grays who gets killed, but how many have you all saved?"

She didn't answer. She just held onto him. They sat silently, neither speaking for a few minutes.

Suddenly, she pulled back and looked up at him. "You're leaving, aren't you?"

His eyes fixed on hers, and he could see the tears she was struggling to hold back. "Yes," he said simply. There was no easy way to put it.

"You don't have to, you know. You could stay, help me lead the Grays. And when the war is over we could go back to the Galadan. You could have a home there, you could have love. Maybe children one day. Is that so bad a life?"

Blackhawk paused. He could see the sadness in her eyes, the realization even before he responded that his answer would be no. "Cass, that would be a wonderful life. Part of me aches for that, to stay with you, to live each day in peace, to work honestly and enjoy the fruits of my labor." He put his hand on her face. "To share a life with you."

He looked down at the ground. "But that is not me, Cass. There is much you don't know about me, about the burdens I carry. I am not the man you think I am…or at least I am not only that man. There are reasons I must keep moving, why I can never settle down." He paused. "And I would rather you didn't know more. If you understood my past, who I am, you would think very differently about me…and I would rather part from you with affection in your gaze and not revulsion."

"I don't care about your past, Ark. We have all done things we're not proud of."

Blackhawk looked back up at her and forced a weak smile. "You say that not knowing the truth, the scope of what I have done. I don't doubt your affection, Cass. And I want you to know that I return your feelings. You are an amazing woman, one I will never forget. But I still have to go. I have unfinished business with General Lucerne…and then I will leave Celtiboria. I must find myself, who I am now, and I can't do it here. I need to be alone, to face the demons inside me. Hearth and home, love and children…that is something I cannot have, at least not until I gain control over the monster that lives inside me. Even if only for fear that one day that beast would escape, that I would become what I once was."

Cass looked back at him. He could see a mix of feelings in her eyes. Sadness, loneliness…and sympathy. She didn't know the details of his past, and he would never tell her. He couldn't be with her, but the thought of her hating him, of looking back as she stared at him with fear and revulsion in her eyes was something he didn't want to imagine. But even without the full story, he could tell she understood the amount of pain he carried with him.

"You will get over me, Cass, forget me. You have your Grays, and I fear you will find that responsibility will only grow heavier."

"I will never forget you, Ark." She smiled, but he knew it was false, that only sadness lay behind it.

He paused. There was nothing else he could say, at least nothing that would ease the sorrow. "At least this old fort will be a good refuge. We're lucky to have found it so quickly." The ancient castle was mostly a ruin, almost entirely covered by the sand over the centuries since it had been occupied. But it was large enough, barely, to accommodate the Grays, at least those who had survived.

Blackhawk knew Cass' numbers would continue to dwindle. Her people were facing harder times, greater danger. Even with her leadership, with the elan she'd fostered in them, some of the Grays would begin to drift away. Some would come to her, tell her they were going home. Others would slip away by night. But without a source of new recruits, he knew Cass faced a very uncertain future. It tugged at him, made him want to ignore all he had told her, stay behind and make sure she was okay. But it simply wasn't possible. He knew very well he could easily become the greatest danger of all to her.

"It will have to do. But we lost everything. Supplies, weapons, ammunition. All we have now is what we carried with us on the raid."

"Supplies are replaceable, Cass. Your people aren't."

There was a knock on the door, soft, tentative.

"Enter," she said, taking a deep breath.

One of the Grays walked into the room. He stood, looking at Cass.

"What?" she said, struggling, with considerable success, to banish the sadness from her voice. "What is it?"

"Cass, Orema has just returned. She is on the way here." Orema Callen had led the group taking the captured convoy to the river cities to sell.

"Well? Did she get a good price?" The caravan wasn't a rich one, but it had been a bit better than Cass had expected. She knew they should have gotten a decent price.

"Ah…yes. Much better than we expected."

Cass straightened up, staring at the man. "Much better? From the black marketeers?" Cass had long chafed at the low prices her people got for the goods they risked their lives to obtain. The underground guilds that bought the contraband paid a price they said was half the final value, though she knew it was usually less than a third. But there were no other options, so she'd come to accept it, even if she didn't like it.

"No, Cass…she sold to another party, a representative for

one of the Warlords."

"One of the Warlords?" Cass' voice was thick with concern.

Blackhawk was sitting silently, watching. Dealing with one of the combatants was probably a good idea, at least in terms of securing the best pricing for their goods. But it was hazardous too. The black marketeers were dangerous enough, a syndicate of gangsters more than willing to resort to violence when it was necessary. But to the Warlords, violence *was* their business.

"Yes." It was a woman's voice, coming from the doorway. Orema Callen walked into the room. She was clearly excited. "They paid full market value plus ten percent, Cass! In hard currency! And they said they'd buy everything we could bring them. It looks like the war is back on, and they're trying secure supply sources."

"You did well, Orema." There was concern in Cass' voice. Blackhawk could tell she was nervous about dealing with a Warlord. "Which one?" she asked.

"It was one of General Lucerne's officers, Cass. He gave us intel on upcoming caravans as well, offered to buy anything we can take."

Blackhawk's head snapped around at the mention of Lucerne. He'd allowed Lucerne to fool him once…he had no intention of doing it again. Or allowing Cass to believe anything Lucerne said.

"What was the officer's name, Orema?" Cass was also suspicious. Blackhawk could tell the instant the words left her mouth. She knew of Blackhawk's vendetta against Lucerne, of course.

"He was a major, Cass, one of General Lucerne's top advisors. His name is Aton Pellier."

Blackhawk froze. Something was wrong. He'd seen Aton Pellier die in the desert, shot down by Ghana's men…

"I want to be careful, Orema…the Warlords are dangerous, all of them." Cass turned toward Blackhawk. "Ark, I know you have a fight with Lucerne. Do you think he is…" Her words stopped as soon as she saw the expression on his face. Arkarin Blackhawk was a hard man, sometimes a cold man…but in the time Cass had known him, she'd never seen him look less than certain about anything. Until now.

Blackhawk was staring back at Cass, but his mind was else-where, analyzing memories, going over the attack in the desert in meticulous detail. Lucerne's men had all been killed. Only Black-hawk's superior abilities had enabled him to survive, to come close to escaping. And he'd seen the spray of blood when Pellier had been hit, watched him go down.

Is this a mistake? No, how would Orema know that name? Pellier.

"Ark?" Cass was staring at Blackhawk.

But if Pellier isn't dead…

He could see Cass' face, hear her words, but they were far away. His mind was sharp, his thoughts moving quickly, meticulously.

Could someone be pretending to be Pellier? No, why would anyone do that? The Grays have no idea who Pellier is…

"Ark, are you okay?" Cass reached out, put her hand on Blackhawk's shoulder.

"Yes," he said, his tone soft, distant. "I am fine."

If Pellier is alive that means…

"Don't, Cass," he said. "It's a trap. Don't trust Pellier."

"Ark, I know you have a dispute with Lucerne, but he…"

"No," Blackhawk said sharply. "Not Lucerne. I was wrong about Lucerne. It was Pellier."

"What?" Cass looked over at her two comrades then back toward Blackhawk. "What do you mean it was Pellier."

Blackhawk's stare hardened, and his gaze seemed to chill the room. "It was Pellier, not Lucerne." His voice was like death itself.

"Pellier?" Cass looked at him, an expression of surprise on her face as she saw the darkness, the pure rage in his eyes. "You know this Pellier?"

"He was my guide. He was taking me to Ghana's headquar-ters, to conduct a mission for Lucerne."

"You worked for Lucerne?" Cass pulled back, staring at Blackhawk with a look of confusion. "I thought you hated Lucerne."

"I thought Lucerne betrayed me. But it was Pellier." His

mind was racing. He'd have killed Lucerne, his rage fueled not just by his reaction to treachery but by his own anger at himself for being fooled by the general.

But maybe you weren't fooled, at least not by Lucerne. The general may be the honest man you believed him to be. And that means…

"I have to get to General Lucerne's headquarters." Blackhawk stood up abruptly. "As quickly as possible."

If Pellier is a traitor…

"I thought Lucerne didn't betray you?" Cass took a step back toward Blackhawk, reaching out, putting her hand on his arm.

"He didn't." Blackhawk's face hardened, frozen rage behind his withering gaze. "Pellier is the traitor. He faked his death, turned me over to Ghana's people." He took a few steps. Then he stopped and turned back. "I have to go, Cass. Now. I have to warn Augustin. Before…" He let his words trail off. He reached out, took her in his arms. "Be careful, Cass. Stay away from Pellier, ignore any intel he gave you. He works for Ghana, I'd bet anything on that. Don't go after those caravans…and don't sell him anything else. Anywhere he sends you is a trap."

He pulled away, turning toward the door. "I need a vehicle… one of the captured transports."

Cass was looking at Blackhawk, her face a mix of confusion and sadness. "Give him whatever he needs," she snapped. The she looked up into his eyes. "Be careful, Ark. Take care of yourself."

"I will," he said as he dashed out the door, too distracted for an extended farewell.

She waved for her people to go, to follow, to give Blackhawk whatever he needed. But it was more than that. She needed to be alone. She stood for a long time, staring at the door, fighting the sadness. She'd known Blackhawk was planning to leave, but she'd expected to have more time, enough to put her words together, to make a proper goodbye. She didn't know if she would ever see him again, and if she didn't, she knew she would always lament the haste with which they were parted.

Good luck to you, Arkarin Blackhawk. Wherever fate takes you.

Then a single tear streamed down her cheek, the first she had shed since the fateful day her father died. Then another. But that was all she would allow herself. She was a leader, and she would be strong. Whatever that took, whatever it cost her.

Chapter Nineteen

Lausanne Valley
East of Rhiombe City
Northern Celtiboria

Jellack watched as the soldiers marched. The mercenary companies were forming up, preparing to set out under his command...on paper, at least. Though he carried the rank of colonel, he was not a real soldier, and certainly not an officer who could effectively command one hundred thousand troops. He was sure Carteria would send someone to lead the mercenary forces, even if that officer technically reported to him. And truth be told, he couldn't wait until that happened. The pressure, the stress of worrying about every aspect of running an army was too much for him. Numbers were his domain, wheeling and dealing. But commanding fighting men? It was a skill that evaded him.

It would take another few weeks, perhaps a month, before the army was ready to march east. The companies were still gathering, calling in soldiers who'd been granted indefinite leave in the absence of employment. The companies generally operated on a shared contract basis, each soldier receiving a portion of any payments commensurate with rank and other considerations. But most of the mercenary forces guaranteed their soldiers a minimum level of sustenance, whether they were contracted or not. Few commanders wanted to lose their veteran troops in the periods between battles, so they made sure they were fed and given at least some semi-worthless scrip, at least enough to gamble with men of the other companies, and perhaps fund an occasional trip to one of the many brothels in the Soldier's Ward in the city. But even this minimal expense level could quickly become ruinous if a new job didn't appear relatively quickly.

Jellack had been in his element negotiating with the merc commanders. They'd tried to intimidate him, to roll over him, demanding enormous pay rates in any contract. But Ganz Jellack had conducted hundreds of negotiations, and he'd always come out on top. The mercs acted tough, clearly trying to rattle him with fears of his own safety...but he was smart enough to realize that none of them would dare raise a hand to Carteria's man. The Marshal didn't have any real power on the Northern Continent—not yet, at least—but everyone knew he was a vindictive man, one who wouldn't hesitate to put a price on the head of anyone who offended him. A price so large, half the men under an officer's command would climb all over each other to kill their boss and collect it.

In the end, Jellack had won the victory, securing the services of one hundred two thousand soldiers, mostly veterans of the battles along the west coast, for less than half what their former employers had paid. He'd allowed himself a moment of self-congratulation after the merc commanders had all agreed to the terms...and a day later Carteria's communique confirmed that the Marshal was pleased as well with what his subordinate had accomplished. Jellack didn't serve Carteria by choice, and he had no affection for his commander, but he knew his quality of life was linked to the esteem in which he was held.

"An impressive array, wouldn't you say, Colonel?" Yuri Dolokov walked up the grassy knoll toward Jellack. "I've not seen a greater combined force of the companies."

Jellack nodded. He knew the soldiers assembling in the valley were almost all veterans of the western wars, but they had served half a dozen masters there, and many of them had fought against each other. He was amazed, as he often was, by the way soldiers could embrace their recent enemies as allies.

If the leaders could behave that way, maybe this world could reclaim its place as the leader of the Primes, and the strongest planet in the Far Stars. Instead of a hell with nothing but eternal war.

"Yes, Colonel Dolokov. It is that." Jellack turned to face the mercenary officer. Dolokov had served him well, been invaluable in reaching out to the other companies, to adding their thousands to the men of the Wolves. All it had taken was a commission—a surprisingly small one, kept secret of course from Dolokov's comrades, who might have inconveniently expected him to treat it as company revenue rather than his own personal slush fund.

Dolokov stopped and stood there, silent for a moment. Then he said, "Colonel Jellack, I must ask you…"

"I have just received a communique, Colonel Dolokov, confirming that the convoy has departed." Jellack had known just what was on Dolokov's mind. The companies had begun assembling before receiving the coin for their first six month's service, an uncommon display of confidence in a new paymaster. That had been part Jellack's doing…his skillful manipulation of Dolokov and the others, his subtle—and not so subtle—reminders that he was well aware they lacked other options. But Jellack knew he'd had advantages going in. The Carterian forces didn't have a presence on the Northern Continent, but the Marshal's name carried weight everywhere on Celtiboria…and Jellack had done nothing to quell the speculation of the mercenary commanders that a major military move was underway. It served his purpose for them to ponder whether they wanted to be on Carteria's side…or to take whatever erratic pay the besieged native Warlords would be able to offer.

It hadn't hurt that Jellack had brought a secret shipment with him, nearly two million ducats, in pure bar form, Celtiboria's most sought-after currency, save of course for imperial crowns. It wasn't a sufficient sum to pay the companies in full, or even close to it. But it was enough to grease the senior officers…and to allow them to issue a preliminary donative to their soldiers, a gesture that was working wonders in bringing the men back to the colors quickly.

"That is good news, Colonel." Jellack had convinced the commanders to rally their forces, to take the arrival of the payment on a certain amount of faith, but the worry in Dolokov's voice was clear. Mercenary officers weren't a group to whom trust came easily.

"As I said before, Colonel, if you would prefer an electronic transfer, we could do…"

"No, Colonel…that will not be necessary. We appreciate the haste with which you have arranged the silver shipment."

Three centuries of constant war had created an odd state of affairs on Celtiboria. The planet was technologically-advanced, it engaged in interstellar trade and its science was highly advanced, at least by Far Stars standards. But the protracted disruptions had created a number of relapses, resulting in a strange combination of the high tech and the primitive. And money was one area where commerce on Celtiboria had regressed. Decades of fraud had rendered electronic transactions almost non-existent, especially for large sums…and with no central government backing, paper, such as the scrip often used to pay soldiers, was little better. Hiring a hundred thousand veteran mercenaries required hard currency…gold, silver. And a lot of it.

"I trust the preliminary payment was well-received by your men." A subtle jab, a reminder that Jellack was aware how desperate things had been for the mercs before he'd arrived.

"Indeed, it has, Colonel. I am still impressed that you were able to travel so far with a small escort…and keep two million ducats a secret."

Jellack nodded. "I am just gratified that the ready availability of my coin has helped stabilize matters, pending the arrival of the second payment."

"Any estimates on timing?"

Jellack forced back a smile. For all the niceties, even the good faith payment he'd made upfront, he knew Dolokov and the others wouldn't be truly comfortable until they had the forty million ducats they were owed. "Not long, Colonel. Perhaps two weeks…possibly even sooner. I'm sure you understand the precautions necessary for transporting such a sum. It takes more than simply filling a few satchels with coin."

"Certainly." Dolokov nodded. "Two weeks will be highly satisfactory…and sooner even better. We should be ready to march as soon as the shipment arrives."

"Please ensure that you are, Colonel. The Marshal was very clear…he wants the campaign to commence as soon as possible."

Dolokov stared back. "Well, we wouldn't want to upset the Marshal now, would we?"

"No," Jellack said, offering a tiny smile. "We wouldn't."

You have no idea how much we don't want to upset the Marshal…

* * *

"Are your men ready to march, Colonel?" Ghana stood outside the armored vehicle he used to travel on campaign. There were columns on the hillside behind him, regiments moving forward, toward the front lines…or at least what would likely be the front lines if open war broke out again between the armies. Which looked likely.

"Almost, General. A day, perhaps two." Eleher's voice dripped with the arrogance so common to the Carterians, especially their senior personnel. Ghana bit down on his response. The truth was, more than anything, he wanted to smash this snotty colonel's face in. But he didn't dare.

"A day, Colonel…" Ghana paused, realizing he was speaking as he would to one of his subordinates. He wasn't sure where Eleher fit in the hierarchy, but he reminded himself to never forget the danger of further angering Carteria. "…if possible. It would be extremely helpful if your people could be on the move sometime tomorrow."

"I will see to it, General. Do you believe General Lucerne will really attack, that he will violate the truce?"

"He will attack, Colonel. It is to his advantage to do so, at least based on the intelligence he likely has available. That makes your arrival on the field even more vital. My forces are unlikely

1880

88   Jay Allan

to prevail without your intervention."

Ghana sighed. He'd fought Lucerne with everything he'd
been able to muster, but it hadn't been enough. He knew his
adversary was an honorable man. Lucerne's ultimatum had been
opportunistic, perhaps, but Ghana had to admit, at least to himself, it was correct based on a strict reading of the cease fire
agreement. He might try to manufacture propaganda out of
events, blame Lucerne for the resumption of hostilities, but he
was well aware his intrigues with Carteria had given his enemy a
legitimate casus bellum.

If Lucerne knew everything, I wonder what he'd have to say...

Eleher's soldiers were a destabilizing element in the fight,
and almost certainly enough to ensure the defeat of Lucerne's
forces.

*Especially when Pellier makes his move...which should be any day
now...*

Ghana had planned his operation well. Massive reinforcements, a double agent in his enemy's headquarters...it was all
perfect. Save for the fact that his new troops weren't the mercenaries he'd expected them to be, they were Carteria's veterans.
And Ghana didn't trust the Marshal. Not one bit.

"Then the war in the Badlands ends in the next few days...
with our total victory."

Ghana could hear it in Eleher's voice. The scheming, the
arrogance. He was certain the Carterian had an agenda beyond
helping defeat Lucerne. But what was it? A demand for a greater
share of Badlands trade revenues? That he could tolerate. Or
was it something more?

He'd been uncertain before, he'd wanted to believe Carteria
was simply supporting him, and not seeking to supplant him.
But now he felt he was starting to see things clearly. Lucerne
would die by Pellier's hand...and his army would be defeated by
the intervention of the superbly-trained Carterian force.

*And then will I die next, killed by Eleher...or some assassin lurking
in his entourage?*

He could see Eleher staring at him, and now as he looked
back he saw his own destruction in the Carterian officer's gaze.

Was it just paranoia? Or was this finally true clarity?

Whatever it is, I brought this on myself. But how do I get out of it?

"I'm afraid I must be going, Colonel," he said abruptly, look-ing at the Carterian officer for a few seconds before turning and stepping toward his armored car. "Tomorrow, Colonel…if you can have your men on the move by tomorrow, I will be greatly appreciative."

"Tomorrow, General."

Ghana smiled and nodded as he climbed into the vehicle and shut the hatch, but once inside, a frown came over his face. He was uneasy, his mind going over every detail, every word Eleher had spoken, every expression on the officer's face. There was something about the Carterian, a feeling Ghana got every time the colonel spoke. It was mistrust, certainly. But there was more.

He believed he would win a victory against Lucerne, but he wasn't sure it would truly be his…or what role he would play after it was won.

If I have any role at all…

He felt more and more certain, his fears hardening into judg-ment, expectation.

Carteria will have me assassinated, even as I suborned Pellier, planned Lucerne's death. And then my loyal officers will be purged…and those who have betrayed me, taken the Marshal's coin, will be placed in command, to lead my army into the Carterian service.

Ghana felt sick, and the same thought kept repeating in his head.

How do I get myself out of this?

* * *

Khal Thorn stood outside his shop, watching the move-ments up and down the Place D'Alhas. He hadn't seen such traffic on the broad avenue in years…and certainly not since the peace along the west coast had left so many of the mercenary companies unemployed. Something had changed. Suddenly. The companies had found employment, at least some of them. That much was obvious.

Thorn sold imported leather goods from a large store at the head of the D'Alhas, though his establishment barely broke even. His true businesses lurked more in the shadows...secret interests in establishments less reputable than the leather trade. Including silent partnerships in several of the brothels in the soldiers' district.

He'd discounted the foot traffic at first, writing it off to the movements of a few companies, a moderate contract of some kind, perhaps with the armies fighting in the Badlands. But then he began to hear from his partners. The brothels had been struggling for months now, the idle soldiers lacking the coin to pursue their desired form of recreation. But over the last few days, business had soared. The soldiers were packed into the establishments, coin in hand, waiting in long lines for their chosen companions.

It was more than could be explained by a few companies taking service with Badlands Warlords...and the more Thorn poked around the more convinced he became that every mercenary plying his trade in the river cities had recently been hired. The other brothels were as busy as his own, and the bars throughout the district were packed as well, full of soldiers drinking, gambling, brawling. They'd gotten coin somehow...and that could mean only one thing.

Someone has enough resources to pay over a hundred thousand mercenaries...but who?

It didn't make sense. The west coast Warlords had fought themselves to exhaustion and bankruptcy...and Ghana and Lucerne and the others in the Badlands weren't far behind on that road. There was no one—no one on the Northern Continent—who could afford to hire so many rifles.

He'd wondered what to do. Was this a danger to him in any way? An opportunity? The information seemed valuable...but to whom? Ghana? Lucerne? One of them *had* to be involved somehow. The other might pay well for what Thorn knew, but how could he determine which to approach? And how could he get to them at all? Word had reached Rhiombe that the armies were on the verge of resuming hostilities. Thorn was a man who knew how to recognize opportunity, but he also believed in lowering his risks whenever possible. So he decided not to make any rash moves. He would learn more before he did anything.

He started in his own back yard. He bribed the women in his establishments to get what they could from their clients, and he put his people in the bars, to buy drinks, loosen tongues...and report back to him on anything they heard.

The information came slowly at first, but then he started piecing things together. Someone had indeed hired all the companies based in the river cities...and they had paid them small advances. That explained the soldiers' descent on the bars and brothels. And there were mentions of more coin on the way, a vast treasure caravan carrying six months' wages for over one hundred thousand men.

He'd pushed harder, spread some ducats around...and slowly he learned more. It was Marshal Carteria who had hired the mercs, and the convoy carrying their pay was coming across the Badlands, around the armies to the encampments where the companies were mustering outside the cities. It was a vast fortune, an almost unimaginable amount of coin in one place. It almost begged for someone to take advantage of the information. But who?

It was too risky to deal with the armies. One of them was most likely working with the Marshal, and Thorn had no idea which. But there had to be a way...

Cassandra...

One of Thorn's other businesses was providing intel—often obtained in the bedrooms of his brothels—to Cassandra Cross and her Grays, mostly schedules of trade caravans moving from the sea to the markets of Rhiombe and the other river cities. Cross had always been straight with him...and she'd never failed to pay him his agreed upon cut, even when his info had proven to be only partial, when her people had endured harder fights than they'd expected. She knew how to maintain a clandestine relationship. Perhaps she could use this information about the mercenaries. She was much closer to the armies on the scene... she might know more than he did. And if she was able to profit, he was sure she would pay him his due.

If her people can capture the convoy…take all that silver…

He knew it was far-fetched. That much coin would be well-protected, with enough guards to fight off Cassandra's band of raiders. But perhaps she could make a deal with one of the armies…or band together the other groups of bandits.

"Gaj," he yelled.

Yes, he thought. *I will send word to Cassandra.*

"Gaj!" he yelled louder, just as his apprentice came running into the room.

"Yes, Master Thorn." Gaj Tryll was young, barely twenty, an orphan Thorn had plucked off the streets five years before, taking him from life as a beggar to work in his store. It had been a good deed, a reaction to something Thorn had seen in the boy, a quality he couldn't have described but felt nevertheless. And his instincts had been true. Tryll had displayed unflinching loyalty, and Thorn had come to trust the young man with aspects of his business far beyond the sale of exotic leather goods.

"I want you to go find the Grays. I have information I want you to give to Cassandra Cross."

"Yes, Master Thorn. I will go at once."

"My message is for Cassandra's ears only, Gaj." He knew Cross' people were loyal, but he wasn't taking any chances, not when a potential windfall of this size was at stake.

"Understood." Tryll turned to leave.

"And Gaj…take some guards with you. Half a dozen." Muscle wasn't a fringe benefit of the leather trade, but it was one of the side benefits of his interests in prostitution and lending. "Go see Hurin at the White Willow. I will call him and have reliable men waiting for you."

"Yes, Master Thorn."

Thorn just nodded, and then he watched his aide slip out the door. Then he reached down and punched a code into his com unit. "Hurin, it's Thorn. I need six of your best men to take a trip. Basic guard duty…nothing too bad. They'll be gone two weeks, and I'll pay them triple what they normally get." He paused. "It's potentially a very profitable trip, so I only want your best."

"Yes, Mr. Thorn. I'll have them ready in ten minutes."

Thorn closed the com unit. He was a skeptical man, not prone to letting his hopes get the better of his. But if Cassandra could figure a way to take that caravan...

Chapter Twenty

Near Lucerne's Headquarters
"The Badlands"
Northern Celtiboria

Blackhawk raced along the tiny ridgeline, staring out into the deep dusk, his eyes scanning for guards, patrols. He'd already slipped past two groups of Lucerne's men, and he knew the general would have more of them out protecting the approaches to his headquarters.

He'd considered just walking up to the front gate, asking for Lucerne. After all, the general had sent him on his mission. But he couldn't chance it. Pellier would be there too, and he almost certainly knew Blackhawk had escaped from Ghana. That meant he would be on his guard. And the sentries would obey him as unquestioningly as they would Lucerne.

No, he had to get inside, reach Lucerne. Even then, he didn't underestimate the challenge that faced him. Aton Pellier had served Lucerne for years. Blackhawk was a drifter, a man in whom the general had placed some confidence, but not one he was likely to believe when he accused a longtime officer of treachery. And Blackhawk knew he had no proof.

He felt an urge to stop, to go back to the Grays, leave Lucerne to his fate. But he couldn't. He'd felt rage toward the general, sworn to destroy the man. But he'd been wrong. He was certain now, Lucerne hadn't had anything to do with his capture…with the trap Pellier had led him into. Now he thought back, to the man he'd spoken to in his cell, the leader he'd eaten with, agreed to serve. His old impressions raced back, pushed aside the false anger and need for vengeance that had so consumed him.

Lucerne was a friend. That was an odd realization for a man who had no friends…who had never had any. And now he felt the overhead of friendship, the obligation, the need to help a friend in trouble. The whole thing felt strange…and somehow right. He'd sacrificed comrades before, coldly, ruthlessly. Victory had been his mistress. But now the idea of leaving Lucerne to his fate was unthinkable.

He reminded himself how ready he'd been to blame the general for his capture, how easily he could have killed his new friend, only to discover after the fact he'd been wrong. It was unsettling, and it drove his need to save Lucerne with even greater intensity.

He jerked to the left, slipped down behind the ridge, an almost instinctive reaction as his eyes caught motion in the near-darkness, another patrol moving across the open desert. He paused, peering over the small crest, his eyes fixed on the soldiers, assuring himself they hadn't spotted him. Then he moved forward again, with the low ridge between him and the sentries.

Lucerne is a cautious man…his headquarters is well-patrolled.

His admiration grew. Blackhawk tended to be daring, a man willing to take risks…but he respected a meticulous warrior. And from what he knew of Lucerne, the general was also willing to gamble…when the odds were in his favor.

He could see the dark shadow ahead, the ancient castle Lucerne had adopted as his main base. It was perched on a rock outcropping, overlooking open desert in every direction. It wouldn't be easy to sneak up undetected, but Blackhawk had been bred and trained from birth for this kind of thing. He moved coolly, steadily across the sand, slipping around toward the back of the great edifice, to the only approach that offered some meager cover.

He climbed back up on the rocky spine, crouching, keeping his head down. He peered out over the desert. The patrol was moving away…but he wasn't going to take any chances. The ridge rose slightly, ending just up ahead in the spur of rock forming the base of the castle. He crept along on the far side, keeping his head below the crest. It was difficult footing, but he managed it well, even at a near run.

A few minutes later he was under the walls of the castle, looking up. It was a long way, a difficult climb, especially without any equipment. He moved closer, looking at the wall. It had been smooth once, but the centuries had taken their toll. There were cracks, holes in the thick stone. A dangerous climb…but a possible one.

He reached up, feeling around with his hands, getting a grip. Then he stepped up, sliding the front of his foot into a crack. It was tenuous, difficult, a slow climb. But it was the only way he could get in undetected.

He continued up, slowly, meticulously, testing every handhold, every perch for his foot. About halfway up, his foot slid, the stone under it giving way. He felt the rush of adrenalin, and his body reacted, instinct and conditioning responding faster than conscious thought. His hands clenched hard, and he drove his other foot deeper into the small crack where he'd shoved it. His heart rate jumped, and for an instant he thought he might fall. But he held…and he pulled himself up, jamming the fallen foot into a higher perch.

He'd moved to the side, following the location of the cracks and holes in the wall, and now he was directly above the small ridge. He paused, rested for a moment. He looked down. It was a long drop, enough to kill a man. He knew his body was strong, sturdy, that his genetics allowed him to survive things other men couldn't. But he knew a fall meant at the least critical injury. And ending up a cripple on Celtiboria would be far worse than death. He'd seen the soldiers, the men maimed and disabled in the endless battles. Some of the Warlords cared for their wounded veterans, at least to an extent, but most of the amputees and other disabled troopers eventually ended up in the cities, begging in the streets. Blackhawk had found himself shocked at that reality, though he'd immediately realized he had never concerned himself with the fates of wounded soldiers who'd fought alongside him in the past. Now that he considered it, he realized they had likely fared no better...and quite possibly worse.

He took a deep breath and heaved himself upward, scrambling up the last section of wall to the top. He swung himself over the battlement and looked all around, scanning for guards, for anyone who might have seen him.

His eyes locked on a sentry, just as the man turned and saw him. He reacted instantly, and before the soldier could pull his rifle off his back, Blackhawk was on him.

This is Lucerne's man, he thought as he lunged forward, and he caught himself, pulled back the lethal attack his training and conditioning had been about to deliver. His hand lunged out, a quick hard chop to the neck...but far enough from the killing zone to ensure his victim's survival. The man crumpled to the ground, and Blackhawk reached out, grabbed him to ease the drop, and to make sure he didn't fall off the battlement.

Blackhawk scanned the area again. The walkway was narrow here, barely enough for two men to stand one next to the other. There was an inner wall, waist high, and beyond a courtyard of sorts. To the north was a cluster of buildings...and the main castle hall itself. That had to be it. He scrambled across the battlement, to the next tower, and he ran down the stairs, emerging onto the dirt and patchy grass of the courtyard.

"Okay, General Lucerne...where are you?"

* * *

"Get my bags to the transport, Corporal. I'll be leaving within the hour. I just need to get something from the general's quarters."

"Yes, Major."

Blackhawk heard the voices from outside the room. Then he saw the light from the corridor, as the door opened. He was crouched down behind the bed, but he knew his cover wasn't good. Lucerne's quarters were sparse, simple. Blackhawk had been surprised when he'd entered, and somehow, the simplicity of it all made him respect Lucerne all the more.

Please…don't make me kill any of his people…

The door opened completely, and an officer walked in, his head down, reading from some kind of small tablet.

"Don't move." Blackhawk's voice was firm, threatening. "Hands out to your sides."

The officer froze. He didn't run, didn't recklessly reach for his pistol. He just did as Blackhawk asked, even as his eyes whipped around the room, locked in on the threat.

"Major!" The voice came from behind, from the hall. Then the sound of boots on the stone floor.

Blackhawk felt his body responding to the threat, the battle trance coming on him. *No*, he thought, fighting back against his instincts. *You can't go gunning down Lucerne's men.*

"Corporal, hold!" It was the officer. Blackhawk could hear the discipline in his voice, the lack of fear he displayed. "If this man wanted me dead, I'd be dead by now."

Blackhawk was impressed. The officer was courageous, and he kept his head in a dangerous situation. "I do not wish to harm you," Blackhawk said, walking out of the shadows. "I have come to speak with General Lucerne. My name is Arkarin Blackhawk. I have vital information to share with him."

"Mr. Blackhawk…" The officer stood where he was, returning Blackhawk's gaze. "The general told me all about you. I am Major DeMark…Rafaelus DeMark. I'm afraid the general is not here. He left yesterday with the main field force."

Blackhawk stood firm, his pistol still aimed at DeMark. Then, slowly, he lowered it. "I am sorry, Major. It was not my desire to hold you at gunpoint."

DeMark lowered his arms. "That is quite alright, Mr. Blackhawk. I have been through worse ordeals, and I will recover from this one." DeMark paused, a weak smile slipping onto his face. "I suggest you tell me what is so urgent that you felt compelled to infiltrate our headquarters to reach the general instead of simply walking up to the front gate."

Blackhawk paused. He'd come to tell Lucerne that Pellier

was a traitor. That had promised to be a difficult task with the general, with whom he'd had some kind of connection. Now he had to convince an officer he'd never met that one of his comrades was a traitor...perhaps even an assassin planning to kill Lucerne.

Might as well be direct...

"Major Pellier is a traitor. He is in Ghana's employ, and I believe he may be planning to assassinate General Lucerne."

Can't get much more direct than that...

Blackhawk stared right at DeMark as he continued. "I wanted to get to the general myself because I was concerned that Pellier would block my access if he could."

He braced for the backlash, for DeMark's impassioned defense of his comrade. But there was nothing of the sort. The officer just stood silently for a moment. Then he asked, "Do you have any evidence to support this claim?" The question was simple, straightforward.

"The party escorting me toward Ghana's base was ambushed, destroyed. I saw Pellier go down, shot by the enemy soldiers. Then, weeks later, I heard that he was alive. There was no way he could have escaped...not unless the whole thing was a setup. Your men died in that attack, Major, innocent soldiers from your ranks. At least I assume none of the others returned. Just Pellier, right?" Blackhawk paused. "All so he could turn me over to Ghana...and return to remain close to Lucerne. Until it was time."

DeMark took a deep breath. "That is not exactly proof, Mr. Blackhawk." His voice was far less doubtful than Blackhawk had expected. "But I do not trust Pellier. I have long disliked him, and while I never considered the possibility he was Ghana's creature, I do not find it difficult to believe."

He turned back toward the guard standing in the door. "Go," he said. "Now. I want the transport ready to leave in five minutes."

"Yes, sir," the non-com snapped back, pausing for just a second, clearly reluctant to leave DeMark alone with the still-armed Blackhawk.

"Go," DeMark repeated, waving with his hand. Then he turned back to Blackhawk. "Come. This is not something we can trust to a communique. I will take you to the general…and we will get to the bottom of this." Blackhawk could hear the tension in DeMark's voice, enough to tell him he'd at least gotten the major's attention.

"Let's go, Major," he said. "My gut tells me we don't have much time."

* * *

"We're in trouble, Jinn. Deep trouble. These Chrono-damned Badlands are going to destroy us before we're done here."

Ghana's voice was rough, defeat heavy in his tone. He stood on a small hill next to Barkus, staring out over the army's camp as the last rays of sun slipped below the horizon. The war was on again, but that wasn't the source of his despondency. It was his ally, not his enemy, that fed his hopelessness.

"Perhaps we can prevail against Lucerne's forces, General. They are capable, there is no question. But we have fought many battles too. The men will fight hard for you, sir."

"I know that, Jinn," Ghana said, his deep voice soft. "They are not what concerns me, nor even Lucerne. I wish I had offered him a half share in the Badlands when the fighting first began. He would have made a truly worthy ally, one a man could trust. Instead of a dangerous enemy. Had I been able to put aside ego, to resist the sickness of greed and pride, we would have formed a powerful bloc…and the trade routes would have been ours. Now we destroy each other…and open the door to another."

"Carteria? You're worried about Carteria's forces. Do you think he has designs beyond assisting us? A greater share of the trade revenues?"

Ghana took a deep breath, staring out over the camp without answering. Then he said, "The heat here…it is like home, yet so different. I miss the warm breezes coming off the sea, Jinn. The lushness of the inland rainforests."

He turned and looked at his officer. "When I was a boy, I would go deep into the forest, hike for days. There are animals there, Jinn, birds and wild cats, like nothing you've seen. We fight over this world, my old friend, we spill blood and kill thousands…yet do we ever take the time to appreciate what we struggle to rule? Celtiboria was a paradise once…and now it is a battlefield. Our ancestors stood above the Far Stars, our world first among a hundred, the most powerful by far. Now we are drawn inward, almost completely withdrawn from the interstellar scene. We digress, our civilization declines. Our world produces less than half what it did three hundred years ago, Jinn, and what we do still make is inferior. The armies of the first Warlords were armed to a standard we couldn't hope to match today. Like gods they would seem to us now, their descendants, fallen so far from their greatness."

Barkus stood silently, listening to Ghana. He looked as though he might speak, but then he just stood there.

"I know, my friend. You have never heard me speak thusly. No, I long ago lost the gentle simplicity of youth, succumbed to the illness that afflicts the Warlords. I didn't even recognize the chance to gain a worthy ally, rare creature that such a thing is, and I turned him to an adversary instead. An honorable man, Jinn…can you imagine such a thing? Why did I not realize this before we clashed as foes? Why did I not sit with Lucerne, look with him over a map, drinks raised high in the air in a toast as we drew a line down the middle…and formed an alliance that would have strengthened both of us? Why could I see only total domination? Victory or death?"

"That is the way it has always been, sir." Barkus spoke softly, tentatively, clearly trying to come up with something to say.

"No, Jinn. Not always. That is man's affliction, no doubt, and I suspect it will always plague him. But Celtiboria wasn't always a battlefield. We were a republic for centuries, my old friend, and even before that, under the kings, peace flourished. Now we destroy each other…and a creature like Carteria rises to power."

"General, Carteria's forces will give us the victory, they will…"

"They will give Carteria the victory, Jinn. That roads leads only to slavery for us, my friend. Or death." Ghana paused. "But perhaps we yet have a chance. A last hope to right the wrongs we have committed, to claim the path back to the light."

"Sir?"

Ghana stared back over the camp, his mind drifting away again. "It has been two years, Jinn, since I have seen my wife. Two years."

"Yes, sir." Barkus was nervous, clearly unsure how to address Ghana's introspection.

"She is beautiful, Jinn, her skin like polished ebony, her eyes dark, as deep as the sea." The sadness in his voice was overwhelming. "I married her for gain, Jinn…just as I have done everything else in my life. She was the path to control of her father's lands and retainers…and she had many suitors. I won her hand, Jinn, through every means I could devise, though it was greed and not love that drove me."

Ghana turned and looked right at Barkus. "I do love her, though, Jinn. I do. Her father's strength and nobility runs heavily through her blood, and she is a fit companion for any man… soldier, Warlord…even a king, I have fancied." He paused. "But does she know that, Jinn? Did I ever show her my true feelings?" Another pause. "I would give away all, position, power, all of it…just to live my days with her, to feel her warmth next to me, to lie together listening to the waves of the sea crash against the great boulders."

"You will see her again, General. We will return home after the campaign…and she will be there, waiting with your children."

Ghana managed an odd smile. "Would that it were so, my old friend. You are a good man, Jinn Barkus, and I fear I have ill-used you at times, that I have failed to repay your loyalty as I should have."

"That is not true, sir. You have my service and my devotion…now and always."

"I would ask you to do something for me, Jinn. I trust no other to do this as I do you."

"Anything, my general. Command me."

Ghana reached into his jacket and pulled out a data crystal. "This is a message, a proposal offering peace. It is what I should have done two years ago. Go to General Lucerne's headquarters. Order Pellier to stand down. And deliver this message to the general."

"Yes, sir." Barkus straightened up, snapping to attention. "I will see it done, sir."

"Hurry, Jinn. You must get there before Pellier strikes. It was a particular bit of evil in my soul that drove me to send an assassin to achieve what I failed to win on the field."

"I will get to him, sir."

"Jinn, I am sorry I must send you to do this. General Lucerne is a merciful man…he will allow you to return. Or, if he does not, he will keep you in comfortable captivity. But…"

Ghana looked at Barkus, and the expression on his face was one of guilt, of regret. Of fear.

"If Pellier has already struck…there is no way of knowing how Lucerne's officers will react." He paused. "I fear I am sending you into great danger, my old friend."

Barkus stood firm, staring back at his commander. "I am honored, General, that you entrust this to me." A pause. "With your permission, I will leave at once."

* * *

"The latest reports confirm it. Ghana's forces are on the march." Lucerne was staring down at the map laying across the large table in front of him. "We're looking at a battle in the next couple days, two or three at most." Lucerne's voice was soft, introspective. He sounded sorry, sad…though he'd manipulated things to create just this situation. As a tactician, he knew the sooner the climactic battle came, the likelier he would have the victory. Time would only give Carteria's forces more time to prepare, to join with Ghana and tilt the scales. But as a soldier, a man, a comrade of the thousands of men who would die when the guns again shattered the dawn calm, he couldn't help but view the return of battle with a grim sorrow.

"Yes, General. The final battle cannot be long delayed. At last, the campaign nears its end."

Lucerne looked up from the map, over toward his aide. There was something about Pellier's tone he found unsettling. He couldn't place it, but he felt a wave of concern, as if there was some danger lurking.

Calm yourself. It's just the looming battle working your nerves...

"I had intended to strike the day after tomorrow..." Lucerne's eyes dropped back to the map. "...but I think we have an opportunity to gain an advantage, to defeat Ghana before Carteria's troops can reach the front. A night's march may give us surprise and victory." He looked down at the map then snapped his eyes back up toward Pellier.

"What is it, Aton? I can see something is troubling you." Lucerne still felt uneasy. He wondered for an instant about Pellier, about whether he could really trust the aide. But he put it out of his mind, feeling a wave of guilt for even considering it. Pellier had been with him for years...and he'd been wounded in action twice. He deserved the trust Lucerne had always given him. But still, there was something...

"It is nothing, sir."

"You are not telling me the truth, Aton. Now what is troubling you?"

Pellier paused. "Well, General...the idea of a night march concerns me. The men will be tired when they engage." Another pause. "I feel it is too great of a risk."

Lucerne's instincts went wild.

He was acting strangely before I mentioned the night march...and the men have had long marches before. Why would he be so concerned after they've just come off an extended rest period?

What the hell is going on here?

His eyes moved quickly over his aide, noting the pistol at his side. That wasn't all that strange. He had no official regulations against his officers being armed in his presence, but still, something didn't seem right.

You're letting your imagination run wild...

He couldn't shake the feeling. His hand moved slowly down

to his side. Nothing. He'd left his own sidearm in his sleeping quarters. His eyes moved back to Pellier. He considered calling for the guard, but then he stopped himself.

How would I explain that when it proved to be nothing? My officers trust me...do I want them thinking I'm worried about every strange face they make, constantly suspecting them of something?

He looked back at Pellier. The officer was tense, fidgeting back and forth on his feet.

He's probably edgy about the way you're acting...

"We've had forced marches before, Aton...and the men are well-rested. I think they can handle one night move. Do you have any other concerns?"

Lucerne could see the tension in his aide as he waited for a response.

Something is definitely wrong...

"General, I just think caution is advisable. We have the edge in the campaign...I can't see how taking any unnecessary risks would be in our interests now."

There was noise out in the hallway now, voices, someone talking to the guard outside the door. Then shouting, arguing. Lucerne's head snapped around. He'd told the sentry he didn't want to be disturbed...but someone wasn't taking that well.

Lucerne saw the motion, Pellier's hand dropping to his side, pulling the pistol from the holster. In an instant, his suspicions were confirmed. His body flooded with adrenalin, his combat instincts reacting on their own.

He moved quickly, his body pivoting toward the table, diving for cover. But he was late. He was fast...but not fast enough.

The pistol cracked loudly, and Lucerne felt the impact, pain. The round had hit him in the shoulder, and he fell back, his hands reaching out, trying to stabilize himself as he went down hard to his knees.

His mind raced.

What did I miss? How could I have not known?

Lucerne was a man who inspired loyalty, a commander who was fair to all his people. He was slow to give his trust, save only for his inexplicable feeling about Blackhawk, but when he did it was usually returned with loyalty. He'd never had a traitor before in his inner circle, and even as his combat reflexes struggled to save his life, his mind raced, wondering where he had gone wrong, what had caused Pellier, an officer to whom he'd given rank, privilege, wealth, to turn on him. To try to kill him.

And he is going to kill you, you damned fool. You've got no escape route, no weapon...no way out of this...

Chapter Twenty-One

South of the Main Battle Zone
"The Badlands"
Northern Celtiboria

"Get these trucks moving, Captain. We must reach our destination in eight days...and that means fourteen hours of constant travel each day." Bulg Trax was covered in sweat. He'd stripped off his uniform jacket, and he stood there in his under-shirt, the thin fabric soaked, plastered to his massive body. The trip across the ocean in the sea planes had been uncomfortable enough, but this blasted desert...

He looked out over the column of transports as the soldiers slowly climbed back aboard. It was only the second day from the coast and already they were looking tired, worn. Trax didn't like it. They had to be alert, ready for anything. Their presence was a closely kept secret, but that was far from foolproof. And while his escort should be strong enough to repel any attack they were likely to see, he wasn't about to let his guard down. Forty million ducats was a lot of coin.

He had allowed a half hour meal break, but that was all he was giving his out-of-shape troops. Carteria's guards hadn't seen any hard field duty in a long time, but Trax wasn't about to indulge them the way they had been back at headquarters. No way. It was time to get the convoy on the move, for his men to become reacquainted with the field, to learn how to sweat the fat off their pampered carcasses.

"Yes, sir." The captain stood in front of Trax, clearly intimidated by his superior. Bulg Trax was not only a legendary warrior—and a virtual giant of a man—he was one of Carteria's oldest and most trusted comrades. There were a dozen ways getting on his wrong side could destroy a man. And it wasn't hard to get on Trax's bad side. The big man had a legendary temper.

"Now, Captain. We do not have time for this leisurely pace." Trax knew the soldiers protecting the transports were the best in the Carterian service, members of the Marshal's own guard…at least that they were considered the best. But Trax tended to prefer teams handpicked directly from the field forces. The guards were selected in just that way, from veterans in the field armies, but Trax felt that their plush lives at court and the lack of combat action quickly dulled their efficiency. They were good troops at their cores, no doubt, and their loyalty was beyond question. But Trax wondered how they would fare against experienced desert fighters, warriors who'd never experienced the luxurious barracks and other benefits Carteria's personal soldiers enjoyed.

Hopefully he wouldn't find out. They were two day's hard march south of the armies…and all intelligence suggested a final battle was imminent. And while the Badlands was and area plagued by bands of raiders, none of the outlaw groups was likely strong enough to take on his column. Still, he was nervous.

"Captain, I want the flank guards doubled."

"Yes, sir."

Trax looked out over the desert, his eyes squinting under the intensity of the midday sun. He could barely see his flankers, a dozen men to each side, on high speed bikes, keeping watch on the approaches to the column. The desert was wide open in most places—and no one should know they were there—but Trax wasn't taking any chances. He had forty million ducats to protect, and he knew his mission was pivotal to launching the campaign to conquer the Northern Continent. He wasn't going to take any chances.

"And send the daily communique to Colonel Jellack. Advise

him we are on schedule."

"Yes, sir."

* * *

"I have just received an update, Colonel Dolokov. The payroll will be here in six days." Jellack stood outside the small shelter that had served as a combination of quarters and office for the past week. He'd advised Dolokov that the funds were on the way, hard currency as promised. He'd withheld details, a bit of caution he felt was warranted, but he had kept the mercenary commander at least somewhat in the loop.

Dolokov had been straightforward with him so far, at least as far as he knew, but he wasn't ready to test a new relationship on something as tempting as a massive convoy of coin. Forty million ducats was a lot of money, especially on the Northern Continent.

The mercenary officer nodded. "That is excellent news, Colonel Jellack." He paused and looked out over the sprawling camp. The gathering of mercenary troopers was growing every day, as men who had wandered off on leave during the hiatus were recalled to the colors. "We should be fully mobilized by then. As soon as the payment is received, we will be ready to march." He looked over at Jellack. "Will you be in command?"

Jellack nodded. "Perhaps," he said, a tiny smile appearing on his lips. "But I am certain the Marshal will send another officer to replace me once the organizational aspects are under control." He paused. "I am a man of numbers, Colonel, as I'm sure you can tell...not a combat officer."

"Your organizational skills are not to be underestimated, Colonel. Nor your negotiations. You have assembled the largest single force the Northern Continent has seen deployed in one location in a century or more...and for all that forty million ducats is a large sum, it is actually a bargain for a fully-equipped force of over one hundred thousand veterans."

Jellack nodded. "A deal is a deal, Colonel." He flashed a glance at the mercenary. "One I expect will be honored," he added, the slightest bit of concern in his tone. He'd had too many people try to renegotiate deals after the fact…and he never forgot that he was surrounded by Dolokov's soldiers and the other companies.

"You needn't worry, Colonel. I am a man of my word. It is part of our trade. A mercenary company that didn't honor its contracts wouldn't last long."

"I wouldn't worry, Colonel Dolokov. You were at a disadvantage in negotiations this time, but Marshal Carteria is very generous to those who serve him well. If our initial campaigns are successful, I am sure you will do well when it comes to renegotiations."

"We shall see." Dolokov's voice was calm, businesslike, but there was something else there. A hesitation…a hint of discomfort."

"What is it, Yuri? What troubles you?"

Dolokov hesitated. "It is nothing, Colonel…just…"

"Just what?" Jellack had an idea what was on Dolokov's mind, but he wanted the officer to say it first.

"There is some concern, Colonel." Jellack had told the mercenary he could call him Ganz, but Dolokov had continued to use his rank when they spoke.

"Concern?"

Dolokov paused again. "Yes, concern about the future of the Northern Continent, about whether we should be aiding an outside power making a move to conquer it."

"Conquer the continent? Who said we were going to conquer the entire continent?"

Dolokov stared back at Jellack. "I know you are not a tactician, Colonel, but I don't believe you are unaware of your master's intentions. He hardly needs this much force to win the fight in the Badlands. So, what else can we infer as to his ultimate goal?"

"And that troubles you?"

Dolokov paused, a thoughtful look on his face. "Yes, Colonel. No doubt, such a war would be long…and it would be lucrative while it lasted. But if your master does unite—conquer—the continent, we would be out of business, would we not? Many give lip service to the desire for a united Celtiboria, but how many, like us, owe everything to the very turmoil people so often curse? If we help your master conquer the continent, we destroy our own utility."

"While I feel you are inferring far too much from the Marshal's actions, even if such a sequence of events did occur, would that much really change? Would you be damaged, stripped of an uncertain and variable livelihood? Or would you gain something longer lasting, more stable? I was not born to the Marshal's service, Colonel, yet here I am, prosperous, wealthy, carrying a high rank. Should Marshal Carteria become master of the continent, I can assure you that he will remember those who made it possible, and the rewards will dwarf whatever you feel you have lost."

Dolokov stared back at Jellack, nodding slightly after a moment. "Perhaps, Colonel." A few seconds passed then the mercenary repeated himself. "Perhaps."

Jellack just nodded.

"Well, Colonel, I'm afraid I have duties that will not wait. If you will excuse me…"

Jellack nodded again, wordlessly.

Dolokov turned and walked down the small hill, back toward the center of the camp. Jellack watched him go, but in his mind his thoughts were bitter.

Yes, Colonel, Marshal Carteria always recognizes skill he can put to his own uses…and he knows how to create loyalty, at least of a sort…

His mind drifted to his family, to his wife and children and the gilded palace that served as their prison. Jellack was well treated, and he knew he would serve Carteria to the best of his ability. But was it loyalty when it was driven by fear? When his allegiance was accompanied by images in his mind, of his children murdered, crucified in front of their opulent home, of his wife raped by Carteria's guards before she too was nailed to a cross to die slowly, the price of his disloyalty?

Or even my failure…

No, I cannot fail. I hate Carteria, but that is of little consequence. I will succeed, I will use all my skills to aid his conquest…for my family…

Cass sat quietly, staring at the wall. She was deep in thought, sad. Her people had been headquartered in the tunnels below the eastern mountains for over a year, and it had become somewhat of a home, at least a temporary one. She realized now that she had become complacent, allowed the Grays to stay for too long in one place. She knew it was luck alone that had prevented the enemy from finding them, from destroying them. But logic didn't prevent her from feeling out of place in the new hideout. The subterranean ruin of the ancient fortress was a poor substitute for the extensive network of tunnels under the ridgeline, and it lacked the improvements her people had made to their old headquarters. It was uncomfortable—and much smaller—and that was made worse by the fact that she'd insisted her people lay low, at least until the armies engaged each other again. They were going stir crazy, climbing all over each other in the restricted confines of the new base.

She was also thinking of Minth Samis. From what she'd been able to piece together, guesswork mostly, he'd ignored Blackhawk's instructions to create a diversion, and he'd tried to seize the caravan by himself. It had been foolish beyond imagination, but it was the only explanation. His people had been killed or captured by the security forces…and the ones taken prisoner had undoubtedly been questioned. She'd never know if that had been the source of the enemy's intelligence or if they had finally simply tracked the Grays down, but the old refuge had been destroyed…including the supplies and weapons she'd stored there.

Her people had escaped—save Samis and those he'd led to destruction, of course—but they were in worse shape than they'd been since she had first led them into the Badlands. They were even short of basic provisions. She had sent a group of her people to Rhiombe with coin taken from one of their secret stashes to buy food and medicine, but now she realized how much a feeling of security she'd felt from their old headquarters, with its secret supplies and deeply-hidden tunnels. She felt like her people were naked now, out in the open…though on some level, she realized they were actually safer than they had been.

She felt sadness for Samis, and anger too. The fool had gotten nine other Grays killed or captured. She had trusted him with an important mission, and he had let her down. She knew, of course, that Samis had a crush on her. He had no doubt thought he was subtle, but it had long been obvious. But Cass had always kept herself apart from the others. She was their leader, and though she lacked any kind of training, much of it seemed to come naturally to her, not the least of which was the realization that the commander was alone. Always.

She'd scrupulously avoided even the hint of romantic involvement with any of her people…and if she'd ever chosen to relax this policy, it wouldn't have been with Samis.

It wouldn't have been with any of them. *I love them all, I would give my life to save them…but they are all boys.*

Cass had felt the crushing burden of command for too long, the guilt at every death, at each plan that failed. Her thoughts were filled with tactics, strategies…and responsibility weighed on her every sleepless hour. It had aged her, scraped away the last vestiges of the cheerful young girl she had once been. She was a warrior now, grim and deadly. Like Blackhawk.

Blackhawk. Another source of her sadness now. He had gone—as she'd always known he would—but though his departure was far from unexpected, now that he was gone she felt the loss acutely. He'd become her lover, and she'd found a brief escape in his arms, in the deep stillness of the desert night. But there was more there too. He was like no one she'd ever met. She didn't know much about him really, but she had sensed enough. He carried his own burdens, scars from a savage past…and she had connected with that part of him. She'd imagined a future she knew could never be, one where they helped to heal each other's wounds. But that was just a dream. Neither of them had reached the end of their own struggles, and she wasn't sure they ever would.

And some wounds are simply too deep to ever heal…

She took a breath, her thoughts drifting to events to the west, to the armies her scouts had reported were now on the march. She wondered if Blackhawk was there, with Lucerne's army. Had he confirmed that Lucerne had not betrayed him? Or had he taken his vengeance, killed the general?

Or perhaps he had failed. For all she knew, Blackhawk could already be dead. But she didn't believe it. She knew it was nonsense, but somehow she was sure she would know.

He is still alive…

"Cass…" It was Jarvis Danith.

"Jarvis," she said, sounding groggy though she hadn't gotten a moment's sleep.

"I'm sorry to disturb you, but the night scouts have returned…and they brought someone back with them. They found him near the old headquarters. It's a miracle Ghana's men didn't get him first."

"Who is it?" She reached down, grabbing her jacket and putting it over her shoulders. She'd never gotten used to the temperature swings in the desert, how cold it could get even after a blisteringly hot day.

"He says his name is Gaj Tryll…that Khal Thorn sent him."

She straightened up, paying close attention now. Khal Thorn was her best contact in the river cities…and his information had always been accurate.

"What does he have to say?"

"He won't tell us, Cass. He says his instructions are to speak only to you directly."

She felt a sense of concern, a passing worry that this was some kind of trap. But Thorn had never given her cause to doubt him…and she had always paid him his due and then some.

"Bring him in, Jarvis. I will speak to him."

"Alone?" Now it was Jarvis' turned to worry.

Cass reached down under the pile of blankets that made up her bed, pulling out a small pistol. She checked it quickly, and shoved it under her robe.

"Yes, Jarvis. I will see him alone. Now."

"Major, may I have a moment?"

Barkus stopped. The phrasing was polite, but the tone was… unsettling.

He turned, looking into the darkness. He could see one face, familiar. But there were others too, hovering back, just out of view.

"What can I do for you, Largon?" Largon Kieves was another of Ghana's longtime officers, a major like Barkus.

"You can help me help the general, Jinn. Help the army."

Barkus felt his stomach knot. He'd known Colonel Eleher had been spreading coin around, but he hadn't realized the Carterian had managed to suborn officers as close to Ghana as Kieves.

"And how would I do that, Largon?" Barkus tensed, and the thought crossed his mind to resist, to strike first. But he let it pass. There were at least three others in the shadows, and probably more. He might take down Kieves, but the others would finish him.

"The general is fatigued, Jinn. He is making poor decisions. We must save him from himself." A pause. "Give me the data chip. And remain here…there is nothing to be gained by going to Lucerne's headquarters."

"Nothing? What about peace? A negotiated end to this ruinous war?"

"We will have an end to the war tomorrow regardless. Without yielding to Lucerne."

"So we yield instead to Carteria?" Jinn cursed himself the moment the words slipped out of his mouth. He didn't suspect it would change things at all, and it was a foolish outburst.

"The Marshal has been enormously helpful, Jinn. Without his aid, we would be facing defeat even now."

"And how much silver did he give you, Largon? What was the price of your betrayal?"

"You always were difficult, Jinn. An idealist, a man incapable of reacting to change. You would follow your master to destruction…and do nothing to prevent doom. You and I are different. I understand that change is sometimes necessary."

"You and I are different indeed, Largon. I am a soldier, and loyalty is my creed. You are a blackhearted traitor, a man with no honor."

"This doesn't need to go this way, Jinn."

Barkus took a deep breath. He'd served with Ghana since the day after his seventeenth birthday. That service was all he knew. He had lived by it. And he was prepared to die by it.

"Yes it does, Largon." His hand dropped to his side, fingers gripping his pistol. His eyes focused on Kieves, and he saw fear there. The other officer realized what was happening, and he reacted. But too late.

Barkus' pistol whipped upward, firing once…twice. Kieves fell back as the projectiles slammed into his chest.

Barkus spun around, firing into the darkness, targeting the shadowy figures the best he could. He hit one, perhaps two…he was sure of that. But then he felt the impact, the first shot slamming into his shoulder, his body twisting hard. Then the pain.

He stumbled, and his arm went weak, the pistol dropping to the ground. But he managed to stay on his feet…for another second or two. Then continued fire, the sounds of weapons discharging…and more impacts. A shot to his leg…then falling to his knees. Then another shot…in the neck. Gasping for air, blood filling his throat, pouring from his mouth.

His vision was blurry. There were sounds, but it was a confused jumble, nothing intelligible. Then more pain. He'd been hit again. He couldn't tell where, but then he felt himself falling, the impact, hitting the ground. Hard. Painful.

His thoughts were floating around, images of his assailants…mixed with faces from long ago, family, old comrades. He was lost, slipping away…falling into the darkness.

Chapter Twenty-Two

General Lucerne's Field HQ
"The Badlands"
Northern Celtiboria

Lucerne let his body fall forward, seeking the cover of the table in front of him. He had to buy time. The guard outside… it was his only hope. He knew the sentry would respond to the shot, that he would burst into the room any second. But he had to survive, at least until then.

He dropped hard, hearing another shot whiz by, just over his head. He was down on all fours now, in tenuous cover, denying Pellier a clear line of fire for the killing shot. The assassin would have to move, to get around the desk…and that would take time.

Then the door burst open, and the guard came running in, his assault rifle leveled. But Pellier was no fool…he knew as well as Lucerne the soldier would come. He had moved quickly, toward the wall, around the corner from the small hallway leading in from the door. The guard saw that Lucerne was down and ran to him, reacting too late to the general's warnings. Pellier's gun cracked again. Twice. Two shots to the back. The guard dropped, hard. Lucerne felt as though he'd been punched in the gut. He knew in an instant the man was dead. But there was no time now to mourn one of his own. He was fighting for his life.

Pellier lunged across the room toward Lucerne, his pistol

out in front of him. There were alarm bells in the distance…the guard had given the alert before he'd rushed in.

He's not firing.

Then: *No, of course not. He needs me alive to get out of here now. A hostage.*

He gritted his teeth, his determination, his anger coalescing into a single thought.

That's never going to happen…

He would die here if need be, but he would never let a traitor like Pellier take him prisoner. Never.

Lucerne knew he could use Pellier's need to take him captive. It was a tactical edge, the only one he had. He twisted, shielding his wounded side from the onslaught. He reached out, striking…a hard punch, just as Pellier reached him. He could feel the impact; he knew he'd hurt his adversary. But Pellier stood firm, absorbing the painful blow, striking back…then turning around behind him, shoving the pistol hard into Lucerne's back.

"Don't move, General." Lucerne stood frozen, his mind racing for a move that could extricate him before Pellier could pull the trigger. But there was nothing. "And you too, DeMark…stay where you are or the general dies. And drop the weapon."

Major DeMark had been rushing through the door, pistol in hand. His eyes locked on Lucerne's, and then on Pellier standing behind him. He paused, not moving at all, but he didn't drop the pistol.

"Now, DeMark," Pellier said, shoving his gun into the small of Lucerne's back. "Drop that weapon or the general dies."

Lucerne shook his head. "No, Rafe, don't…he can't ki… oooph…"

Pellier's hand had come down hard on Lucerne's wounded shoulder.

DeMark stood still, watching. Lucerne shook his head again, and Pellier punched the injured spot, harder this time. Lucerne almost crumpled to the ground, but Pellier's free arm slipped under his shoulder, holding him up. His other hand held the pistol, pressed right against Lucerne's back. "Drop it. Now. Or I'll blow off one bit of him at a time."

DeMark hesitated for another few seconds, unmoving. Finally, he let the gun slip out of his hand and drop to the floor.

"Over, against the wall."

DeMark hesitated again. "Pellier, you're never going to get out of here…you know that. Why don't you make it easy on yourself? You know the general is a fair ma…"

"Shut up and do what I say. Now…against the wall." Pellier's voice was ragged, tense. He was afraid, and it showed.

DeMark moved slowly, his eyes darting around, taking stock of the situation each minute. Stopping again. "Pell…"

"Now!" Pellier roared. "Or the general loses a leg in two seconds…"

DeMark moved to the side. "Come on, Aton," he said, keeping his voice soft, even. You're trapped, and you know it. There is no escape. Let the general go, and we'll let you leave. You can go to Ghana's camp…wherever you want. But this is a dead end you're on now."

"You think I believe that, Rafaelus? That you would just let me leave? After this?"

"I wouldn't," the officer responded. "I want to see you on the ground bleeding to death, you stinking traitor." His voice was hard-edged, angry. "But the general is more merciful than I am."

"I *will* let you go, Aton." Lucerne's voice was ragged…he was in a lot of pain. But there was sincerity there too. "Just put the gun down. I'll give you a transport, you can take your things and go. Join Ghana…or head to the river cities. Go wherever you want."

Pellier hesitated, his grip loosening slightly. Lucerne was waiting for the right moment. His move would be hampered by his wounds. And any miscalculation probably meant death. Then he saw a flash of motion behind DeMark, at the doorway. A dark shadowy figure, rushing into the room.

Lucerne saw the movement…another guard he assumed. He prepared himself. His guards were good, but Pellier was behind him, mostly hidden by his body. He would only need an instant to pull the trigger. His man would be hesitant to fire, to risk hitting him. And even an instant's delay could be fatal.

Then there was a loud crack, a single shot that took him by surprise. He tensed, twisting hard, moving away from Pellier. Then he felt something on the side of his face…warm, wet. Pellier fell away from him, dropping to the ground.

He turned, amazed, staring down at the body of his captor, his hand moving to his face, pulling away, streaked with red wetness. Blood. Pellier's blood. The officer lay on the ground, a red pool expanding around his head. What was left of his head.

Lucerne snapped back around, looking at DeMark…and the man standing behind him, just inside the room, his arm still extended, holding a pistol.

Blackhawk.

His new ally was still alive. And he had saved his life.

* * *

Ghana sat at the makeshift desk, staring off into the semidarkness of the tent. It was the eve of battle, late into the deep night. At dawn, just a few hours away, his soldiers would engage Lucerne's army. He had no doubt his forces would fight well, but he was equally certain they would be pushed back. He'd used the truce to rearm and reorganize his army, but he hadn't secured the coin he needed to hire more mercs…and his army unaided had already been thrice defeated by Lucerne's veterans.

Perhaps defeat would be a blessing, an end to this war. Lucerne is not a savage…there are worse men to have in control of your fate…

But there would be no defeat, Ghana was confident of that. Carteria's troops were half a day's march back, and as soon as Lucerne's forces were fully engaged, they would hit the enemy flank. Ghana had learned to respect Lucerne's troops, and he wagered man for man they were more than a match for the Carterians…save for their equipment. Lucerne's army was outfitted like Ghana's…but the far wealthier Carteria had provided his soldiers with advanced weapons, systems Ghana, Lucerne, and the rest of their Northern Continent brethren could only dream about. He'd even heard rumors the Carterians had some imperial tech, weapons of a power that far exceeded anything of Celtiborian manufacture.

When twenty-five thousand superbly armed Carterians slammed into their flank, even General Augustin Lucerne and his proud veterans would be defeated.

Victory. So long sought. Yet not mine.

He'd wrestled with his expectations. What would Carteria do once Lucerne was gone? He'd tried to believe his ally would continue to back him, but Bako Ghana was no one's fool. In his heart he knew he would be the next to go. His mind bounced around, wondering which of his people Carteria had already bribed, who had been promised his place.

He'd hoped his desperate gamble, his outreach to Lucerne would extricate him from the mess he'd created for himself. But there had been no word. None at all. Could Barkus have been turned…had Carteria's coin gotten to his aide?

No. Not Jinn Barkus. He's been with me practically since he was a boy…

He wanted to believe…but he wasn't sure. Everything was falling apart around him, and he didn't know who he could trust. His rational mind said Barkus was solid…but he was beginning to doubt everything, even his own judgment. Still, one thing was clear to him. The Marshal would wait until the battle was over… he wouldn't risk unsettling the army before the final fight. But then Carteria would have Ghana killed, either by an assassin…or at the hands of one of his own men. That would be the ultimate defeat, to be gunned down by one of his own officers.

He didn't know what to do. Not unless Barkus returned. Had Lucerne taken his messenger prisoner? Was Barkus waiting in Lucerne's camp for an answer? Had some patrol or sentry captured him…or worse? He just didn't know. But there was nothing he could do. Nothing but wait. And hope Barkus returned before battle was joined. Once blood was spilled it would be far more difficult to make the peace.

Jinn…where are you?

Chapter Twenty-Three

The Ataphor Basin
"The Badlands"
Northern Celtiboria

The "Battle of Ataphor" – First Phase

The dawn was clear, cold. All across the field, the sun's first rays were touching the ground, bringing light, and the first warmth to drive away the night's chill. It had rained the evening before, a rare bit of precipitation this time of year in the deep desert, and the sand was dark, wet. There were puddles in a few low lying areas, small stretches of open water that would not long survive the day's coming heat.

It was early, very early, but the soldiers had been on the march for over an hour. Columns moved almost silently over the rolling hillsides, and staff officers scurried around, delivering orders too sensitive to trust to vulnerable com transmissions.

General Lucerne's army had risen before the sun, his veteran warriors emerging from their tents into the cold darkness. They had eaten a hasty breakfast, and then, as they had so many times before, they formed up and marched forward. To battle.

Lucerne hadn't awakened early like his soldiers. He had never slept. The general was a restless soul who rarely got more than three or four hours of sleep a night, and almost never a wink on the eve of battle. His dynamic leadership in the heat of combat seemed spontaneous to those around him, orders flying rapidly from his mouth, almost as if his decisions were instantaneous. But that was a misleading impression. In truth he spent hours in the near darkness, huddled over his desk, reviewing scouting reports, maps, battle plans…working deep into the night. His reputation had been earned, as much in those quiet hours as on the field itself, pistol in hand, leading his troops into the heart of the struggle.

"Does it always feel like this?" Blackhawk walked up behind the general. Like Lucerne, Blackhawk was a poor sleeper.

Lucerne turned and nodded as his new colleague climbed up the hillside, stopping right next to him. "You should know. Your past is still a mystery to me, but I'd bet my last ducat you're no stranger to the field of battle. You know how it is…the danger, the tension. The guilt for those you sent to their deaths."

Blackhawk just nodded. He'd fallen a little under Lucerne's spell, but he realized the general couldn't possibly understand a man like him. Like he had been. It was true that the battle-field wasn't new to Blackhawk…but a lot of what he was feeling was very new. He was tense, nervous…and he felt for the men he knew would not survive the day. Before it had been different. He'd been confident, always commanding greater resources than his foe…and he'd viewed the casualties as numbers on a spreadsheet after the fact, nothing more.

Blackhawk had been running from himself, from who he had been, but now it seemed to him things had been simpler before. Still, he wouldn't go back…indeed, he would fight with all he had to ensure that he never again became what he had been.

"Your troops look sharp. How do you feel about the battle?"

Lucerne sighed softly. "My people will defeat Ghana's army…though I hesitate to imagine the cost." The general paused, looking off into the distance.

Blackhawk could tell there was more on Lucerne's mind, something troubling him beyond the threat of Ghana's soldiers. "What is it?" he said softly.

"Carteria's troops...they are the unknown," Lucerne replied, turning back toward Blackhawk. "If there are no more than ten thousand, we can probably handle them...but if there are more..."

He took a deep breath. "This is going to sound strange... but I feel something. There have been scouting reports...nothing conclusive, but my gut tells me that force is larger than we think. I've sent out three flights of drones, but all they've spotted are tents...rows and rows of tents. More than there should be." He paused. "I think Carteria may be making a more aggressive move, perhaps the start of an invasion of the Northern Continent."

"Maybe the drone flights picked up some of Ghana's own reinforcements. He may have scraped up some levies from back home." Blackhawk's tone suggested he didn't believe that any more than Lucerne.

"Perhaps. I've had no reports that he has acquired the services of any mercenary companies...and unless my intelligence is woefully lacking, he does not have troops to spare from other locations. But..."

"But you can't ignore this," Blackhawk interrupted. "Even if it's just a hunch. So, what are you doing?"

"What can I do? I'm holding back a few veteran regiments to deal with anything unexpected." He paused. "I'd call off the battle entirely if I could, withdraw and redouble my scouting efforts. But that's not an option."

Blackhawk nodded. He knew Lucerne's situation, probably much better than the general would have expected. "You need a victory...an end to this war."

"Yes. I have extended my resources to the breaking point. This was a gamble, a desperate one...my play to break out, to become more than a small regional Warlord. But it took everything I had to mount this campaign." He turned and looked at Blackhawk. "For me, it is victory or a deep slide into ruin. And I don't have much time left."

Blackhawk just nodded, and the two stood for a while, silent, looking out over the field as the army continued to form up.

Then he turned back toward Lucerne.

"I will scout behind Ghana's lines, General. I will find out what he has back there in reserve and get word to you... somehow."

"That is a suicide mission."

"Dangerous, perhaps. Suicide? I wouldn't go that far. As you seem to have observed, I am no stranger to the battlefield."

"I'll send a company with you."

"No," Blackhawk snapped. "I appreciate the offer, but I will be relying on stealth..." And my own abilities that your men can't match. "...I will be better off on my own."

Lucerne looked as though he might argue, but then he just nodded. "Thank you, Arkarin. Your offer of assistance is greatly appreciated. What can I do to help?

* * *

"I want fire on that hill...now!" Clarkson Wells crouched down in the shallow foxhole his troops had dug in the shifting sand. The ground had been wet when they'd first taken the position, but the sun had dried it out, and now the walls of the makeshift trench were beginning to collapse in on themselves.

Wells was a captain, but he held a major's billet, the command of one of Lucerne's veteran battalions. His troops were on the vanguard of the attack, driving a wedge between Ghana's right flank and his center. They'd moved forward for two hours, pushing the enemy before them, barely pausing to regroup before continuing their attack. But now they were stuck. Wells had sent two attacks forward, and both had been driven back with heavy losses. His people were facing one of Ghana's oldest battalions right now, and they were dug in on high ground.

"Yes, Captain."

Wells turned back and watched as his aide pulled out his com unit. "All mortars, open fire," the lieutenant snapped off. "Target Hill 107, maximum rate of fire."

There was a pause, a very short one. Then Wells could hear the familiar, high pitched sounds of mortar shells heading toward the enemy positions. He had stripped his companies of their heavy ordnance platoons and combined them together, the closest thing he had to a grand battery.

He looked out across the field, watching as the first shells began to land on the hill. His gunners were dead on, the first volley hitting all around the target…but the enemy was in a strong position, and he knew it was going to take more than some shelling to drive them off. Sooner or later—and probably sooner—he was going to have to send his troops back in…and that would be a bloody business. But Wells knew, as did all his veterans, that a victory here would make this the final battle. Ghana had extricated himself from defeat three times before, but no one, from the General Lucerne himself down to the foot soldiers in the ranks, intended to let that happen again. They would drive as hard as they had to, suffer what losses it took… but the war would end here.

He crouched lower as shells began to land around his own positions, the enemy answering his bombardment. He could see the difference in the two forces immediately. His own mortars were targeting a tightly-focused area, their accuracy sharp. The enemy shells were landing over a much wider area, their fire clearly less accurate. That didn't mean they weren't dangerous, but it meant his people were likely to take fewer losses than their enemy…and in the end, it would be the strength and resolve at the point of decision that would decide the result.

Still, taking that position is going to be brutal…

"Lieutenant, call HQ again…repeat the request for air support."

"Yes, sir." He could hear the doubt in the aide's voice. Wells had already requested bombing runs twice, and the only response had been a vague, 'as soon as assets are available.' General Lucerne's air forces were small, limited, as were most of those commanded by the Warlords, by lack of resources. It was an expensive branch of service, and it relied on controlling industrial centers or establishing reliable trade routes to ensure a steady stream of ordnance and replacement parts. Wells knew Ghana's forces were in the same boat…and he also knew

Lucerne's few available squadrons were up there even now, battling the enemy wings for control of the air. That was the first priority. He understood—he even agreed. But he'd have killed for a single flight of airships making a strafing run on the target.

"Sir," the aide said, "HQ reports all air assets are engaged. It will be at least an hour, Captain."

Too long…

"Looks like we're going to have to do this on the ground," Wells said grimly. He stared off across the field, at the explosions as his mortars continued to impact all along the enemy line. He didn't kid himself…he knew it looked worse than it was, that the damage would be relatively light. But hopefully the enemy would at least be a little disordered, shaken.

"All units prepare for battalion assault." He'd sent companies to attack before, but now he was going all in, five hundred soldiers of the battalion moving forward as one.

"Yes, Captain."

He could hear the tension in the aide's voice, the fear. Lieutenant Stoor was a veteran, but it was a common misconception that experienced troops weren't afraid in battle. Only lunatics weren't afraid in battle.

"All companies, report ready, sir."

Wells took one last look, watching as the shells continued to smash into the enemy line. Then he turned back toward Stoor. "All mortars…cease fire."

The aide repeated the order, and in a few seconds the weapons fell silent. The enemy line was obscured by smoke, the trenches torn apart in a dozen places where mortar rounds had impacted hard. He knew from experience there was no way to be sure how much damage he'd done, how many casualties his shells had inflicted, how many enemy autocannons had been silenced, driven away.

But it was time to find out.

"All companies, prepare to charge…"

He reached down and scooped his assault rifle from where he'd set it down. One thing for sure, he wasn't sending troops forward again, not alone. This time he was going with them. He snapped a cartridge into place, and he looked back toward Stoor, nodding once. Then he turned, facing toward the enemy…and he said one word.

"Charge!"

* * *

Blackhawk moved quickly behind the low ridge, hopping along the row of boulders hugging the edge of the small rocky crest. His hands dropped to his side for the third or fourth time, feeling the familiar belt, the pistol and sword he'd carried for so long. When Lucerne had asked what he needed, apart from half a dozen grenades and an assault rifle, all he'd asked for was his own equipment, the gun and sword he'd left behind when he had set out on his mission to infiltrate Ghana's headquarters. It was foolish, he knew, but he somehow felt complete now, ready. They were just weapons, he knew, but in a way, they were like a part of him.

He'd left Lucerne's camp almost immediately after he had agreed to investigate Ghana's reserves. He had a long way to cover and not a lot of time…and even his rugged constitution would be worn down by long stretches of jogging in the searing heat of midday. He'd pushed hard, and he'd already moved around the flank of the enemy army…two hours of exertion that taken him a distance equal to a full day's march for a normal soldier.

His senses had been on edge, his eyes and ears straining for any signs of enemy reinforcements, an approaching force that might turn the tide in the battle being fought even now. He'd had one close call, a flight of Ghana's airships moving toward the front. He'd heard them coming from a distance, and he'd hit the ground, lying under an overhanging boulder while the low-flying planes roared overhead. But since he'd slipped past Ghana's main army, he hadn't seen so much as a scout or a fading trail of footsteps in the sand.

Until now.

He stopped suddenly, crouching lower, behind the cover of

the rocks. It had been a sound, vague, almost nothing. But he'd learned to trust his instincts. He leaned forward, controlling his breath, clearing his mind and listening. There was nothing, at least for the first few seconds. Then he heard it again. Then again, louder now...and he knew what it was. The sound of a transport...no, more than one. A column of trucks approaching.

He moved up into the rocks, peering carefully out from his makeshift cover. He could see them now, distant, no more than a glint or two of the bright sun off the chassis of the approaching vehicles. The sounds were louder now as the convoy approached. He stared for a few more seconds, his mind filling in the blanks, the details he couldn't yet see...and he knew exactly what he was looking at. A column of mechanized troops moving forward. A big one.

He felt the rush of adrenalin...satisfaction that he had found what he'd come to seek, and also tension, alertness. This was a threat to General Lucerne, a very dangerous. He had to get word back. Now. But he needed more specifics...a reasonable estimate of the enemy strength. He could see now it was larger than the ten thousand he and Lucerne had discussed. But how much larger? Double, at least, he guessed...and maybe bigger. He stared for another moment, counting transports...doing quick calculations. He had an urge to push forward, to get a closer look, but he knew that would be too dangerous.

He'd brought a small com unit with him, but now he was reluctant to use it. It was too subject to interception...and if these troops picked it up he'd have a hundred men on his tail in an instant.

Besides, Lucerne doesn't have the troops to handle a force this large, not in a straight up fight. Not when he's still fully engaged with Ghana's main army. We need surprise...we need the enemy not to know we're aware of the size of this force...

His eyes were still fixed straight ahead. He'd made his decision...he would take the report back himself. He would push as hard as he could, get back as quickly as possible. He was just about to turn away from the enemy force and start back when he froze. There was something different about these soldiers.

Something wrong…familiar.

That is not normal Celtiborian ordnance…not all of it.

His eyes were fixed on the closest transport, on the turret affixed to its top. He'd seen that kind of weapon before, but not here, not on Celtiboria.

A particle accelerator. An imperial particle accelerator.

Blackhawk's mind raced, wondering what Ghana must have paid to smuggle imperial weapons to Celtiboria. Such things weren't unknown in the Far Stars, but they were rare…very rare. And they commanded a king's ransom. More than Ghana could have…no…not Ghana.

Carteria. There are all Carteria's soldiers…twenty thousand, maybe thirty, and armed with imperial tech…

His eyes looked back, from the first truck to the second, and the third. All similarly armed. Only one Warlord on Celtiboria could afford to import imperial weapons. Suddenly, he knew… he understand fully. Carteria wasn't just backing Ghana. If he was committing this kind of ordnance to the fight it could mean only one thing. He was beginning a move on the Northern Continent itself.

I have to get back to Lucerne. Now.

Then he heard it. Scrambling, voices. He spun around, looking through a crack in the line of rocks. There were soldiers, half a dozen, and they were moving his way. A scouting patrol…and they'd spotted him!

His mind raced, calculating the odds, devising a strategy in a matter of seconds. He couldn't run, not with those guards so close on his heels. They'd come over the rock outcropping, and they'd have a clear field of fire. No…he had to take them out first.

He spun around, quickly, without hesitation, his body acting almost on its own. He slid the assault rifle off his back, bringing it around to aim. The enemy had spotted him, but he still had good cover…and they were out in the open. His rifle spat, one shot after the other, and with each one a soldier dropped. In two seconds his pursuers were all down, not a shot fired his way.

But he'd warned the enemy, given up his location. He could

hear transports moving forward, speeding up. He could see dozens of troopers dismounting, moving in his direction, firing sporadically as they advanced.

Fuck!

He turned and spun around, taking off across the desert. He was a skilled warrior, a veteran, genetically-enhanced…but he couldn't take on an enemy army. Escape was his only choice. And right now it was looking like a longshot.

His legs pumped hard, accelerating his pace to a dead run, staying close to the rocks as he put as much distance as possible between him and his pursuers. The wound in his leg was still tender, but his constitution had done its job once again, and it was mostly healed. What little infirmity he still had from the injury was overwhelmed by massive flows of adrenalin coursing through his blood. He knew he could outrun Carteria's soldiers…and he could outlast them in the heat too. But they had transports, and if they wanted him badly enough they could get past him, cover his escape routes, surround him.

His hand dropped to his side, pulling the small com unit from his belt. He hadn't wanted to break radio silence, but secrecy was blown anyway…and Lucerne had to know what was coming, whether Blackhawk made it back or not.

"This is Arkarin Blackhawk calling for General Lucerne," he said, his voice strained as he continued to run full out across the baking sand. "This is Arkarin Blackhawk calling for General Lucerne," he repeated.

Nothing. Just static, heavy, unrelenting.

Fuck. They're jamming me.

"This is Arkarin Blackhawk calling for General Lucerne… do you read me?"

Still nothing.

Blackhawk turned and looked over the small ridge. He could see the transports moving, faster now, gaining on him.

He sucked in a deep breath of the hot air and pushed harder, his legs scrambling over the rocky sand.

General, Captain Wells' men have broken through. They've isolated the enemy's right flank."

Augustin Lucerne stood outside the large truck that served as his field headquarters. He had a seat inside the transport, even a small office. But he'd never been able to sit down at a desk when his troops were in battle.

He'd led his first combats from the front, advancing at the head of the thousand retainers he'd inherited from his father. But those days were behind him, and even he had acknowledged that a modern army of tens of thousands of soldiers couldn't be effectively commanded that way. He needed information, a constant flow of it, and he needed it in a timely manner. His staff had to be around him, with access to maps, data banks. He was responsible for the whole army, for the overall outcome of the battle...and gun in hand, he could only lead a small force. While he was crawling in the dirt with single battalion the rest of his army would be on its own, effectively leaderless.

Still, he always felt the guilt. Somehow it had been easier to accept the casualties when he had accompanied the men, shared the same dangers. That wasn't possible for him anymore, and he knew he'd only hurt his people through pointless bravado...but he still felt it.

"Casualties?" Lucerne, turned and stared back at his aide.

"Heavy, sir," the officer replied. Then a pause. "Very heavy. He estimates forty percent in his forward units."

Lucerne nodded, sighing softly, almost imperceptibly. He knew the cost of war, of victory. But he still didn't like it. And he was pushing his people hard, ignoring casualties to try to defeat Ghana's army before...

Before whatever Carteria sent here attacks us...

Lucerne hated trading lives for ground, losing more men to save a few hours. But there was no choice.

"General, Major Quarn reports the enemy air forces are breaking off. He requests permission to pursue."

Lucerne paused, just for a moment. Then he said, "Negative, Captain. I need Quarn's squadrons to run strafing mission for the ground forces."

It's costing us too much to do this a footstep at a time. The boys on the ground need air support…

"General…"

"Yes, Captain, I'm well aware that Major Quarn's birds have an opportunity to crush Ghana's air forces. But the cost is the men on the ground. We've got three thousand dead already… at least. I want those airships running ground support missions now!"

"Yes, sir."

Lucerne pulled back a little. He'd let his anger get away from him. Quarn had only been doing his job…and any of Ghana's airships that escaped and managed to rearm and return would be a problem. But he couldn't help but think of the losses Wells' people had suffered. His army couldn't take that for long, not across the whole field. No, they needed air support, and they needed it now. He'd worry about Ghana's regrouped and resupplied planes later.

He turned and started walking back toward the transport.

"General…"

He spun around. "What is it?"

"I think it's Blackhawk, sir. He's very garbled…almost like he's being jammed."

Lucerne moved toward the captain, reaching out for the headset and slapping it on.

"Gen…enemy…mov…large…"

Lucerne listened, trying to make out the words. His hands moved over the controls on the headset, trying to clear up the signal as much as he could.

"Blackhawk, is that you? Do you read me?"

"Gen…Blackha…being…pursued…"

Lucerne knew something was wrong. What had Blackhawk found?

Then the signal cleared for a moment…and Lucerne felt his stomach clench.

"…pursuing me, General. Twenty-thousand at lea…imperial weapons…" Then the signal was gone.

Twenty thousand. At least. Imperial weapons.

Lucerne froze. He'd felt victory within his grasp, but now he knew, with a cold feeling in his stomach, it was slipping away.

What the hell was coming his way?

And how was he going to defeat Carteria's forces armed with imperial tech?

Chapter Twenty-Four

Deep Southern Desert
"The Badlands"
Northern Celtiboria

"Chrono…" Cass stood along the rocks, looking out over the wide, sandy valley. She felt naked now, exposed, her Grays stripped of their makeshift home, and of the underground conduit they had used to such effect for the past two years. All gone, found by Ghana's soldiers. Her people still knew their way around the desert, but it was more difficult to travel now, more dangerous.

"Yeah," Jarvis said, his voice stretching out the word as he said it. "There must be hundreds of guards down there. There's no way we can take that convoy, Cass. Not a chance." He paused. "Hell, they must have scouts out all around…we're taking a hell of a chance just staying here."

"Yeah, you're right, Jarvis…" There was a hitch in her voice, an unwillingness to give up on the target, even though it was clear they had no choice. "But…"

"But what, Cass? There's barely sixty of us left…and those guys down there are armed. Heavily armed. Even if we could get close enough in the open desert, slip by whatever scouts they have out…we wouldn't last two minutes. It would take five hundred troops to hit that convoy, Cass. Maybe a thousand."

She nodded. Everything Jarvis said was true. But she was still determined to find a way. Even a small portion of that convoy would guarantee the people back home a life. If could do more than feed them for a while, buy medicine for the sick. It could rebuild the farms and mills...all that the soldiers had destroyed. There had to be a way.

"I know what you're thinking, Cass, but even if we could reach all the other raiding teams—and if they talked with us instead of just opening fire—we still wouldn't have enough strength. We're the biggest group already...even all the rest of them wouldn't add more than a hundred in total. If that."

She started shaking her head. "No," she said, her eyes dropping to the ground as an idea came to her. "Not the other raiders...and certainly not us alone." Her eyes snapped up to Jarvis'. "Blackhawk."

Jarvis returned her gaze for a few seconds then he sighed. "Cass, I know you became attached to Blackhawk...but what do we really know about him? You're talking about risking all of our lives on a desperate attack. Do you really trust him with everyone's lives? I broke out of Ghana's prison with him...I saw what he can do. But he's only one man, Cass. He doesn't have followers, an army."

Cass stood unmoving, thinking. Blackhawk had been her lover, at least for a short time, and she felt affection for him. But she didn't know much about the man, that was true. Still, she had to trust her instincts, her gut. And that told her she could trust him.

"Not Blackhawk alone, Jarvis...he's with Lucerne's army by now. And Lucerne has thousands of men."

"You can't be serious," Jarvis said, his voice incredulous. "You would trust a Warlord? One of the monsters who ravaged the Galadan? It was a Warlord's men who killed your father, Cass. Don't tell me you've forgotten that?"

"No," she snapped, her voice heavy with anger for a moment. "You know better than that," she added, calming down somewhat...but far from completely. "But you also know as well as I do that General Lucerne never came through the Galadan. And by all accounts, he is different from the others, more just."

"So much so that Blackhawk couldn't wait to leave so he could go kill him. Until he changed his mind."

She flashed her eyes back at Jarvis. "That is unfair. You know Blackhawk had misinformation. The mistake he almost made should teach you...he thought worse of Lucerne than the general deserved. Should we make the same mistake?"

"Cass...we came to the Badlands because you asked us to follow you, because you led us here. To save our families, to try to undo some of the damage that had been done to our homeland. And I have given you my loyalty...always. But to trust one of the Warlords? Or even Blackhawk? How much do we rely on his judgment?"

Cass reached out, put her hand on Jarvis' shoulder. "My old friend, we cannot allow ourselves to be ruled by prejudices. The fighting here will end soon, no matter who is the victor. And when it does, we will be driven off, we will no longer be able to survive in the disorder created by the Warlords' struggles. Do we stay, await destruction, so that none of us returns home? Or do we leave, go back to the Galadan, to its ruined farms and poisoned wells, to see how long the supplies we sent last before we again watch our families starve?"

"What if Lucerne just has us killed? There are death sentences on all of us, after all. Under all of the Warlords, I believe." He paused. "It is time to ask yourself, Cass. How much to do you trust Blackhawk. Really?"

She stared at Jarvis. "I trust him, Jarvis. You have to ask yourself, do you still trust my judgment?"

"Of course, Cass. I've been with you from the start. But even if you trust Blackhawk, are you're sure he is in Lucerne's good graces? That he is able to intervene on our behalf...to convince Lucerne to listen, and even when he does, to share the convoy with us and not just take to for himself and give us nothing but a bullet between the ears?"

"No, Jarvis, I am not sure. I cannot be. But I intend to go to Lucerne's camp, to find Blackhawk. I want a share of that treasure convoy, Jarvis. I want to send enough home, to truly rebuild the Galadan. But even more, I want it stopped…before it gets through the Badlands. You know that is blood money, on its way to pay mercenaries, soldiers who could easily march across the Galadan, to bring to hell of war back down upon us. We must see those transports intercepted, whatever deal we must make… with whatever devil. Even Augustin Lucerne."

Jarvis didn't look satisfied, but he didn't argue with her any more either. He just stood silently, an unhappy look on his face.

"I want you to stay, Jarvis. I want you to take command of the Grays while I am gone. And if something goes wrong…"

"No, Cass…I'm not going to let you go do this yourself."

"Please," she said, her voice soft. "I have to do this…but I also have to know my people are okay. If I don't come back you have to promise me you will lead them home, back to the Galadan. There will be nothing left here but war and death."

"Cass…" His voice was soft, almost distraught.

"Please, Jarvis. Do this for me."

He stared back at her. He looked as though he might speak, but then he just nodded.

"Thank you, my old friend. Keep ahead of the convoy… don't take any chances. And if I'm not back in four days, go. See that our people all get home. We have lost too many of our number already." She paused. "I am counting on you, Jarvis."

He closed his eyes tightly, then he reopened them, unable to force himself to look into her eyes. Finally, he just nodded again.

She stood for a moment and looked at her friend. She'd known Jarvis since they'd both been young children. She trusted him. He would mourn if she didn't return, but he would see that the others got home. And knowing that made it easier to go, to do what she had to do.

Then she reached down and scooped up her pack…and she took off across the desert.

* * *

"We buried the bodies out in the desert, Colonel. Far enough that no one will find them." Massen Roan stood opposite Eleher, staring at the Carterian officer. He was trying to keep his voice firm, but he was troubled, the images of Jinn Barkus and Largon Kieves floating in his mind. Roan was one of the cabal of officers who had conspired with Carteria's deputy, who had followed as Kieves and the others had taken foreign coin to buy their loyalty. But now Kieves was dead, at Barkus' hand, and Roan had taken part with the others in killing Barkus in turn.

He felt sick, unclean, and the thought of his dead comrades, both of them, made him want to vomit. But he had made his decision, and whether or not he now regretted it, there was no turning back. His own survival rode on the success of the coup. He'd considered for a fleeting moment taking a stand on honor and going to Ghana with the truth, but he had quickly realized he lacked the courage for self-sacrifice.

He'd tried to convince himself he'd made his choice out of concern for the army, that the money had been a secondary concern. But watching Barkus stand firm, incorruptible, invulnerable to the bribes and pleas to turn him aside from his duty—even killing Kieves rather than betraying his oath to Ghana—had stripped Roan of that pleasant fiction. He'd sold his honor, his loyalty, and he'd done it for coin...and for the power Carteria would give him in reward for his betrayal. For better or worse, he was part of the cabal, and his old comrade's blood was on his hands.

"Very good, Captain," Eleher said softly, looking around them as they spoke. "Our forces are almost engaged. In less than an hour we will turn this ignominious retreat into total victory. And then we will deal with General Ghana." He paused, surveying the expression on Roan's face. "There is no other way, Massen. I know it is a burden, that you still have sympathies for Ghana...but you made the right choice. Any other route leads only to destruction for your army, for all your comrades."

Roan nodded slowly. "Yes, Colonel," he said unconvincingly. He was fighting off the guilt, his mind alive with the vivid memory of Barkus' eyes wide open as he'd looked down on his slain comrade.

Eleher reached out his hand, gesturing toward a shadowy

figure at the base of the hill. The man turned and walked up toward the two conspirators.

"This is Zoln Darvon, Captain." Eleher paused. "We will wait until after our forces are fully engaged and the victory is assured. Then Zoln will handle General Ghana. It will relieve you and your comrades of the discomfort." He paused. "Remember, you are doing this to save your army. Mr. Darvon here has an offer for the general, a comfortable and honorable retirement."

"Yes, Colonel." Roan wanted to believe that, he wanted to convince himself that General Ghana and his family would live out their days in peace and comfort. But for all his faults, he'd never been a fool. He knew Carteria couldn't allow Ghana to live, not when he planned to take control of the general's army and lands. And he'd never allow Ghana's sons to live either. No, there would be no easy way out. His betrayal would come at full cost, the price of his treachery paid in Bako Ghana's blood. And Massen Roan's honor...his self-esteem.

"I will see to it, Colonel."

Chapter Twenty-Five

The Ataphor Basin
"The Badlands"
Northern Celtiboria

The "Battle of Ataphor" – Second Phase

"What the hell was that?" Sergeant Slannen stared off over the open desert toward the distant ridgeline. There were enemy troops there, the scouts had spotted them moving into position. Now they were opening fire.

Lieutenant Bash stood next to his company commander, looking in the same direction. The flash had been almost blinding, visible even in the bright light of the desert afternoon. It had hit behind his line, slamming into a rock outcropping and shattering it. Whatever it was, it was powerful, far more so than anything in his arsenal.

"An energy weapon of some kind," Bash said, trying to hide the concern in his voice. Softer, mostly to himself: "I hope they don't have too many of those…"

As if in response, a dozen of the weapons fired in a coordinated volley, electric blue light arcing across the sky. There were impacts all along the line. Most of the shots hit in the rear, slamming into the boulders and sandy ridgeline behind Bash's troops, but three of them smacked right into his shallow trench line. He saw the closest impact, ripping into the front edge of the position, caving in a large section of trench.

Soldiers were climbing out, disordered, pulling wounded comrades behind them. He could feel something he didn't often sense among his troops. The beginnings of panic.

The weapons fired again, their accuracy improving, more of them smashing into the troop positions. His com was crackling to life, frantic reports from all along the battalion's frontage. Wherever these troops were from, they were better-equipped than Ghana's men, that much was certain.

Better than us too…

He snapped his head back and forth, looking up and down the line. Bombardments were always difficult to endure, hard on the morale that kept an army together. And it was even worse when the barrage was coming from high tech weapons, ordnance you couldn't hope to match. His first instinct was to pull back. There was a ridgeline not too far back, one that would provide decent cover, at least. But he'd leave a hole in the line, expose the flanks of the units on either side if he just pulled out…and General Lucerne's soldiers did not leave their comrades behind, unsupported.

The enemy weapons fired again, most of them trained now on the line, tearing apart sections of hastily-dug trenches and blasting groups of his soldiers to bits. He hadn't gotten any casualty reports yet, but all he had to do was look to see that a lot of his troopers were down. He had to do something. He couldn't stay here…and he couldn't retreat either, not unless the whole wing fell back. That only left one option…

"Sergeant, get your company ready. We've got to take that position. Now."

"You mean charge?" Slannen was a hard nut, but even he sounded unsettled at the new enemy weapon…and even more so at Bash's idea of how to deal with it.

It was unusual for a sergeant to be commanding a company, but Slannen was a rock solid veteran, one of the Thousand, the semi-reverent name the army had for the first retainers General Lucerne had inherited from his father. It hadn't been exactly a thousand, of course—just under eleven hundred, in fact—and many of those originals had since fallen in battle. But Slannen had been there since the beginning, one of those dedicated non-coms who resisted advance to commissioned rank at all costs. General Lucerne had humored Slannen's not uncommon eccentricity with regard to the rank insignia on his uniform, but he'd put him in command of a company nevertheless.

"It's that or pull back." Bash didn't sound like he felt much better about his plan. "But those guns are opposite us...and we can't stay here and let them blast us to atoms. We've got to take them out."

Slannen just nodded. "Yes, sir." He turned and raced over toward his troops.

"All company commanders, this is Captain Bash." Another volley of the enemy weapons crashed along the line, including one uncomfortably close to Bash. He hunched forward, down below the lip of the shallow trench, belatedly taking cover. "We are going to charge that ridgeline and silence those weapons," he continued a few seconds later. "Whatever it takes."

He reached around and pulled the assault rifle from his back. "In twenty seconds..."

Bash stared down the weapon, double-checking that he'd put a fresh clip in.

"Ten seconds."

He took a deep breath. His mind was trying to be rational, logical, calculating the chances of his battalion getting across the open ground and taking out the enemy weapons before they were wiped out...but he stopped himself. The chances were shitty, and he knew it. But retreat wasn't an option, and standing along the ridge while those deadly arcs of light—he was fairly certain they were some kind of particle accelerators—ripped apart his trenches wasn't an option either. So whatever chance an attack gave his people...it was better than nothing.

"Battalion..." He screamed into his com unit. "Charge!"

He threw himself over the edge of the trench, what was left of it at least, and he ran across the field.

"We're getting reports all along the left flank, General…units under heavy bombardment. Strange weapons, nothing we've ever seen before." A pause. Then: "Sir, Captain Bash ordered an assault along his sector of the line."

"What?" Lucerne spun around. Eli Bash was one of his most reliable officers, not one he'd expected to run off on some reckless attack without even asking for approval. "Call him back, Captain. Immediately."

"They're already there, General. It appears some elements have reached the enemy position. Estimates are in excess of fifty percent casualties in the assault, sir. And the survivors are engaged with the enemy forces right now."

Lucerne felt his stomach tighten. He could picture the scene. Bash's battalion was shattered, half its soldiers lying dead or wounded in the field between the ridges. Most of the rest were fleeing back, broken, running for the perceived safety of their own lines. But Bash himself, and a few clusters of veterans would have reached the enemy position. They would have ignored fire, losses, pain. They would have run across the burning sands and scaled the low rocky heights to get to the enemy. And when they finally reached their objective they would fight like hell…but they would be outnumbered, surrounded. Most of them would be killed or captured. A few might escape back the way they had come, pushing with all the strength they had left to get back to their own ridge before the enemy fire resumed and cut them all down.

Lucerne had seen it before, in other battles. But no matter how many times he witnessed the tragedy, it hurt the same every time.

"Sir, Captain Javers and Major Vhasa request permission to advance in support of Bash's troops." There was a hint of hope in the aide's voice. The two officers commanded the units flanking Bash's battalion. "Shall I advise them they may…"

"No."

"General, Captain Bash and his…"

"No, Captain. We have no idea what is positioned behind that ridge, no understanding of how many of these weapons they have, or what else they might possess." Lucerne's voice was firm, resolute. He understood his aide's point of view, he even shared it. But he knew better. An attacking force would suffer more troopers lost than Bash had left…and, by the time the relieving force got there, most of Bash's men would be casualties anyway. Sending more troops would be a 'feel good' exercise, but not one that benefitted the army.

Lucerne knew there were times it made sense to ignore the raw mathematics. A dangerous rescue operation, for example. But his left flank was already in trouble…and getting two more battalions shot to pieces would only further jeopardize the army.

And we're already in plenty of jeopardy.

His mind was working rapidly, and it was coming to a single dark conclusion.

Carteria is making a full scale move on the Northern Continent. There is more at stake than the Badlands, more than defeating Ghana…

That had to be it. There was no one else on Celtiboria with the wealth and offworld connections to secure imperial weapons…and Marshal Carteria was too capable a strategist to carelessly deploy the limited quantity of advanced tech he did have. If he had put his priceless weapons into the field, it was part of something big. Carteria might send Ghana money to manipulate events in the Badlands, but imperial weapons were expensive, even for Celtiboria's most powerful Warlord. Lucerne knew it could only mean one thing.

He's planning a move on the Northern Continent. It has to be. Controlling Badlands trade is a valuable prize, but not worth this kind of commitment. It has to be more. And if he can take advantage of the disorder on the continent now, he just might bag the whole thing. And if he does that, nothing will stop him from conquering the entire planet…

His mind reeled. What was Ghana thinking? Lucerne had been Ghana's enemy for two years now, but he'd always maintained a level of respect for his adversary. How could he have been so foolish to seek Carterian troops, to expose the Northern Continent to domination by an outside power?

We shouldn't be fighting each other. We should be uniting to drive Carteria's forces into the sea. But we're not…and if Carteria's forces destroy my army there will be no one near the coast to resist them. He'll have hundreds of thousands of troops here before anyone is ready to fight him.

Suddenly, Lucerne knew what he had to do. He had to keep his army together at all costs…to survive. Somehow.

"Captain, all units are to execute an immediate withdrawal from the combat zone."

"Sir?" There was shock in the captain's voice. Lucerne's army was used to victory…and they had seemed so close to a complete triumph in the Badlands.

"I said we're retreating, by Chrono. Now!" Lucerne glared at the officer. He didn't like it any more than his aide. But he knew, deep inside, the game had changed dramatically. He wasn't trying to win the battle now, nor even to fight for control of the Badlands. No, he realized he was in a different struggle now, one for nothing less than the survival of his army.

* * *

"General, we have reports coming in from all over the field. Lucerne's forces are retreating, sir. All of them."

Ghana nodded. "Thank you, Captain." Then, a moment later. "That will be all."

Ghana sat at his desk, staring down at his hands as the officer turned and walked out of the room.

The implements of your own destruction, he thought grimly, turning them over and looking at his palms. You brought this about, through your own failings, your foolishness. You could have shared the Badlands with Lucerne, but greed drove you, pride did. You could have negotiated a peace while you still had bargaining power, a disadvantageous one perhaps, but not disastrous. But instead you doubled down for victory…extended a hand to the devil to make it possible…

Ghana knew he was confined to his headquarters. He'd never received any notice of that, of course, nor any explicit order directing him to stay. No, Eleher was too diplomatic for that, far too smooth to allow a scene. The Carterian troops had come bearing the message that they'd been sent to secure his headquarters, to protect him against any breakthrough by Lucerne's troops. It was like any good lie, just plausible enough to be true. But Ghana knew it wasn't.

His mind had been wandering as he sat, drifting back to the past. To his family, to those lost long ago…friends, his parents. He thought about his wife, the brilliant marriage that had launched his career, the foundation upon which he had built his realm. The great General Ghana, who would likely as not have spent his life shucking cane in the sugar fields had he not married a Warlord's daughter.

Sinase. She'd been so beautiful…with dozens of courtiers seeking her hand. Most of her suitors had far more to offer than Bako Ghana…wealth, lands, rank. But Sinase had been taken with the brash young warrior, and her words had softened her father's will. He'd resisted the marriage at first, but in the end Sinase wore him down…and she and Bako were married. Thus, a soldier with no coin, no lands, became the heir to a Warlord.

Old Rajdan would have been proud to see how the lands he left me have grown, how his old army was now twentyfold its size at his death.

Ghana sighed softly.

I wonder if he would have approved as well of his daughters life, of his heir's performance as a husband and not a general.

Ghana could see Sinase's image in front of him, still beautiful after so many years…as least when he'd last seen her.

When I last saw her. Two years ago? Almost three?

He had married her for gain, to sate his ambition. To claim a beautiful and noble bride, another brick in the wall of power and grandeur he built around him. But he'd come to love her too, after his own fashion and now, sitting in his headquarters, he truly realized what she meant to him. He thought grimly of what would become of her and his children if Carteria succeeded in destroying Lucerne…and then him as well. If the greatest—and most coldly savage—Warlord on the planet marched across the Northern Continent, destroying all in his path.

Sinase will die. My sons will die. And none of them easily.

He felt a wave of sadness, of fear. And then something else. Resolve.

No, I will not allow this to happen.

He knew what he had to do. He felt a pit in his stomach, heard the beat of his heart pounding in his ears. Fear, uncertainty. This would be his greatest test…and he steeled himself to meet it.

He sighed softly. He couldn't do what he had to alone. He would need help.

He thought for a moment, wishing he knew where Jinn Barkus was…and wondering who he could trust with a mission this important. Finally, he turned and leaned over his com unit, punching in a direct access code.

"Jangus, I need to see you in my quarters. Now."

* * *

Massen Roan walked silently, the strange Carterian following right behind. Lucerne's forces were in wholesale retreat all across the line…and the word had come from Eleher. The battle was as good as won. It was time to deal with Ghana.

Roan had been dreading this moment. He'd taken the Carterian coin, sold his allegiance, his pride…but he'd never really considered the true consequences of his actions. He'd agreed to help a stronger power bring the army more victories…and to gain his own advancement in that new order. But he'd never imagined selling the lives of his comrades. Of his friends. Of the general.

It had been Jinn Barkus' dead eyes staring back at him that had shaken his resolve, made him realize what a fool he'd been. But it was too late…there was no escape for him. He had to see the whole thing through, whatever that meant.

And now he was leading a killer to Bako Ghana, the man to whom he'd sworn allegiance so many years before. Eleher had maintained that Zoln Darvon would merely escort Ghana to a plush exile, but Roan couldn't fool himself into believing that. Not anymore.

The two men walked into the portable shelter that housed Ghana's battlefield command post. Roan stared down at the officer at the front station. "I need to see the general at once, Captain," he said, trying to sound business-as-usual despite the fact that he felt as if he might vomit at any moment.

"I'm sorry, sir. General Ghana said he is not to be disturbed under any circumstances."

Roan turned back toward Darvon. "Perhaps we should come back…"

His words were clipped off as Darvon leapt forward, jumping behind the desk, and wrapping his arms around the officer's neck, twisting hard in one quick motion.

Roan stared in shocked, cringing at the sickening sound of the aide's neck snapping.

"Stay here. I will handle this." Darvon's voice was cold, brutal. Roan froze.

This is what you signed up for…this is the cost of your treachery…

He watched as Darvon pulled a pistol from under his jacket and moved toward the door, shoving it open and stepping inside.

Roan retched, feeling the burn on the back of his throat, the foul taste of bile rising up in his throat…

* * *

"We've got to find a strong position, someplace we can hold while we figure out exactly what we're facing." Augustin Lucerne had never known defeat in battle. Until now. His army was reeling from an enemy that outmatched it in ordnance, one that had struck his own victorious but exhausted troops in the flank with thousands of fresh soldiers.

Blackhawk stood behind Lucerne, looking at the map on the table. He'd burst through the door a few moments earlier, his fatigues soaked through with sweat, his long brown hair a stringy, dripping mess. He'd somehow managed to elude his pursuers and make it back.

"They hit us just in the right place…and their timing was perfect." Blackhawk took a step forward, turning toward Lucerne.

"And those are Mark VI particle accelerators…one generation behind currently-deployed front line imperial support weapons. They pack a hell of a punch, General. You're going to need a very strong ridgeline if you want effective cover. Those guns will obliterate most of the little rocky spurs that snake their way across this desert."

Lucerne's eyes fixed on Blackhawk's. "You seem to be more familiar with this ordnance than any of my people." Blackhawk knew Lucerne had questions about his knowledge, about how the visitor knew so much about imperial weaponry. But the general didn't ask, he respected Blackhawk's privacy. "We need to come up with our best counter," he said, "and we need to do it now." A pause. "Can you offer any advice?"

Blackhawk's eyes flashed back to the map, though he'd already memorized the terrain. There was a ridgeline that looked like a promising position, but it was at least two day's march to the rear, and he just wasn't sure Lucerne's people could get there before the enemy caught up with them…and cut them to ribbons in the open ground.

"Make for here." Blackhawk pointed to the ridge.

"What about the fortress?" Lucerne looked down at the small star representing the castle he'd procured as his main headquarters.

"Abandon it." Blackhawk knew his advice would be difficult for Lucerne to follow. But he also knew what the general was facing. "Those Mark VIs will tear the fortress to rubble in half a day, General. And there's no solid cover near there…" Blackhawk almost stopped, but then he continued, "You can't let yourself get caught in the open. Your army will be wiped out before it can get to another position it can hold."

Lucerne was still staring at the map, but his head began moving slowly, nodding. Finally, he said, "You're right, Blackhawk. We'll make for the ridge." He turned toward the small cluster of aides who had been watching the exchange. "All units are to retreat to this location." He pointed down at the map. "Forced march, no stopping. And send orders to the fortress…the garrison is to abandon it immediately and link up with the main army."

He took a deep breath. "We need to get there in thirty hours, to concentrate all our forces on that ridge." He glanced at Black-hawk and then back to the map, muttering to himself, "Or we'll never get there at all…"

* * *

"It is time Bako Ghana."

Ghana looked up from his desk toward the man who had just walked into his office. He was dark, clad in a deep charcoal gray, in sharp contrast to the light desert gear soldiers typically wore in the Badlands. And he held a pistol, calmly, expertly, as thought it was part of his hand. Ghana knew immediately. An assassin.

It wasn't his own death he feared, at least not mostly. He'd known Carteria would send his killers, but he'd hoped to have more time. Time to complete his plan. But he was too late. He felt a wave of despair, of hopelessness. All was lost. The army would fall to Carteria…his lands too. And Sinase…his sons…

He sat opposite from Jangus Sand. He could see his officer's eyes, glancing off to the side, to the hook on the wall where he'd hung his own weapon. Ghana knew Sand was considering a leap for his pistol…but he also knew the officer didn't have a chance.

Ghana could see the assassin's weapon, pointed right at him. There would be no ceremony with this man. Bako Ghana knew his life was over. He swallowed hard, painfully, struggling to maintain his calm, to die with dignity as least. With defiance.

Then he heard the shot, a single crack, loud, echoing through the room. There was blood on his desk…but he was still sitting there, unharmed. Then he heard the crash, looked forward as the assassin fell to the ground. Massen Roan was standing in the doorway, his own pistol in his hand.

Roan's face was a mask of shock of fear. He dropped the pistol and walked into the room, falling to his knees, tears streaming down his face. "I am so sorry, my General," he said miserably. "I was weak, driven by greed, by ambition. I allowed

myself to be fooled, to believe you would be retired, not murdered." He paused, sucking in a deep breath through the tears.
"Jinn Barkus...he is dead. We killed him." He fell to the floor in
a broken heap, sobbing piteously.

Ghana stood up, motioning for Sand to stand back. The
security chief had leapt up the instant Roan had fired, and he
was standing against the wall, his own pistol now in his hand
and aimed at the sobbing man on the floor. Ghana could see the
scowl of anger on Sand's face, and he knew the newly-promoted
major was ready to put a bullet in Roan's head, despite the fact
that the treacherous officer had just saved their lives.

Ghana felt a confusing wave of emotions. Anger at the
betrayal, of course. Gratitude that Roan had repented and saved
his life. Distrust for a man who had turned traitor...and respect
for the risk Roan had taken to return to his old allegiance. But
mostly...the realization that he needed Roan, that his plan would
require him to rely on this man.

"Jangus, no." His voice was calm, so much so that it surprised even him. "We have much to do if we are going to salvage
the situation. Carteria's men are all around this headquarters. If I
try to leave...if they find out their assassin is dead, we are lost."

"But how are we going to get you out of here, General?"
Sand moved toward the desk as he spoke. His voice was shaky,
filled with concern.

"We're not, Jangus. I'm not going anywhere. But you are."
He looked over at Roan. "And you are as well, Massen...if you
are serious about aiding me...the army."

"Yes, General, what can I do?" Roan sounded nervous,
but Ghana took that as a good sign, evidence of sincerity.
"Anything."

He'd be calmer if he was just planning to bolt...

"Jangus, Jinn Barkus was carrying a communique from me
to General Lucerne, a proposal for peace, an attempt to prevent
battle." He paused. "It's too late for that now...and we now
know Jinn didn't make it. But if you're willing to carry it, I'd like
to try again with a new message. I have an idea how to end this,
how to save the army." He paused. "But it will be dangerous..."

"Yes, General. I will carry your message." Sand took another step forward. "I will leave as soon as it is ready."

"I will record it now, Jangus. The sooner you go the better." He turned toward Roan. "And Massen, I have an even more difficult and dangerous task for you, one I believe will be made possible by your former participation in the cabal against me." Another pause. "If you are willing to do this for me. Your life will be at great risk."

Ghana stared at the repentant traitor. It was troubling, deeply unnerving, to entrust the future of the army, the survival of his family...everything...to a man who had conspired against him. But he had no choice...and he knew Roan didn't either. He'd killed the Carterian assassin. There was no going back for him.

"I will prepare an address to the army, Massen. And when it is ready you will take it to the comm tent...and you will transmit it over the main channel."

Roan shifted nervously. "What message?"

"That is not your concern. You will go...and come back in one hour. The data crystal will be waiting here for you. Just take it and see that it is transmitted." He paused. "I know this is dangerous, Massen, but I am counting on you. You are the only hope of stopping Carteria from gaining control of the army and the Badlands...indeed, of the entire Northern Continent. I know you faltered before, you made an ill-fated decision. But if you do this, you will earn forgiveness, from me...and from every soldier in the army. From every resident of the Northern Continent."

Ghana could feel the tension, the fear. If Roan didn't come through, it was all over. His lands, his family...all gone. He had a hundred men he would have trusted more than the treacherous officer standing in front of him...but none who could get to the communications tent with Carteria's men watching. None save Roan.

The officer stood, frozen, and for a moment his expression was uncertain. But then his features hardened, and Ghana could see the decisiveness taking hold. "Yes, sir," Roan said, "I will do it."

Chapter Twenty-Six

The Ataphor Basin
"The Badlands"
Northern Celtiboria

The "Battle of Ataphor" – Third Phase: The Retreat

"Keep up your fire…and stay the hell down." Blackhawk
was on the sand himself, staring out at the approaching enemy
troops. They were good, well-trained, though no more, he
guessed, than Lucerne's. Less, actually…or at least lacking the
same elan. They were arrogant, certainly, but that wasn't the
same thing. But there was no question they were better equipped,
an amount of money lavished on their weapons and support
gear that Lucerne's footsore legions could only dream about.
And that had been the difference in the battle. Victory had been
within the general's grasp, at least when only Ghana's legions
had stood before him, but it had been ripped away by Carteria's
magnificently equipped expeditionary force.

"We can't get a good line of fire from here…Major." The
lieutenant's voice was stilted, uncomfortable, the resentment in
his voice clear as he addressed Blackhawk by his new rank.

Advancement in Lucerne's army was something soldiers
earned. There was no patronage, no nepotism…only success
in battle mattered. Courage, attention to duty. Yet Lucerne had

inexplicably—at least from the perspective of his officers and men—bestowed a major's commission on his newest ally. The act had taken Blackhawk by surprise as well, and he'd almost refused. But then he'd realized it was an accommodation, not a long term commitment. If Blackhawk was going to help the Warlord extricate himself from this mess, he'd need some level of authority.

"Neither can they, Lieutenant...and their weapons are a bigger threat than yours." Blackhawk had volunteered to lead the rearguard, to buy whatever time he could for the rest of the army to get away. It was dangerous duty, but he knew if Lucerne's people were going to have any chance, they needed his experience directing the holding force. He knew the enemy weapons, better than Carteria's men knew their own ordnance, he suspected. And he understood just what they could do to a disordered, retreating army.

Blackhawk had tried to think of a way to fight against the enemy's imperial weapons. If they'd been in the mountains, the jungle, anywhere but here, maybe. But the desert was too wide open. Save for a few rocky ridgelines, it was a perfect killing ground, a nightmare for a broken, fleeing army. He'd only come up with one idea. The imperial particle accelerators were powered by small nuclear fuel rods...and the reloads were breathtakingly expensive. Even Carteria, with all his wealth, could only afford a limited number of cartridges. And Blackhawk was willing to bet he'd only committed a limited number to his Northern Continent expeditionary force.

"I want the squad assault guns set up and firing, Captain. Now!" Blackhawk intended to buy time for Lucerne's battalions to retreat...but he had another thought, one that was purely a gut play. If he could make the enemy burn through their imperial ordnance, he could blunt the enemy attack, possibly even allow Lucerne to reorganize his troops and counterattack.

It was dicey business, guessing how many reloads the enemy had. But Blackhawk tended to follow his hunches...and the four hundred soldiers Lucerne had placed under him were about to get a lesson in how it felt to be commanded by a true madman, one far colder and more willing to spend their lives for victory than Augustin Lucerne. And there was no question in Blackhawk's mind…his force was a target, one he would use to draw as much enemy fire as possible.

* * *

Ghana was alone at his desk. Roan and Sand had hidden the assassin's body in a supply room before they'd both gone. Sand had slipped away with the message for Lucerne and Ghana's plea to move as quickly as possible. And Roan had gone with instructions to come back in an hour. Ghana figured he had at least that long before anyone came looking for Zoln Darvon…and the army was committed, its orders clear, to pursue Lucerne's retreating forces.

He'd only needed a few minutes to record his address to the army, but he'd given himself the whole hour. It was a selfish decision, but he'd wanted time to think, to remember. To create another message, a private one. To Sinase, some things he'd wished he'd said long before. And a few words to his children. He could only hope his plan was successful, that his messages were delivered. That Lucerne was victorious and heeded his plea to spare his family.

He'd watched the recording he had made, the address to his troops, and then he placed the recorder on the desk, right where he'd told Roan to find it. He wondered again how he'd ever gotten so desperate as to trust a traitor with something so important…with the survival of his army, his family, even the Northern Continent itself. But something inside told him Roan would do what he'd asked.

He glanced down at the desk again, scooping up the image of Sinase he'd set down earlier. It was an older photo, taken a few months after the birth of their first child. It had been a relatively peaceful period in his career, one that had seen him home for a far longer time than usual. As he looked back now, he realized it had been the happiest he'd ever been, indeed, perhaps the only time he had been truly happy. He'd felt the elation of victory many times, but now it all seemed pointless, empty. He had reached the end of that road, and now all he felt was a longing for those simpler days, to walk along the shoreline, to hold his wife's hand as they watched the waves. He closed his eyes, trying to remember the jasmine scent of her, the sound of her voice in the still of the night, but it had been long, and the freshness of his memories had faded.

"I am sorry, my love, that ours wasn't a different life. I am sorry, my children that you grew up without me there, that mine was a passing presence in your lives. Will you mourn me? Truly?

His eyes glanced at the chronometer. Five minutes left. It was time.

He reached down, opening the desk drawer, pulling out a dark object. A pistol.

He set it down softly, putting his hand on the switch to activate the recorder.

"My beloved soldiers, I have told you what you must do, and I beseech you to carry out these orders...my last orders." He paused, looking into the camera. "As I tape this, I am a virtual captive in my camp, surrounded by Carteria's soldiers. I have already survived one assassination attempt...and it will not be long until another is made. Or worse, until I am taken captive, used in some way to control your actions. I would not live that way, a prisoner, watching my soldiers yield to slavery in an effort to save me."

He took a deep breath, his hand moving slowly across the desk. "So, my soldiers, know by my actions now that I am with you, as I always will be. Go now, all of you. Fall upon Carteria's troops, attack them everywhere you can. Destroy the invader, drive them back into the sea. Do not fight General Lucerne and his soldiers. Stand together with them against the Carterians... and then I beg you all, swear yourselves to him, to his service. For though we were enemies, I know that Augustin Lucerne is a man of honor, and I trust that he will care for you all...as I can no longer do."

He picked up the pistol and turned it toward his head. "Farewell, my brave warriors...and serve me one last time, follow my orders now and free yourselves."

He took one last deep breath, savoring the air, the feeling of his lungs filling. He pressed the gun to his temple, steeling himself, putting all that remained of his courage into this last act. Then his finger tightened...and it was over.

Bako Ghana was dead.

* * *

Roan walked across the sandy dirt track that formed the main street of the camp. The headquarters was a small group of shelters, perhaps twenty prefab buildings dropped in an almost haphazard layout. He stared straight ahead, trying to look as natural as possible as he walked back to Ghana's office, though inside he was barely holding it together.

He'd stayed away one hour after he'd left, and now he had returned, precisely on time. He was on his way to pick up the message the general had asked him to broadcast. He walked into the outer office, his eyes panning around the empty room. He and Sand had hidden the body of the murdered aide along with the assassin's, and now the room was still empty, the station unmanned. Ghana had made it clear he didn't want to be disturbed, and it appeared he had indeed been left alone for an hour.

Roan walked up to the inner door and knocked twice before he opened it and let himself in. His eyes panned the room, and it took an instant before they focused on the desk...and the dark form slumped over there. He felt a wave of panic as he saw it was Ghana, focused on the blood still pooling on the surface, running down in rivulets along the side of the desk. His first thought was that Eleher had sent another assassin, one who'd succeeded this time. He spun around, checking the room in a near panic, his hand dropping to his belt, pulling out his own sidearm. But there was no one else there, no sign of any struggle.

He almost turned and ran, sickened at the thought of what had happened. But he looked down, noticed the pistol on the floor where it had fallen from Ghana's hand, and clarity came to him. The general had killed himself.

Roan was shocked, standing utterly still for a few seconds in stunned surprise. But then it began to make sense to him. He remembered Ghana's tone earlier, his words. He realized he had listened to the general, but failed to truly hear. Now he understood. This is what the Warlord had intended all along.

Of course, he thought...*it makes sense. Whatever happens, he was never getting out of here. The Carterians are everywhere. There was no escape for him. Only a chance for us...for the army.*

He felt a fresh wave of guilt. He'd succumbed to the advances of the Carterians because he'd allowed petty resentments to cloud his judgment, to wear down his loyalty to Ghana. He'd been upset at the recent defeats, and he'd blamed the general for the humiliation, for the friends he'd lost in the fighting. He'd convinced himself he'd been denied a promotion he felt he deserved...and the Carterians had known just how to come at him. Ghana had lost his edge, they said. He was a danger to the army. It was time to force his retirement, to send him to comfortable pasture. For the good of his comrades.

What a damned fool I was.

He stared at the body of his commander, the man he'd served for half his lifetime. He remembered the feelings he'd felt years before, when he was young and his loyalty was new, not worn down by hard service and defeat.

I am sorry, General...I will not fail you again.

Roan found himself invigorated, a feeling of urgency to see Ghana's last orders carried out. The guilt over his treachery had turned around, become a driving force now, filling him with determination. He had to do what he'd promised the general. He had to get Ghana's last message out, save the army from falling under Carteria's dominion.

He reached over to the desk, pulling the data crystal from the camera. He turned, his eyes dropping to his fingers, red with Ghana's blood that had splattered over the device. He walked over to the wall, wiping his hand, leaving a trail of red behind as he did.

His stomach was in turmoil, fear at the danger of what he must do, regret at Ghana's death, uncertainty over what would happen in the hours and days ahead. He took a deep, ragged breath, struggling to calm himself as he stepped into the outer office and then, a few second later into the waning light of late afternoon. He could hear the sounds of battle, fading now, distant. Lucerne's forces were in full retreat, and the Ghana's battered units that had been driven back earlier had rallied and begun to pursue. There were officers running about, the business of the camp in full swing.

General Ghana had left orders he was not to be disturbed, but Roan knew it was only a matter of time before someone entered his officer shelter...and discovered what had transpired, that Ghana was dead, along with his aide and one of Carteria's operatives. When that happened, the shit would hit the fan... and Carteria's people would clamp down on the camp, take full control and arrest—or kill, Roan didn't know which—the loyalist Ghanan officers and men.

He hurried his pace, moving steadily toward the comm shelter. There were two guards on duty outside, and an officer, Dal Fragus. The sentries were normal, but Roan knew Fragus was one of the conspirators, obviously there to keep an eye on the communications center. He felt a chill, a ripple of fear running down his spine.

Okay, keep cool. Fragus thinks you're one of Carteria's supporters. Just act like you have business in the com center.

"Dal," Roan said, nodding as he walked to the door.

"Massen." Fragus' eyes moved over him.

Roan felt himself freeze, but he fought to resist, to move smoothly through the door. He knew Fragus had no reason to suspect him, but it took all he had to keep himself from shaking uncontrollably.

"Are you okay, Massen? You don't look so good." Fragus had moved up right next to Roan, and he was whispering into his ear.

Roan stopped, his stomach twisted into a tight knot. He was busted.

"I know, Massen..."

Roan forced back the bile, clenched his fists as he fought to keep his stomach from emptying its contents.

"You know what, Dal?" He managed to get the words out, calmly...or at least something close to it. He stood in place, dreading the answer. He had a sudden urge to run, to flee for his life. But he kept enough control to realize there was no chance he'd get away. No, he had to see this through, try to allay any suspicions Fragus had.

"I know it is difficult," Fragus said, his voice even quieter, his lips right up against Roan's ear. "Killing Jinn Barkus couldn't have been easy...and I know you're beating yourself up over it."

Roan felt a massive wave of relief. Fragus didn't know why he was here...he was just sympathetic about the incident with Barkus.

"Yes," he said softly. "It is difficult...but we do what we must, don't we?" He paused. "Right now, I've got some business inside."

Fragus stepped back and nodded.

Roan returned the nod, and he walked through the door.

Almost there...

Chapter Twenty-Seven

The Ataphor Basin
"The Badlands"
Northern Celtiboria

The "Battle of Ataphor" – Last Phase: The Counterattack

"My soldiers, we have fought long together, we have marched until our feet were raw and blistered. We have celebrated victories and mourned lost comrades. But now our great campaign is at an end. It is to this place, this blasted desert, so valuable for its location, that I have led you, but alas, it is not I who will lead you out of here."

Blackhawk was on the ground behind a small rock outcropping, listening to the transmission. It was being broadcast wide, in the clear, pushed to every channel and frequency available to both sides.

The rearguard had fallen back steadily, moving from one meager bit of cover to the next...and suffering badly as it did. But it was also doing its job, forcing the enemy to expend large quantities of its enhanced ordnance. The rate of fire of the particle accelerators had fallen by more than half...conservation measures, Blackhawk guessed, as supplies began to dwindle. Soldiers were still dying, victims of the imperial weapons, but the ammunition expended for each kill had risen sharply. That was good news, at least after a fashion, but Blackhawk was conflicted, torn between his cold analysis and the newer feelings, the regrets for men killed following his orders.

"I have made a terrible mistake, my soldiers, placed you all in grave peril. For I enlisted aid in our struggle, but instead of gaining an ally, I have sold our futures. Sold your futures. And that I cannot allow to stand."

Blackhawk glanced over the small rocky spur toward the enemy lines. The fire was still coming, and even as he lay there, several arcs of blue light slammed into his positions, along with a volley of more conventional ordnance. His soldiers were pressed up against the cover, holding their fire. He'd ordered them to stand firm…but to fire only when the enemy advanced. Between charges, they were to hunker down, do all they could to stay in cover.

"I am a prisoner as I tape this message, in all but name. This transmission is possible only through the courage of one of our own, who has risked his life to bring it to you."

Blackhawk heard the word 'prisoner,' and he understood. Carteria had taken control of Ghana's army. Perhaps not openly, but effectively nevertheless. And this was Ghana's attempt to strike back, to…

Suddenly Blackhawk knew what Ghana was going to do. Had already done.

"I cannot escape, my soldiers, and I will not allow myself to be used as a tool…or to be murdered by an assassin's hand, as has already been attempted once. So, listen to me now, and obey this, my final order."

For a moment, Blackhawk felt as if he'd been with Ghana when the general had spoken those words. Ghana had never been anything to him, save perhaps an enemy. Not even, more the enemy of his new friend, Lucerne. But now he understood, he felt the emotion driving the address, the raw defiance. Ghana would die before he would yield…and Blackhawk couldn't help but feel a wave of respect for the cornered Warlord.

"I have sent a communique to General Lucerne, an offer of peace…and more than that, a request to him that he take all my positions and ranks, my lands and titles, my commands and my responsibilities. I beseech all of you, my beloved soldiers, to swear faith to General Lucerne, to serve him as you have served me. Though he has ever been my enemy, he is an honorable man, and one I know I can trust to look after all of you."

Blackhawk could see what was happening. He hoped Lucerne was listening, that the general understood the opportunity he was being offered. The retreat had to stop, now. It was time to destroy Carteria's forces. Losses would be high, very high. But the victory was there, waiting to be plucked. If Lucerne had the stomach to spill the rivers of blood it would take to win.

"Attack, my soldiers. Now. Fall upon Carteria's forces. Fight them, take them by surprise…attack in the flank, the rear. Fight, my brave warriors…fight as you have never fought before. And trust that General Lucerne and his men will join you. Together you will save the Northern Continent. You will drive the invaders into the sea."

There was a long pause, the transmission silent. Blackhawk knew Carteria's forces would try and block the signal, but he also suspected they had been caught by surprise…and that had given time for Ghana's words to reach his entire army, and Lucerne's as well.

"Goodbye, my soldiers. Do as I command, win the future for yourselves. And now, I will do all that I can, the only action left to me to ensure I can never be made a tool to use against you." Another pause. "I love you all, my brave warriors."

Blackhawk knew what was about to happen, but he still found himself startled at the blast. Bako Ghana was dead.

He also knew how Ghana's soldiers would react. Ghana hadn't been a match for Lucerne, but the man had been no fool. His death would inspire his men, anger them. They would fall on the Carterians with unbridled fury…and if Lucerne's forces stopped their retreat, returned to the fight…the invaders would be caught between two forces. Even their enhanced weaponry wouldn't save them.

Blackhawk could feel something growing inside him, a calling, the drive of a feral beast. He pulled the small com unit from his belt. "Major Blackhawk...calling General Lucerne." His voice was deep, thick with focused rage.

"Yes, Major." Lucerne's voice lacked the raw bloodthirstiness of Blackhawk's, but the determination in it was unmistakable. "I saw the transmission. And I received General Ghana's personal message. I've issued orders to halt the retreat. The army will attack."

Blackhawk felt old feelings, drives he'd suppressed for the past few years, rushing over him like a tidal wave. They came from a dark place inside him, cold, emotionless. The mantra that had driven him for so long. Victory. At all costs.

At all costs. He turned and looked over the survivors of the rearguard. He'd been pulling back steadily, doing his best to minimize losses, to force the enemy to expend ordnance, trading space to save casualties. But now that would stop. These few hundred men would stand here, fix the enemy army in this place. There would be no further retreat. None. It would be costly, indeed few would likely survive. But those few would hold this patch of ground...and the army would win the victory. Carteria's forces would be defeated. And that was all that mattered.

Was it all that mattered? Should it be? The answer was clear...at least in Blackhawk's mind. Yes...it was all that mattered. For the alternative to victory was defeat.

The jumble of emotions he'd experienced recently was pushed aside, Cass, her people, his admiration for Lucerne's soldiers. The thoughts, the emotions were still there, but they were driven deep, subsumed by the inner warrior. This was war, and he had a command, a job to do. There was nothing else now for him, nothing save victory.

A part of him struggled against the coldness, but the wave of battle had taken him, and all else was subordinated to it. The drifter, the lone wanderer he'd become, the man awakening, finding purpose in aiding Lucerne and affection with Cass... that man was gone, the cold blooded warrior back in his place.

He was what he had been, what he'd run so far to escape.

"Open that door, now." The Carterian officer's voice was harsh, angry. Roan stared at the locked door, his hand shaking, fingers tightly gripped around his pistol. He'd done what he'd promised, transmitted the message to the armies. He'd taken the Carterians by surprise, and he was almost certain he'd gotten the whole thing out before they'd managed to jam his signal. But now he was trapped, cut off.

His eyes scanned the room, glancing down to the body lying half under the main station. He'd chased the two other crew members out of the hut, locking the door behind them. But he hadn't taken any chances with the Carterian he'd found in the room.

He was scared. He had agreed to transmit Ghana's message because he'd been ashamed at his treachery…to save the comrades he'd almost helped to sell into servitude under Carteria. Only now that he'd completed his mission did he realize the true cost he would pay. Ghana had known, of course. Had he found it amusing, ironic…to send his traitorous officer to almost certain death even as he struck his final blow against Carteria?

Would the desperate effort even succeed? Would the army respond to the words of their dead general? Would the scattered units, the officers in command of battalions and regiments come together, join with their recent enemies to fight the Carterians?

Or have I come here…will I die here…in vain?

Roan sucked in a deep breath, struggling to control the shivering. He wanted to live. He'd been a soldier, an officer for many years, but he'd served mostly in staff positions. He'd been on the battle lines before, had a few close calls. But now a cold truth was becoming clear to him. He was about to die.

Maybe I can surrender…perhaps they will keep me alive. No…I have threatened their entire plan, killed one of their men. I took their coin and then betrayed them, even as I had betrayed General Ghana in joining them.

He turned and looked around the small shelter, though he knew it was hopeless. There was only a single entrance, and even now, those who would be his killers were banging against that door, demanding entrance.

He took a step back…then another. He felt wetness on his

eyes, tears streaming down his cheeks. He was terrified. He didn't want to die. The thought that he had only moments—perhaps even seconds—to live seemed unreal, and he began shivering uncontrollably.

"No!" he shouted, feeling as if he was about to go mad. He had to escape, somehow. He had to open the door…if he waited until they blasted the thing open they would kill him for sure. Maybe if he surrendered, begged for mercy…

No…your choices have brought you here. You must face this. General Ghana stood firm…he sacrificed himself. For the army. For his family and his lands. The man you were prepared to betray for base coin. Now you must decide…will you die a coward and a traitor? Or weapon in hand, true to your commander and your comrades?

He heard the sound against the door, the soldiers outside, battering against it. The entrance to the communications center was heavily armored, but he knew that wouldn't keep his killers out for long. He stepped back again, bumping into the consoles along the wall. Nowhere left to go. Nothing to do. Save wait.

He heard the sounds of assault rifles firing into the thick hypersteel door. Then silence, the soldiers outside stepping back. He took a deep breath, prepared himself.

You have lived poorly, made bad choices. If you do one thing now… die well.

There was a massive blast, the door blown from its place, a twisted heap of metal, slamming into the comm station next to him. He flinched, fell back onto the equipment behind him, even as soldiers poured in through the thick smoke.

He began panicking, losing control, but then he felt something. A strange calm, focus. He reached out his arm, firing the pistol. One of the troopers went down. Then he fired again, another body falling, this one almost at his feet.

He could hear the return fire, automatic weapons. His body was thrown back, hard into the wall. But he felt nothing, no pain. Only a strange floating sensation. And then darkness.

"Advance!" Rafaelus DeMark lurched forward, climbing out of the crater and advancing across the field. The enemy fire was heavy, but it was beginning to slacken as the Carterians pulled back, blasted by the repeated sorties conducted by the remnants of the now-cooperating air forces of the two armies.

DeMark had thirty-two hundred men at his back, veterans all. They had seen the damage the Carterians had inflicted on their comrades, the brutal toll the enemy's imperial weapons had claimed…and they were here as avenging angels, come to destroy those who had killed so many of their friends. They were oblivious to their own losses, and their charismatic leader urged them on, leading by example, from the first rank.

DeMark had expected the enemy to hold up his advance for hours, perhaps days, to defend the approaches to the battle now raging between Ghana's forces and the main Carterian army. But Blackhawk had somehow held the enemy back, penning them against the edge of the original battlefield, thwarting their pursuit of Lucerne's retreating soldiers. His handful of troops had nailed themselves to their ridge, and they had driven back charge after charge. By the time it was over, barely one man in five was standing. But they were still on that ridge. And DeMark's troops and the rest of Lucerne's army were able to forcemarch back to the field unhindered, arriving in a matter of hours instead of after days of vicious combat.

DeMark was a veteran warrior, one of Lucerne's most trusted commanders. He'd fought in his share of bloody battles, but he'd never seen anything like Blackhawk's grim determination…and the perseverance he'd extracted from the men under his command.

Eighty percent casualties. And they are still there, fighting…

He wondered if he could have done the same thing, if he could have ordered his soldiers to stand so long in a maelstrom, watching most of them die, without yielding, pulling back. He admired the tenacity of his new ally…and he felt disapproval too. He was a warrior, certainly, but now he knew he had witnessed the ultimate demonstration of cold blooded determination. Of butchery, unrestrained by human weakness, compassion. The singleminded pursuit of victory, unimpeded by any other considerations.

Those men were your comrades…and they are dead now.

But their sacrifice made this attack possible. If they'd faltered, we might have been held back for a day, even two. What losses would we have suffered then? And if Ghana's forces might have been defeated before we got to the fight…

DeMark pushed the conflicting thoughts aside. This wasn't time for philosophy, nor for facing the profoundly confusing morality of war. He would take a lesson now from Blackhawk. It was time to fight. Time to win the victory. To forget everything else.

He jumped down, into another crater, staring out at the battlefield in front of him. The Carterians were on the defensive, but they weren't defeated, not yet. The fire from the imperial weapons had slacked off, barely half what it had been earlier. But he could still see the deadly arcs of light ripping across the field, killing his men, blasting vehicles to scrap. The particle accelerators had a longer range than his own autocannons, and that meant his men had to push forward and endure all the enemy could throw at them before they were able to respond. But now his units were coming into their own range…and he had two companies moving around the enemy flank, seizing a section of high ground where they could take the Carterians in enfilade.

His eyes dropped to his scanner, noting the mounting losses as the casualty reports continued to come in. He tried to ignore it, to focus on the objective…and not on the thousands of men who would die—who were dying even now. He was conflicted, and he knew his thoughts were contradictory. He wanted to disapprove of Blackhawk, to be shocked at the coldness the stranger displayed in combat, his indifference to the suffering of his soldiers. But he knew there was more to it than that. They weren't fighting now for coin, even for strategic gain. This was a battle for the Northern Continent itself, to keep their homes free from Carteria's subjugation. It was a sacred goal, one worth the loss of every soldier in either army.

He flipped at his com unit, calling up the commanders of the flanking companies. "Gwan, Tyllen…are you both in position?"

A second or two passed, then he got the answers, one right after the other. They were ready.

"Open fire." He flipped the com unit to the wide channel. "All units…fire."

The flat area between the armies erupted, first DeMark's autocannons opening up, a hundred heavy weapons firing almost as one. Then the Carterians responding, their own standard guns joining in with the imperial particle accelerators.

The Carterians had a decent position, along a ridge with some natural cover. DeMark's people would have been more in the open, save for the fact that the field itself had been the scene of fierce fighting the day before. There were craters, great rents torn into the ground, and his veterans used them all to great effect, sheltering from the enemy fire, leapfrogging forward from position to position.

The battle raged on, and DeMark's forces bled strength, hundreds killed as they moved forward, and more wounded, some carried back by the overworked corps of medics, but most left to live—or die—by themselves, alone on the field, hurt, bleeding, afraid. It was war, stripped of the glory, the pomp and ceremony…only the raw suffering and the determination it took to prevail.

"Keep moving," he growled into the com, wondering as he did how different he was from Blackhawk, from the coldness he'd been so ready to condemn a few moments earlier. He hurt for every man he lost…but he knew his loyalty was to Lucerne. And the general needed his people to break through here. No matter what it cost.

He lunged up out of the crater, crouched low, keeping the great mounds of displaced sand between him and the enemy positions as he moved forward.

Forward…to the enemy. To victory.

"General DeMark reports the enemy is in full retreat. He is pursuing."

"Very well." Lucerne nodded. "Order the 8th and the 11th forward to reinforce the general." Lucerne didn't have much left in reserve after releasing those two regiments, but he had an idea of the losses DeMark had suffered driving so deeply into the enemy positions. He knew he had to keep up the pressure, and DeMark's dwindling force was the tip of the spear. The Carterians were hurt, but they were still dangerous…and Lucerne had no intention of allowing them to regroup, of throwing away the victory his soldiers had bought with their blood.

"We're getting communications from General Ghana's units as well. They are also reporting the Carterians are fleeing." The aide turned toward Lucerne. "And they are offering their allegiance, sir, just as General Ghana requested."

Lucerne sighed softly, turning and walking back to his chair, sitting down hard. He was tired, exhausted. The past few days had been like nothing he'd ever experienced…an all-out attack, followed by victory then defeat. Then the death of his former enemy…and the army he'd fought against for over a year joining his forces, striking the Carterian invaders.

"Advise all of General Ghana's units that we welcome them as friends and allies." Lucerne had been stunned when he'd first received Ghana's message. His rival had made him his official heir, bade him take control of his soldiers, his lands. The general had asked almost nothing…just that Lucerne take care of his family and his soldiers, that he look after the people in the areas Ghana had ruled.

Lucerne had expected a trick at first, but then Ghana's broadcast to his troops had come in over the com. He had listened in stunned amazement, just like everyone else in his headquarters. Ghana had been his enemy, but there had been no hatred there. He'd always considered the rival Warlord to be an honorable foe, at least to an extent. But Ghana's final act had impressed him…and he knew he would always remember the general with respect and honor. And he would grant his rival's final requests.

Indeed, his foe had given him a great opportunity. Ghana

had ruled over lands almost twice as large as he had. Lucerne knew Ghana's bequest would triple his holdings in an instant… and give him full control over the Badlands trade routes. It was a victory beyond anything he'd dared to imagine when he'd first come to the Badlands.

Assuming he could extricate his people—old and new. There was still fighting to do, Carterian refugees to pursue, defeat. And the battle had been a cataclysm. It had drained supplies at a far faster rate than he'd expected. All the careful logistical preparations during the truce had proven grossly inadequate. His troops were low on supplies, on ammunition. The field hospitals were overflowing, running out of medicine. It would take everything he had to secure his position, to stabilize the situation…both in the Badlands, and in Ghana's home territories.

"We are receiving acknowledgements from General Ghana's commanders, sir. They are accepting your offers of amnesty, of service."

Lucerne just nodded. For all the gains the victory promised, he was uncomfortable. Ghana had hired mercenaries, impressed troops from areas he'd controlled tenuously. Lucerne's soldiers were almost all from his home region, loyal veterans who had volunteered to follow him. He knew Ghana had many good troops, men he would welcome under his banner. But he was also aware there were thousands who had no place in his army.

He'd almost refused the entreaties of the officers offering their services, tried to put off the matter until he had time to set up some system of review to pick and choose the troops he wanted. But he quickly realized that wasn't possible. He needed Ghana's men now, allied with his own…or Carteria's forces might rally and snatch back the victory.

He would handle things differently, less directly than he would have preferred. He would weed out the soldiers he didn't want over time. He would retire them, offer pensions when he could afford them, grant farms…or less important jobs in the civil governments in his lands. He would spread them around, dilute any potential for organized resistance to his rule from those who would offer false oaths.

He would make it work, gradually, subtly, without making it a rallying cry for the former Ghanan forces to resist him.

"General Lucerne...there is someone here requesting to see you, sir." The officer's voice pulled Lucerne from his thoughts. The aide's tone sounded doubtful, as if Lucerne would order the petitioner sent away. Or, just as likely, shot.

"Who is it, Lieutenant?" Lucerne had been hunched over a folding table holding a large map, but now he stood up and turned around.

"A woman, sir. She claims her name is Cassandra Cross, that she is the commander of the Grays."

"And she is here?" Lucerne was surprised. He hadn't struggled with the Grays the way Ghana had, but he found it hard to believe the pirate commander would have come to see him, alone, without at least some prior guarantee of her safety.

"Yes, General. Shall I have her arrested?"

"Certainly not, Lieutenant. If she is here, she is here on a parlay, whether such was formally declared or not...and we will respect that." He knew the Grays weren't a military unit, that the rules of war, to the extent that they were ever respected, did not apply. But Lucerne was a man of honor, and if the Grays commander was indeed in his headquarters, come of her own free will to see him, he would speak to her. He couldn't imagine she had anything to say he would find compelling, but he would listen to her at least. And then he would let her leave.

Chapter Twenty-Eight

General Lucerne's Field Headquarters
"The Badlands"
Northern Celtiboria

Blackhawk strode across the rutted and dusty road running through Lucerne's field headquarters. The general had moved his command post forward, onto the plateau originally occupied by Ghana's frontline forces. There had been heavy fighting all around the location, and while most of the bodies had been removed, the ground was still badly torn up and covered with shattered weapons and discarded bits of equipment.

Lucerne had called Blackhawk directly, asked him to return to headquarters immediately. Blackhawk noted the general had requested his presence, he didn't order it. He ran his fingers over the major's insignia, remembering that he'd accepted the temporary commission Lucerne had offered him, and that it gave the general every right to order him to return at once. The restraint, the cautious respect, was another sign of Lucerne's natural leadership, his perception into how to handle his subordinates and allies.

Blackhawk was unsettled, his normally controlled mind disordered, as if part of him was at war with another part. The battle had taken him fully, the old parts of him, those he had struggled so hard to suppress over the past few years, returning in full force. His four hundred men had accomplished miracles, held back enemy attacks that outnumbered them ten to one. Blackhawk had been everywhere along the line, urging the troops when they seemed to waver, joining in the fighting on the front line...even shooting two men who had tried to run, branding them deserters and swearing to the others they would meet the same fate if their courage failed.

Sixty-three.

Sixty-three of his four hundred men were still on their feet, all the others killed or seriously wounded. But those sixty-three had held the ridge until the end...until Rafaelus DeMark and his soldiers had arrived, and launched the counterattack that broke the Carterian line.

Blackhawk, the new part of him, longed to feel something, anything. But he didn't. Not regret at the losses, not elation at the victory. He had merely done what he'd had to do. What he'd been born—created—to do.

He wrestled with the thoughts, wondering if his flight to the Far Stars had been for naught, if his quest for a normal life, to live as a man with emotions, with a conscience, was a hopeless dream.

Am I nothing but an automaton, a machine built to kill?

He took a deep breath as he walked toward the shelter housing Lucerne's office. He wanted to believe there was more to him, that his quest was not in vain. But he was drowning now in doubts.

He opened the door and walked inside.

"Major Blackhawk," the aide said, "go right in. The General is waiting for you."

Blackhawk nodded and walked toward the door, stepping inside as it slid open.

"Ark, thank you for coming so quickly."

Blackhawk nodded, and it struck him again how well Lucerne seemed to understand him. The general's willingness to treat him as an ally and not a subordinate, despite the fact that he bore Lucerne's insignia, affected him deeply. He was not a man who followed others easily...indeed, at all.

"Congratulations, General. My understanding is that the Carterians are fleeing across the line." He paused for a second. "I suggest you not let up on them. If they are able to regroup..."

His words stopped suddenly as his eyes caught the figure sitting at a table on the other side of the room. The recognition was immediate...and he felt a wave of thoughts, emotions flooding into his troubled mind, throwing him into greater confusion, turmoil.

"Cass," he said, unable to keep the surprise from his voice. "What are you doing here?"

The Grays' commander stood up and walked across the room, hurrying her step as she got closer to Blackhawk. "Ark, I'm so happy you are okay. I was worried about you. The reports on the fighting in your sector..."

She walked right up and threw her arms around him. He hesitated for an instant, and then he returned the gesture, pulling her into a tight embrace.

"I'm glad you are okay too, Cass." He loosened his grip and pulled back a step, his eyes finding hers. "But, what are you doing here?" he repeated. There was an edge of concern in his voice, and his eyes darted over toward Lucerne. A Warlord's headquarters wasn't the safest place for the most wanted raider in the Badlands.

"Don't worry, Ark." Lucerne said. "Cassandra and I have had a long talk...and we've settled what differences we might have had."

Blackhawk looked over at Lucerne and then back to Cass. "You allied yourself with one of the Warlords?" He couldn't keep the surprise from his tone.

She nodded and smiled. "Leadership requires an open mind. I figured if you believed General Lucerne was an honorable man then I could give him a chance as well."

"The Galadan will be under my protection, Ark," Lucerne interjected. "Any who would march there, victimize its inhabitants, will find themselves at war with me as a consequence. The Warlords in that area are all local powers. I do not believe any of them would wish to pick a fight with me, especially not after I absorb Ghana's lands."

"But the region is still in ruins, dependent upon the proceeds of the raids. And you will now control the Badlands trade. How can the Gray's continue to support their people without being at odds with you?" Blackhawk couldn't see a solution to that paradox, and it made him uncomfortable. He wasn't used to being confused.

"The Grays will stop their raiding immediately, Ark. They will be given a choice, return and help rebuild the Galadan…or join my army."

"But how will the Galadan be rebuilt? From what Cass told me it will take a fortune, several million ducats at least. I know your resources are strained…and the people there have already lost everything."

"Cass has solved that problem as well, Ark. Or at least offered a possible solution." Lucerne smiled. "I should have known your taste in women would run to the capable as well as the beautiful."

Blackhawk was still uncertain, and he looked over at Cass.

"We will make one more raid, Ark," she said softly. "There is a convoy, and it is carrying something very special." She looked back over at Lucerne. "It is a grave threat to the general and his army, and for that reason alone, it is essential that it be stopped." She paused and glanced back at Blackhawk. "But it will also solve our problems with funding the reconstruction of the Galadan."

"What convoy is this?"

"Carteria, Ark. It is Carteria's convoy." Lucerne's voice was deeper, more serious than it had been. "Cassandra brought valuable intelligence with her…crucial information. Indeed, she may have saved the army."

Blackhawk glanced at Cass and then back to Lucerne, but he remained silent, listening.

"One of Cassandra's informants in the river cities sent word that all of the mercenary companies have been hired…*all of them*. With no other information, we could be sure that was Carteria. No Warlord on the Northern Continent could afford such a mobilization. But there is more. The convoy the Grays found contains silver, hard currency to pay the mercenaries…forty million ducats."

Blackhawk understood immediately, and he started to nod. "We will have to move quickly or the convoy…"

"Or the convoy will get through…and Carteria's beaten forces will be reinforced by more than one hundred thousand veteran mercenaries." Lucerne stared at Blackhawk, a deadpan expression on his face. "And then we will be defeated, driven from the Badlands and destroyed far from home." Lucerne's tone was deadly serious now.

"How strong is the convoy? It must be heavily protected."

"Hundreds of soldiers, Ark," Cass said. "I saw it myself. They are heavily armed, with a whole column of armored vehicles. It will take a thousand men to attack it…which is why I came here in the first place."

"Will you go, Ark?" Lucerne asked. "Will you go with Cass and Rafe DeMark and take this convoy for me while I pursue the remnants of Carteria's army?"

Blackhawk nodded. "Yes, Augustin, of course. But we will never catch it. If Cass came all the way here, they must be halfway to the river cities by now."

"That is why I need you. I would give Cass her thousand soldiers to take the convoy, or two thousand or three…but I cannot get them there. Not on the ground, not in time. And my airship squadrons are shot to pieces. Even with the surviving planes from Ghana's army, we can only move two hundred men by air. It will be several hours before the ships can return and reload… which means our attacking force will be outnumbered. We can't delay…every hour that passes, we risk the mercenary forces moving east, linking up with the convoy." He paused. "We must take that coin before the mercs get it, before Carteria is able to buy his hundred thousand men."

Blackhawk stood silently for a moment. He'd never shied away from a fight, and he wouldn't now. But there was something else. He remembered the feeling that had come over him in the battle on the ridge, the old drives pushing out from the dark places into which he'd confined them. Seeing Cass, feeling her embrace…it had brought him the rest of the way back from what the fight had awakened in him, pushing away the dark impulses once again. But now he had to go back into battle. He wasn't afraid, not of death. Part of him would even welcome his demise, welcome it as a release from the exhaustion, the pain.

It wasn't the outcome of the fight that troubled him either. He didn't doubt victory…outnumbered, outgunned…it didn't matter to Blackhawk. He was confident he would find a way to win. Whatever the cost. But it was just that cost that worried him. What would he do to secure victory? Drive Lucerne's soldiers to their deaths? See DeMark gunned down leading a desperate charge? And Cass? What would he do with Cass and her people? Would they become cannon fodder, a diversion to win his victory? Would he find himself standing on the field of battle, staring down at a bunch of dead farmers whose lives he had coldly expended to gain the victory?

"I will do it," he said, his voice grim. He knew there was no other option. He was exhausted, his body crusted with dried sweat and dirt from the field. His leg was mostly healed, but it still throbbed, and he was covered with cuts and scrapes, the wear and tear of a vicious fight. He'd been in the thick of the fighting for three straight days, without rest, with hardly a gulp of water and a bite for two of food. But there was no time to waste, none at all. "But we cannot waste time. We must go. Now."

Lucerne nodded, clearly feeling guilty about sending Blackhawk back out again so soon. "Thank you, Ark. The planes are ready to go…and Rafe DeMark is gathering the first two hundred men. They are the best of the best, Ark, my oldest veterans." He paused. "Take good care of them."

"We'll get the convoy, Augustin. Whatever it takes." Lucerne had done his duty, expressed concern for his men. But Blackhawk knew the general understood as well as he did…nothing was more important than taking that convoy before it reached the mercenaries. Whatever the cost.

He turned. "Cass, you don't have to go. You did enough binging us this news. Stay here. This is liable to get…" Blackhawk paused. "…ugly." Please stay…

"Don't you tell me to stay behind, Arkarin Blackhawk. General Lucerne has promised two million ducats from the convoy to rebuild the Galadan…and I have promised all the Grays can do to help…and nothing is keeping from this mission." Her voice was tinged with anger, but mostly it was determination Blackhawk heard in her words.

He sighed softly. He turned toward Lucerne, and for an instant he considered asking the General to keep her behind, making her safety a condition of his own involvement. But something stopped him. He was fond of Cass, and he wanted to protect her, to keep her out of the bloody fight he knew was coming. But she was right. He had no place keeping her from this struggle. The battle would save her people, both the Grays and the farmers back home. It was all she'd left the Galadan to achieve, and if it was successful, she would have saved her homeland. He had no right to try and keep her from this fight. However much he wanted to.

"Okay, Cass…but promise me you will be careful. These are probably good troops we'll be facing…this is going to be a tough fight."

"Don't worry about me, Ark."

He looked over at her and forced a smile. He'd left her once, when he'd come to find Lucerne, but now he wondered how he would do it again. He was still trying to understand his emotions, struggling to grasp how he felt…and how to combine those feelings with reason.

Arkarin Blackhawk was a thirty-four year old man, a veteran warrior, a genetically-enhanced killing machine. But he was newly born in many ways as well. He fought to manage the new feelings, the stimuli he hadn't had most of his life, not until he'd broken his conditioning. And as he pushed through it all, he was trying to understand one thing especially. He had strong feelings for Cassandra Cross…but did he love her? Did he even know what love was?

He looked at her and nodded, saying nothing. He hated the idea of letting her come, but he knew he couldn't stop her. She had a right to be there.

Chapter Twenty-Nine

Deep Southern Desert
"The Badlands"
Northern Celtiboria

Blackhawk jumped out of the airship's hatch, rifle in hand and twenty of General Lucerne's best veterans behind him. He felt his feet slam down on the sand, and he lurched forward immediately, running toward the line of rock outcroppings ahead. It wasn't much cover, but it was something…and it was the only thing but open desert for two days in either direction. He'd ordered the airships to circle for almost an hour until the convoy reached that location. That meant a delay before reinforcements would arrive, but Blackhawk wanted that cover. If his people could take out enough of the defenders from that vantage point, maybe he could even the odds a little.

"Let's move. To the rocks…grab some cover and then open fire." He was shouting back to his small group, but also yelling into his com unit, to the soldiers jumping from the other airships. He snapped his head to the left and right, confirming what he already knew…two hundred of Lucerne's crack veterans were on the ground. The battle for a fortune in coin, for the control of an army of mercenaries large enough to turn the tide in the fight for the Northern Continent, had begun.

He'd wanted to keep Cass close to him, imagining that he'd

be able to protect her somehow, keep her safe. He knew there hadn't been much truth to that hope. The battlefield was a dangerous place. But the urge had been strong anyway...and ultimately futile. She wasn't there...she was on the far side of the convoy, with one airship full of Lucerne's soldiers, linking up with the rest of the Grays. Her people had been shadowing the convoy since they'd discovered it, staying just outside the perimeter the enemy's scouts patrolled.

There hadn't been a doubt what Cass would do, that she would go and link up with her people, lead them into the fight. She hugged Blackhawk and gave him a passionate kiss...and then she walked away and boarded a different airship. Blackhawk had almost followed, gone with her, but he knew he had to be with the main attack. He would do more to protect her by ensuring the outnumbered force prevailed in the fight.

He ran up to a large boulder protruding from the sand and peered carefully around the edge. There was some fire...the convoy guards had heard the airships, and they'd deployed to face the attack. He watched them move, and he knew immediately.

Those are crack troops...

He pulled his rifle around and aimed it toward the convoy. They were too far out for reliable aimed fire, at least most of his troops were. Blackhawk stared down the barrel, targeting a man in an officer's uniform. Crack. His rifle spat and the soldier fell, clutching at a gruesome neck wound.

The return fire was light, but it was increasing in intensity as more guards rushed to the threatened area. Still, things were going well so far. At least a dozen of the convoy troops were down already...and Blackhawk hadn't seen a casualty among his men.

That won't last...

He fired again...and again, two more hits. He glanced down the line. His troops were all along the rocky spine, crouched behind the stones and perched atop the larger outcroppings. They were firing steadily, but the convoy guards had fallen back, taking cover behind the trucks.

The fight raged on for at least another ten minutes, Blackhawk and his troopers taking a steady toll on their enemies. But the bloodless fight was long over, and at least four of the attackers were down now, two dead for sure, the others badly wounded. Blackhawk suspected his losses were higher, but half of the platoon leaders were reporting to DeMark.

He kept firing, picking his shots, now shooting as often to suppress enemy fire as to score hits. Then he heard the sound overhead, the last two armed and operational ground attack craft in Lucerne's army. They were out of bombs, but their autocannons were fully loaded, and they came screeching down from the sky, like deadly birds of prey. Their weapons opened up, spat death on the defenders as they raked the enemy positions and shot up the transports.

Blackhawk knew the air attack was limited, that a single strafing run by two planes would fall far short of destroying a force of five hundred. But the attack had a different purpose, and as he watched the disorder below he knew the pilots had done their part, scattering the defenders and pulling their attention from the infantry threatening them. It was time.

"All units…forward now. Charge!"

He leapt from behind the stones, running hard over the small rocks and then the sand. The enemy fire was slow, sluggish, their formations distracted and disordered by the air attack. But Blackhawk knew they were good troops…and his chance to close would be brief. If his people delayed, even for an instant, they would be caught in the open by the full firepower of the defenders…and that would be the end.

He fired as he ran, shooting small bursts all across the enemy position. "Fire," he yelled into his com. "Suppressing fire…keep them pinned." He heard the volume of the assault rifles pick up all around him as he ran. He was halfway there…in another few seconds it would be a close range fight.

He saw a soldier fall, off to his right. Then another. And one to the left. The enemy had been hard hit by the strafing run, but now the soldiers were reacting to the charge. The resumed their fire, slower and more ragged than it had been perhaps, but deadly enough to soldiers running in the open. Blackhawk had known the mission would be a costly one, and now he was seeing that first hand. But there was nothing to do, nothing but continue onward, to fight to the end.

"Forward," he screamed again, pushing his legs, running out in front of the formation. It was a reckless move, but he knew Lucerne's men didn't know him...they didn't trust him as they did their longtime leaders. So he would motivate them the old fashioned way, gun in hand, out in front.

He began aiming his fire as he got closer, targeting the enemy troopers closest to him, picking off any of them reckless enough to peer around from behind one of the transports.

"Fire, men...and forward. Take the convoy!"

* * *

"Cass, this is suicide." Jarvis was right behind the Grays' commander and he reached out and grabbed her shoulder. "We'll be wiped out."

Cass and Jarvis had watched the strafing run, and they'd been listening to the sounds of the fighting down below. She knew Blackhawk would be in the battle already, and it was almost time for her people to hit the engaged enemy from the other side.

"This is why we're here, Jarvis," she snapped back, her intensity sounding almost like anger. "General Lucerne's men are fighting...and it's our job to hit the enemy in the rear while they are fully engaged."

"Is this even our fight, Cass? What do we care who hires mercenaries, who controls the Northern Continent?" There was bitterness in Jarvis tone, the anger of a man who had buried both parents and a sister after the Warlords had ravaged the Galadan.

"You'd better care, Jarvis. You came here with me to save our people. I know the losses you suffered, my friend. But we can't let ourselves assume the Warlords are all the same just because we're angry at what happened. They are not the same...and if Carteria comes to this continent, we will see firsthand the difference. I also would have the Galadan independent, free of all of them if I could. But that won't happen, Jarvis. It's not something we can attain. And Augustin Lucerne is by far the best option. He promised me two million ducats from the convoy…enough to rebuild every farm in the Galadan."

"And you believe him? You trust him?"

She paused. "Yes," she finally said. "I do. And if you trust me, accept my judgment. We're going to lose friends today, Jarvis. Not all of us will survive this…but the ones who do—and those who fall as well—will save our people."

Jarvis stared at her silently for a few seconds. Then he shook his head. "I don't know, Cass," he said. Then, after a long pause: "We'll be lucky if half of us come through this, you know. It is much to gamble on the word of a Warlord you hardly know. But if you are sure, I will trust what you say. I wouldn't take a piss on a rock for Lucerne—or for Blackhawk for that matter. But I will do anything for you."

Cass turned toward Jarvis and gave him a weak smile, the best she could manage through the fear and tension. "Thank you, Jarvis. For this. For everything. Your loyalty has been one of the crutches that has gotten me through the last two years."

Cass held Jarvis' gaze for a few more seconds then she looked out, down at the convoy. It was time.

"Alright, everybody," she said, turning her head back and forth, yelling to her gathered Grays. "This is it. Everything we have done up until now has led us to this. Success today will ensure a future for the Galadan, for our friends, our families. Not just food, supplies, sustenance, but complete rebuilding. Our courage here, our victory, will signal a new future for our people, one of prosperity, of plenty."

She took a deep breath, her hands tightening around the assault rifle. All her people had the sleek new guns. General Lucerne had sent her back with a cache of weapons, and the Grays were equipped with military grade ordnance, equipment they couldn't have dreamed of before.

She moved forward climbing over the gentle crest her people had been hiding behind. "Now," she shouted…and she ran down the hillside, right into the maelstrom.

Blackhawk spun around the end to the transport, his eyes fixing on the closest enemy soldier. He squeezed the trigger, and the trooper fell back hard, taken in the chest by the close ranged shot. His snapped his head around, scanning the area. Nothing. Then he turned toward the back of the truck, his weapon trained on the hatch. He reached up, pulling open the door slowly. His senses were on fire, the battle trance fully engaged. He was ready to fire, but there was nothing inside…nothing except a pile of metal chests. He felt a wave of satisfaction, the knowledge that those chests likely held the coin he'd come to seize. He felt an urge to jump inside the truck, to open a chest and confirm that expectation. But his discipline intervened. He had to win the battle first…when the enemy was defeated, the spoils would remain.

He crept to the edge of the transport, peering around, looking quickly both ways. There was combat going on all along the column, soldiers firing at each other at close range, even hand to hand struggles with rifle butts and survival knives.

His people had gained the initiative, at least to a point. The strafing run had done considerable damage to the enemy, and his charge had taken the defenders by surprise. But Blackhawk's troops were still outnumbered. Each of them could kill two enemies for every one of their own that fell, and they would still lose the fight. Lucerne's men were long service veterans, experienced killers with nerves of steel. But the troops they were fighting were elites too…some kind of guard unit, Blackhawk guessed. They didn't have the raw edge Lucerne's people did, but they were solid fighters, and their morale was strong. They held firm, refusing to give ground despite the losses suffered in the air attack and the surprise of the subsequent charge.

Blackhawk panned his eyes around, looking for threats, targets. Then his rifle snapped up, almost on pure instinct. It fired once, twice. The shot was a dangerous one, the bullets ripping right past the head of one of his own…and slamming into the Carterian beyond who was about to fire. The soldier had recoiled from the sound of Blackhawk's shots, but then he turned, nodding a silent thanks to the stranger turned officer who had just saved his life.

"Blackhawk, what's your status? We're pinned back here, almost surrounded. We need support." It was Rafe DeMark on the com, and his usually calm voice was thick with tension. Blackhawk didn't know DeMark very well, but he'd liked the officer from the moment they'd met. And he knew if the veteran major was calling for help, his situation had to be downright critical.

"On the way, Major," Blackhawk snapped. "I'll grab some men and be right there."

"Roger that, Blackhawk." DeMark paused, and Blackhawk could hear the sounds of heavy combat in the background. "Hurry," DeMark added. Then he cut the line.

"Sergeant Fillon, get your men and follow me to the rear of the convoy."

"Yes, sir," came the non-com's gruff reply.

Blackhawk turned and headed back toward DeMark's position. He ran along the edge of the transports, his eyes darting back and forth, his hands moving almost on their own, aiming his rifle and picking off enemy soldiers who came into his field of fire.

He could hear the sounds of the enemy rifles up ahead, higher pitched than those of his men. The sounds of combat were intense. Blackhawk's troops had run into less resistance than he'd feared, and now he knew why. DeMark's wing had run into the heavy fighting.

Not just DeMark…

Blackhawk's pace increased, pushing him ahead of the cluster of troops following him. DeMark's force had attacked the rear of the convoy…but that was also where the Grays were coming in.

They should be in the fight any minute…

Perhaps they even are already…

"Sergeant," he snapped out, "keep your men moving, and catch up with me when you can." Then he gritted his teeth and pumped his legs hard, unleashing the full capability of his enhanced muscles. His leg ached where he'd been wounded, but he ignored it. He had to get to the fight. The Grays were there. Cass was there.

* * *

Cass could hear her heart pounding in her ears, feel the sweat dripping down her neck, her back. She knew what was behind it all...fear. She was scared to death, and every fiber of her being was screaming to her to run, to flee from the swirling melee and find someplace to hide.

She'd been in combat before, of course, but never like this. The Grays' raids had involved fighting, but the battles had been short, and the Grays had mostly fought against private security forces who were quick to surrender. Even when her people had encountered Ghana's forces and suffered losses, the struggles had still been brief. But this was a full scale battle, with grim veterans on both sides, experienced troops armed with military-grade weapons. It was a bloodbath, a killing zone the likes of which she had never seen. None of these soldiers were going to surrender. This was a fight to the death.

She glanced back over her shoulder, confirming what she already knew. Some of her Grays had run. She wanted to be angry, to brand the routers as traitors, but she couldn't bring herself to go that far. Her people had come here with her to the Badlands, and they had stayed for two years, fighting, hiding, living off the sparse land. But they weren't real soldiers, not most of them at least. They were farmers, brave men and women when forced to be, but not warriors who could endure an inferno like this.

But you are a warrior...

The thought echoed through her head, a shout back at the fear trying to break her resolve. She wasn't sure if she'd always been a true fighter, or whether it was a metamorphosis that had come over her as she watched her father's life slip away. But suddenly, she realized. There was nothing in the Galadan for her anymore. A visit with her mother, perhaps, but no kind of life.

As a girl she'd sought escape in the promise of university—and she'd briefly dreamed of life on the farm with Blackhawk—but now she knew. Her place was the field of battle.

She spun around, let her newly-discovered instincts take control. She was firing, almost without thinking, her eyes darting around, picking out targets as she ran. Her marksmanship was only average, and most of her hurried shots went wide. But she took down one enemy trooper...and then another.

She could hear firing from just to her left, Jarvis, keeping up with her, spraying the ground ahead with automatic fire. It felt right for Jarvis to be at her side. He'd been a friend for most of her life, and he'd been a reliable companion since her people had left the Galadan. There had never been anything romantic between them, but she thought of her comrade as a brother. Closer even.

Her people were almost to the trucks. There was a firefight going on just on the other side of the convoy, Lucerne's veterans faced off against at least a hundred of the Carterians. There were dozens of men lying on the ground, many dead, others wounded, and the fighting was still raging.

She took stock of the situation. Lucerne's forces were fighting well, but they were outnumbered.

Still, they might hang on...

Then she saw it...a shadow at first, and then the image, the largest man she had ever seen. He had an autocannon in each hand, and he was hosing down the line of Lucerne's troops. At least half a dozen fell, and the others dove for cover. The fire all along the line sputtered to almost nothing as the attackers fell back to escape the streams of death coming from the giant's guns.

She snapped her head around, seeing her people slow to a stop, staring at the massive warrior in awe. She knew the Grays were at their limit, and watching this monster gun down Lucerne's veterans was too much for them.

They're going to run, she thought grimly. *She looked behind to the right. Even Jarvis...*

That monster is going to turn the tide here, almost singlehandedly. I've got to do something…

* * *

Bulg Trax was consumed with rage. His convoy was under attack…and the soldiers coming at him had to be Lucerne's veterans. They were too good, too rock solid to be anything else. And that meant Varn Eleher had fucked up. He was supposed to be engaged with Lucerne's army even now, pinning them down if not destroying them outright. The convoy had run on strict radio silence, but he didn't need a dispatch to tell him Eleher had fouled things up. Otherwise he wouldn't have Lucerne's planes strafing his column…he wouldn't be watching Lucerne's toughest troops coming at the pampered lapdogs of Carteria's guard.

I will break that fool in two when I get to him…

Trax's arms were flexed hard, each of them holding a heavy autocannon. The recoil of the two weapons was fierce, and it took every bit of his enormous strength to hold steady, to unload the terrific firepower on Lucerne's line. Lucerne's soldiers were a crack formation, that much was obvious. Better man for man than his own house troops. But he had numbers…and he was going to lead the counterattack himself, break the back of this enemy formation. He would see these soldiers dead, every one of them, if he had to kill them all himself.

Lucerne's men hadn't broken yet, but the relentless blast from his autocannons sent them diving to the ground and lunging for whatever meager cover they could find. He had singlehandedly almost shut down their fire, and now it was time for his troops to move from the defensive. To attack.

"Forward," he roared, "everyone. Destroy these raiders."

He stood where he was, firing both guns, grunting hard from the exertion of holding the massive weapons. His troops were moving ahead all across the line now. He saw a few drop, but his fire was pinning most of Lucerne's survivors. As soon as the Carterians reached their enemies it would be two and three to one at close range…and that fight wouldn't last long.

Then he heard something…more soldiers. Coming from

behind.

He swung around, bringing one of the autocannons to bear to the rear. There were about twenty-five of them approaching. They were a ragged lot, not ordered like Lucerne's men. They had no uniforms...they looked more like farmers than soldiers, most of them clad in gray cloaks of some sort. But they were armed, and they were firing.

He saw two of his men drop, shot from behind by the newcomers. He felt another wave of rage, and he opened up on them, firing on full auto.

The attackers started to drop, half a dozen of them going down in a few seconds. About half of the others wavered... then they turned and ran. But the rest were still coming, perhaps half a dozen.

He felt a sharp pain in his shoulder, and he dropped one of the autocannons. The hit wasn't that serious, but it hurt like hell, taking his fury to a crescendo. His head turned, his eyes locking on the source of the shot. It was a woman. She was tall, thin, a riotous mass of dark brown hair hanging out from her cap. And she was almost on him, a gray-clad man at her side.

Trax whipped around, swinging his remaining autocannon around as he did. He wasn't going to bring it to bear quickly enough to fire, but he smashed the heavy weapon into the man, breaking his arm like a twig. His target screamed and fell back, dropping to the ground. But the woman was on him.

He reached out, swung at her as she came on, but she ducked, avoiding his blow. She had a pistol in one hand and a knife in the other. She struggled to bring the pistol to bear, but Trax grabbed her arm, twisting, turning the weapon aside.

She howled in pain as he jerked her arm, breaking her wrist and then twisting again. Trax smiled, staring down at her face, tears streaming from down her cheeks, and he yanked hard again, pulling her savaged arm. She screamed in pain, looking up at his laughing face with terror in her eyes.

He pulled hard yet again, lifting her off the ground by her broken wrist, laughing as she cried in agony. But then he felt it, a jab in his leg. He looked down, his anger flaring again as he saw it. She had planted the knife in his thigh. She'd lost her grip on it, but the blade remained, stuck deep in his leg.

He pulled her around with one hand and slammed his other fist into her head, sending a cloud of blood flying all around. Then he threw her hard to the ground.

He paused, leaning down, gripping the knife and pulling it from his leg. He moved forward, holding the blade and standing over her. Blood was pumping from his wound, but he seemed to ignore it. He glared down at her and kicked hard, his huge booted foot slamming into her side. She yelled in pain and coughed hard, spitting blood from her mouth as she did.

He leaned down, staring right into her eyes, savoring the look of pain, of fear he saw there. This woman, this raider... she was a brave woman, a capable fighter. But she was no match for Bulg Trax.

He lowered his face, his eyes right above hers as he held her own blade to her gut...began to push it slowly into her...

* * *

Blackhawk threw the assault rifle aside, his last clip expended. He reached down, pulled out his pistol. He fired twice, taking down a pair of enemy soldiers who had jumped out in front of him. He was almost to the rear of the convoy, and from DeMark's ongoing coms, things had gone from bad to downright critical.

Blackhawk had taken a hit, a slug to the side, and his uniform was soaked with his blood. He could tell the injury wasn't too bad, but it still hurt like hell. He ignored the pain, and he pushed himself forward. There would be time to mend his wounds later, but right now, battle called.

He ducked between two transports, spinning around, coming out behind the last truck. He stopped abruptly. The field before him was a nightmare, covered with the dead and dying. DeMark's troops had been driven back, and the Carterians were rushing the battered position even now.

He reacted on instinct, firing, almost like a machine. Crack.

Crack. Crack. He was targeting the Carterians moving on DeMark's position, taking down at least a dozen before he emptied the clip. He was about to reach for a reload when he heard a scream.

He turned to look, but even before he could there was another yell, louder than the first, piteous. And he recognized the voice.

Cass!

He swung around, looking for her. Nothing. There were a couple of the Grays still standing—he hoped that wasn't all who had survived—but not Cass. And there was a giant, a Carterian as large as any man he'd ever seen.

Then he saw. Cass. Lying on the ground under the big man. And his hand…driving a blade into her gut.

"No!" he screamed, dropping the pistol and pulling his sword from the sheath. He was already moving, running across the field toward the giant.

"Carterian," he screamed, desperately trying to draw the man's attention from Cass. "Turn and fight me, dog." Blackhawk's voice was angry, elemental. There was no doubt what part of his psyche was in control now…and his voice was the essence of pure rage.

The Carterian turned, grabbing for his own blade as he saw Blackhawk moving toward him. He stepped forward himself, slashing hard as soon as he came into range. His face had been twisted into an angry scowl, but that changed to a look of surprise as Blackhawk shifted his body, expertly parrying the blow.

The two combatants switched positions as Blackhawk's momentum carried him past his adversary. He felt an almost irresistible urge to turn, to check and see how badly hurt Cass was. But he held firm. It was the dark side again, he knew, saving him from his own weakness. The newer thoughts were fixed on Cass, on the need to go to her…but his older self was in control now, and that part of him was single-minded. Kill the enemy.

He looked at the Carterian. Blackhawk was a large man, tall and muscular, but his adversary seemed almost like a giant come alive from the pages of some ancient myth. He was tall, tower-

ing above Blackhawk, and he was enormously muscular. Blackhawk knew this was a dangerous opponent, even for him.

His body tingled, his system pumping huge amounts of
adrenalin into his arteries. He stared at his enemy, eyes focused,
his mind watching for the slightest movement, even a hint of
which way his foe would come at him. This was the battle trance
in its purest form...Blackhawk alone, facing a deadly enemy.
One he knew could kill him.

The world was gone, thoughts, memories, motivations...all
vanished. There was nothing now, nothing save the fight, the
call of battle.

The Carterian stood for a moment, still surprised at the skill
Blackhawk had shown in evading his attack. His face was twisted
into an enraged scowl, but his eyes were focused, controlled.

This is no immensely strong idiot. This is a skilled warrior.

Then, the Carterian moved, quickly, suddenly. He came
straight ahead, his sword in front of him, driving straight for
Blackhawk's body.

Blackhawk reacted, saw the first hints of movement. His
enemy was lumbering straight at him, like a wild beast...feral,
controlled by rage. For an instant he thought he'd overestimated
the man, that for all his size he was nothing but a brainless giant,
lacking cunning, finesse.

But there was something else, deep in Blackhawk's mind. A
warning. Do not underestimate this foe.

Then he saw the move, felt shock at how quickly the immense
mountain of a man could shift his body, alter his momentum.
The Carterian swung sharply to the side, his blade dropping low
as his body twisted, the blow coming in under Blackhawk's own
sword.

Blackhawk saw the move, almost too late, and he jerked his
body hard, away from his enemy's sword. His own blade came
around, adjusting to the Carterian's move, but too late. He felt
his foe's blade bite into him. He'd almost avoided the slash, but
it caught him in the side, barely, just a shallow cut. He knew it
wasn't serious, but it hurt like hell...and the fact that his enemy
had drawn first blood tore at him deep inside, where his war-

rior's pride lived.

This is a capable opponent, you fool…and it has been far too long since you faced an enemy more dangerous than drunks in a tavern or footsoldiers in the field…

Blackhawk's eyes were fixed on the Carterian's, his hand tightly clasped around his blade. He had lost the first round… but he wasn't going to give his enemy another opening.

He took stock of the warrior. The Carterian was big, strong…but Blackhawk knew his own genetic enhancements would equalize that. The giant would be surprised when Blackhawk revealed his true quickness, strength. That was an advantage, one he intended to use to the greatest effect.

He stumbled back, appearing as though the slash had hurt him worse than it had. But he didn't overplay it. He knew his opponent was a veteran, that he would know the wound was minor.

The giant lunged forward, pressing his advantage. Blackhawk held out his blade, parried the blow. The Carterian's strike was hard, and Blackhawk's armed ached as he held his sword firm against the attack. His enemy pulled his sword up, struck again. Blackhawk realized the man was used to overpowering his enemies. Strength, not finesse was his game.

Blackhawk parried blow after blow, analyzing the Carterian's every thrust, his every step. He was on the defensive, watchful of his surroundings, looking for any enemy soldiers who might try to intervene. But the Carterians were occupied. The troops Blackhawk had brought with him were pouring into the fight… and DeMark's people had leapt out of their meager cover and charged back in. The battle raged all around, even as Blackhawk and the Carterian commander fought their own private war.

Blackhawk felt rage, anger that this man had hurt Cass. He craved his enemy's blood, and he knew one thing. There would be no quarter in this battle.

The Carterian was becoming angrier with each parried blow, throwing all his strength into repeated attacks, each a bit less controlled than the last. Blackhawk was drawing his enemy on, tiring him. His own arm ached, fatigue and pain from fending off the repeated blows taking their own toll. Blackhawk's endurance was strong, and he knew he could outlast his enemy. But there was no time for that. This was no arena, it was a battlefield, and victory hung in the balance. And Cass. He needed to get to her, to help her.

He twisted hard to the side, the Carterian missing him entirely, sword slamming into the ground. Blackhawk' lightning countermove caught the giant unprotected, a sharp stab to the side, the razor point of his blade sinking deep into his enemy's thigh.

Blackhawk pulled the blade back from the wound, and twisted his body hard again, coming around, ducking just as his opponent swung hard.

That was close…he's tiring, but he's not done yet. This man could still kill you…

He took a step back, resetting himself. But his attention wavered despite his warning to himself. His eyes darted toward Cass, trying to get a look at her, at how badly she was injured. It was an error, a lapse, and his enemy was on him, another swing. This time the giant connected. Blackhawk felt the impact, the blade hitting him in his midsection. The edge of the sword had turned, caught on his coat, but the force of the heavy metal weapon hit hard. He wasn't cut, but he knew immediately his opponent had hurt him again. He had broken a rib at least, and perhaps worse.

Then he felt something, his mind emptying, all thoughts gone save the death of his enemy. Suddenly, the struggle between his old persona and the new one was gone. There was nothing now, no thoughts of Cass, of Lucerne, of the battle raging around him. Just coldness, like the depths of space. His time in the Far Stars, the years of aimless wandering, his allegiance to Lucerne…it was all gone. He was as he had been years before, on battlefields far away. Death personified.

He lunged at his enemy, eyes focused like lasers. He heard the clang of the blades as his enemy barely parried. But then his sword moved again, fast, a blur. His side hurt, the gash on his shoulder pumped blood down his side, but he ignored it all.

There was nothing. Nothing save his enemy…and his sword.

He swung again, knocking the Carterian's blade to the side, then he turned, kicked his enemy hard, sending the giant falling to his knees. Then another swing, even harder, with all the strength he could manage. The enemy, raising his own blade just in time…and the hypersteel of Blackhawk's expertly-crafted weapon slicing through, snapping his foe's sword with a loud clang.

Blackhawk could see the surprise in his enemy's face, the shock. And something else, something he suspected this man was not used to feeling. Fear.

Blackhawk suspected this man would refuse to surrender… but he didn't care. There was no pity in him, no mercy, not even the respect for a worthy adversary. No, he was a killing machine, and nothing more.

He looked down into his beaten foe's face, savored the terror he saw. This was victory, distilled to its pure, brutal essence. He was death, come to deliver another enemy to the deepest dark.

His sword flashed, moving so quickly no eye could follow it. For an instant, his enemy knelt, unmoving, still staring at him. Then his head slid slowly to the side, severed, falling to the ground a second before the body followed, blood erupting from the neck. Blackhawk felt a wave of emotion, satisfaction. This was what he'd been born to do. He reached down, scooped up the Carterian's severed head, holding it by the hair.

"Death to them all," he screamed, holding the head before him as he stared out at the melee. "Death to the Carterians." There was frozen venom in his voice as he screamed to the soldiers surrounding him. He hurled the giant's head into the melee and charged in himself, leaning down, picking up a rifle from one of the dead.

He fired…then again. And with each hit he felt a wave of satisfaction. He fed from the death, from the pain and despair of his enemies. This was victory. Total domination, destruction. Even the treasure convoy was unimportant. Only one thing mattered. The Carterians must die. All of them.

Chapter Thirty

Deep Southern Desert
"The Badlands"
Northern Celtiboria

Blackhawk stood on a mound in the middle of the battle-field, surrounded by the bodies of his enemies. He was wounded in several places, covered in blood. Some of it was his own, but most had come from the men he'd killed. Dozens of Carterians had fallen by his hand, and the rest by the soldiers he had led. There had been no quarter, and not a man from the convoy still lived. Soldiers, guards, drivers, laborers...Blackhawk had ordered them all slain. Some of Lucerne's men had resisted, especially toward the end when the last of the Carterians tried to yield. But in the end, Blackhawk had held his pistol to the head of a lieutenant and assured him he would only repeat himself once. In the end, his orders had been obeyed.

His memories were hazy, vague reminiscences. He had killed the Carterian commander, he remembered the combat with the giant. It had been like a rebirth, waking him from a long sleep. Then he'd plunged into the battle, shooting, hacking, killing enemies with abandon. His thoughts were new...and old. He had awakened, and the elemental energy of combat flowed through him.

He was unmoving, like a statue, staring out over the detritus of battle, hundreds dead, carrion birds flying overhead, swooping down to pick at those around the perimeter of the field. It was all that was dark and cruel about war. But it was not disturbing to him. There was comfort in it. He was home. But he was not Arkarin Blackhawk, as he had been moments before…he was another, one born of the darkness.

He stared at the field, at the bodies of his own men, Lucerne's men, and he was emotionless. They were the cost of victory, nothing more. For spouses and children and parents back home, who would miss these soldiers, cry in the night for their loss, he felt nothing.

But there was something else, from deep inside, a spark. It was pain, sadness for the losses his soldiers had suffered. Loyalty, satisfaction at the victory, but regret for its cost. The man who had fled from all he'd been, who had wandered lost and aimless…until he'd found Augustin Lucerne. Blackhawk was still there, hanging on, but the cold, heartless killer was in control.

"Blackhawk…"

He spun around, reached out, grabbing the speaker by the throat.

"Blackhawk," the startled man rasped, "…it's Jarvis Danith, from the Grays…" The voice was clipped. Something was wrong.

The spark that was Blackhawk flared inside, struggling with the frigid warrior that had taken control. A battle raged in his mind. The dark side had seemed supreme, but now the Blackhawk persona was driven onward. It had seen Jarvis, the expression on the pirate's face. And that focused him on a single thought.

Cass!

Suddenly he remembered. Cass. The image of her lying on the ground as he fought the enemy leader. He'd forgotten, the part of him that cared for her completely subsumed by the dark warrior. But now the emotion roared back, pushing the Blackhawk persona forward, forcing the frozen side of him back down, into the dark place it lived. Visions of Cass appeared, flickering remembrances of her in the confines of the Gray's old headquarters, standing in the desert smiling at him...but they all faded back to the same thing. Her, blood-covered form, lying on the sand.

His hand was still holding Jarvis, choking his stunned comrade. He released his hold.

"I'm sorry, Jarvis..." Blackhawk was going to explain, but then he realized there was no way he could, not without hours to tell the tale. Not to someone who would never believe the incredible story anyway.

"Cass?" It was a question, but he already knew the answer. He looked at Jarvis, the cold strength gone from his eyes, replaced by sadness, distress.

"You have to come now, Blackhawk." A pause. "Please... she's calling for you."

Blackhawk felt as if gut had turned inside out, the image of Cass, of her broken body suddenly clear, as memory flooded back into this thoughts.

He turned and ran down the small hill, outpacing Jarvis as he raced back to the scene of his battle with the giant...back to where he'd last seen Cass. He leapt over a series of small craters, twisted around a pile of bodies. Then he saw the corpse of the giant, sprawled across the spot that had been their battlefield. And beyond, Cass, right where she'd been before. Before he'd somehow forgotten about her, plunged wildly into the swirling melee without any thought of her at all.

Three of the Grays were kneeling next to her. His eyes focused on their expressions, grim, angry. There were tears streaming down their faces. He ran over, dropping to his knees next to her.

"Cass," he said, leaning over, his eyes darting over her almost still form. Her body was broken, he could see that in an instant. He was overcome with grief, with frustration, but he wasn't a man who could fool himself, even to forestall pain. Cassandra Cross had led her people to the Badlands, fought with them for two years. She had reached Blackhawk deeply, more even than Lucerne had, helped to pull him from the lost wreck he'd become. Though he still didn't understand his emotions, not fully at least, he thought he loved her.

And now she was dying.

"Ark…" Her voice was soft, weak. She looked up at him, her eyes dull, hazy.

Blackhawk's looked down at her, his hand moving to her cheek.

"I'm so sorry, Cass…"

"I thought I was a warrior…"

Her voice was weakening. Blackhawk struggled against the feelings rising within him. Futility, guilt…grief.

"You are a warrior. And a leader. You have proven that."

He reached down, took her hand in his.

"Make sure my people are taken care of…please."

"I will," Blackhawk said softly. "I will see to your comrades. And that the money the general promised you gets to the Galadan. You have saved your people, Cass. All of them."

She forced a weak smile but it vanished a few seconds later as her body convulsed. She moaned in pain, and tears began to pour down her face.

"I love you, Ark. I would have spent a lifetime with you."

Blackhawk felt the emotions in his head, but they were still foreign, beyond his control. He wanted to tell her he loved her too, but he didn't know. He didn't understand himself well enough. Perhaps one day, but not today.

He opened his mouth, resolved to tell her anyway, to let her hear what she desperately wanted to hear, but he couldn't bring himself to say it. He just leaned down and kissed her cheek, still trying to force the words from his mouth. Then he heard her exhale hard…her last breath.

Cassandra Cross was dead.

* * *

Blackhawk stood next to Lucerne as the general addressed the assembled soldiers. His thoughts were bleak, grim. Cass' death weighed on him, pain at her loss, guilt at himself for losing control in the battle and not rushing to her side.

And for not telling her he loved her. He was still struggling to understand some of his emotions, but he raged at himself for not saying the words, letting her hear what she had wanted to in her final few seconds.

What a miserable bit of comfort, and you still couldn't give it to her...

Blackhawk knew Lucerne had to be struggling himself, exhausted, overwhelmed with the surprise events of the past few days, but he wasn't showing it as he stood before his men, both new and old.

The army had suffered grievous losses, but it had gained new recruits as well. The ranks of soldiers standing before him included men he had called enemies just a few days before, soldiers who had followed General Ghana for years.

Blackhawk was impressed, staring at the scene and truly realizing that Augustin Lucerne was indeed an extraordinary commander. He'd wandered aimlessly for a long time, and it had been fortune alone that had led him to that tavern, to the encounter with Ghana's soldiers that marked his turn down this path. Since that day he'd found purpose...he'd found himself, the man he'd become. He'd almost lost it himself as well, surrendered to the monster he'd once been. And he'd found love, or at least the closest he could come to that storied emotion. He'd lost that too, and it had been replaced with grief and regret. But even that suffering marked a difference in him, in what he'd become. And for all it tore at him, he was grateful for it too.

"Soldiers," Lucerne said, his voice strength itself, "many of you have fought with me for years now. Some were among that first thousand men who marched at my side from our ancestral lands...to fight, to carry forward with honor as well as conquest. To bring justice as well as rule to those we conquered." He paused. "And some of you are new to these ranks. You have known of me before, but as an enemy. We have fought each other, struggled on the field, spilled each other's blood...but that is now at an end. We now move past the losses, the fallen comrades, and we step into the future, where we shall fight as brothers, move ahead together."

Blackhawk's respect for Lucerne had only grown over the

past several days, a time that had seen the general's forces swing from victory to defeat…and then to victory again. Blackhawk knew Lucerne's triumph owed much to his own skills, both in forging his army into the tool of victory it had become, and also in his calm and effective leadership during the battle. But he realized there had been more to this struggle. It had been Bako Ghana as much as Lucerne who had engineered this outcome. Blackhawk knew Ghana had made foolish mistakes, but in the end he had to admit the general had redeemed himself, sacrificing his life to save his army…and protect the Northern Continent from conquest by an outsider. Blackhawk's entire being pulsated with the instinct to survive, to struggle to the end. He couldn't imagine killing himself, even in the face of certain destruction. But he had to admit that Ghana had died an honorable death, and he'd prevented himself from being used as a pawn by his enemies. There were worse ways to die.

"To you men who fought under the banner of General Ghana, know that though I fought your old commander, ever did I respect the man. He will be buried in his homeland, with full military honors. His wife shall live out her days in her home, provided for and protected under my personal guarantee of safety. General Ghana's sons shall become my wards, and I will see to their care and educations. When they are old enough they shall have the option to serve in my forces…or to make whatever other lives they choose. Never shall they want for anything."

Blackhawk had been surprised when Lucerne had told him he would spare Ghana's sons, put them under his own protection. He had imagined the general might spare the defeated Warlord's wife, perhaps keep her in some kind of comfortable confinement, but the sons? Ghana's sons were his heirs, and however Lucerne handled them, they would always present a potential danger. Blackhawk knew that few men in Lucerne's shoes would have allowed the boys to live. He was certain what he would have done in the past…and he had to admit to himself there was more than a little chance he would have executed them even now. They were just too dangerous, and there was more at stake for Lucerne than personal aggrandizement. He was responsible for thousands of soldiers, millions of civilians... indeed, with Ghana's lands and his soldiers, and the Badlands as well now his, he was one of the most powerful Warlords on the Northern Continent. Could he risk all that just to offer mercy to two young boys? To grant the last request of a dead enemy?

But look at the faces on Ghana's men, the effect Lucerne's words are having. Honor is a burden, but perhaps it offers its own benefits...

"We have many battles ahead of us, my soldiers. I would like to say that everyone here will survive them all. But we know that will not be the case. Many of us will fall, as will comrades who have not yet joined our ranks. I cannot promise you victory, nor wealth and long life. But I can swear that all I have I will give to our cause, and with my last breath I will lead this army, sacrifice anything to its survival and victory."

Lucerne paused, and the soldiers erupted in a loud cheer. Blackhawk noted that Lucerne's old soldiers might have been a second or two quicker, devoted to him as they had already been, for years in many cases. But the new troopers, Ghana's men, came right behind their new comrades, and in their voices Blackhawk heard sincerity, enthusiasm. He knew in that moment that Lucerne had somehow done it, he'd turned thousands of enemies, men who until the day before had sought to destroy him... and he had turned them into loyal followers.

Blackhawk watched in amazement. He knew Lucerne would have to be careful, that among the converted thousands there would be a few, the resentful, the angry. It would take time to weed them out, and diligence to ensure they did no serious damage while they were there. But he didn't have the slightest doubt that the vast majority of those present had set themselves on the road behind Lucerne, and that they would remain there, wherever that path led.

Blackhawk had led soldiers before too, though there had only been one tool to control them—fear. But Lucerne had made no threats, used no force. He'd shown these men mercy, respect, honesty. He'd washed away the past, the enmity between them. He had sliced through their hatred, their resentments, their anger. And they had responded.

You must learn from this man. You must come to know different ways than those of your past if you would win the admiration of those around you, the respect.

Blackhawk stood in awe and stared at the crowd…and within a moment he realized he too was cheering for General Lucerne.

Chapter Thirty-One

Outskirts East of the River Cities
Just West of the Badlands
Northern Celtiboria

Augustin Lucerne stood in front of the group of officers,
clad in his finest dress blues. He wore the emblems of all his
lands…including his newest ones, those along the Palm Coast
that had belonged to General Ghana. His boots were black, polished to a mirror shine. Lucerne wasn't a man who normally
paid much attention to such things, a footsoldier's general, more
apt to wander the field in an enlisted man's overcoat, threadbare
and splattered with mud. But now his purpose required this,
the splendor of war, the frill and glitter so many mistook as the
badges of true power.

He knew most of those present, at least he was aware of
who they were. Most of the mercenary commanders of the
Northern Continent were there…along with another man, unfamiliar, strangely dressed in exotic civilian garb.

The Carterian.

"I have asked you here under flag of truce," he said, his eyes
scanning the group, looking for reactions, signs of what the officers were thinking. "I have done this so you may learn of news
you might find relevant." Lucerne paused. He was unassuming
for a man of his power and accomplishments, and he despised

braggarts. But this time he had come here to boast of his own victories, at least after a fashion, and to use them to win yet another, hopefully without a shot fired.

"To the east my army has prevailed. Ghana is dead. I now command both my own forces and those soldiers formerly sworn to serve my rival. Our forces have already joined, and they are camped close to this spot, along the edge of the Badlands."

He could see varying levels of surprise on those standing before him. He knew some word must have reached them of what had transpired, but he was sure they couldn't know everything. Not yet. But they would in a moment.

"The Carterian force sent to bolster—and then betray—General Ghana has also been defeated. Half its soldiers have been slain, and the rest are my prisoners. Not one man in fifty escaped, and what fugitives successfully fled the battle are lost in the deep desert, pursued by my hunter teams."

He could see that last part had been unexpected, though he wasn't sure if it was the defeat of Carteria's forces or their very presence that surprised the mercs.

Whatever...it doesn't matter. This will be a surprise...one cutting close to home for them.

"And my forces have intercepted an armed convoy, one carrying silver ducats...funds intended to pay your forces, I believe." His tone changed, becoming harsher, a hint of anger slipping in. "Your wages, your base pay...for serving a foreign master, one you would have helped to conquer the Northern Continent. Your home." He didn't try to hide the disgust in his voice.

He could see the discomfort in the faces of the officers. There was a hint of fear, but it was ephemeral. His reputation was well known, and the mercenaries knew he would never violate a flag of truce. Even if they believed he would enjoy ordering them gunned down...

"General..." The voice came from the center of the group, but it faded off, as if the speaker had wanted to say something, to make an argument of some kind. But the words didn't come.

"Colonel Dolokov, in my experiences you have never been a

man to fumble with his words." Lucerne glared intensely. "Have you nothing to say to the man who has the silver, the coin you promised to your men? What will they say when you tell them their payroll is not coming? That they have gathered here under false promises. What will they do?"

Lucerne was speaking boldly, proudly. But Blackhawk knew the general hadn't lost sight of reality. His position had its strengths certainly, that much was clear. But there were weaknesses too, and his strategy here was half bluff. Even with Ghana's men, he had barely forty thousand combat-ready troops nearby that he could put in the field. The final battles had been bloodbaths, and beyond the thousands dead, the field hospitals were overflowing with wounded and sick. And the men he did have in the ranks were exhausted and low on ammunition, half of them Ghana's people, new to his command, to fighting alongside his veterans.

The mercenaries had at least one hundred thousand troops fully mobilized, and they were the better supplied of the two forces now. They were short of funds, and they couldn't last long in the field without financial support. But if Dolokov and his associates had the courage to stand up to Lucerne, to threaten an invasion of the Badlands unless he released their coin, it would have been a deadly danger.

Blackhawk didn't know what Lucerne would do if it came to that. He didn't know because the two men had talked the night before, and the general himself had confessed to Blackhawk that he simply didn't know what he would do.

Lucerne just stared, his eyes boring into the mercenary's, and Blackhawk saw no hint of any concern the mercs would stand up to him. Whatever doubts he harbored, Augustin Lucerne was broadcasting pure strength, almost arrogance.

"What will *you* do, General?" Lucerne stepped forward as he spoke.

Blackhawk saw the doubt on Dolokov's face, and he knew immediately his ally had won the battle of wills. Lucerne was prepared to give Dolokov an out, and now Blackhawk had no doubt the mercenary would take it.

"Will you serve this distant Warlord for no pay?" Lucerne asked, taking a step forward as he spoke. "Would your soldiers follow you if you did?"

Lucerne paused. "Or would you follow me instead? Will you join my cause?" Lucerne stared at the officers, his gaze cold, hard. "I will hire no mercenaries, no freebooters who sell their swords to the highest bidder. But if your men will swear an oath to serve me—if you and your fellow officers will so swear—then I shall welcome you all into my service. I shall accept you as friends."

Dolokov stared back at Lucerne, unable to hide the shock in his expression. Blackhawk didn't know what the mercenary had expected to hear, but he was pretty sure this wasn't it. It was a good offer under the circumstances, and making it required another leap of faith by Lucerne, to allow men into his service without his usual vetting process, to rely on his leadership abilities, and the elan of his men, to turn these swords for hire into loyal soldiers.

Blackhawk wasn't sure what the mercs would do. A year before, Lucerne's reputation had been one of a capable general, leading a small but effective army. He was respected, but not feared. But things had changed over the past few days. If Lucerne added over a hundred thousand more veterans to his army, he would jump to the top of the Northern Continent power struggle...and his new soldiers, and their officers, would go with him, become part of the strongest power in the hemisphere.

"The Red Wolves have existed for over a century, General Lucerne. Some of the other companies for even longer periods. You expect us to abandon our legacy, case our colors...swear oaths to you?"

Lucerne stared at Dolokov. "Yes, that is exactly what I expect. Times change, Colonel. Men change with them...or they fade away." He paused. "We can win battles together, honorable triumphs. We can make a difference." Another pause, longer this time. "Or we can be enemies. We can seek to destroy each other. There is no other ground here."

Blackhawk was startled by the last bit. He looked at the mercenary commanders, hard men all, expecting them to scoff at Lucerne's idealism. But there was nothing, not a hint of mockery or doubt. Only fear. And respect.

"You speak of lofty things, General Lucerne. But as you noted, our forces have not been paid in many months. Would you expect them to join you, and wait months more, even years before your next campaigns provide booty to fund their wages?"

"No, Colonel Dolokov, I would not expect that. I have booty now, millions of silver ducats, courtesy of Marshal Carteria." A pause. "And I will pay the wages of any man who signs on to my service."

There was a hushed murmur from the officers. Dolokov turned and looked back at the others before returning his gaze to Lucerne. "You are keeping the Marshal's silver?"

Lucerne stood stone still, his voice loud booming. "Indeed, I am, Colonel. The Marshal has committed acts of war against me, supporting my enemy, sending soldiers to fight my own, hiring mercenaries to battle against me. By all rights, I should embark my army, travel to the Southern Continent, bring the fires of war to his homeland as he has brought them to ours. But I shall not demand such harsh reprisals. I will keep the coin, sent here for dishonorable purposes, and accept it as just compensation for the wrongs done to me."

The field was silent, the stunned faces of all those gathered locked on Lucerne. Carteria was by far the strongest Warlord on Celtiboria…and he was regarded with dread everywhere on the planet. But Augustin Lucerne stood like a statue, speaking boldly and betraying not an iota of fear to anyone around him.

"And from it I shall pay a bonus of six months' wages to all men who take my service. And then we shall embark on a great campaign…to unite the Northern Continent. For too long Carteria has held himself above the rest of us, wielded power no other Warlord dared to challenge. It is time another power rises, one that can face the Marshal, meet him on equal terms."

Lucerne paused, looking out over the group of officers, and behind him, at his own people. There were stunned faces everywhere, all of the men assembled. Save one.

Blackhawk's face was cold, unreadable. His eyes were fixed on Lucerne, and inside his respect grew again. Blackhawk admired courage. It was one thing that spanned both his old and his new personas. And Augustin Lucerne, whatever else he was, was a courageous man.

Dolokov stood quietly for a moment, exchanging glances with his fellow commanders. Finally, he looked back at Lucerne. "General, may we have a moment to discuss your offer?"

Lucerne nodded. "Certainly, Colonel Dolokov." He gestured behind him. "I will be at the base of the hill with my officers when you are finished."

Blackhawk watched the exchange, understanding it for what it was. Dolokov and his people would talk, then the mercenary would return with a list of conditions, minor guarantees, face-saving concessions. And then they would accept the offer.

Augustin Lucerne's victory was complete.

* * *

"Here it is, Jarvis. Two million silver ducats, as promised."

Blackhawk stood off to the side, watching as Lucerne presented the surviving Grays with their share of the booty. He had kept his word, followed through on what he had promised Cass.

"And I will honor all the promises I made to Cassandra. Henceforth, the Galadan will be under my protection. None now will dare come and victimize your people, for such would put them at war with me." That was a significant threat now. Lucerne commanded his and Ghana's troops, both the forces that had fought over the Badlands, and all the garrisons and other armies stationed throughout the two Warlord's domains... and to that he had added 95,000 former mercenaries, almost all the men in the companies that had contracted with Carteria. Altogether, 320,000 soldiers followed his banner, and he ruled over lands covering twenty-five percent of the continent.

Trade flowed again across the Badlands, freed of both the threats of war and the raiding of the Grays, and even now, two weeks after the end of hostilities, revenue from caravans was flowing into Lucerne's coffers, helping with the monumental task of supporting an army so large.

"Thank you, General," Jarvis replied. "For everything. I know Cass would have…" The ex-raider paused for a moment. "I know she would have been pleased…and grateful."

"It is I who am grateful, Jarvis. I only knew her for a very short time, but Cassandra Cross was an extraordinary woman… and she will not be forgotten."

"Again, thank you, General." He turned and looked at a small cluster of uniformed figures, six of them. One third of the Grays who had survived…and the members of the company who had chosen to join Lucerne's army. Elli Marne stood in front of them, their leader now despite her young age. Lucerne, too, had looked past her years, and he'd put a lieutenant's bars on her shoulders. Her first mission would be to lead a company to the Galadan, to protect the silver convoy and establish a fortress to watch over the province, to protect it from any who might come again and ravage its rich farms and fields. Lucerne was sending more than money, more than soldiers. He had hundreds of thousands of soldiers to feed now, and he had agreed to buy all the grain the revived Galadan could produce.

"Good luck to you, Jarvis." Lucerne reached out, shook hands with the Gray. Then he turned and walked back toward the main camp.

"Good luck from me as well, Jarvis." Blackhawk's voice was soft, clipped. He had trouble facing the man who had served so closely with Cass, who had seen his own behavior in those fateful moments on the battlefield.

"Thank you, Blackhawk." Jarvis' voice was unemotional, and Blackhawk knew that was the best he could hope for. He knew Jarvis resented him, but he'd come to wish the new leader of the Grays his best anyway. It's what Cass would have wanted.

Blackhawk was sad as he thought of her. He felt he had let her down, hurt her in ways he wished he hadn't. Leaving her the first time, refusing her when she asked him to stay, to settle with her in the Galadan. And later, on the battlefield…where she'd lost her life. Where he'd been unable to say the one thing he knew she'd longed to hear.

He watched as Jarvis turned and walked away, led the rest of his people as they set out for home. He smiled as Elli Marne snapped her commands. Cass had been fond of both Jarvis and Elli, and he knew it would have pleased her to see them now, to know they had made it, that the Galadan was safe.

Cass was gone, but she'd left one hell of a legacy, and he supposed there were worse ways to go. He felt a grim satisfaction that she hadn't died in vain, but the emptiness was still there inside him, the sadness. Such feelings were new to him, and though the pain was almost unbearable, he knew his ability to feel it was a step forward for him. One more thing he owed Cassandra Cross.

He watched the Grays for a few more minutes, as they made their way south, back toward home. Then he turned and headed back to the camp, following Lucerne.

Chapter Thirty-Two

Marshal Lucerne's Camp
Just West of the Badlands
Northern Celtiboria

Augustin Lucerne stared into the flames, sitting silently. He and Blackhawk sat in the great hall of the manor house he'd appropriated for his headquarters. The lands east of the river cities were considerably richer than the wastelands of the Badlands, and they provided more comfortable lodgings for the army.

The fire's warmth was welcome as the dusk had given way to a late night chill. Blackhawk had spoken long, and he had told Lucerne things he'd never confided to anyone, recollections he'd barely faced himself. He'd told the general of his past, all of it. From his beginnings, through all the deeds he'd done. He hadn't intended to be so thorough, but by the time he'd finished, he had turned Lucerne into his confessor.

He had waited to have this talk, until things had calmed, until the tumult from the Badlands Campaign had slipped from the present into the recent past. The wounded were healed, or at least on the mend, the army's logistics had been patched together.

Now that all that was done, Blackhawk knew the time had come for him to leave. He knew Lucerne couldn't afford peace for long…he had built a massive army, and if he was going to pay for it in the long term, he had to use it. And Blackhawk had to be gone by then…for reasons that had become very clear to him on the battlefield. He was not ready to lead men in battle, to stand in the halls of power. It was too great a temptation. He had to learn to understand himself first.

He had been uncertain how Lucerne would respond to the things he had just confessed. His past was dark, ugly. And Augustin Lucerne was now the only other person who knew the truth.

"I knew you had a past, Ark…but I confess, I hadn't imagined anything close to the truth." Lucerne's voice betrayed his surprise, but there was none of the disapproval Blackhawk had expected.

"I broke my conditioning, Augustin. I am not that man anymore." He paused uncomfortably. "But he is still inside me. That is why I must go, Augustin. Not because I wouldn't serve you, wouldn't stand at your side and help you reunite Celtiboria. There is no man I respect more than you." He paused.

"But you didn't see me on the field. I lost myself, every time battle was joined. I slipped back into what I was. That man is not one you would want at your side, my friend, however great his skills. He wouldn't serve you. He would seek to replace you, to take control. He would think nothing of putting a bullet in your head to serve his purposes." Blackhawk hesitated, took a breath. "I must be alone, Augustin. I must not command armies, for proximity to such power would surely destroy me. I would wander the Far Stars alone, a friendless drifter, before I would allow myself to become what I once was."

"To wander aimlessly? For a lifetime? Does any man deserve such a fate, no matter what he has done?" There was still no recrimination in Lucerne's voice. Indeed, to Blackhawk's astonishment, he thought he heard compassion.

"Perhaps not for a lifetime. I must understand myself better, what I am, what I was. I must learn to face the monster that lives within me, to destroy him once and for all. And until I am able to do that, I cannot have a home…no matter how much I might want one."

Lucerne looked over at his friend. "And Celtiboria reminds you of Cassandra…"

Blackhawk winced. He was unsettled at how insightful Lucerne was, how the general seemed to penetrate his very thoughts.

"Yes. Her shade is heavy here." He looked down at the floor. "She offered me a home, a life at her side. As a farmer. Perhaps that was my chance, Augustin, to live a quiet life, to grow crops, avoid the battlefield that feeds my dark side." He paused and sighed softly. "But I spurned her. I told myself I had to find you, to redress the ill I thought you had done to me. Then I made other excuses. But the truth is, I don't know how to be anything other than what I am. I couldn't do that to her, tie to her to me. I don't even know what I am, what I can be. She deserved better, Augustin." His voice was soft, and he sat silent for a moment. "Instead she got nothing, no life at all. Just death on the battlefield."

"You suffer my friend," Lucerne said, "You blame yourself for much. Perhaps some of that is just, and some you seek to feed your self-hatred. Perhaps there is justice in that, a penance of sorts. But promise me this, my friend…don't stop looking for redemption. You will find it one day. I believe that with all my heart. You are not fated to live your life alone, without love, without friends. Do not make it so by your own actions when it need not be that way." Lucerne paused. "And never forget, Arkarin Blackhawk, you have a home here on Celtiboria. Return to us one day, my friend. If ever you need aid or succor…or just rest, a place to hide, it is here.

Blackhawk just nodded. He appreciated Lucerne's thoughts, the general's hopes for his future, but he wasn't sure he believed it. He didn't know what the future held for him, but he'd resolved to take things a step at a time. But he felt something, a bit of peace, of contentment.

Perhaps this is what it is to have a friend. A home.

Blackhawk walked slowly across the dirt road, toward the small line of trucks ahead. It was a routine convoy, heading to Rhiombe to pick up supplies...but it was also Blackhawk's ride. General Lucerne had offered to fly Blackhawk to Trattoria or Columbia, the cities that housed the Northern Continent's two spaceports. But Blackhawk had refused, saying he would obtain his own transit in Rhiombe. Lucerne's battered air force was already thinly stretched, and besides, he was going to have to get used to being on his own. In Lucerne's camp he was an officer, a friend of the Warlord. But when he left he would be a wanderer again, a friendless drifter. He wasn't the same as he'd been before, and he was grateful for that, to Lucerne, to Cass, to all those who had helped pull him back from the abyss...but his path was still a solitary one.

He was confused, still struggling to deal with his new emotions, with the grief over Cass, but he felt something new, something good. He had been a part of Lucerne's victory, he had fought for a cause, for more than personal gain. He liked the way it felt, the joy at aiding a friend, of winning something meaningful. He'd relished victory before, but this was something different, something less cold than what he recalled.

His friend had become a very powerful man, and he wondered how the next few years would progress. Lucerne could handle any local enemies, he was sure of that, but eventually he would have to face off against Carteria. He'd avoided that war for now, through luck and deft maneuvering. He had returned the fifteen thousand survivors of Carteria's guard, unharmed and without demanding any tribute. He knew an honorable gesture alone wouldn't be enough to sway Carteria, but the Marshal had lost half his elite soldiers, as well as forty million ducats in silver...and Lucerne had grown vastly in strength. It was in Carteria's interests to postpone any move against Lucerne and the Northern Continent, and the Marshal took the prisoner repatriation as an excuse to make peace...just as Lucerne had predicted.

Lucerne had gained one other thing from Carteria, an asset

beyond more soldiers, more lands. Ganz Jellack had come to the Northern Continent to organize Carteria's mercenary army, and he'd been left with a small cadre of guards when the mercs deserted him en masse. Lucerne had taken his entourage prisoner, promising to return them to the Southern Continent as quickly as he could. But he quickly noticed Jellack's gifts for organization and financial management, and he offered him a place in his own service.

The Carterian had declined, though he'd been clear that he had no loyalty to Carteria, that the Marshal guaranteed his loyalty by holding his wife and children as hostages. Blackhawk had seen a certain sense in Carteria's actions, a brutal logic, but Lucerne had been outraged...and he'd sent Rafe DeMark and a team of elite commandoes on a mission to rescue Jellack's family. DeMark and his crew had dressed as pirates, approached from the sea. Surprise had been total, and Jellack's wife and children were retrieved almost bloodlessly.

Jellack had been stunned when Lucerne brought his family to him and repeated his offer, and this time he enthusiastically accepted. He would have to keep a low profile at first. Lucerne didn't want to inflame the situation with Carteria by disclosing that he'd infiltrated and attacked one of the Marshal's facilities. But Blackhawk knew it had been more than a minor coup. Jellack was a genius in his field, and with the massive expansion of Lucerne's holdings, the general would desperately need a skilled finance minister.

"Ark..." The voice was instantly recognizable. Blackhawk had already said his farewells to Lucerne, but the Marshal had come to see him off.

"Augustin." He turned. Lucerne was standing in the road behind him, a young girl following along behind him. Blackhawk had seen her in the headquarters before, running around with orders, working in the field hospital. She was perhaps ten years old, but there was something about her. He saw it in her eyes, a piercing stare, a gaze that broadcast intelligence.

"I just wanted to see you off, my friend." He paused, looking down at the girl. "This is my daughter, Ark." Then: "Astra, this is

Arkarin Blackhawk. He is a friend. Without his help the victory would not have been possible."

"Hello, Mr. Blackhawk. It is a pleasure to meet you."

Blackhawk returned the girl's gaze. He hadn't spent much time around children in his life, but he'd seen enough of them to realize how different this girl was. She spoke like an adult, and he was even more convinced now that she was extremely capable.

"Hello, Astra. I assure you, the pleasure is all mine." He smiled, glancing up at Lucerne and back down at the girl. "Can you do a favor for me, Astra?"

She looked up at him, an expectant look on her face. "What do you want me to do?"

"Take care of your father when I am gone. He is a good man, Astra, but he needs help. He carries much on his shoulders...and I am sure you are a great comfort to him."

She smiled. "I will, Mr. Blackhawk. I promise."

"Astra," Lucerne said softly, "I need to speak with Mr. Blackhawk alone. I will meet you back at out quarters in a few minutes."

"Yes, father." She turned toward Blackhawk and gave him a warm smile. "Goodbye, Mr. Blackhawk. Come see us again one day." Then she turned and jogged back toward the manor house.

"She is an extraordinary child, Augustin. I didn't know you had children."

Lucerne nodded, a somber expression on his face. "Only Astra, I'm afraid." A sadness fell on Lucerne's face. Blackhawk could see there was more to the story. "Come back as Astra says, Ark. When you do, it will be my turn to share my shame and sadness, and yours to be confessor."

"That's a bargain, Augustin."

There was a short pause then Lucerne spoke again, his voice normal, the sadness pushed aside. "I came to ask you once again to take more coin with you. This victory wouldn't have occurred without you, Ark. Indeed, it is likely I would have faced defeat and disaster—even assassination—without your participation. You deserve more."

Blackhawk shook his head. "No, my friend...you need every

ducat you can get. Even that will not be enough to sustain this army. I would not drain resources from you now. You have paid me what you offered when all this began, a thousand imperial crowns. That will be enough for me. That is my last word on it. Consider anything else you would have given to be my contribution to sustaining all of this…for you have declared it my home too, have you not?"

Lucerne stood there, looking as if he might argue. But then he just nodded. The two stood silently for a moment then Lucerne said, "Whatever you might have done in the past, know this…the man standing before me is an honorable one, and one any man would be fortunate to call his friend."

"As are you, Augustin. You cannot know what you have pulled me from…and I shall never forget my debt to you."

Blackhawk stepped forward and put his arms out, grabbing Lucerne in a firm embrace. After a few seconds, he stepped back and looked at his friend for a few seconds. Then he turned and walked away.

He had no idea what his future held, but he knew one thing. It was time to find out.

The Adventures of Arkarin Blackhawk continue in the Far Stars trilogy, published by Harper Voyager and available now everywhere.

Shadow of Empire
Enemy in the Dark
Funeral Games

The Far Stars Series

Book I: Shadow of Empire
Book II: Enemy in the Dark
Book III: Funeral Games

The Far Stars is a space opera series, published by Harper-
Collins Voyager. It continues the story of Blackhawk.

The Far Stars series is set on the fringe of the galaxy
where a hundred worlds struggle to resist domination
by the empire that rules the rest of mankind. It follows
the rogue mercenary Blackhawk and the crew of his
ship, Wolf's Claw, as they are caught up in the sweeping
events that will determine the future of the Far Stars.